Village of Sycamore

Village of Sycamore by Maria Rihte:

The Village of Sycamore is a work of fiction.

Village of Sycamore

A Novel

By
Maria Rihte

iUniverse, Inc.
New York   Bloomington

Village of Sycamore
A Novel

iUniverse books may be ordered through booksellers or by contacting:

iUniverse
1663 Liberty Drive
Bloomington, IN 47403
www.iuniverse.com
1-800-Authors (1-800-288-4677)

ISBN: 978-1-4401-9546-4 (sc)
ISBN: 978-1-4401-9550-1 (dj)
ISBN: 978-1-4401-9548-8 (ebk)

Author photograph: Phoebe Rihte-Kreamer
Cover painting: Richard Kreamer

Printed in the United States of America

iUniverse rev. date: 1/28/2010

For the loves of my life
Phoebe and Richard

Contents

Acknowledgements

This book took many years to complete and it lived in its infant stages through many countries. It began out of utter loneliness in Poland and it is now seeing its daylight in Paris, France.

It has been a long, but very interesting journey and I would like to thank several people who helped me while travelling in the strange land of words.

Thank you to my grandmother, mummi Lea Rihte, who bought me my first colour pencils. You never knew where those pencils would lead me.

Thank you to Mervi Raulos, my friend and my first reader. Your positive reaction and advice gave me the courage to finish my withering project.

Thank you to my editor Mary Newberry, the guardian angel of editing and the master of finding the main line of thought in the jungle of words. Without you this book would not be as good.

Thank you to my husband Richard Kreamer and to my daughter Phoebe, who did not complain about my absentmindedness, the meagre dinners, the lack of clean clothes and a very dusty house, while I was in the midst of my book. Without you two, this book would not have seen the daylight.

In memory of Aino and Ahti. You both are missed in many ways.

Chapter 1

Coming Home

We are all forced to go through a doubtful period or two in our lives, when we try anxiously to find an answer to our own uncertainties; what if I would have, what if I had or maybe had not, should have, ought to, and all those other self analyzing questions that haunt our existence like ghosts that hover above our sad bent heads. These often repeated questions don't help at all, but they make the extra drink or the extra piece of chocolate seem so right for the occasion.

Those were the exact feelings of Jacqueline Callaghan when she stepped into her late grandmother's cottage on a cold windswept, sparsely populated island. Doubtful, miserable, guilty, uncertain but, perhaps, slightly optimistic in a very tentative, reserved kind of way.

'I'm trying to like my mother, but I'm failing miserably,' thought Jackie as she dropped her bag onto the dusty floor. It fell heavily, bending the old, creaky floorboards. A dense cloud of dust rose into the air and it made Jackie sneeze. She waved her hands in front of her, trying to clear the air.

'I can hear her voice right now,' she thought anxiously. '"Why would you go back to that tiny house which I left as a young girl for a better life in the city?"' Her mother's sharp voice echoed in her mind as she coughed out the last stubborn particles of old dirt.

'Well beats me,' Jackie said to herself, more cheerfully than she felt. She wiped off the gritty dust, which covered her face and draped her eyelashes, while trying to shake off the guilty feeling and her mother's words clinging to her skin like the dust—unwanted but nevertheless present.

It took awhile for her eyes to adjust to the darkness of the room. She stood in the ray of light coming in from the wide open front door, listening to the chirping birds in the garden and watching the specks of dust dance in the bright midday light. The shapes of the furniture slowly took form. It was an old house, an old room, filled with old furniture. The house smelled of must and forgotten ground coffee beans.

Jackie could see a yellowing lace cloth on the three-legged table; in the middle sat a vase of plastic flowers. The chairs still had the fabric arm covers and the sofa had a set of crocheted pillows placed neatly against the armrests. It all looked so familiar, bringing back memories from long gone summers when the most important thing on her mind had been to get to the table on time for lunch, and then run out again as soon possible without seeming to be completely without manners. She could almost feel the sun, the soaking wet bathing suit and the itching mosquito bites on her legs. The memory made her scratch her calves. She hated the mosquitoes with a passion. Her friend Jill called them the last living remnants of the vampire empire.

Jackie began walking toward the kitchen, fighting back the increasing sense of panic. She remembered her mother's sharp voice, engaged in normal conversation with the neighbour, penetrating the walls and travelling upstairs to the room where Jackie sat by her school desk.

'That girl has a mind of her own. What can I do?' Her mother would say without waiting for the polite dismissive response from the confused neighbour. 'When she has something on her mind, she'll fight for it. She never thinks of anybody else except herself.'

Jackie shrugged her shoulders. The guilt left her for a moment, soon replaced by a slight resentment. She opened the door to the kitchen. The hinges cried with a deep shriek and orange rust flakes rubbed off onto the floor of the narrow hallway. Bright light flooded the room from the big windows that looked onto the garden. The uneven wooden floor groaned as Jackie walked into the middle of the kitchen. It looked just like it had every summer of her life when she had visited her grandmother during her holidays. Jackie felt grief take hold of her as her eyes wandered around, taking in all those objects from her childhood: the tea kettle, dented pots and pans and the Formica table with a wobbly leg that had been evened out with a folded piece of cardboard stuck under it, waiting to be fixed someday when there would be more time. She opened the cupboard; there were all the lovely teacups in blue landscape pattern with sheep and girls in beautiful dresses. She had always loved the one with a girl swinging, the hem of her skirt flying high. She remembered trying to create the same romantic atmosphere by dressing up in her grandmother's old underskirts and how the pub owner's son had laughed when he had seen her patterned underwear peaking through the layers of elegant lace. They ended up in a big fight—a far cry from romantic.

She started looking for that one particular cup when she heard the front door open.

'Hello!' A strong woman's voice called. 'Anybody home?' The voice continued while its owner and her heavy footsteps approached the kitchen. Where else could a person be if there was nobody in the garden, and the car was parked in front of the house? It was part of the island's customs: one light knock on the open front door was enough to let yourself in. No separate invitation needed. The footsteps seemed to follow an old familiar pattern.

'Over here in the kitchen,' Jackie answered tentatively, her words echoing in the room. She stood facing the door and waited for the owner of the voice to enter.

A big, robust, cheerful woman walked, or rather stomped, into the kitchen. Her hugeness was not created by her being overweight; she simply was a very, very big person. She had a lovely broad face and the presence of a man. Her hands were large and adorned with many gold rings that seemed to be several sizes too small. Her voice was loud and warm and without effort filled the air. It was the kind of voice you hear in 1940s films when there is a scene in a school room. The busty headmistress stomps into the classroom wearing a dress with the buttons on the front stretched to their utmost limit and the happy voices of the children die down, and yes, you could hear a pin drop.

Right now it was so quiet that you could truly have heard a pin drop as Jackie stared curiously at her first visitor and waited for her to say something.

'Let me look at you,' the woman cried enthusiastically, surprising Jackie with her familiarity. 'We had been wondering when you would be coming back, because as you know, once an islander, always an islander.' The woman continued speaking with a loud voice and suddenly grabbed Jackie by her shoulders to have a better look.

'Oh?' Jackie mumbled, unable to move in the firm grip of those hands.

'Yes, yes…nothing stays private here, darling.' The woman moved a bit closer to Jackie and stared seriously into her eyes. 'And I mean nothing.' She leaned back again and then added, 'A good thing to keep in mind.' She gave a knowing look, pursing her lips and raising her bushy eyebrows.

Jackie stared; what should she say? She was about to mumble something in the line of—'oh, thank you'—when the woman exclaimed loudly: 'So you have come back then.' She clasped her hands together tightly and began walking around the kitchen. Her weight made the old floor creak sadly with each step she took.

'You got tired of that bustling city life and wanted peace of mind and a more economical place to live.' The woman stated and winked, looking over her gold rimmed glasses.

'I guess,' Jackie said tentatively and stared at the strange woman in her kitchen.

'Yes that's what we all came here for.' The woman continued: 'All of a sudden the whole island filled up with people who wanted to stretch a penny a bit further.'

Jackie's eyes were glued to this woman who was opening and closing her grandmother's cupboard doors looking for something.

'Have we met?' Jackie finally had to ask, because, as much as she tried, she could not remember meeting this woman before.

'No, not really, but I have heard a great deal about you and your mother,' answered the woman, as she took two teacups from the cupboard while exclaiming cheerfully, 'There you are!' She walked to the sink and turned on the taps. The water gurgled in the pipes before shooting forcefully out of the faucet. The woman let the water run for awhile, till the colour of it was not so horrifyingly rusty. 'Tea?' She asked as she rolled up her sleeves and revealed two thick forearms.

'Uh...tea...yes, why not,' Jackie mumbled absentmindedly. 'My mother?' She fixed her eyes on the woman. 'You knew her then?' A surprised disbelief showed in her voice.

'No, goodness no.' She laughed loudly. 'I'm a newcomer here. I have lived in this village only for ten years now, but I have heard many stories about her.' The woman chatted cheerfully while she washed the cups in the sink, splashing the water generously over the sink and onto the counter.

'Stories...?' Jackie stared at her. She knew no stories of her mother whatsoever. Her mother had done nothing in her whole entire life that could be called a story. As far as Jackie knew, her mother was the epitome of correctness and had no connections to stories, gossip or fantasy. Her mother believed in accuracy, facts and a certain place in the much valued social hierarchy.

'Oh, yes.' The woman sighed loudly. 'Your mother was the wild one, if there is any truth to the stories I have heard in the pub. Very wild indeed. Your grandmother apparently went grey overnight when your mother crashed the car into the tree just outside the gate over there.' She nodded quickly toward the dust streaked window.

Jackie stretched her neck to look out the kitchen window. A big old oak tree stood there by the fence stretching its majestic branches over the little cottage. Jackie stared at the tree for a long time trying to digest what she had just heard. It was as if her whole life had been turned upside down. Her mother a wild girl? It just didn't sound right. It didn't sound like her mother at all.

'Now really, you can't be serious,' she finally uttered in profound shock. 'My mother a wild girl? You must be joking. She considered a skirt without pleats vulgar.'

The woman let out a deep, rippling laugh. 'You Callaghan girls always had a strange sense of humour, but pleated skirts, now that's funny.' The woman filled up the kettle and began the search for teabags. 'Now where an earth did she keep her teabags?' The strange woman opened the doors of almost all the cupboards until finally she cried out. 'Ah, found them.' She straightened up slowly, leaning with her big hands on her knees and cursed her weak back. 'What would you like? Earl Grey. Though you probably have no milk in the house…let me see…or strawberry, chamomile…good for your nerves, by the way…or…green tea?' She looked at Jackie. 'What would it be?'

'I think I need something stronger than tea,' Jackie mumbled scratching her head and darting her eyes between the strange woman in her kitchen and the big oak tree outside. 'But considering I just sold my apartment in the city, left my boyfriend, lost my job, had my thirty-second birthday, and buried my grandmother, I probably should go for chamomile.'

*   *   *

The next morning, when Jackie woke up she could not immediately remember where she was. She had slept peacefully in the guest bedroom, papered a long time ago with floral wallpaper. Thousands of tiny blue and pink flowers danced on the walls and on the ceiling. The air had a hint of old lavender with musty undertones, and the thick quilted floral blanket was heavy and slightly damp. She had forgotten how wet the island air was. She sat up in her bed stretching her hands over her head and letting her eyes slowly wander around the room. The cool morning air was fresh, and she could hear the seagulls in the far distance.

'Not bad,' she said to herself. 'Could be worse, much worse in fact.' She fell back onto the bed and stared at the slightly slanted flowered ceiling, slowly collecting her sleepy thoughts.

Her grandmother's house was in a quiet corner in a small village just off the busy main street. She could not hear the waves of the sea, but she smelled the salt in the air. She still remembered the shortcut to the beach through the neighbour's yard and she wondered if the mean dog was still alive. Probably not. Last time she had been to the cottage was many years ago as a teenager. After that her grandmother had bought an apartment on the mainland because island life in the winter had been too hard for her old bones. After a bridge had been built to replace the old ferry, it had become easier to visit the cottage even during the winter, but by then her grandmother was too ill and only went to the cottage for a few weeks in July.

Jackie could hear a neighbour trying to start a lawnmower. On the third try the machine did spring to life and the neighbour began noisily cutting the grass. 'It was a comforting sound in a strange way,' Jackie thought, just as the smell of cut grass drifted into the room through the slightly open window.

She had missed the island, she realized now. She had missed it without even knowing. Her grandmother had left the cottage to Jackie in her will, much to Jackie's mother's dismay. Her mother had wanted to sell the 'nasty piece of useless mould,' but Jackie had decided by then to move into the cottage and start her own business. What was there for her to lose? She had nothing to hold onto in the city. She had no job since the design company she had worked for had gone bankrupt. Her boyfriend was not much of a boyfriend, and she had inherited a beautiful cottage on an island which was becoming a very trendy summer tourist area with its vast sandy beaches and gentle rolling hills. 'Why not? Why not leave it all behind and start a new life?' She had asked her astonished and utterly shocked mother, who for once, was left without an answer.

Jackie smiled sleepily in her bed and turned around to look at the clock on the nightstand. It was early yet. The lace curtains were moving in the breeze and the lawnmower was coughing its way through the weeds on the neighbour's yard.

Her grandmother had always said that her heart belonged to the island, no matter how long she had been away on the mainland. She had also said, looking at Jackie with her kind green eyes, that Jackie was an islander as well, though she might not have realized it yet. Jackie remembered most fondly the many conversations they had over a cup of tea. Jackie's grandmother had always asked her about her life, the ups and downs and about the nice level ground. It had been a well-known fact that Jackie's mother was more interested in the ups of Jackie's life, things that would be easy to talk about in cafes while drinking a frothy latte macchiato. So Jackie bared her soul to her grandmother. From her mother, for practical reasons, she withheld everything.

She lay in the bed with the pink and blue flowers around her for a while longer before going downstairs to make a cup of coffee and begin her new islander's life. There was no food in the house, but she thought she would walk to the local store later on. In the cupboard she found a jar of hardened sugar and was able to scrape some off with the side of a spoon to sweeten her coffee.

She walked into the garden and sat down on a bench by the flowerbeds. The garden had grown wild during the absence of her grandmother. The flowers bloomed together with the weeds and hardy vines. The rosebush resembled a knobby tree and the lamb's ear had grown roots everywhere in the garden.

As a child Jackie had helped her grandmother weed the flowerbeds, and together they had planted a summer vegetable garden. She had loved those two months that she spent with her grandmother. She had taught Jackie how to paint, first with watercolours, and then later on with oils. They used to sit together on the old bench under a tree in the garden and paint flowers.

It was purely through her grandmother's influence and financial help that Jackie had gone to art school. The fact that her choice had made her mother furious had proved to the two of them that their choice was the right one.

'Betsy dear, Jackie is very talented,' her grandmother had said to Jackie's mother, who had snapped back icily, 'My name is Belinda, mother, not Betsy. B-e-l-i-n-d-a.' She had spelled slowly, while licking her lips angrily.

The cold mossy ground under Jackie's bare feet brought her back to the present. Unexpectedly she heard the gate open. The old hinges cried loudly making the neighbour's dog bark. A small older woman walked briskly in carrying a basket in the crook of her arm. She noticed Jackie in the garden and hollered cheerfully, 'Good morning. Wonderful day isn't it?'

'Yes it is,' Jackie answered, and then suddenly became aware of her clothes. 'I really have to buy a decent pair of pyjamas, or at least a robe,' she mumbled as she pulled the hem of her shrunken T-shirt down as much as she could. Holding onto her shirt she walked to the woman who was waiting for her on the front steps of the house.

'I thought you probably didn't have anything to eat in the house, so I brought you some muffins,' the woman said and gave Jackie a warm paper bag.

'Thank you,' was all Jackie could say as she held onto the parcel of muffins.

'They are blueberry muffins; I hope you like them.'

'I…I do,' Jackie mumbled.

'Oh, I'm sorry,' the woman laughed. 'I'm Muriel. I met Harriet yesterday, and she said that you had arrived and probably had no food in the house, so I thought I would just bake some muffins for you and drop them off on my way to the store.'

'Thank you. That was very kind of you,' Jackie said. Now she knew the name of the woman who had made her tea last night. By the time she had left, it had been too late to ask for her name. Jackie knew that in some way she should have just plainly asked, dropped the question there and then, but somehow she just couldn't find the right moment to form the words.

'I knew your grandmother and I'm happy to see that you have decided to move back to the island.' Muriel looked at the house and the garden. 'You have a lot of work ahead of you with this house. It hasn't been lived in permanently for a long time.' She pointed to the garden. 'If you need any plants, just come to my house. I'll be happy to give you some seedlings.'

'Thank you,' Jackie said again. She was touched by this older woman, who wore sensible walking shoes and a warm cardigan. 'Would you like some coffee?' She offered and waved her cup in the air. 'I have made plenty.'

'No no. I know you will be very busy getting this house in order, so I won't bother you any longer. If you need anything, I live in that white house around the corner.' Muriel pointed to her house. 'Drop in any time,' and with these words she left, closing the creaky gate behind her. The neighbour's dog continued his incessant barking with newly found vigour.

Jackie walked back to the bench under the tree and ate two of the muffins and finished her coffee while enjoying the cool and damp summer morning. She hadn't had such a lovely breakfast for as long as she could remember. She listened to the busy sounds of the village slowly beginning a new day. Somebody else started cutting the grass farther down the street, a radio was being switched on somewhere, the birds were singing in the trees and children were squealing with laughter. There were no angry car horns, no traffic jams, no echoes from the walls of the high-risers; there was no hot exhaust circling her legs when waiting for a bus on a busy street. Instead, there was tranquillity, and clean, crisp early morning air. Jackie took a deep breath, leaned her back against the old bench and closed her eyes.

She felt happiness spread slowly through her body. Perhaps she was an islander after all.

After having a shower, Jackie stepped out again. On her doorstep she found bread, butter, jam, a dozen eggs and a litre of milk. There were no notes to tell her who had brought all this food.

She took the food into the house, placed it on the old wobbly Formica table and looked skeptically at the old refrigerator in the corner of the kitchen. It looked as if it had been in a coma for the last ten years. She couldn't even begin to guess its age and she was terrified of opening it. Fortunately it was not so bad, and she found an old kitchen sponge that didn't look too disgusting and cleaned the fridge with a generous splash of antibacterial liquid. After that she stood back and closed her eyes as she inserted the plug into the wall socket. The loud churning of its motor began as the fridge sprang to life. Jackie was relieved to find that it still worked and she listened contentedly to its steady, though loud, humming while eating one more of Muriel's muffins. The kitchen had a fresh summer breeze blowing through it, making the white lace curtains dance in the wind and, outside, Jackie could hear the seagulls' hungry calls.

'The floor needs a good scrubbing,' she thought while licking the last bits of blueberry off her fingertips. 'And so do the counters and cupboards. Everything actually.' She looked around her kitchen and felt like a child playing house, but instead of mud pies, she was eating a real blueberry muffin.

As the word spread round the little village that Evelyn's granddaughter had returned, people dropped by to welcome Jackie back into the neighbourhood; in their eyes she had never left, only been accidentally away for a few years. Once an islander, always an islander. By the late afternoon Jackie realized that she really didn't have to go to the store, because somehow the old refrigerator had filled itself.

At five o'clock Harriet walked in with a champagne bottle under her wide arm. She took one look at the food on the table and said, 'Word of warning. Miss Kendal's meat pies are pretty deadly.'

'Oh,' was all Jackie could say as she watched Harriet open the cupboard and take out two glasses.

'Don't eat them unless you have at least two bottles of antacid in your cupboard.'

Jackie nodded and bit her bottom lip.

'Sit down,' Harriet said and opened the champagne. The cork flew into the sink with a loud pop. 'How was your first day here in Sycamore?' She poured the foaming champagne into the glasses.

Jackie sat down. 'Nice. It was nice.' She pushed her spider-web covered tangled hair away from her eyes and smiled. 'It was fantastic, actually.'

'Good to hear.' She gave Jackie a glass of champagne. 'Cheers! Welcome to the island.' Harriet winked as they clicked glasses together.

There was a knock at the kitchen door and a tall man walked in. He had black hair that fell on his well-proportioned face, and he had a very mischievous smile.

'Thomas!' Harriet yelled as she stared at the tall man, 'You smell champagne miles away. You are like a bloody bloodhound.'

Thomas grinned and bent down to kiss Harriet on her cheek. Then he turned to Jackie and handed her a small parcel.

'Welcome,' he said. 'It's nothing special, just a small something to welcome you into the neighbourhood. Aha, Miss Kendal's meat pies!' He also noticed the pie on the table. 'Don't eat them unless you have an iron stomach.' He sat down, folding his long legs under the table.

Jackie thanked him for his gift and for his well-meant advice.

'Could it be that you gave her something made out of glass, Thomas?' Harriet laughed and pushed his arm comradely.

'Could be.' Thomas grinned. 'Most likely. Well...' He hesitated for a moment. 'Most definitely,' he finally added, while slowly rubbing his chin.

Harriet got up and took a third glass from the cupboard and poured Thomas some champagne. 'Welcome to the island!' Thomas said as he lifted his glass in the air. 'Cheers!'

Jackie opened Thomas's present slowly. It was a beautiful small glass bowl. Jackie admired it honestly. She stared at the twirling spirals of translucent cobalt blue and emerald green. 'Thank you,' she finally uttered. 'You shouldn't have. I mean, I love it, but you really didn't have to bring me anything, honestly.'

'Oh, don't worry. I heard that you are a woodworker, so consider that gift as bribery. You might find me on your doorstep asking to borrow this and that in the future. After all we are all suffering artists and craftsmen.' Thomas winked cheerfully.

'Thomas is a glassblower, you know.' Harriet said to Jackie.

'Really!' Jackie grew excited. She was happy to know that there were other artists on the island.

'Yes, I have a glassblowing studio in the old fire station just outside the village. Drop in anytime. I'm there most of the time, since I live above the studio.'

'And if he is not there, then you can find him in the pub.' Harriet smiled.

'Now, now, Harriet. I might call that a slight exaggeration.' Thomas sighed and shook his head.

'I think not.' Harriet rolled her eyes and chuckled.

Thomas looked at Jackie and repeated his earlier words. 'In any case, drop in anytime.' He took a sip of champagne and continued; 'There are quite a few artists and crafts people here on the island. Life is more affordable here than in the city and the summer tourists' trade is quite good. The more studios we have, the more tourists we get. That's the way I think about it, anyway. So welcome fellow sufferer.' Thomas smiled his pleasant, slightly crooked smile as he lifted his glass.

'Thank you,' was all Jackie could say. She took a sip of champagne and looked at these two people in front of her in her own kitchen. She had been living in her grandmother's house less than a day and already people walked into her house as if she had been living there for years. One of her main worries had been a fear of feeling lonely on the island. It didn't look like she was going to suffer from solitude.

'So, tell me, Thomas. I heard that you are going through the young women in this village alphabetically, now.' Harriet enquired suddenly. 'What letter are you up to?'

'I'm meeting Emma later tonight at the pub. That's all.' Thomas answered defensively, running his long fingers through his tousled hair.

Harriet fixed her eyes on Jackie. 'This charming man here is not to be dated. He has no morals, but he does have a lovely soul.' Harriet smiled in a motherly way and slapped him on his leg. Thomas winced. Harriet was not known for her gentle touch.

'And you, Thomas. You leave this nice girl here alone, you hear.' Harriet was waving her finger in front of Thomas's face.

Thomas smiled and gently patted Harriet on her shoulders. 'Well I'm off to the pub. You two joining me?'

'Well...' was all Jackie managed to say before she was whisked to the pub.

All she could remember of that evening, when she finally fell into her own bed, was that she had met a pub full of new and interesting people. She had been introduced to everybody, warned about some people and given friendly advice all the way round.

She had met Nick, the owner of the pub, who was not the red nosed, overweight, burly man you would expect, but rather a friendly looking young man with an easy smile on his honest face. Nick lightheartedly reminded Jackie about their famous fight in Jackie's grandmother's backyard when they were children. Jackie stared at Nick for awhile before remembering the laughing freckled-faced boy with hard fists. She was about to apologize for the black eye she had given him on that hot summer day long ago, when George the hardware owner grabbed her by her arm, and promised her a discount because he had just heard that Jackie was a woodworker. George was pushed aside by Hilary, the beauty parlour owner who told Jackie that her hair needed trimming and that she should drop in any time. Hilary promised, with a very sombre tone, that she would bring out the woman in her. Jackie stared at Hilary's rather red lips and her gravity-defying bleached hair. Jackie was scared what Hilary might bring out of her. She wasn't even sure what kind of woman was lurking inside her, but she was quite sure that it wasn't the one Hilary had in mind. She escaped Hilary's friendly offers with the help of an old, but not frail, man named Russell.

Jackie had been promised a kitten and a puppy by somebody she no longer remembered. Thomas had already borrowed some money from her, and Harriet had given a strong speech about a better money management plan. The pastor had not been offended when Jackie had told him that she rarely went to church. She had softened her refusal by offering him a pint, which had made Jack Wilkinson, a man permanently fused to the table he shared with his best mates, call her a diplomat, which in turn ignited a deep, heated discussion about the latest news on the political front and had absolutely nothing to do with Jackie's abilities as a diplomat.

Chapter 2

Bankers and Bills

Jack Wilkinson was, as always, sitting at the table by the window whenever Jackie happened to step into the pub. He would greet her with his generous grin and periodically call her a diplomat, especially if he was in need of a pint or two.

'Never bite the hand that feeds Jack Wilkinson.' He smiled shamelessly and gave his advice freely to anybody who was near enough to hear him.

And, as always, Nick was there behind the bar, happily weeding around the exaggerated truths of Jack Wilkinson's stranger than life stories. Thomas still owed Jackie some money, and she still bought the pastor pints when she felt slightly guilty for not going to church. She had mysteriously acquired a dog and a cat and she had learned how to kindly refuse offers for more kittens and puppies.

Her grandmother's house had become her home, her own first real home. Just like the second morning in the village, she still, once in a while, woke up with an aching head and told herself not to drink that very last pint at the pub ever, ever again.

Jackie had slowly cleaned up her grandmother's house. The moving van had arrived a few days after her arrival, and she had unpacked everything in one day, which made her realize how very little she owned. She still slept in the guest room, and those tiny blue and pink flowers were still there on the walls and on the ceiling looking at her when she woke up. Felix the dog had a basket beside her bed, and Oscar the cat brought her mice after his wild nocturnal travels in the neighbourhood.

In the mornings she made herself a cup of coffee and walked around her garden with the hot mug warming her hands. She loved how cold and damp the grass felt on her bare feet. It was cool in the shade under the trees, and she was still amazed at how quiet it was. This coffee walk had become her morning ritual, after which she usually worked on her future studio beside the house.

She had used the left over money from the sale of her apartment to remodel the old barn behind the house into a studio. Gallons of white paint and countless hours of back-breaking work had been needed to transform the old building into a working studio and a brightly lit gallery. A steady line of friendly advisers had daily been walking through the small barn. She had been told many things—things she could do and things that would be unadvisable to do. She had been the talk of the pub, the post office and the flower shop for months till the gallery was finally finished. Nothing had fallen down, and the roof had remained in its original place, much to everyone's surprise. Jack Wilkinson had lost the bet, and Thomas had collected the winnings with a grand smile on his face.

Jackie had been very proud of that moment when she had finally hung the sign in front of her gate: Jacqueline Callaghan Gallery. She had celebrated by inviting Nick, Thomas and Harriet for a dinner, which they ate happily in the kitchen sitting at the old Formica table with the wobbly leg. Jackie had made it less wobbly by folding a brand new piece of thick cardboard and putting it under the slightly shorter leg. She promised to fix it as soon as she had more time.

'Not bad,' Thomas had said after looking around the gallery. 'Not bad at all.'

Jackie had taken his words as a compliment. Nick had been very impressed, and Harriet had not stopped saying, 'Fantastic, girl, absolutely bloody fantastic!' especially after they had opened the second bottle of champagne.

Jackie loved the architectural feeling of her gallery. She loved the plain white walls and the old wooden beams that cut that pristine white surface of the slanted ceiling. She loved her stainless steel table and bright halogen lights. She even loved the small basket where she kept all of her pencils. She had placed her business cards in neat stacks on the little table in her gallery. The cards had felt shiny under her fingers and they had that new paper smell, which Jackie loved. Jackie enjoyed sitting at her gallery table drinking her cup of tea at night and looking at the results of her hard work. She felt the joyous pounding of her heart and let her eyes wander around the room. She smiled.

After awhile, small orders began to come in from the galleries and gift shops she had contacted. The tourists that came to the island to spend their summer vacations had found her gallery. Nick had helped by sending anybody who was even slightly interested in arts to visit Jackie's gallery. Jackie's gallery was open six days a week during the busy summer months. When there weren't too many customers, she worked in the studio making peppermills.

She was making a living. She wasn't rich by any means; getting new galleries to represent her work was difficult and demanded a lot of smiling, even when the answers she had expected to be positive had turned out to be negative. It was far easier to design and make things than to sell them.

Her mother had come for a quick visit. She had looked around the village, and then she had shaken her head with slight distaste and sighed sorrowfully. 'For the life of me, I do not understand how you can possibly live on this god-forsaken island. But if you must, you must, though I find it an absolute waste of time.'

Jackie had taken her words as encouragement because that was as close to an endorsement her mother would ever be able to give.

'It's so quaint,' her best friend Jill had said about the village when she came for a weekend visit with her husband Robbie.

'Loved the pub,' Robbie had said, and then, rubbing his temples with his fingers, he had added weakly, 'maybe too much.'

Later on Sunday afternoon when Jill and Robbie were getting into their car to drive back home, they were surprised when one of the villagers walked to the car and brought them a puppy. Apparently, Robbie, while drinking his sixth pint, had more than eagerly agreed to take it since he loved dogs so very much. At least those were the old man's words. Jill sat in the front seat with the adorable drooling puppy on her lap, as Robbie traced those murky midnight moments in his pounding head and tried to avoid Jill's piercing looks.

*   *   *

After drinking the third cup of coffee, cleaning the house, washing the laundry and chatting with Jill on the phone while doing the dishes, Jackie had to face the now unavoidable task of sorting through the bills and bank statements. This was the once a month inevitable nightmare that she always tried to avoid. She said to herself, very unconvincingly, that 'maybe the money will somehow float in, or there is money in the bank that I have forgotten to count or, even better, maybe the bank will suddenly decide to give an amazingly high interest rate to their customers.' Sadly the answer was always 'no.'

She carried her cup of coffee to the table and switched on the computer. She stretched her neck and told herself not to get too depressed. Somehow the total amount of money in her bank account never reached Jackie's hopes and aspirations, never mind how many times she calculated and re-calculated. She loved her work and her studio. She said to herself that she could even deal with her strangest, most demanding clients, if she knew that there would be some money left in the bank at the end of the month.

Money was scarce, and while that had been the acceptable norm when she was in her twenties, now in her thirties that scarceness had an underlying nastiness attached to it. Bohemian turned into a bankrupt thirty-something. She grunted and thought fleetingly about setting up a pension plan and then went to make another cup of coffee, hoping for someone to call her and interrupt her misery.

She was putting water in the kettle when the phone rang.

'Lovely.' Jackie smiled and rushed to the phone. 'The best scenario would be an order for peppermills,' she fantasized as she answered the phone. 'The worst would be…' She didn't have time to finish her thought before she heard an all-too-familiar voice.

'Jackie, it's me.'

'Good morning, Mom,' she said as she stared at the wall. 'How are you?'

'Fine, just fine. I'm going to a luncheon later on today. I have just a few minutes before I'll have to be on my way.'

'Oh,' Jackie said and wondered why on earth her mother would call her if she was so busy and pressed for time.

'You know that Penny's daughter is going to get married this fall. We received the invitation for the engagement party this morning. I called Penny immediately and she said that she has been on the phone all morning long. The poor woman is quite tired. His name is Charles and he is a banker.'

'Banker...that's what I need,' Jackie thought dreamily while her mother continued her monologue.

'Yes, can you imagine? A banker! He's six feet, five inches tall and loves to play tennis. You should start playing tennis, dear. Next time you are in town, I'll take you to the tennis club. That's where Charles and Tracy met. Do you have tennis shoes?'

There was a half a second silence that caught Jackie by surprise. 'What? Sorry, Mom. I missed you right there. Do I have what?'

'Tennis shoes. You can't wear your running shoes to play tennis, you know. It's bad for your ankles.'

'No, Mom. I don't have tennis shoes.'

'Well, that's all right. We'll go and get you some when you are in town next time.'

'That won't be necessary.' Jackie managed finally to put a few words in. 'As you know, I do not know how to play tennis.'

'Oh, that doesn't matter. You just hit the ball over the net and wear a miniskirt. That's what Penny said Tracy did, and, quite frankly, you have much nicer legs than Tracy. She has always been a bit on the plump side. Penny had a nice figure when she was young. I don't know what happened to Tracy. Must be from her father's side...So anyway, the Curtises are coming and so are the Flemings. Do you remember Jamie, their son? He's coming as well, and you should receive an invitation any day now. You need to come earlier because we need to go and buy you a nice new outfit for the wedding. Last time you were here, you were wearing a pair of jeans, and it just does my head in that a girl with legs like yours would hide them in baggy pants! You have a lovely figure, Jacqueline, and you should make the most of it now that you are still young-ish.' Jackie's mother let out a long, deep, meaningful sigh. Jackie could imagine her mother shaking her head sadly, feeling sorry for herself for having an unmarried young-ish daughter.

'Well I better run now,' her mother continued. 'Nice chatting with you. I really miss you, Jacqueline, and I miss our nice daughter-mother chats. Penny talks to Tracy everyday, now with the wedding and all. Penny said that Tracy should just move back home till the wedding takes place. There's so much work to be done—invitations, the cake, the dress, and everything, you know. Well bye for now, dear.'

She was gone.

Jackie put the phone down and thought about the bank statements that were waiting for her on the kitchen table. Somehow the work ahead didn't seem that bad anymore. What could possibly be more intimidating than a phone conversation with her mother? She bent down to fix the sock that had a hole in it and thought fleetingly about miniskirts and tennis. If her mother could see her and her torn sock right now. She laughed to herself and slowly picked up the electric bill from the table. The loan payment for the machinery was next, then the telephone bill and the plumber's bill. Lord, how she had started to resent the sight of the plumber's bright yellow van in her driveway. 'Luckily there is no gas bill,' she murmured and grabbed the remaining stack of bills: Internet connection, lumber, shipping account, bill for the bubble wrap needed for packaging, bill for the grinder parts for the peppermills, wood glue, sandpaper, wood stains, light bulbs, lacquer. There didn't seem to be an end to the list. It went on and on. Jackie stared at the numbers. They were not lying. She was not meeting her budget and the pension plan would have to be postponed indefinitely. She placed her chin in the cup of her hands and looked intently at the computer screen. Maybe she had mistakenly left a zero out? Hope flickered in the air for awhile and then disappeared without a trace. No, there was no mistake. She was extremely bohemian and exceptionally poor.

She was expecting some money in a few weeks, but these kinds of numbers scared her. She would have to call a few galleries and inquire after the money they still owed her. She hated that even more than balancing the books. Then she would have to go after new clients and galleries. She would have to take new photos of her new production line and then, for a while, play the role of a salesman.

'Oh, lord,' she sighed heavily. 'I hate being poor. Obviously I need to learn to play tennis, wear a miniskirt and marry a rich, tall banker.' She laid her head on top of the bills and stared at the peeling wallpaper on the opposite wall. Felix licked her bare toes, and absentmindedly she scratched him behind the ears.

After wallowing for a while in sadness and desperation, she had another cup of coffee and began thinking about her money problems seriously. It was a desperate situation and drastic measures needed to be taken. Unfortunately, feeling sorry would not fix anything.

'How did that saying go again,' she mumbled and bit her bottom lip. 'If the mountain does not come to you, you go to the mountain... something like that.'

She went to her studio and sat down at her worktable, chewing the end of her drawing pencil vigorously with uncertain determination.

'I need to bring an effing big mountain to my front door.' She stared at her corkboard on the wall; pinned onto it were drawings of her previous designs. She looked at them with the end of the pencil still in her mouth, thinking and swivelling in her chair.

She needed new designs that were fast and easy to produce. She made mostly peppermills, but what she really wanted to make was unique furniture, like the table she had just finished; but not many people ordered unique furniture.

'Think small and efficient,' she said to herself. She continued staring at her previous designs, speaking to herself and thinking absentmindedly about weddings and her mother.

'Salt shakers! I will need to start making salt shakers to match the peppermills...couples, weddings...pairs.' She took the badly chewed pencil from her mouth and tapped it against the table, pleased to have gotten an idea. 'That could work.'

She grabbed a sheet of paper and took her coloured pencils out. 'It could work,' she mumbled as she drew lines onto the paper. 'I need to think about simplicity and something poignantly unique.'

She worked until it was time to take Felix for a walk. She felt better already. Having a plan was definitely better than no plan, even though she did not know if it would work. But then again, people got married every day, and somebody might want to have a bride and groom salt shaker and pepper grinder set. 'Thank you, mother, thank you, Tracy, and thank you Mr. Banker.' She said inaudibly as she left the gallery, still a bit worried that she might have entered into the world of kitsch. She bit her lip, looked at the new design drawings pinned to the corkboard and then thought about her empty bank account. A desperate situation needed, indeed, a desperate solution. No, the design was just rogue enough not to cross the border into kitsch. She was safe.

She whistled for Felix and they began walking their normal route by the sea. She looked at the few tourists walking along the beach. It was still very early in the season. The yacht club was busy with people preparing their boats to be put into the water, and the smell of paints and sealants drifted along the shore.

The village needed to bring more tourists into the area, extend the summer season and tap into the pre-Christmas season. If she could somehow make it possible, maybe then the bank manager would start smiling at her once more. She was deep in thought as she walked with Felix. Suddenly she had an idea. Maybe there could be a way. She felt around in her pocket and found a crumpled-up piece of paper that she had stuffed in there a month ago. She sat down on a rock on the beach and let Felix run loose. She straightened the brochure against her knee and stared at it for a long time. The wind blew her hair around her face. She wrapped her loose hair around her hand and closed her eyes, letting the wind caress her face. Maybe it could be done, just maybe. An idea was slowly beginning to form in her head, but she needed to talk to Thomas first—just to try her idea out before she would begin working with it. She opened her eyes and put the piece of paper back into her pocket.

She was on her way to Thomas's glass studio in the old fire station on the east side of the village. The street was nice and cozy with a touch of old-fashioned neighbourhood feeling that involved laughing children in pastel dresses and dark blue pants running peacefully down the street. On the left side of the street was a bed and breakfast with a sign in the front garden, painted in muted colours with a simple flowered border. The sign said 'East End Bed and Breakfast.' Outside the door were two equally well-groomed, slightly city-looking but friendly and attractive men with a dog on a leash. The men stopped for a moment as Jackie passed by with Felix.

Jackie waved her hand and hollered, 'I just finished your new breakfast table. The varnish still needs to dry over night but I'll bring it over tomorrow.'

One of the men answered and an expectant smile spread over his face. 'Great. See you tomorrow.'

Jackie continued walking. A group of teenage girls were walking toward her giggling like teenage girls do and bumping into each other for no particular reason.

'Hi girls!' Jackie said.

'Hi Jackie!' the girls giggled a bit more.

'Do you know if Thomas is still working?'

This time the level of giggling was deafening. Amongst the laughter, Jackie could hear, 'Yes, he is.'

There was more giggling and nudging. The teenagers seemed to fuse together into a moving mass of hilarity, where one hand intertwined with the other's body. You couldn't really tell who was who in the group since all the girls were wearing denim, creating a singular cloud of giggling indigo.

'Well, thanks girls. You all have a good night.' Jackie was amused.

'You too, Jackie,' said the indigo cloud. The girls continued walking toward the centre of the village when they looked back at

Jackie and then whispered something to each other which caused them, again, to burst into uncontrollable giggles.

Jackie remained standing still and looking at the vanishing girls. She shook her head at the thought of how young the girls seemed to be, and then immediately got scared at the thought of how old that would make her! She shivered and wondered if she had behaved like that when she was a teenager. She couldn't quite remember, and that irritated her.

The fire station was an old building that had been expertly and elegantly renovated. On top of the double doors was a bright sign that said: Thomas Stockwell Glass Studio Gallery.

Jackie opened one of the double doors and stepped into the dimly lit gallery. She could hear the humming sound of the glory hole. There was a slit of light coming from the darkened studio and she could hear Thomas singing along with his CD.

'Jesus!' Jackie said to herself. 'He is still listening to Bryan Adams.' She heard Thomas wailing along with the 'Summer of 69' song. In all honesty it could not be called singing. Jackie put Felix into Thomas's office and walked into the studio. It was too dangerous for a young dog to run free in a glass studio.

Jackie had been very interested in glassblowing and Thomas had taught her how to make small things. Now, when she stepped into the glass studio, she knew what was what and what it was for.

The glass was melted in the furnace. The glory hole was where the pieces were reheated to make them hot again so that it was possible to form the glass into the desired shape. The blowpipes were used to blow air through them to make the piece of hot glass hollow from the inside. Then there was the puntil rod that Thomas attached to the bottom of the piece he was working on to be able to open the front of it. There were also the paddles, shears and odd scissors. The list continued endlessly. It had taken a long time for Jackie to learn to use the correct names of the tools. She was always concentrating so hard on avoiding a disaster that the names just slipped out of her mind. She drove Thomas crazy by calling the annealer an oven.

'We are not baking fucking muffins here!' he used to shout before launching into a detailed technical description of the importance of an annealer 'It is called an annealer,' he would say slowly with a newly acquired teacher voice that was so irritatingly calm and condescending that it made Jackie want to make faces at him. 'It is the place where you slooowly cool the glass pieces down to room temperature.' Jackie hid her yawn behind her dirty hand and murmured, faking enthusiasm. 'Oh, really? How very fascinating!'

Glassblowing was a very technical art form and Jackie did admire Thomas for his skill and perseverance, but of course, she could not say that to him. He already had a very high opinion of himself, which he freely and constantly expressed to Jackie. Jackie's response was inevitably, 'Bugger off!'

Thomas stood up and stepped in front of the glory hole to reheat the piece of glass he was working on. As soon as he opened the door, the scorching orange glow hit his face.

'Hi Thomas!' Jackie said. 'Are you still listening to that 80s crap?'

'Oh, hi Jackie!' Thomas looked quickly over his shoulder. 'For your information, it is not crap. It is retro rock.'

'Retro crap,' Jackie repeated and laughed.

'Perfect timing! Bring me a bit, will you.' Thomas was back sitting on his workbench, rolling the blow pipe on two metal arms attached to the bench. It all looked very medieval, but served its purpose perfectly.

Jackie sighed and took off her jacket, scarf and hat and put on an extra pair of safety glasses from the nearby table.

'You could ask nicer, you know,' Jackie said as she walked to the glass furnace.

'We retro-crap men don't talk pretty,' Thomas grinned from his workbench and waited for Jackie to bring him the hot glass bit.

Jackie stood in front of the furnace, 'How big of a bit?'

'Not too big.'

'Well that's very helpful crap-man,' Jackie murmured under her breath. She opened the door of the furnace and immediately the immense heat hit her face. It burned her cheeks and all the moisture disappeared from her lips. She pushed the metal rod into the mass of golden molten glass and then turned the rod very quickly with her fingers and at the same time she pulled it outwards with hot glass gathered onto the end of it. It always reminded her of scooping honey from the jar.

'Come on. I don't have all day,' Thomas told her impatiently.

'Oh, shut up, will you?' Jackie retorted. She closed the furnace door with her elbow and kept turning the rod in her hands so that the molten glass would not fall off. It looked much easier than it was. She walked to the bench where Thomas was standing, resting the blowpipe's one end on the top of his shoe, while holding the hot end pointed up toward the ceiling.

Jackie lifted her rod up with the molten glass wrapped around the end of it. Thomas grabbed the rod with his tools that reminded Jackie of crab claws, and attached the soft, hot, pliable glass confidently onto the bottom of his glass piece, and then cut off the rest. He sat down again and began turning the blowpipe, and, at the same time, he pushed the still elastic glass bit firmly, fusing it to the glass piece. He looked at the result and smiled proudly. 'When you got it, you got it.' He smirked at Jackie, got up, and went back to the glory hole to reheat the quickly cooling piece of glass.

Meanwhile, Jackie put the used rod into a big metal barrel with the other rods. She could hear the sharp sound of broken glass grinding against the side of the barrel. Jackie observed Thomas carefully. She was waiting for him to say something.

'Okay, you take the piece. Give it a short ten seconds, reheat it in the hole…'

The barking order came as she expected.

Jackie did not move. Thomas looked at Jackie, puzzled, raising his eyebrows. 'Please,' he added tentatively after awhile.

Jackie smiled and walked to the bench and took the glass piece from Thomas. 'See how easy it is to be civilized. You should try it more often.' She laughed cheerfully. 'It might suit you, you know.'

'Stop yapping, woman!'

Jackie smiled. The two of them were by now such good friends that they could be murderously brutal with each other. When Jackie had first moved to the village, the rumours had begun circulating almost instantly about her dating Thomas. But as Jackie put it to

Harriet, 'Thomas is too much in love with himself to be ready to date anybody, never mind to love them.' Then she added almost as an afterthought. 'And he is too beautiful a man for me to date; just look at his long eyelashes and voluminous black hair.'

Harriet had laughed heartily and, after her quick but informative visit to the post office, the rumours had died down. Though once in awhile, during the cold and damp winter months when there was no other gossip available to keep people's blood from freezing, they became an item again. That was until something else worth talking about happened.

Thomas walked to the furnace and opened its door. He gathered a small piece of glass on the end of the rod with the confident moves that only come after many years of perfecting his craft.

Jackie was sitting on the workbench waiting for Thomas. It was very warm in front of the furnaces.

Thomas was very proud of how he prepared his punty, which was crucial for holding onto the almost finished piece. A bad punty would mean an end to hours worth of hard work. Thomas whistled and cheerfully lectured Jackie about the importance of doing things properly in the glass studio. Jackie faked yet another yawn and told him politely to shut up. Thomas shrugged his shoulders and walked to the bench with his perfectly made punty. He attached it to the centre of the newly made foot. For a moment everything stopped—the rolling glass piece, now with two metal pipes attached to it, and the two pairs of working hands. Nothing moved. Then, as if given a signal, Thomas began to turn his end of the pipe slowly, and Jackie's hands swiftly followed his movement. They broke the piece off from the blowpipe with a one slight bang from an ancient-looking metal tool. The glass piece was cut off from the neck of the pipe where the opening of the vase would be. The nascent vase was now attached only to the puntil rod, which Thomas was holding and swinging in the air in an attempt to get a better grip while balancing the fragile piece.

Jackie leaned against the wall to watch. 'How come I always have to work when I come to see you?' She inquired.

'It's hard to say no to free labour.' Thomas laughed. 'Thanks for your help.'

Jackie sighed and walked into the dark gallery next door. She flicked on the lights. The effect was dramatic. The colourful glass objects on transparent shelves were lit from behind with bright lights. The gallery was a vast, glowing sea of orange, yellow, blue, green, purple and red against the pristine white background. The colours sparkled and shined, creating new colours where they overlapped. Jackie stood in the doorway and admired the sight. She could hear Thomas in the background sorting out the studio after finishing off. There was a sound of banging and crashing and then a sudden silence. The glory hole had been switched off, the constant humming had stopped and the studio had become eerily silent.

Thomas walked into the gallery clasping his hands together. 'Hey, you want a beer?'

'Sure, why not.' Jackie responded.

Thomas disappeared into the small office. He greeted Felix and continued talking to Jackie with a loud voice while rummaging through his fridge in the corner. 'You know, you would make a decent glassblower...'

'Thanks for the compliment, but I'll stick to my woodworking, if you don't mind. It's less hot.'

Thomas came out of the office carrying two cold beers. He smiled with his head tilted to one side. 'But woodworking is so dusty...Now glassblowing. That is an ancient art form where physical challenges meet aesthetic desires.' He handed the other beer to Jackie.

'Thanks. Your poetic soul frightens me.' Jackie opened her beer and took a sip. 'Is that the way you pick up your girls? I always thought of you more like, "fancy a shag?" type of man.' Jackie smiled into her beer and fought back giggles.

'No respect at all.' Thomas grunted. 'A man tries to be poetic and all he gets back is sneering.'

'Sorry.' Jackie laughed out loud, not sorry at all.

Thomas's 'no respect' mumbles went on as he swigged back his beer. Jackie smiled and watched him for awhile before beginning to explain the reason for her visit.

'You know,' she said tentatively testing the air before saying too much. 'I have a crazy idea.'

'Idea?' Thomas pretended to gulp air in astonishment.

'Oh, cut it out, you big...' Jackie pretended to think hard. 'You know, I have run out of sufficiently insulting words to describe you.' Jackie shook her head from side to side pretending to show feelings of great sadness.

Thomas rolled his eyes, 'Okay, what you got on your mind, girl?'

Jackie hopped onto the table and looked at Thomas seriously. 'You know what a studio tour is?' she asked him.

'Yes, I think so.' Thomas rubbed his chin where the late afternoon shadow was beginning to show. 'Isn't it some kind of artists' studio open house that brings many, many tourists to one area to see artists and their studios so that they can chat with the artists and hopefully buy many, *many, many* pieces of art...something like that?'

'Yes, the general idea is to increase tourism during the slow times on an island like ours, for example.' Jackie nodded her head. She was happy that Thomas seemed interested in her idea. It showed promise.

'With heavy emphasis on the buying and selling aspect.' Thomas was now smiling, showing his beautiful white teeth.

'Now you are getting it.' Jackie lifted her bottle and saluted Thomas.

'I love it already. Anything that promises to make me a rich man makes me happy.'

Jackie took the crumpled brochure out of her pocket and handed it to Thomas. 'Look at this and tell me what you think?'

Thomas put his beer down on the table and opened the brochure, glancing quickly through it. Jackie played with her bottle while waiting for Thomas to finish. She shifted nervously in her seat and started tapping the side of the table with her fingers.

Thomas took another sip of his beer, scratched his chin. 'Well...' He let the unsaid words float in the air.

'I think we have enough artists in this area for a good tour.' Jackie cut in animatedly.

'How many studios are we talking about?' Thomas enquired and studied the cover design of the brochure while waiting for Jackie's answer.

'I don't know...ten...twelve?'

'Who did you have in mind?' He looked up at Jackie, and then suddenly an unpleasant thought came to his mind and caused him to shake his head in disbelief. '*No*, not the Clay General, I'm begging you. Not the bloody marching music Clay General! Please. Have mercy on my poor, *poor* soul.' Thomas's face expressed deep desperation.

'Oh, come on, Thomas. Sheridan is a very talented potter and he is also quite well known...never mind his taste in music,' Jackie said solemnly. Poor Thomas! Sheridan was perhaps the only person in this world who absolutely rubbed him the wrong way. Not that Sheridan regarded Thomas very highly either. 'Besides, you don't have a soul.' She pointed out merrily and tapped softly on Thomas's chest.

'You are a mean woman, Jacqueline Victoria Callaghan. Very mean.' Thomas breathed in dramatically. 'And I do have a soul.' He continued speaking, slowly emphasizing every word. 'I might even go as far as to call it a sensitive soul.' He lifted his chin theatrically and placed his hand over his heart. He looked dashingly ridiculous.

'Now you are just making me sick.' Jackie shook her head and was forced to laugh. 'Seriously though, Sheridan is a good artist.'

'Yeah, unfortunately you're right. We do need the bugger.' Thomas sighed.

'Just promise me you'll behave yourself.' Jackie warned Thomas.

Thomas did not look too happy at the thought of behaving well in front of Sheridan, the Clay General.

'Anyhow I was going to go and talk with him on my way home and I thought I would have a chat with Nick, as well, about using the pub as a sort of a base camp.'

Thomas mumbled something and gave Jackie a sideways glance that was meant to demonstrate his hurt feelings.

Jackie was amused. 'So, Tommy-boy, will you help me?'

Thomas stared at Jackie with a slight smile spreading across his face. 'Okay, you can count me in. I'll give you all of my moral support and, if you want, my not so moral support.'

'You poor, poor sick man.' Jackie put her empty beer bottle down, and shook her head sadly as she went back into the studio to get her jacket.

When she returned to the gallery Thomas was still sitting on his desk drinking beer. He watched Jackie put her jacket on. 'I might be poor, but I'm not sick. It is called a healthy sexual appetite.' Thomas grinned with a wide smile, banishing any possibility of a leer from his appealing boyish face.

'Here's an apple for you, then.' Jackie snapped. She grabbed an apple from a bowl on the table and, as she walked to the door, she threw it at him. Thomas caught it easily. She walked out the gallery door with Felix at her heel. Thomas vigorously wiped the caught apple onto his jeans and took a hungry bite. He was still chewing when he hollered loudly and cheerfully after Jackie.

'See you later, Eve!'

'I seriously hope not.' Jackie said and slammed the door shut behind her.

Chapter 3
The Birth of an Idea

Jackie walked toward the centre of the village with Felix prancing behind her. She stopped in front of an old Victorian house which had a meticulously painted sign in the front garden: Sheridan Watson Artistic Ceramic Atelier. Jackie had helped him make the sign. Sheridan had originally wanted to add the words 'High Quality,' but the sign hadn't had enough space. Reluctantly he had settled for a much shorter version. The word 'studio' apparently had too much of a folksy feeling, and he had been afraid that that people might think of him as a hobbyist.

'As you know, I am a serious artist,' he had said to Jackie, speaking very slowly in order to make his words sound more meaningful.

Jackie stared at the sign, and then let out a long sigh as if that sigh could have expelled her nervousness. Not that she was afraid of Sheridan; she just wasn't sure if she would be ready for the complications. Sheridan was noted for his passion for minuscule details. She bit her lip, walked in through the gate and rang the doorbell with a stronger outward determination than she felt.

An older man opened the front door and loud marching music blasted into the still evening. Sheridan Watson stood in the lit doorway in all of his mighty height and width. He took his pipe slowly out of his mouth.

'Aha! Jackie! What a surprise!' He bellowed with a deep gurgling voice as he pointed his pipe toward her. 'And to what do I owe this pleasure?'

Sheridan Watson was dressed all in khaki. He was generously plump in the middle, giving the impression that his head and feet were proportionally too small for his rotund body. He stood very straight, like a general. You could easily draw a straight line from the back of his head to the heels of his shoes. His toes, however, due to his wide girth, were in permanent shadow. The colonial-safari look about him made Jackie smile. She stared at him and tried to hear what he was saying. It was almost impossible, though, because of the blasting marching music that made her eardrums vibrate.

'Good evening, Sheridan. I hope it isn't too late,' she yelled as politely as one can possibly yell.

'God no!' Sheridan shook his head. 'Please come in.'

'Thank you,' Jackie said and stepped into the house as Sheridan closed the door behind them. Felix sneaked in and Jackie told him to wait by the door. Sheridan was not too keen on dogs unless they were hunting dogs and, therefore, of some use. Felix was disappointed. He had wanted to search the kitchen floor for crumbs, but that would have been a futile quest: the house was immaculate. Even the pillows on the sofa were orderly and evenly placed, leaning a perfect forty-five degrees to the right.

'Please, come in, come in.' Sheridan beckoned and turned off the blasting marching music by banging his hand heavily against the CD player's buttons. The CD player, certainly, was off, but both doors of the tape deck simultaneously flew open. There was nothing quiet and settled about Sheridan.

'Sit down, sit down, Jackie. It's a cool night out there.' He slammed his hands together loudly and rubbed them vigorously. 'Would you like to have a glass of cognac with me?'

'I wouldn't say no to a small one.' Jackie sat gingerly on the edge of the sofa between the organized pillows, trying not to knock them down like a set of dominos.

Sheridan opened the cabinet doors and took out a bottle of cognac and a pair of glasses. He poured the cognac while slamming the door closed with his knee. When finished, he thumped the bottle down, and put the cap back on. He handed one glass to Jackie and then sat down heavily on a chair beside the sofa.

'Now, my girl, what brings you here?' he asked, after taking a long drink from his glass. He folded his round fingers on the glass and leaned back in his chair, ready to listen.

Jackie thought for a moment about how she should start her explanation. She moved hesitantly on the firm sofa, put her glass on the table, and placed her hands on top of her knees tapping them slightly.

'Well, I was wondering if it would be possible to arrange a studio tour here on our island?' Jackie took the brochure out of her pocket.

'Studio tour?' Sheridan put his glass down on the table with his usual bang. He lit his pipe and puffed while staring into the distance, narrowing his eyes.

'I have heard of those things.' He took his pipe out of his mouth and once again pointed it at Jackie. 'Now, that sounds quite interesting, quite interesting…uh…more tourists…' He put his pipe back into his mouth and seemed to be completely absorbed in smoking. 'Interesting…' His voice trailed off. 'More spending power…extra income to the area businesses…huh.' He took his pipe out of his mouth again and continued. 'As a member of the area's business association, I really cannot say no to that.'

He leaned with some difficulty toward the table to grab his glass of cognac, his firm unyielding waistline causing some trouble.

Jackie showed him her brochure, and Sheridan studied it carefully, huffing while reading about the artists—some of whom he thought highly of, and some of whom he thought were quite shockingly amateurish. He grunted his approval and then handed the brochure back to Jackie. As Sheridan took a sip of his cognac, a disagreeable thought occurred to him. He looked up at Jackie. His already small eyes were formed into two narrowing slits, and his lips had acquired a strange purplish hue.

'Who were you thinking of inviting?' Again, his pipe was pointed menacingly at Jackie. 'Not that Pretty Glass Boy, I hope.'

There was a pause, and Jackie quickly collected her thoughts while listening to a cuckoo clock croak six times in the other room. 'Well, to be totally honest with you, Sheridan, I just came from his studio.' Jackie swallowed hard and stared intently at her glass, avoiding Sheridan's eyes.

Sheridan resumed smoking and was now staring at the ceiling. His stout, short feet were sticking out as if unable to bend. 'Uh…I guess we would need him…too bad, too bad.' He stammered as another plume of smoke billowed out of his pipe.

Jackie stared at the cloud of smoke and then suggested shyly. 'I believe his studio would fit in very nicely, wouldn't you say?'

'Yes, yes, unfortunately you might be quite right.' Sheridan sighed deeply, as he spoke with an obvious strain in his voice. 'You just might be right.'

'So I can count you and your studio in?' Jackie was sounding carefully optimistic. She was looking for firm ground to stand on. Sheridan did not answer right away, so Jackie added quickly, not wanting to lose the momentum. 'Because we really need your talent. It would not be as good without you.' She looked at him as if listening to his mood. 'You know that I'm right, Sheridan. You are an expert in your field.' She added, shamelessly flattering him.

'Yes, yes, you are quite right.' He shook his head as he spoke. 'I can't let you down, young girl.' He put his pipe down and got up slowly, leaning on his knobby knees. 'So count me in.' He offered his hand to seal their agreement with a firm handshake. 'Yes, yes, count me in.' He said once more.

Jackie took his hand and looked very pleased. 'Great! I'll give you a call later on this week.' She drank the last sip of her cognac and got up hastily, adding, 'And any ideas are greatly appreciated, Sheridan.' She walked briskly to the door before Sheridan could have time to change his mind or suggest another idea. 'Bye for now and thank you for the drink, Sheridan.' Jackie waved her hands as she stepped outside with Felix right at her heels.

Sheridan was standing in the doorway still puffing his pipe. 'Good night, Jackie. See you soon!' He closed the door with a loud bang.

As Jackie started walking toward the gate, she heard the music turned on again in the house. The 'Colonel Bogey March' blasted into the still night.

The night had fallen as Jackie set out toward the pub from Sheridan Watson's house. There was a strong wind and the air was slightly damp. The remnants of the past winter were still in the air, twisting their invisible cold fingers around every living thing. Jackie pulled the scarf more tightly around her neck and pushed herself determinedly against the wind. She loved the dark starry night sky against the brightly lit houses. She enjoyed walking in the village, and she had acquired the country habit of slightly lengthening her neck to see past the bordering hedges—just to have a look at the gardens inside.

Mrs. Jefferson's front lawn puzzled her with its ever expanding collection of wooden whirly-gigs. The bird with whirling wings had been joined by a business man with a spinning attaché suitcase, who had been joined by a woman bending over, exposing her polka-dotted underwear and gigantic behind.

The Scotts, on the other side of the street, had a continuing fight over the garden gnomes that Mrs. Scott loved and Mr. Scott hated with all of his might. She bought them, put them in the garden, and he hid them late at night while she was sleeping, blaming the drunks going home from the pub. Whether she believed him or not, nobody knew, but the garden centre was making a good profit selling gnomes.

Luckily for the island, most of the extensive remodelling the village had undergone was more subtle after word spread of the area's natural beauty. Tourists came for the long winding beaches and for the unspoiled nature of the island. The old pathways by the sea and the rolling hills had become famous bicycle and hiking trails. Some farms offered holidays for families with children, and there was a birding group that met once a month. The yacht club had expanded to accommodate the boats of the summer island residents, enabling the club owner's wife to spend her winters in Mexico. She never suffered from the dark, cold winters and was permanently tanned.

Her skin was an extraordinary orange and the most wrinkled Jackie had ever seen. She drove the only convertible car on the island listening continuously to Spanish conversation tapes. She greeted everybody with a cheerful 'Hola,' flashing a big, almost blindingly white smile.

The main street was lined with B & Bs and many small shops. Honey's tearoom had bright pink cushions on the wrought iron chairs. The tearoom served cakes and muffins, and during summertime its main income was ice cream. In the window, Honey had a miniature Eiffel tower with red Christmas lights wrapped all around. She had said that she wanted to bring a bit of Parisian culture to the island. The people of Sycamore were still waiting for fresh croissants, while eating, without complaints, the home baked muffins. But they did rename Honey's tearoom 'Little Paris.' All of this had to be explained to outsiders. Every time anyone asked directions to Honey's tearoom, explaining the nickname took far longer than telling how to get there. Even so, there was confusion, and tourists were often found wandering up and down the main street looking for a little Parisian café and staring strangely at the blinking Eiffel tower in the window of a small tearoom called 'Honey's.'

O'Neill's' pub was right near the town hall between Peter's fish and chips and the church. It was therefore possible during one Sunday afternoon to satisfy all of your religious, gastronomic and dehydration needs within one hundred metres. The pastor was very pleased about his church being so happily situated. Being already a religious man and being single, he was, therefore, most often found either at Pete's or at O'Neill's.

Suzy Jenkins had recently opened a store called 'The Cozy Corner.' Her shop was filled with all the pretty little things that you didn't actually need, but once you saw them you wanted to have them and could not fathom a life without a matching apron, napkins and address book. Kathleen, on the other hand, at Candles, Scents and More was none too pleased about this sudden new competition.

The village also had a book store, called 'Books'N'More,' which was open mostly on rainy summer afternoons and cold winter days, when it was impossible for its owner, Dan Finch, to go sailing. How he managed to stay in business was a mystery to everybody.

Hilary Pike owned the beauty parlour across the street from the book shop. It was a known fact that Dan Finch would like to take Hilary sailing but had never asked her. Instead, while he actually was in the shop, he spent most of his time peaking through the window trying to catch a glimpse of Hilary.

By the sea was a fish and tackle store owned by John Smith. It sold everything for your fishing needs but was seldom open, since John loved fishing more than anything else in his life. He had heard about a worm vending machine from his cousin, who had travelled widely, and John had tried to make one himself out of an old coca cola machine he had bought in an auction. He hoped that he could simultaneously be in business and out on the sea. The machine had not worked very well and the masking tape that had covered 'coca cola' had fallen off. Now, the beaten up and rusted machine said 'John's coca cola worms.'

Beside John's fishing shop was the Sycamore Yacht Club, whose owner, Charles Prescott, was not too keen about John's machine expelling worms in coke cans. They had had many loud arguments over the coca cola worms, and Charles Prescott had even offered to buy John's store, but in vain. John's fishing shop gave John a purpose in life, if not the income.

The island's two main sources of information were found in the centre of the village. If you wanted to clarify the rumours you had heard in the post office, you only had to step into Mary's Flowers where Mary Cullighan could verify if there was any truth to the gossip and stories circulating the island. Pam Johnson, the postmaster and rumourmonger extraordinaire, and Mary Cullighan had a daily exchange of information over lunch while watching the traffic out of the window of Mary's shop. It was from there they had the best overall view of the village. The pastor had acknowledged the strategically important position of the flower shop and had made a habit of going to the pub through the back alley during the daylight hours.

Outside that very pub Jackie saw an old riding lawnmower parked neatly beside the front door. It had muddy tires and its rusty, flaking metal was full of small dents. The seat was ripped at the seams and had foam sticking out causing problems on rainy days. Often you could see the lawnmower sitting there in front of the pub in a rainstorm with a plastic bag wrapped around its worn out seat. The lawnmower belonged to Jack Wilkinson and so did the parking spot. It didn't have his name on it, but everyone in the village knew it as his spot. Nobody knew exactly how long it had been his spot. What everyone did know was that since he lost his driver's license Jack Wilkinson had always had a riding lawnmower and that it had always been parked there in front of the pub from afternoon till closing time.

Jackie pushed open the pub's heavy door and walked in. 'Hi boys!' she said without even looking around her.

A little mumble was heard from the far corner of the pub where Jack Wilkinson was talking with three other men: Howard, Calvin and Glenn. These three men were called 'the boys' by everyone in the village, though they had left their boyhood long behind them. Felix dashed to the three men. He was ready for a good belly rub. Nick was working at the bar as always. He was drying glasses and he had tossed the white towel over his shoulder as he reached up to hang the wine glasses upside down from the racks above the bar.

'Hi Nick! How's it going?' Jackie sat down and folded her jacket on the nearby chair.

'Good, good, and how are you?' Nick tossed the towel into the corner and leaned on the counter with his hands outstretched. He was solid looking and wore a flannel shirt, jeans and a pullover.

'Good...can't complain, let's put it that way.' Jackie smiled.

'That's nice to hear. A pint?'

'Not tonight, thanks, Nick. I actually came to talk business with you.'

'Ah! What kind of business?' Nick handed Jackie a cup of coffee instead.

Jackie thanked Nick and smiled. She added sugar to her coffee. 'Studio tour business,' Jackie said seriously. 'I believe that we could easily attract more tourists to this area by arranging a studio gallery tour in the fall, just before Christmas. We could easily extend our season since we already have everything we need: the studios, hotels, B & Bs, restaurants and pubs. She paused and took the crumpled brochure out of her pocket and spread it open on the table for Nick to see. 'See here, this one.' She pointed to an article. 'It's a small community just like ours, and they arrange fall and spring studio tours. Some of the studios are even offering workshop weekends during winter.' Jackie stopped to take a sip of her coffee. 'And it looks like they are even offering cooking classes here in this little village,' she added while pointing enthusiastically to a colourful advertisement.

Nick had been watching Jackie intently. He liked how her cheeks became slightly scarlet as she spoke and her words fused into each other in her excitement. He took the brochure from the table and quickly read it through. It advertised a place called Hodgin's Greens which offered various courses, including watercolour painting, with a dinner included, in a local traditional pub complete with live music. Nick looked at Jackie over the edge of the paper. Jackie did have a brilliant idea. If a little village similar to their Sycamore had done it, why couldn't they?

'You're right,' he said slowly, smiling approvingly at Jackie. 'It's a fantastic idea. You can use my pub anytime for meetings, and if I can help in any way, just let me know.'

'Thanks, Nick.' Jackie smiled. If Nick believed that she could make this happen in Sycamore, then it felt like a legitimate dream. 'What's your slowest night at the pub?'

'That would be Monday night.' Nick rubbed his chin and looked around. 'It's not full, as you can see.' His eyes stopped to gaze at the three men and Jack Wilkinson in the corner of the pub. Jackie followed Nick's eyes, also glancing around the empty pub. It was not only she who needed more income.

'How about I arrange a meeting here at the pub next Monday?'

'Sure. That will be fine with me.' Nick leaned against the counter with his elbows and poured himself more coffee. On Mondays, especially, he needed a lot of caffeine to stay awake till closing time.

'Great!' Jackie took a sip of her coffee. It was hot and her hands were nicely warming around the cup.

'Who have you asked to come to the meeting?' asked Nick.

'Well.' Jackie sighed and her smile disappeared. 'Thomas is in and so is Sheridan.' Nick raised his eyebrows. It was not often that you heard those two names spoken in one sentence. Jackie returned his surprised look with a wry grin and shrugged her shoulders.

'I still have to talk to Russell, Nancy, Daisy, Harriet and Janet.' Jackie was using her fingers to count the people she was talking about. 'Now who did I leave out?' she asked Nick while staring at her fingers and pursing her lips. 'Uh…of course…Kenneth and Caroline and the church quilting group.' She remembered triumphantly. 'And then…Rosalind and Alistair.' Her face suddenly distorted as if she had tasted something vile.

'Oh, yes…Rosalind.' Nick sympathetically blew air out through his lips as he slowly pronounced Rosalind's name, hanging onto every consonant.

'Yes, Rosalind.' Jackie repeated and covered her eyes for a moment with her hands.

'That's a good group.' Nick said trying to cheer Jackie up. 'Not too big and not too small, just like in this brochure.'

'Now I just have to persuade everybody else to join the tour.' Jackie sighed, resting her chin on her hand.

Nick glanced at her over his coffee cup and said slowly, more thinking to himself than saying the words to Jackie. 'That's easier said than done.'

Chapter 4

Herding Cats

The next morning Jackie woke early. She had an odd pain in her stomach, just like she used to have when she was a child in school, and the feared math teacher was passing out the exam papers. You knew that you knew the answers, but somehow they were inaccessible in the deepest part of your brain, paralyzed by uncontrollable fear.

She made herself a cup of coffee and decided to rid herself of the horrible feeling and walk to Alistair's house immediately. She was tempted to take the scenic way in her pathetic attempt to postpone the inevitable a moment longer. In the end, though, she steeled herself and strode briskly to the house of the McKay's, which sat slightly back from the street and was surrounded by a sharp white picket fence.

Jackie walked around the house to the kitchen door at the back and hesitated for a moment as she slowly lifted her hand to knock on the door. She closed her eyes for a second, pursed her lips, and then knocked sharply three times, held her breath and waited. Perhaps nobody was home.

As she was ready to leave, she heard the sound of footsteps and, to her great dismay, the door opened. An older woman in her late fifties was standing in the doorway. She was dressed in black, a large, elaborately fashioned silver necklace hanging from her neck. Her white hair was sculpted, rather than combed; Jackie marvelled at the shiny helmet effect and wondered how strong the wind would have to be to move even a single hair out of place.

Rosalind's voice rang out, quickly snapping Jackie back. 'Jacqueline, what a nice surprise!' She had a shrill voice and her words didn't match her facial expression, which remained detached, almost scornful.

'Hi Rosalind! How are you?' Jackie inquired civilly.

'I'm fine. I just came from the city…back to this little island life.' Rosalind waved her hands expressing her mild but continuous distaste for country living.

Jackie spoke as if she was following an invisible manual for a polite conversation in stressful situations. She was asking many questions and answering very few. 'And how is Alistair?'

'Oh, he is fine, fully immersed in his work as usual.' Rosalind sighed. 'You know how these geniuses are. I don't even think he noticed that I was away.' Rosalind seemed to find this idea very amusing and let out a sharp little laugh, which despite the upturned lips did not sound at all happy.

Jackie decided to ignore the attempted joke, since joking was not a talent Rosalind was well known for. It seemed safer to stick with the business and know as little as possible about the personal life of Rosalind McKay. 'Could I talk with him or…is he too busy?'

'He is in his studio,' Rosalind said sharply and shook her head as if this thought would bring anguish into her life. 'I'm not sure if he would like to be disturbed at the moment.' She looked at her watch. 'But, tell you what. You tell me what is on your mind, and I will forward your message to him…if needed.'

'Oh, all right.' Jackie bit her lip, willing herself to be polite. She moved a bit on the tiny carpet in front of the door and looked at her old muddy boots. It didn't look like Rosalind was going to invite her to come in. Jackie cleared her throat. 'I have an idea about arranging an artists' studio tour next fall here on the island and I would like to invite you and Alistair to the first meeting at the pub next Monday night at seven.'

'A studio tour? It's a wonderful idea.' Rosalind was excited, which for a moment lifted Jackie's spirits considerably. Maybe, just maybe, there was a god in heaven, and maybe Rosalind wasn't the evil witch from hell who had been sent to torture Jackie for the rest of her earthly life.

'My Alistair has been talking about a studio tour for a few years now. He is such an original thinker.'

Jackie stared at Rosalind with a blank face that, surprisingly, did not show any of the dangerously aggressive feelings she was experiencing.

'I'll tell Alistair and we will be there if we don't have anything else on our agenda.'

'Great!' Jackie's *great* sounded anything but great and her voice was oddly thin. Jackie was about to say 'See you there, then,' when Rosalind cut her off. 'Who have you invited to this meeting?'

Jackie studied her boots for a while before answering. 'Thomas and Sheridan have already agreed to come, and I will talk to Russell, Nancy, Daisy, Harriet, Janet, Kenneth and Caroline later on this week.' Jackie was counting the people with her fingers. She tried not to forget anybody. She went through the list of people again in her mind. 'Aha,' she exclaimed. 'And also Muriel and her quilting group.'

'Oh, so you are thinking of inviting Nancy, are you?' Rosalind looked as if she had tasted something very foul and sour. Her nose seemed sharper than usual.

'Yes, I think she would add a nice variety to the group, don't you?'

'Variety, maybe yes, but…well, I for one have never thought of dried flower arrangements as being a high and sophisticated form of art…never mind that friend of hers who seems to paint anything she finds around in her house—what's her name again?' Rosalind's face was pinched.

'You must be talking about Daisy.' Jackie fixed her burning angry eyes on the forsythia bush next to the steps.

'Yes, that's the one. Those horrid mail boxes that seem to be popping up in every corner in this village nowadays. Couldn't we stop that…make a bylaw of some kind…to demand sophistication?' Rosalind sighed deeply and then added as an afterthought. 'I better talk to Sheridan…maybe he could bring it up in the next council meeting.'

Jackie was still staring at the bush. She was looking for the right words, which, perhaps, were not the words she wanted to say but were the words she needed to say. When she answered, her voice was soft but firm. 'This is a small island, Rosalind, and I don't think we can leave her out of the group without hurting her feelings and causing a great deal of trouble. And, frankly, I don't think a studio tour should divide our community; it should, in fact, do just the opposite.' She stopped and looked at Rosalind and waited for her answer, which she knew might be, and most likely would be, upsetting, as Rosalind was not well known for her generosity and tact.

Rosalind's long nose quivered as she spoke. 'Well, it's a good thing we are going to have this meeting, because obviously we'll have to set some kind of guidelines for this studio tour group. If we don't stand firm, we will have all sorts of stone painters and watercolourists without any proper artistic education claiming themselves as artists.' She coughed the last words out with the deepest distaste. Her lips were straighter and tighter than even before, making her mouth a thin pencil line.

'I'll be off now.' Jackie turned to leave and in that very moment Alistair McKay walked up the steps.

He was an older man dressed in a black turtleneck pullover. He looked like a sailor on dry land—confused and lost. He had no time to greet Jackie, because Rosalind pulled him quickly into the house and pushed Jackie out at the same time.

'Oh, you don't have to waste your precious time, dear Jacqueline. I'll explain everything to Alistair. Goodbye.' Rosalind closed the door.

Jackie stared at the closed door and then slowly shook her head sideways. She looked up to the sky and let out a long cry.

'Why, oh why! Of all the villages in the world, why did she have to move into mine?'

* * *

The telephone rang in Jackie's studio. Jackie dropped her pencil onto her worktable and rushed to the phone. Maybe it was the gallery owner with whom she had talked yesterday about an order. Jackie glanced upwards and silently mouthed the words 'please, please, please' and crossed her fingers.

'Jacqueline Callaghan furniture design,' she answered the phone and then held her breath.

'Is that you, Jackie?' She heard an all-too-familiar woman's voice. 'Do you have a cold or something? Your voice sounds so strange.'

'Hi, Mom.' Jackie's words fell off her tongue with a long, painful sigh. 'No, I don't have a cold. I wasn't expecting you to call. That's all.'

'Whose call were you expecting, then?'

'Well.' Jackie hesitated for a moment. She wasn't sure if she wanted to tell her mother all the little details of her life. She was tempted for a few seconds to say a call from an on-line dating service, but she knew her mother would not appreciate the irony. 'I was expecting a call from a gallery.'

'Well, if you sigh onto the phone like you have a cold, I don't think the gallery owner would have been very impressed.' Her mother's voice trailed off into the distant corner of Jackie's mind while she stared at the ceiling and cursed herself for being honest.

'Are you going to meet this gallery owner?' her mother asked impatiently. 'Because if you are, make sure to dress neatly and look her straight in the eye, and, for god's sake, do not slouch. And remember! A firm handshake. There is nothing worse than a soft, lifeless handshake. Remember your great-aunt Julia's husband, Geoffrey? His hands were like old wilted lettuce. Tragic! No wonder he never did anything with his life. So, remember, Jacqueline. Nice and firm handshake.'

'Yes, Mom. I'll do that.' Jackie slipped into her well-rehearsed role of saying yes to anything her mother suggested. This was a lifelong practice that had made life easier and had brought a quicker end to the occasional professional torture by her beloved mother without causing permanent damage to their already frail relationship.

'How's Bob?'

'Jacqueline, you do know that your stepfather would rather be called by his real name, Robert.'

'How's Robert, Mom?'

'He's fine; thank you for asking. He has his sixtieth birthday party next month. I thought you did not need the fancy invitation in the mail, so that's why I called. You need to buy something nice for yourself. Last time we saw you, you were wearing those awful jeans again. I swear, you looked like you had joined the Hells Angels, or something equally vulgar. Do promise to buy something nice, will you? All of Robert's friends will be there, and he has asked Andrew to come as well. Do you remember Andrew? You met him last year. He's the son of Robert's accountant and he works for Robert. Nice man. Wears nice ties and has a brand new Audi. Jacqueline, are you still there? Why so quiet?'

Jackie exhaled noisily, giving herself away.

'Were you listening to me at all? My god, I call you all this way and you don't even bother to listen.'

'I did listen to you, Mom. Yes, Andrew is a very nice man and, yes, I will wear something nice.'

'Good. Now I don't have to worry about what Robert's friends might think.'

'Good,' said Jackie and bit her fingernail.

'Are you biting your fingernails?'

'How does she do that?' Jackie thought, completely in awe. 'No I'm not,' she lied. 'It was Felix. He just woke up.'

'Felix? Who's Felix?'

'My dog.'

'When did you get a dog?'

'Six months ago or so.'

'How come you never said anything to me?'

'I thought I did. I'm sure I did. I must have told you.'

'Well, maybe you did. Just don't let the dog sleep in your bed. I hate that dog smell on people. You know Mrs. Falk. Nice woman. Seems perfectly normal but smells like a wet dog. It does not matter how much perfume she puts on. The smell is still there. It makes our charity luncheons unbearable. The same with cats. I can't stand them. I never go to Elaine's anymore. The cat smell is just like in a zoo. Oh, look at the time. I have to run. I'm meeting Suzanne for lunch. Remember to get something nice for yourself. I'll call you next week.'

And she was gone.

Jackie stared at her dust-covered jeans. She knew that her mother would not have approved of them. Neither would she have been thrilled to see that Jackie's hair was in braids. The safety goggles would surely have had her panting for air, and the steel-toed shoes would have marked Jackie as a biker with lesbian tendencies. It was alright for other families to have their strange offspring with peculiar habits—the perfect topic for a lengthy before dinner discussion over drinks. But for Belinda Bloom, the only word she liked, and approved of, when linked to her own family was the word *normal*, combined perhaps with words like affluent, successful...normal. Her family was the one that should be the subject of envy and not ridicule. It wasn't by accident that Betsy Callaghan had married Robert Bloom; a respected business man.

'Andrew,' Jackie thought. 'Why do they always want me and Andrew to get together?' Though, she already knew the answer. Andrew's family had money and position, which was everything that Jackie's mother wanted and lived for.

Andrew was nice. You could say that without lying, and then you could not think of anything else to say about him. Nice. Very nice. Extremely nice. Very, *very* nice. And that was just about it.

Felix barked and Jackie looked at him. 'You're a good boy, Felix.' I guess Andrew could be called *a good boy* too. Good and nice. But there was no spark. Only clammy soft hands and nice ties. She couldn't remember what his handshake was like. Maybe it was lettuce-like. Nice crispy iceberg lettuce. But enough of Andrew. There was the studio tour to be organized and she still needed to talk to the rest of the island's artists, and she might as well do it now, since her thoughts were everywhere but on her work and new designs.

A nice drive in the countryside would do her good, and also it would keep her mother out of her thoughts. Jackie grabbed her keys and stepped outside. She walked to her car which was parked in front of her house.

Her car was a very old beat-up station wagon that had been used to bring miscellaneous supplies to her studio, and it clearly showed. It was a history channel on four wheels. Jackie was not sure what the original colour of the car had been. It had been patched so many times during its lifetime that the initial coat of glossy paint had vanished without a trace and was now supplemented by an ever growing collection of rust specks. Nevertheless, the car worked most of the time. Jackie was not thinking of buying a new one, not that she could afford one. Her mother, of course, hated her car with a never ceasing passion, and when Jackie went to visit her and Bob in the city, she had ordered Jackie never to park it in front of her house, even if it was an emergency.

'Remember always wear a nice pair of underwear, because you just never know when you are going to end up in a hospital,' she had said to Jackie many times, and somehow, the car belonged to the same group in some odd, twisted kind of way. 'You never know who is going to walk by, and my god, if an ambulance were to come, what would the paramedics say if they saw that heap of junk at my front door?'

So Jackie was defeated, and she had been directed to park the pile of rust masquerading as a car as far away as possible from her house, just so that her mother would avoid the embarrassment of having her family linked to such a vile vehicle.

Jackie drove through the green hills spotted with black and white cows and populated by wind-bent knobby trees until she came to an old farmhouse gate. As she opened the car door, she could hear loud barking in the distance. She stood by the gate not daring to open it. The sound of howling and snarling dogs was coming closer and closer. She congratulated herself for leaving Felix home.

A burly man's voice called loudly for the dogs to be quiet as he briskly walked through the pack of dogs to the gate. The ear splitting barking suddenly stopped and, instead, there were wagging tails, lolling tongues and happy brown eyes. 'Good morning, Russell.'

'Good morning, Jackie. Come in, come in. These dogs won't hurt you. Don't worry.' Russell beckoned to Jackie and opened the gate for her. The dogs were all over her—licking, sniffing, pushing her. She tried to push them gently away, but as soon as she got one dog off, another one eagerly pushed in his wet nose.

'Lovely day. Isn't it?' Russell bellowed happily and then clapped his large hands together loudly. 'Lovely day.'

'Yes…uh…' Jackie mumbled. A small terrier began pulling her shoelaces apart. Jackie yanked her right leg, dragging with it the feisty dog.

'I was chopping firewood over there to keep my missus and me warm.' Russell flung his arm toward a small cluster of trees.

'My missus likes to sit in front of the fire…and I keep the home fires burning…if you know what I mean.' Russell stopped and turned to look at Jackie. The old man winked, and then chuckled at his own thought.

Russell yanked the front door open and Jackie found herself trying to get through the doorway with all the dogs doing precisely same thing at exactly the same time.

'Jane! Visitor!' Russell boomed and tapped the passing dog on its back.

'I'll be right down,' a small, frail voice answered from upstairs.

The hallway was narrow and dark. Its walls were covered with paintings, realistic renditions of dogs, birds and wildlife; there were also many portraits of a woman who turned out to be Jane, Russell's wife. They were very good indeed. Russell would make a great addition to the artists' group.

'Your paintings are beautiful,' Jackie said.

'Well, thank you. I used to do illustrations for bird guides and all kinds of other nature books and magazines. Now I just paint for fun. It keeps me busy in my retirement. I can't just sit still.' Russell scratched his scalp through his bushy white hair and stared at his paintings on the wall.

'Now, come into the kitchen, Jackie. I'll put some tea on.' Russell ushered Jackie toward the kitchen where he busied himself with the kettle but seemed unable to find the teabags. He made a lot of noise opening and closing the cupboards but, finally, called for Jane again, yelling as loud as he could. 'Jane! Where the hell are the bloody teabags?'

Jane came slowly down the steps. She was a modest looking woman dressed in beige and brown. She showed her age, unlike her boisterous husband. Her hair was kept short and it was combed back, away from her grey eyes. Russell had beautifully captured her quiet essence in his paintings. 'Oh, for heaven's sake, Russell. Keep quiet. Let me get them for you.'

Russell straightened his back and looked up. 'Oh, there you are. I was starting to wonder when you would be coming down.' He pointed to Jackie, 'This girl here is Jackie.'

Jane smiled warmly. 'Very nice to meet you, Jackie. I'm Jane, Russell's wife.'

'If you just give me a minute, I'll fix us some tea.' Jane opened a cupboard to take the cups out while the water began to boil in the kettle. Her movements were soft and hushed.

'Oh, no, that isn't really necessary. I just came to…' Jackie had no time to finish her sentence, when Russell cut her off with his thunderous voice.

'It is so bloody cold and damp outside, girl. You'll need to have some hot tea in you, and that's that.' He pulled out a chair for Jackie and signalled for her to sit down. Jackie was going to have some tea and that was that.

Russell sat down opposite Jackie. He was scratching one of the dogs behind its ear, and the dog began thumping its leg rhythmically against the floorboards.

'Russell, I actually came here to ask if you would be interested in being part of an artists' studio tour.'

Jane brought the teacups and a plate of cookies. Immediately there was movement under the table. The dogs stirred at the sound of the cookie plate. Jackie held onto her teacup as the table shook slightly. Russell pushed the big plate of cookies in front of her. 'Oh, no, thank you.' Jackie shook her head politely.

'Rubbish! A woman needs meat around her bones. Have a cookie!' Russell bellowed and pushed the plate of cookies even closer to Jackie. 'Go on! Take a cookie!' he repeated and cheerfully took a big bite out of his own cookie. 'Come on. Go ahead. No need to be shy here. Have a cookie,' he said between loud crispy mouthfuls.

'Well…uh…all right then…thank you. So what I was saying… is…' Jackie paused. She felt brown, alert, hungry dog eyes on her: the unspoken desire brewing under the table.

'I'll be happy to be part of a studio tour. It's a grand idea, girl. I'm glad that somebody is trying something new around here.' Russell banged the table with his big hand. 'Come on girl, eat, drink, make merry,' he bellowed.

'All right then.' Jackie took a bite of her cookie.

'Now, what can I do?' Russell enquired between big gulps of tea.

'Well, the first meeting is…' She had not even time to finish her sentence when Russell jumped in with excitement.

'I'll be there. Bloody fantastic idea! Isn't it, Jane?' Russell banged his hand on the table again. Jane had been drinking her tea, wisely holding her cup and saucer in her hands rather than putting them on the table.

'Yes, yes it is. Wonderful idea, Jackie. Wonderful indeed.' She smiled contently. 'I'll be glad to help as well, if you need me.' She sounded so soft and demure compared to her rowdy husband. Jackie couldn't imagine her banging her hand against the table or yelling at the top her lungs 'bloody marvellous!'

Jackie finally finished her tea and much talked about cookie. 'I'll be off now. Thank you for the tea and…uh…cookies.'

'No, thank you for inviting us to be part of the tour, Jackie. Bloody fantastic, I say.' Russell beamed and loudly tapped his stomach.

Jane looked at her husband. The thirty-odd years together had made her completely accustomed to her husband's loud existence. 'Russell dear, would you keep the dogs inside so Jackie can walk to her car peacefully?'

'Oh, yes, of course. Stay!' He bellowed the word so loudly and unexpectedly that Jackie instinctively moved to cover her ears. The dogs protested but obeyed. Jackie's ears were still ringing when she walked to the front door.

Russell put his hand around Jane's narrow shoulders. 'Till next week,' he hollered and closed the front door with a loud bang and the howling and barking of the dogs followed immediately. Jane turned around to scold her husband but Russell just smiled and squeezed her behind.

*　　　*　　　*

Jackie stared at the list of artists in front of her. Time was running out fast and the first meeting was approaching. She glanced at her watch and then stared out of her car window. The wind had picked up a little. Clouds were travelling fast above the waves. She started her car and decided to visit Janet Nesmith's farm nearby. 'Janet should be at home,' she said to herself, more hoping it to be true than knowing so.

She drove on a tiny winding road by the rocky shore. The gulls' screams pierced the air as they followed the fishing boats out to sea. Jackie stopped her car and got out. She held onto her jacket as the wind tried to tear the buttons open. It was cold and the sharp wind hurt her ears, forcing her hair back. It was a strong salty sea wind that went where it wanted, no permission asked. All its strength it had gathered from its travels and was now triumphantly blasting the shoreline. Her eyes watering and her fingers numb with cold, Jackie climbed back into her car and drove on.

She arrived at the vast yard of an old farmhouse which looked over the small, rocky bay. Laundry was drying in the wind and chickens scurried away. Jackie left her car and hollered 'Hello,' but there was no answer. She looked around the yard and waited awhile before deciding to walk toward the barn. It was later in the morning, so Janet was likely to be working. Jackie stepped into the dark barn and saw a woman in her early fifties cleaning the sheep stalls.

The woman looked strong and honest. Her mouth, a thin line in her sculpted and weathered face——an approachable face, but not overly familiar with laughter and not tolerant of chit chat or wasted time. It was a face that believed in hard work as a natural consequence of being born into this world. She was wearing a beautifully knitted colourful pullover, very old jeans and a pair of men's old green rubber boots. Her greying hair was cut short and it gave her a boyish appearance despite her deeply wrinkled face.

'Hi Janet,' Jackie said quietly as she stepped into the barn.

'Oh, hi Jackie. Mind your step.' Janet looked up quickly and then nodded toward the ground. Jackie looked down and stepped carefully over the pile of sheep manure. She walked toward Janet.

'What can I do for you?' Janet was leaning against her shovel and wiping her forehead with her sleeve.

'I came to ask if you would be interested in joining an island artists' group to organize a studio tour next fall?'

Janet looked at her for a while before answering. 'I have heard of those studio tours.' She finally said slowly. Her voice was stern but not unkind. She was trying to think what exactly she had heard about the studio tours.

'It would be great to have your hand-knitted sweaters and scarves in the tour.'

'Um,' Janet sighed. Her eyes were focused on the stone wall just behind Jackie's left ear.

'Your pullovers are gorgeous.' Jackie said, and pulled slightly on her own pullover's collar to show Janet what she was wearing. She then waited for her answer. She had said all she could say and knew Janet well enough not to try to influence her decision in any way. The island farmers were stubborn and didn't take kindly to pushiness. All in good time and on their own terms. Waiting was sometimes a virtue and not a hindrance.

The sheep were baaing outside in the neighbouring field. The wind whistled through the old barn. The chickens clucked, and Jackie waited.

'Well...I guess...' Janet squinted and small wrinkles formed in the corners of her eyes. She paused, picked a straw off her sweater and dropped it onto the stone floor. 'Well, I never thought to see the day, when my sweaters and knitted things could be called art.' Janet was amused by the very thought. Her late husband would have had a good laugh over that.

'I'm having an information meeting on Monday night at seven at the pub.'

'Well, I guess I'll be there. It would be nice to go out and see somebody else but the sheep for a change.' Janet sighed and looked around the barn. She really didn't mind the solitude, but once in a while she craved to hear people talk and laugh, even if she did not participate. It broke the monotonous existence of farm life.

'Great!' Jackie smiled. 'Well, I better let you get back to work.' Jackie also knew that the island farmers did not like to waste time when there was work to be done.

Janet picked up her shovel again. Jackie was about to leave when she turned around and asked, 'By the way, is that Kenneth's car parked on the road over there?'

Janet peered through the small barn window. 'Yes, I believe it is. He said something about photographing birds when I saw him yesterday.'

'Good, maybe I can get hold of him on my way back to town.'

'He normally walks by the river. You might catch him there.' Janet was already working, her broad back turned toward Jackie.

'Thanks, Janet. See you on Monday.'

Janet responded only by nodding her head this time, letting Jackie know that she had heard her.

Jackie walked out of the barn back to her car. She leaned against its rusty door and admired the beautiful landscape with the bleating sheep scattered in the fields. The air smelled fresh and it had that underlying promise of warmer weather despite the howling wind. You could almost believe that the summer would arrive at some time in the near future.

Jackie got into her car and drove a couple of hundred metres down the road and parked behind Kenneth's car. She got out and began walking toward the river through the fields. She was glad that she was wearing her rubber boots. The grass under her feet was very wet, parting with each step and dissolving into little puddles of brown water.

She saw a man setting up a camera on a tripod by the river bed. He camouflaged well with his surroundings. He was a very tall, thin man with a grey beard and moustache. His clothes were also grey. His hat was a dark green knitted cap that fit snugly, covering his overly large ears. He moved very slowly as if his body needed time to think about its movements before accomplishing them. He had something of an old oak tree about him. Jackie could understand, watching him set up, how he got his surprisingly clear and candid shots of birds. It would be good to have his photographs as part of the tour.

Jackie stepped on a branch and it made a loud snap. The man turned around and saw Jackie. It was difficult to tell whether he was pleased or annoyed by this sudden interruption. Jackie felt apologetic for disturbing this tall, quiet grey man in the middle of this tranquil setting. She lifted her hand slightly and waved hesitantly. 'Hello!' She said slowly, desperately thinking what to say next. 'I saw Janet and she said I might find you here. How are you, Kenneth?'

Kenneth stared at her for a while as if trying to remember who she was and where he had seen her before. 'Been better, been worse.' He answered slowly with a low weathered voice that cracked like dry tree branches in the wind.

'Oh, uh…good then?' Jackie didn't know what to say to such a greeting. She looked puzzled, but Kenneth didn't say anything else. He didn't acknowledge the silence between them. The normal rules of dialogue did not apply with him. To him a deep grunt said everything that was needed, whether it was an agreement or a deep dislike. He didn't seem to have extreme feelings in him. The words giddy and abhorrence did not belong to him. He might describe things as pleasant or rather nice, but never had Jackie heard him say words like divine or awful.

'I just talked to Janet about an artists' studio tour, which I am trying to organize here on the island.' Jackie paused again and waited, in vain, for Kenneth to acknowledge her words. He remained quiet so Jackie continued her strange monologue-dialogue. 'You know about the studio tour concept?' She tried.

'Yes, I might know a thing or two about it.' All this time Kenneth had been looking through his camera lens, but now he stopped and adjusted the tripod again. He straightened his back slowly and stared at Jackie with his small grey eyes, expecting her to continue her speech.

Jackie felt awkward. In her mind, she cursed quiet people; her discomfort was growing; she was panicking, jabbering pathetically.

'Well, well, it would be great if you could come on Monday night at seven to the information meeting. It will be held at O'Neill's pub, not that there are any other pubs in the village, come to think of it.' Jackie let out a fleeting anxious laugh. 'But...' She was about to continue, then decided she had said quite enough. Nervously, she shifted her weight. Her one foot sunk deeper into the wet earth, while the other came free with a loud thwack.

Kenneth continued to stare at her. You couldn't really tell what he was thinking. Was he for the studio tour idea or against it? Jackie had no idea what to talk about next. She began to say something but before the words even left her lips, she had already decided against them. Instead, she put her hands in her pockets, dug her heels into the ground and waited for an answer. 'Even one word would do,' she thought.

She waited and waited. A flock of birds on the way to the river flew over the trees, calling for each other. Kenneth was silently observing their landing on the water. He'd completely forgotten Jackie, or so it seemed to her.

'Well...I'll be off now,' she blurted when she could take the silence no longer. 'But you will come to the meeting, won't you?' She added, hesitantly, as if asking that he, at least, acknowledge her existence.

'I might. We'll see.' He looked at her quickly under his bushy eyebrows.

'Thanks, Kenneth. See you later.' Jackie was all smiles. His noncommittal answer held some promise.

Kenneth nodded slightly, cleared his throat, and then turned his back again. Jackie hesitated to leave, but what else could she possibly say to him? She pulled her feet free from the muddy ground and walked slowly back to her car.

Her rubber boots were noisy as she trod the damp earth, sounding even louder in the unexpected stillness as the wind had died down.

A rumour circulated that Kenneth had been a biology teacher before retiring to the island, attracted by its large variety of birdlife. 'How had he been able to teach with no words,' Jackie wondered. She turned around to look at the contented older man by the river. He almost merged with nature. Only the metal of his tripod, glistening in the weak sunshine, gave him away.

Chapter 5

Tea, Ice and Muffins

Jackie walked down a quiet street in the village toward an old brick house surrounded by blooming spring flowers. Lilacs were happily budding in the nearby bordering bush. The earth was waking up. Jackie inhaled deeply, breathing in the damp and muddy morning air spiked with the strong sweet scent of the lilacs.

She opened the squeaky gate, spotted green with moss, and followed the path behind the house into the ample back garden.

In the far corner of the garden she saw an elderly woman weeding her flowerbeds. She was deep in her spring cleaning. She had on a pair of flower-patterned gardening gloves and she was dressed in loose fitting soft jeans with an elastic waistband, light blue T-shirt, a lilac coloured cardigan and a wide brimmed hat to shield her eyes from the bright spring sun.

Jackie waved her hand and called, 'Good morning, Muriel. Wonderful day!'

Muriel lifted her head slowly to see who had arrived. 'Oh, well, hello, Jacqueline. Yes, yes, it is beautiful, isn't it?' Muriel got up, supporting her back with her two hands as she gradually straightened. She looked content even though her back was obviously giving her trouble. She unhurriedly took off her gardening gloves, pulling them gently over her swollen arthritic knuckles. She began collecting her tools scattered amongst the flowers.

'How are you, dear?' She enquired with a soft, cheerful voice brushing a stubborn lock of hair from her face.

'Just fine, thank you. And you?'

'Splendid! I just love the spring! Too much work for my old bones though, but I cannot resist. So much work, yes. Would you like to have cup of tea, my dear?' Muriel brushed her hands together, gently rubbing her bent fingers to warm them up.

'Oh, you don't need to bother for me,' Jackie protested.

'Well, I would like to have some, and to be honest with you, I could use a break, you see. Come in, dear.' Muriel began to walk toward the kitchen door carrying her basket, which held the gardening tools and flowery rubber gloves, refusing any help offered by Jackie. She set the little basket on the kitchen doorstep and leaned on the railing, catching her breath.

'I wish my back would not remind me so often about my age.' She left her muddy shoes by the door on a mat, which said welcome in large forest green letters.

Jackie followed her into the kitchen. It was a bright room with cascades of flowered curtains framing the windows. The smell of just baked muffins lingered in the air. Muriel put the kettle on and brought out some cookies and still warm muffins. Jackie sat down at the table on a flowered cushioned chair.

'How is the studio tour coming along?' Muriel asked, her back turned toward Jackie.

Jackie was astonished. Harriet had been right; there were no secrets in this village. She looked at Muriel with a surprised smile spreading across her face. 'Well, that is actually the reason I came to see you.'

Muriel brought the teacups to the table and sat down to wait for the water to boil. She looked at Jackie; her veined hands were crossed in front of her. 'What can I do to help?' She asked, while straightening the flowery tablecloth.

'I know you have a quilting club at the Methodist church and I was...'

'Yes, the Bitch and Stitch Club.' Muriel interrupted.

'What?' Jackie was taken by surprise.

'Oh, yes. That is what we call our club…bitch and stitch.' Unofficially of course, but I think it is quite fitting.' Muriel glanced at Jackie with a bemused look on her face.

'Oh,' Jackie mumbled, too stunned to come up with anything else.

'So what would you like us old bitchers and stitchers to do?' Muriel got up to make the tea. She put on a flowery apron with large pockets on both sides and ruffles at the hem.

It took awhile for Jackie to collect her thoughts again. 'Well, I was going to ask you if you would like to make a display of your quilts in the church hall for the tour. You could even have a bake sale if you like.'

'That's a splendid idea.' Muriel smiled. 'I'll talk to the pastor. You don't need to worry about that. The ladies will be delighted and we could raise some money for the church. The piano in the church is in terrible condition, but we have no money to repair it, never mind buying a new one.' Muriel brought the pot of tea to the table and sat down. Her eyes were bright with excitement as she was already planning the quilt display in her mind.

'Thank you, Muriel.'

'Now, please eat some muffins dear…and I'll pour you some tea?' Muriel picked up the tea pot, and then asked with a twinkle in her eyes, 'And you want us to come to the first meeting at the pub on Monday night at seven. Is that so?'

Jackie looked up from her tea and shook her head slightly. She shouldn't be surprised that Muriel knew all the details already. 'Yes,' she said. 'That would be great if you could attend the first meeting.'

'Good,' Muriel said. 'And now, tell me. How is your mother? And what was his name again…Bob…Robert?'

Jackie settled down for a nice long tea break during which time all the new gossip of the village was going to be thoroughly dissected and discussed.

There was no such thing as a quick cup of tea on the island.

*   *   *

'Jackie, what a great surprise. Come in, come in!' Harriet exclaimed as she opened the door. Jackie stepped in and, smiling, braced herself for another cup of tea. There was absolutely nothing quiet and small in Harriet. She was loud and honest in a way that bordered on the brutal, and she expected nothing less from her friends.

'Say it straight, say it out loud, and waste no bloody time going around in circles, because one way or the other the truth will come out, and it's better if it is now rather than later,' she had been heard to say on more than one occasion.

Harriet's house was a great contrast to her great size. It was filled with small, delicate porcelain objects placed carefully on white lacy tablecloths. Jackie wondered how Harriet managed to walk between her furniture without knocking things down. And Harriet always dressed simply, so it had been a surprise for Jackie to see pink table lamps with lacy fringes and porcelain plates lining the flowery walls.

Among the flower and lace were Winston's trophies. They were brightly polished with not a speck of dust on their glittering surfaces. There were plenty of them and they came in all shapes and sizes.

As Jackie and Harriet walked toward the kitchen, a small poodle ran up and sniffed Jackie's legs. Harriet scooped the little dog into her big, strong arms and snuggled him gently.

'Mommy's little beast, aren't you?'

The dog was anything but a beast, and it made Jackie smile as she scratched behind the beast's ear.

'How is Winston nowadays?' She asked Harriet.

'Oh, Winston is just grand. Aren't you, Winston. It was just a bad cold, but luckily we are all better now.'

The little dog wagged his tail and looked about as happy as a dog can be.

'I'm glad to hear that,' Jackie said as they walked into the kitchen. Harriet put Winston down on the floor. 'Sit down, Jackie! I'll make us some tea,' she said loudly but kindly, while filling the tea kettle.

'Oh, you really don't have to.' Jackie made a weak attempt to refuse yet another cup of tea.

'Darling, I know I don't have to make any tea, and I wouldn't have offered any if I didn't want to make it…so there…sit down for heaven's sake.' Harriet shook her head and pointed to a pink chair.

Jackie grinned sheepishly. You could not help but like Harriet. She was bossy, indeed, but her bossiness was meant well. 'In that case. Tea sounds good to me.' Jackie sat down.

'That's a good girl. I knew you would come to your senses. So what brings you here?'

Winston had settled into his bed in the corner of the kitchen amongst the flower-patterned chairs and wallpaper. Winston's bed fabric had poppies and lupines while his pillow was covered with apple blossoms. Jackie stared at the psychedelic colour infusion before answering. 'I have this crazy idea of organizing an artists' studio tour here on the island, and I would like to have you and your porcelain paintings in it,' Jackie said.

'I thought you might come to ask me just that. Splendid! Of course I'll do it. I'll do anything once,' exclaimed Harriet and put two teacups with saucers on the table. They too had flowery patterns on them. Harriet went to fetch the silver spoons from the drawer by the sink.

'Great! Next Monday night there's a meeting at the pub at seven o'clock.'

'I'll be there. Sugar?' Harriet sat down to pour the tea. The chair under her groaned.

'Yes, please.'

'Milk?'

'Thank you.'

'So who's coming?' Harriet enquired, energetically stirring the sugar into her tea.

'So far I have talked to Thomas, Sheridan, Russell, Muriel, Janet and Kenneth, though I really don't know whether he is coming or not.'

'He'll be there, don't you worry. If Janet is coming, so will he.' Harriet lifted the cup up to take the careful first sip of her tea. She liked her tea hot.

Janet and Kenneth? Jackie had never thought of Kenneth being interested in anything but nature photography and birds. She was quite surprised. She paused to think about the impossible and then continued. 'Well, then I have talked to Alistair, or should I say Rosalind.'

'Lord, Rosalind…that woman is so stiff that I swear she has the biggest pickle stuffed up her arse.'

Jackie snorted out loud and Harriet looked at her a little surprised. As far as Harriet was concerned, she had only stated the truth and nothing else. The truth was that she couldn't stand Rosalind, and Rosalind did not think very highly of Harriet either.

'Well, that's one way to put it.' Jackie laughed and then drew in her breath and added as an afterthought, 'Though sometimes she can be nice.' Her voice was slightly hesitant.

'Lord, girl don't you turn Christian in my house.' Harriet almost choked on her tea. She stared at Jackie in disbelief. 'Now really, Jackie. That kind of hypocrisy talk just turns my stomach, and you know that I was a nurse and used to seeing all sorts of horrible things; but hypocrisy, that's just plainly nauseating.'

Jackie laughed at the sight of Harriet's scrunched-up face. Winston let out a sharp yelp and stared at the two women from his flowery bed.

'I'm going to talk to Daisy and Nancy, hopefully, later today and…' Remnants of the earlier laughter were still lingering in her voice, when suddenly Jackie took a deep breath and added gravely, '…then I have to talk to Caroline.'

'Don't worry about Caroline.' Harriet waved her hand brushing away the needless worries. 'Rosalind has filled her up with all the details already. I saw her coming out of Rosalind's house yesterday— or was it the day—before, anyhow, she has received all of the information. You can be certain of that.'

'Gossiping is a national sport here in Sycamore, isn't it?' Jackie sighed.

'I'm afraid it is, dear.' Harriet shook her head in agreement.

'Well, I better be off. I have to run to the post office.' Jackie got up and so did Harriet. As soon as Harriet got up, Winston got onto his four feet and walked eagerly to her. They walked together through the flowery house again and stopped by the yellow front door.

'Thanks for the tea, Harriet.'

'That's nothing, girl. It's always nice to chat with you. Stop in anytime.'

'Same here. See you on Monday, then.'

'Absolutely! Bye.' Harriet had lifted Winston into her arms and they were both watching Jackie walk away.

After Jackie disappeared around the corner, Harriet walked back into her house with Winston at her heels. She went into the kitchen to wash the teacups. In the hallway she stopped for a few seconds to wipe the dust off from two photographs on a small table. Harriet had been married twice and she often said that both of her husbands had been very nice. She kept their photographs on display and visited their graves at the same time. Harriet was fair, extremely fair, and she made sure that she continued to treat both of her late husbands the same.

Her first husband had been a doctor and her second husband had been a patient, which all suited Harriet well, since she had been a nurse. She had worked with her first late husband in a small doctor's office till he died, and then she had taken care of her second husband till he died. There had been a lot of illness and plenty of happiness in her life. 'All in good harmony,' as she said. Now she was content with Winston and the painting of porcelain.

She went to the kitchen and turned on the hot water tap to fill the sink. Winston got a cookie and the hot water got a generous splash of dish soap. She flicked on the radio to listen to the news while doing the dishes. The voice from the radio filled the otherwise quiet house.

*   *   *

Jackie was waiting in the post office line when Caroline Trevor arrived. The door slammed shut loudly behind her, making the windows rattle slightly. The heels of her shoes tapped sharply against the tile floor as she took the few steps from the door to the end of the queue.

Other people in the post office were dressed in their country casuals: boots, thick jackets and woolly hats. But Caroline Trevor had an elegant shawl draped around her thin, pointy shoulders; her black leather skirt came just above her knees, showing off her narrow thighs, and on her feet she wore a pair of shiny black high-heeled boots. In her manicured hands, with studied indifference, she held a stack of letters. People turned to see who had walked in. Jackie had quickly learned this peculiar island habit, and she too turned around at the sound of the door. These curious eyes were met with a cold stare from Caroline's dark eyes.

It was impossible to visit a bank, grocery store, post office or flower shop on the island without having at least two or three separate conversations, since everybody knew everybody on the island. Jackie didn't know if it was a good or a bad thing, but it was a different way of life compared to the anonymity of the city.

Some people, having already conducted their official postal business, were there to finish off conversations. Once Caroline was identified as the person through the door, people resumed where they had left off. Unlike earlier, there were no friendly greetings, no smiles and not even a small bowing of a head: maybe a slight raising of an eyebrow or two and then hushed voices.

Caroline tipped her beautiful head slightly toward Jackie, but didn't say anything. Her eyes were cold and revealed no feelings.

'Hi Caroline!' Jackie began hastily. 'Could I have a quick word with you?'

Caroline lifted one of her finely shaped eyebrows. 'Is it about the studio tour the whole island is talking about?' Her voice was cold and reminded Jackie of metal being scraped across the pavement.

All the people in the post office were now listening with utmost concentration. They were staring at the walls or the neck of the person in front of them. Just the same, they were listening to every single word exchanged between Jackie and Caroline.

'Well, yes it is,' Jackie answered. She wasn't surprised. After all, she had been warned by Harriet.

'I was wondering when you would take time off from your precious busy schedule to pay me a visit. You talked to Rosalind two days ago and I was beginning to think that your charming tour didn't actually need a nationally established painter in it.' Caroline's slightly nasal voice was condescending.

'News certainly spreads fast here.' Jackie sighed and made a pathetic attempt to smile. She felt extremely uncomfortable.

A woman at the desk had finished and she turned around to leave.

'Bye, Suzy.' Jackie said to her as she walked by slowly, putting her wallet back into her handbag.

'Bye, Jackie. Good luck with the tour.'

'Oh, thanks.' Jackie smiled. 'We need all the luck we can get.' She added as an afterthought bordering on a prayer.

Suzy walked by Caroline and barely nodded. Caroline wasn't even aware of her. Her eyes simply looked through her.

The front door opened again and, before Suzy had time to leave, somebody that everybody knew stepped in. The post office came alive again with greetings and inquiries. Jackie listened quietly at what was being said and smiled secretly. The woman between Jackie and Caroline in the queue let Caroline pass her, because somebody at the end of the line mentioned a heart attack. The small room was suddenly filled with loud sighs and many 'dear mother of gods.' Jackie and Caroline waited silently for their turn. Jackie tried to begin a friendly conversation with Caroline, but in the end she was defeated and remained quiet, comforted by the chatty laughter coming from the end of the queue.

Jackie loved to hear the people in the village gossip. The exaggerated sighs, the sharp intake of breath to express utter shock, the dozen no's followed by nervous hands being pressed against lips—it all made her smile. Maybe the silence between her and Caroline was not so awkward, she thought shrugging her shoulders. Finally, Jackie's turn came. She moved to the desk and everybody behind her in the post office took a few steps forward on the cold tile floor. You could hear the sound of the shoes scuffing on the floor and then, there was again the sharp tapping sound of Caroline's high heels.

'Good morning, Pam,' Jackie said cheerfully and lifted her package onto the ledge.

'Sending off your pepper grinders again, are you?' asked Pam Johnson, the postmaster and the gossip extraordinaire. Her ears were like radar trained to hear even the slightest whisper in the post office. Nothing escaped her, and the speed at which she put information into the network of the island was astonishing. A few times the person in question had not even returned home from the post office before a neighbour was already briefed with the delicate new facts, most likely hugely exaggerated and not having much in common with the actual truth.

Pam Johnson got up slowly from her chair and walked to a small door beside her desk and opened it to pick up Jackie's well wrapped parcel.

'Yes, it's a small order, but better than nothing, right?' Jackie smiled.

'Yes, that is certainly true. Hold on a minute. I'll go and weigh your package.'

'No rush.' Jackie turned around to face Caroline again.

'Would you like to come to the information meeting next Monday night and meet all the other artists?' She asked her quickly, looking directly into her eyes. The resemblance to the stare of a snake was quite alarming.

'I might, if I'm not too busy.' Caroline turned to examine her nails.

'Good. The meeting starts at seven in the pub.' Jackie turned around again. Her work was done. Caroline had been invited, and now it was up to her to accept it or not. Jackie could not influence that decision and neither did she want to.

Pam Johnson returned. 'It'll be $8.50 dear and I'll fill in the paper work later for you.'

Jackie took her wallet from her jacket pocket and counted the money. 'Thank you so much, Pam. You really needn't to do that.'

'Oh, that's nothing. It's not really that busy here all day long.' She was writing the receipt for Jackie and let her eyes rest briefly on Caroline who was getting agitated by Pam Johnson's laid back attitude and slowness. Pam Johnson observed this with great pleasure and she handed the receipt to Jackie even more leisurely than usual.

'Bye and thank you, Pam.' Jackie said and stuffed her receipt into her pocket, reminding herself to put it in the expenses file later on.

'Bye for now, Jackie. Oh, I almost forgot I do have a letter for you. It arrived after Simon left to do his daily rounds. Let me just go and fetch it for you.'

The sigh that escaped from Caroline's thin lips was clearly audible. Pam Johnson smiled contentedly and walked unhurriedly to the back of the room. 'It'll take just a minute,' she cheerfully called over her shoulder while going through the mail.

Caroline was staring at the wall covered with postal advertising. She saw nothing, but her loathing toward Pam Johnson increased noticeably during that short period of time.

Pam Johnson returned with a letter for Jackie and handed it over to her with a satisfied smile. Caroline's foot tapping impatiently against the tile floor, counting the seconds that were being wasted by the small and round postmaster, only served to increase Pam's satisfaction.

Jackie thanked Pam and turned around to leave. She stopped for a second in front of Caroline who was now staring with burning eyes at Pam Johnson.

'I hope to see you on Monday night.'

Caroline didn't answer; she only moved her eyes to show that she had heard Jackie's words. She moved quickly forward to the desk and put her letters down with a loud slap.

Pam Johnson nodded to Caroline and smiled victoriously. She loved being the postmaster of the village and making people like Caroline Trevor feel her power. She and Mary Cullighan would have a nice long lunch hour together today at Mary's flower shop.

Behind Caroline, a farmer blew his nose loudly and thoroughly. Caroline Trevor felt the small hairs on her neck stand up and her already strong dislike of the little village and its habitants increased considerably.

After she left the post office, Jackie walked slowly to the other side of the town. She thought about Caroline and nervousness about the upcoming meeting washed over her like the white crest of a big uncontrolled breaking wave. The studio tour idea had been generally well received, but she felt that Caroline and Rosalind would make it as complicated as it could possibly be. Jackie began practising her responses to Rosalind's inquiries and complaints, which were sure to come in the very near future. It was much easier to be horribly insulting in one's mind than in the actual moment. Jackie felt better after coming up with a couple snappy retorts.

She stopped at a house with a beautiful large dried flower wreath hanging on the burgundy front door.

'Well, I'll visit Nancy first,' Jackie said to herself and opened the gate. She followed a pretty garden path to the house and rang the doorbell. She heard the ring echoing in the big house and admired the wreath while she waited. Nancy had a great eye for colour and a very delicate hand. Her wreaths were well known around the island.

Jackie heard footsteps from inside and a slightly out of breath voice exclaiming, 'I'm coming.' The door was opened by an older greying woman.

'What a wonderful surprise,' the woman said with a pleasant, slightly shaky voice. 'Please come in.' She ushered Jackie into the house smoothing her apron at the same time. 'Daisy! Jackie is here!' She shouted toward the open kitchen door.

'Daisy is here? Great!' Jackie smiled. This would make her life easier. 'I need to talk to her as well.'

Jackie wiped her muddy boots on the outside carpet and stepped in where she, despite Nancy's numerous pleas, left her boots by the door.

They walked into the kitchen, where Daisy was drinking tea. 'So nice to see you, Jackie dear. How are you?' Daisy smiled cheerfully with a merry twinkle in her eyes.

'Fine, and y…?'

Daisy cut her off in haste. She spoke so fast that her words almost fused into one long continuous word. 'Have you come here to talk about the studio tour?' She stared at Jackie eagerly holding her breath while her cheeks were getting more flushed by the second.

'Well…yes, but how did you know?' Jackie looked at the older woman who had immaculate grey, almost white curls framing her soft face.

'I went to the post office very early this morning and Pat told me that you were planning a studio tour.' Daisy smiled smartly and took a sip of her tea. 'And then I went to buy flowers from Mary's…' She let her words hang in the air, without the need to finish them.

Jackie shook her head in disbelief. 'That explains it all then. There really is no chance of doing anything secretly in this village,' she said.

Daisy nodded knowingly. 'Yes, I hardly have to read a newspaper anymore. I just pop into the post office or flower shop and I come back home fully briefed with the world and village news.' Daisy giggled softly and fixed her curls with the cup of her hand.

Nancy came to the table holding a teacup and saucer in her hands. 'Have some tea, Jackie,' she said.

'Oh, no, no thank you.' Jackie tried to decline the kind offer.

'Please, Jackie. I baked some muffins this morning.' Nancy sighed and shook her head, slight disappointment colouring her words. Nancy, to Jackie's mind, was the perfect image of a grandmother. She was soft and smelled of muffins and talcum powder with a hint of dusty rose, and you did feel very, very guilty if you ever even considered saying no to her.

'Oh, well, all right then, but just a small cup. Thank you.' Jackie smiled and sat down. Nancy placed a teacup and a plate full of muffins in front of her.

'There you go, dear.' She patted Jackie on her shoulder in a grandmotherly way.

'Thank you,' Jackie put sugar in her tea and looked at the two women in front of her. 'Will you come to the meeting then on Monday night?'

'I want to, but Nancy here is not sure.' Daisy looked at Nancy quickly and narrowed her eyes. She was upset about her friend's refusal to participate and had spent a great many hours trying to convince her otherwise. She couldn't keep the hint of dissatisfaction out of her voice.

'Oh, please, Nancy, we need your dried flowers on the tour, and it is going to be held just before Christmas, and everybody needs a Christmas wreath.' Jackie almost sang her last sentence in her attempt to sell the studio tour idea to Nancy.

'She is right, you know.' Daisy was staring intently at Nancy, who avoided both of their eyes and kept looking at her hands as they restlessly twitched on her lap. She was having a difficult time deciding whether she should join the group or not. She didn't like making these kinds of decisions. It made her feel very anxious and uncomfortable.

'Well, maybe I should…I just don't know,' she stammered and wrung her hands in agony.

'Oh, for heaven's sake, Nancy!' Daisy cried. 'It'll be a hoot. I with my painted things, and you with your flowers. What else do we have to do with our time? We are retired old girls and we need to have some excitement in our life, don't you agree?'

Nancy glanced at Daisy and then looked up at Jackie nervously. She was thinking how she could put her words so they would come out right and not be misunderstood. 'I hate to talk ill of anybody.' Nancy finally sighed and smoothed her apron with her hands. 'But that Rosalind just makes me feel so uncomfortable, and…' She paused for a second before asking the question that had been on her mind since the gossip about the studio tour had began. 'And she is coming…right?' She was afraid to ask the question, in case what she had just said was proven true.

Jackie remained quiet for a while. 'Yes, she is.' Jackie mumbled and an image of Rosalind dressed all in black came to her. 'For better or worse she is coming…but all your other friends will be there.' Jackie was trying to sound optimistic and positive. 'You never know,' she thought. 'It might turn out to be great.' There was that chance, though, that chance was as likely as peace on earth and good will to men.

Nancy was still hesitant but she could not resist being with her friends, and she did truly like Jackie whom she had always treated as her own daughter. She shook her head and breathed out her words rather than saying them. 'Well, all right then…I'll do it.' She looked so scared that Jackie felt sorry for her. She bent over to give an encouraging pat on Nancy's hands. Nancy smiled and looked suddenly very brave. Making up her mind had been the hardest part.

'Great. I'm happy to hear that.' Jackie smiled and Daisy was giddy with excitement and praised her friend for making such an important and correct decision.

'Your muffins smell delicious, Nancy.' Jackie said, as she drank the last sip of her tea.

'Oh, well, take some home with you, then.' Nancy urged her and pushed the plate closer to Jackie.

'No, no I couldn't.' Jackie's words fell on deaf ears as Nancy got up briskly and put a few still hot muffins from the pan into a paper bag. She handed the warm bag over to Jackie.

'Just take them, Jackie. You are always so busy working that I'm sure you don't have any time to bake anything for yourself.' She gave the grandmotherly 'don't you dare to argue with me' look. Jackie sighed and then admitted, 'I'm afraid you're right. Thank you so much, Nancy.' She bent over to give Nancy a kiss on her cheek and then walked to the door carrying the bag of muffins. The two ladies followed her.

'See you then on Monday night at the pub.'

'At seven?' Daisy wanted to make sure she had heard the time correctly at the post office.

'Yes, at seven. Bye and thank you.' She waved her warm muffin bag in the air. The bag was getting slightly damp on the bottom, staining the paper faintly blue.

Nick was lifting chairs down from the top of the tables when Jackie walked into the pub.

'Hi, fighter!' He hollered happily, reminding Jackie again about their childhood fights. He wiped his hands on the back of his jeans. His hair was in its usual state of natural disarray. It stood up stubbornly in the front, no matter how much he tried to comb it down. 'Want some tea?' Nick asked.

'No thank you. I have had too many cups of tea today already.' Jackie slumped down on a chair by the bar. 'This studio tour business requires a hefty bladder.'

Nick lifted down the last chair and then noticed the paper bag in Jackie's hands. 'Ah…Nancy's muffins.' He beamed.

'How did you know?'

'She brings them to me occasionally. They are delicious.'

'Do you want one?'

'Why not?' Nick walked to the bar. 'What kind are they today?'

Jackie peeked into the bag. 'Something with blueberry.'

Nick sat down on a bar stool. It was strange for him to be on this side of the bar for once. Jackie offered the bag to Nick. He picked up a muffin, but before he took a bite he stared curiously at Jackie with a slight bemused smile behind his blue eyes.

Jackie was chewing on her muffin completely oblivious of Nick's stare. She was eating her second delicious muffin today, and her thoughts were only on muffins and the studio tour.

'So all is in order for the next Monday night meeting?' Nick asked, slowly studying Jackie's face for answers, mentally mapping any feelings showing unexpectedly on her face. 'You have talked to all of the people already…even to Caroline, which I take, went extremely well.' Nick took a bite of his muffin, hiding his half smile.

Jackie looked up at Nick. She was baffled and tried not to drop crumbs all over herself. 'How did you know that?' Damn, she had dropped half of the muffin on her lap, and part of it fell on the floor despite her efforts. She stared at Nick who had a wide mischievous grin on his face.

'I went to the post office this morning.' Nick answered finally, in a strange casual way, and then burst out laughing.

Jackie stared at his laughing face and then shook her head slightly. 'Dear, dear, Pam Johnson,' she said and leaned back in her chair brushing the loose muffin crumbs into her hand.

On the other side of the street in Mary's flower shop, Ms. Mary Cullighan and Ms. Pam Johnson were just about to bite into their egg salad sandwiches while keeping a keen eye on the front door to the pub.

Chapter 6

The Meeting

On the day of the meeting, Jackie arrived at the pub an hour early, full of ideas and determination. 'It won't be that bad,' she said to herself, sounding more positive than she felt.

Nick watched from behind the bar. He admired her energy and fortitude, particularly standing tall under Rosalind's watchful and mostly critical eyes. 'It will not be easy,' he thought. Nick had offered to help Jackie earlier, but she had declined politely by telling him that he had helped her already by allowing her to use the pub for the meeting. So Nick stood behind his bar and watched, ready to step in if needed.

Jackie was pushing tables together into a group. The boys were watching from their usual spot by the window. They were full of not-so-useful advice, offered freely and continuously.

'Now then, Jackie, remember to sit right by that black witch Rosalind,' Jack Wilkinson would say and then the four of them would roll over with laughter, only to come up with another as useful piece of advice a moment later.

Jackie ignored them and continued her task with tightly pursed lips. Nick glared at the boys, but they were on a roll. This kind of meeting did not happen often in Sycamore and it needed to be fully lived.

'Maybe if you make Thomas sit beside the black witch,' they suggested and nodded toward the bar where Thomas was having a pint. 'You know, beauty and the beast.' This brought a new wave of hysterical laughter. Howard drank his beer down the wrong way and it took a few strong bangs on his back to bring the coughing to an end.

'Or maybe the apprentice witch Caroline will eat Thomas alive,' Howard exclaimed with new gusto having recovered from his coughing episode. 'Though I don't think she needs much practice. She has scared half the village to bits already.'

Normally Jackie would have laughed a little, because no matter how useless these four men were, they were utterly and so honestly useless that you could not but like them. This time, she was not in the mood. She put her hands on her hips and stepped back to look at the group of tables and chairs. She counted the chairs in her mind. 'We can always pull some extra chairs around, if we have to.' She was talking to herself and biting her bottom lip till it hurt.

Nick was making coffee and tea for the meeting. 'Would you like a cup of coffee, Jackie?' he asked.

'I'd love one,' Jackie answered and walked to the bar. 'That should do, don't you think?' She turned around to have another look at the set of tables.

'Yes, that should be just fine,' Nick answered and handed a cup of coffee to her. 'Careful, it's really hot.'

'If I were you, Jackie, I would start drinking whisky already, because that Rosalind woman is coming down the road all high and mighty.' Jack Wilkinson suddenly exclaimed, stirring excitedly on his window seat.

Jackie turned sharply to look out the window and saw Rosalind approaching. She sighed deeply and desperately, feeling sick to her stomach. 'Nick, there is a slight chance that I might need a wee drop of your whisky after this meeting. Just keep the bottle ready.'

Nick nodded sympathetically and looked out the window as well.

Rosalind was indeed walking toward the pub. She walked tensely, her head held extremely high, looking straight ahead. She stepped over the puddles in the middle of the sidewalk, glaring at them with the disgust she associated with all things rural.

Nick gave Jackie a pat on her shoulder. 'Good luck with the meeting,' he said under his breath.

'Thanks,' Jackie said and walked grimly back to the group of tables with her coffee and sat down. From her bag, she pulled out a pile of brochures and a calendar. She organized them in a neat pile and then placed her pen on top of the papers. She was ready for the storm. She was ready for Rosalind. She was ready for a slow descent into hell.

Rosalind walked into the pub. 'Good evening, Nicholas. How are you?' She said the words automatically, obvious from her voice that she was not really interested in hearing what Nick's answer was going to be.

Nick was his usual polite self. 'Just fine thank you, and you?' He said, cheerfully aware of his low status in Rosalind's eyes—as a pub owner, he did not merit much.

'Fine, fine...' She ignored the boys in the corner completely, and Thomas received only a cold nod as she walked to the group of tables where Jackie was drinking her coffee and staring at her well-organized papers.

Jackie saw nothing but fuzziness. Black dots that became grey and danced on the page, fusing together into broken, unreadable lines. She was trying to avoid looking at Rosalind, in an attempt to buy time before meeting her overly critical eyes.

Finally Jackie had to look up at Rosalind. She had a forced smile on her lips, an odd mixture of pain and politeness with a hint of wishful thinking that, maybe, just maybe, everything would turn out fine.

'Hello Rosalind, how are you?'

'Fine, fine. Where is everybody? Oh, well, you should never expect these people to be on time, now should you?' She sat down beside Jackie and placed her black purse on the chair beside her, reserving it for Alistair.

'Alistair is coming. Don't worry. He has to finish his project first. You know. First things first.' It never occurred to her that Alistair was going to be late, just like the people she so greatly despised. She and Alistair naturally belonged to a completely different category.

'That's all right, Rosalind. We'll wait for him.' Jackie said calmly and continued studying her papers. There was no need to say anything extra to Rosalind. Keep it short and tight had been Nick's advice. Suddenly the door opened and Caroline walked in. She looked at Thomas and smiled coolly with her thin lips stretching across her small teeth.

Her high heels tapped sharply on the floor as she walked confidently across the floor. Jack Wilkinson moved his head from right to left with the rhythm of Caroline's heels. He grinned, but made sure that Caroline's back was turned toward him. He was no fool and he feared receiving her icy stare. The other boys drowned their laughter in their beer glasses. The massacre of Jackie was about to begin and they had the best seats in the house.

Caroline nodded at Jackie coldly. She took off her shawl and draped it on the back of the chair. 'Jackie, I hope everything is ready for the tonight's *very* exciting meeting.' She pronounced the word exciting mockingly, putting the emphasis on the *very*.

'Yes I think so.' Jackie said and added in her mind, 'Or I should say, I hope so.'

'Caroline, how is that exhibition of yours coming along?' Rosalind was eager to chat with Caroline. She had recognized a kindred spirit as soon as she had met her.

'It's a drag, really, but what can you do.' Caroline sat down on the other side of Rosalind and crossed her long, shapely legs, which were, again, dressed in a short skirt and a pair of long black leather high-heeled boots. Caroline began talking with Rosalind closing the rest of the world out.

The boys, despite their fear of Caroline, and ready to spring back at the slightest sign of movement from her, could not but help lean forward to catch a glimpse, so generously exhibited before them, of the best legs on the island.

Across the room, Thomas, as happy and without care as ever, was leaning against the bar telling Nick a funny story he had heard at the post office.

The door to the pub opened once more, ushering in Nancy O'Brien and Daisy Davidson.

'Good evening,' Nancy said with a small hesitant voice that relayed her desire to immediately return home.

Caroline and Rosalind slowly glanced at Nancy and Daisy, raising their eyebrows as if to say that they were already bored with these two 'old girls.'

Nancy made a few hesitant movements toward the front door, but Daisy had her arm in a strong but friendly grip.

Jackie smiled. She was genuinely happy to see kind faces around the table. 'I'm happy you came. Please, sit down; help yourself to coffee or tea.' Jackie was surprised by her own calm hostessing. Nick nodded his head to her encouragingly. Thomas flashed thumbs up from his seat at the bar.

Nancy and Daisy hesitantly sat down as far as possible from Rosalind and Caroline, who did not even acknowledge their existence.

Nevertheless, Nancy and Daisy nodded shyly and politely at them. They might not have liked them, but good manners demanded they at least be polite; in their world people were judged by their manners.

They were pouring tea for themselves when Sheridan Watson marched into the pub. 'Good evening, everybody!' He exclaimed and quickly brushed his prominent moustache with his fingers.

Nick nodded from the bar and Thomas lifted his pint as a greeting then turned and made a face.

Sheridan went to the coat rack, tossed his hat on the top shelf and took off his jacket. He shook it in front of him to make sure it was straight, without any creases in its brown tartan, and then hung it up, seeing that nothing touched it.

He pulled out a comb from his back pocket and combed his thinning hair. He did not comb his moustache, which made Jackie forever grateful.

'I think I will have a cup of coffee before the meeting. First business and then pleasure.' Sheridan let his eyes rest a moment on Thomas's back at the bar.

Thomas made another face, took a slow, noisy sip of his beer and exclaimed in a deep voice. 'Ahh, just what I need after a hard day of hard physical labour.' Sheridan's moustache quivered slightly, and he wiggled his nose to show his gentlemanly dislike of Thomas and his ilk.

Harriet and Janet, visible through the window just past Jack Wilkinson's bent wolf-like head, were walking toward the pub. Harriet pushed the door open to let Janet go in first.

'Good evening, folks. What? Is it beer time already, Stockwell?' She bellowed merrily. Thomas turned around to greet Harriet with a mischievous grin on his face. 'Yes indeed it is. Why, won't you join me, darling?'

'Maybe later I will.' Harriet smiled and winked at Thomas.

She took both hers and Janet's coats and then tossed them on top of the other clothes, to Sheridan's horror. He would need to press his jacket again.

Harriet slapped her enormous thighs as she sat down heavily on the small chair greeting Muriel who was quietly putting her gloves away.

Muriel straightened her skirt and smoothed her sweater before she walked to the table, making sure her broach was firmly attached to her sweater.

'You came alone?' Harriet enquired lifting her one eyebrow higher than the other.

'Yes, I was chosen to be the representative of the bitchers and stitchers.'

'Darling, you can bitch and stitch better than anybody,' Harriet chuckled.

'If that was a compliment, Harriet, I'm pleased,' Muriel answered with a smile that was a combination of demure and teasing. Harriet let out a huge laugh and put her hand on Muriel's shoulders. 'Have some tea, Muriel.' Harriet squeezed her and then poured the tea.

'Thank you.' Muriel was reaching for some sugar when Russell stormed in. He stopped in the middle of the floor and looked happily around as if taking in the whole scene.

'Boy, you have been a busy girl,' he exclaimed and rubbed his hands together readily. 'You got all of these people together. Bloody fantastic! Absolutely brilliant! Swell!' He looked toward the bar, where Thomas was lounging and enjoying his pint.

'Stockwell, having a pint already?' He asked jovially. 'I might just have to join you.'

'Please do, Russell. It is very lonely out here.' Thomas grinned and pulled out a chair for him.

Russell stomped to the bar and hung his clothes on the back of the chair. Nick handed him a pint with a welcoming smile. 'Nice to see you, Russell.'

'Thank you, old man.' Russell took a loud, long thirsty sip from his pint. A happy relaxed smile spread over his weather-beaten old face. He was content. A bit of excitement and a bit of beer. Life was grand. 'Now this Jackie of ours, isn't she something or what.' He exclaimed and put his pint down on the table wiping his mouth at the same time. 'She has gotten all of us here together to make something new happen in our village.'

'Yes, she is something.' Nick looked at Jackie, who was reorganizing her papers in neat piles. She needed the action to calm her nerves. Her face was very serious as if going through an invisible checklist in her mind. All the other people around the table were chatting busily. Nick smiled at the sight of Jackie's pinched, slightly flushed face.

'Yes, she is our little Jackie all right.' Thomas answered Russell's statement before Nick did.

'You know, I had just finished giving my missus this old bone here'—Russell pointed to his groin in the small way of his, nodded knowingly, and then held up his pint in a toast to their manhood and its magnificent capabilities. Thomas almost choked on his beer and Nick turned his head so quickly that a hot flash ran up his scalp. He rubbed his throbbing head while Thomas wiped the spilled foam from the front of his shirt. Russell continued, unaware of the strange silence surrounding him—'when this girl here came by our house to invite me to the studio tour meeting. My god, I said to my missus.

That is a wonderful idea. Just what this island needs. She's got brains that girl and she isn't bad to look at either.'

Thomas and Nick were staring at Russell in awe and didn't even notice that Kenneth had walked in silently, trying his best to slip in unnoticed.

Kenneth glanced at Jackie and walked quietly to the table where the ladies asked him what he would like to have, and then poured him some tea. Kenneth put his jacket on the back of the chair and sat down. He took a handkerchief out of his pocket, blew his nose loudly, and got up again to walk to the bar.

'Could I have small rum, please?' His voice was hoarse, and he had left his scarf on, wrapped tightly around his neck.

'Of course,' Nick said leaning in a bit over the counter to hear Kenneth's hushed words properly. He normally spoke very quietly, and now with his sore throat his voice was almost inaudible.

'It's for my tea. I have a cold, you see,' Kenneth explained, wiping his nose with his large handkerchief again.

'Nothing better for a cold than a bit of rum in your tea,' Nick said sympathetically and gave the glass of rum to Kenneth.

'Me...I'm never sick and you know why?' Russell cut in brashly. He took a loud, slurping sip of his pint and wiped his mouth on his sleeve before getting into the details. 'If you have sex often enough,' he bellowed, 'then those germs don't have a chance. Sex keeps your blood too hot for those germs to make you sick.' Russell nodded, knowingly. He seemed genuinely happy to be able to help others by giving out his expert health advice.

Nick turned quickly to stare at the shelves behind the bar, his back shaking slightly as he tried not to laugh out loud.

Kenneth walked away with his glass of rum, as if he had not heard a thing. Thomas looked up at Russell, suddenly very interested in what more Russell might have to say on the subject.

'Is that so?' Thomas enquired innocently, lifting his eyebrows high and nodding his head, as if he did not quite agree with Russell and needed more information before his mind could be made up.

'Ooh, yes...I have never been sick since my wedding night.' Russell exclaimed proudly.

'Really? Now that's interesting. Now, did you hear that, Nick?' Thomas asked Nick, who was still desperately staring at the wall. 'Fantastic health advice, indeed.'

'Interesting, very interesting,' were the only words Nick could safely say before the laughter made him bend over and he had to pretend to have a violent coughing attack.

Russell looked over the counter at Nick and shook his head sadly. 'There are a lot of colds going around these days, I say.' He clicked his tongue knowingly.

Just then Alistair walked in. He looked briefly at Nick, who was still red-faced and coughing wildly behind the bar. Rosalind lifted her head and pointed sharply to the chair beside her.

Sheridan nodded his greetings to Alistair. A simple grave nod, one great man to another. Sheridan smoothed his shirt front and straightened his pen on the table.

Kenneth was sitting amongst the ladies. He was slowly mixing his rum into his cup of tea. He was such a tall, thin man that sometimes he had difficulties fitting comfortably into the pub chairs. He kept moving his knees and peering under the table to see where he could stretch his legs and not disturb any of the other people around him.

'Great, Alistair is here. We can start now.' Jackie declared loudly. 'If you boys wouldn't mind coming over here? Thank you.' She looked at Thomas and beckoned him and Russell over.

Russell and Thomas walked toward the table. On his way Thomas glanced back at Nick, grinning shamelessly. Nick just shook his red face and tried hard to suppress further laughter that was forcing its way through.

Jackie cleared her throat and let her eyes wander over the people around the table. She was extremely pleased with the turnout. 'Thank you all for coming.' She energetically grabbed a pile of brochures in front of her. 'I have brought some interesting information with me from other studio tours around the country. Could you pass these on, Rosalind? Please have a good look at them and tell me what you think.'

Rosalind took the stack, glaring at Jackie suspiciously. She had a skeptical expression on her pointy face. It seemed to say, 'I already know that anything in these papers is not up to the artistic level I have been used to, but if you insist, I might humour you for a while and pretend to be excited about this whole charade.' Rosalind passed the stack forward as if they might be infected with mediocrity. She immediately began reading the first brochure just to prove to herself, as soon as possible, that her thoughts were correct.

The pile of papers went around the table and soon everybody was immersed in reading them. Jackie sat in the silence broken only with a low murmur and the crisp sound of turning pages. Jackie leaned back in her chair and took a sip of coffee deciding to wait for a few minutes before taking centre stage again.

'I might as well enjoy this moment when Rosalind is actually present but quiet.' She thought with some amusement and let her eyes wander around the table.

Suddenly Rosalind leaned over to Alistair and pointed with her long finger at a picture. 'And she calls that art. I beg to differ.' She pinched her nose in disgust. Alistair looked as bored as ever when Caroline suddenly laughed out heartily. Her laugh was not kind and held no happiness usually associated with laughter.

'Oh my god! This woman here is such a bad painter. Oh, I think I'm going to die.' Caroline showed a picture to Rosalind who joined Caroline's hilarity with pleasure.

Jackie tried to ignore them. Luckily Russell came to rescue her spirits. He had been studying the information in front of him very keenly and finally he had come to a conclusion. He held one of the pamphlets high in the air and then slapped it on to the table loudly.

'These are all good artists here, Jackie. Darn good, I say.' He exclaimed. 'You really think we could make a similar tour here in Sycamore?' He looked at Jackie and waited eagerly her answer.

'Yes, I sincerely do. We are quite a talented lot, in my opinion.' Jackie was very happy to have such a positive reaction, never mind that it was from Russell who generally thought everything was bloody fantastic.

'Well, that depends on one's opinion.' Rosalind's piercing voice cut the air sharply. She was looking at Caroline as she was speaking and they both had slight knowing smiles spreading across their faces.

Jackie stared bitterly at Rosalind but decided, after a quick conversation in her mind, to say nothing. Rosalind turned slowly to look at Jackie. She cleared her throat and she was ready to give her opinion whether it was welcomed or not. 'Surely we have to establish some kind of guidelines about who can be accepted to join our studio tour organization.' Rosalind paused for just a second and then continued with a deep expressive sigh that revealed her sharp front teeth. 'Otherwise we'll be burdened with all kinds of amateurs and hobbyists who call themselves artists after a weekend course at the local club.' She pronounced the words *amateurs* and *hobbyist* with great dislike and she appeared to be looking, particularly, at Nancy and Daisy.

Daisy and Nancy looked down at the brochures on the table in front of them just to avoid looking at Rosalind.

Jackie was struggling to resist the impulse to jump over the table and strangle Rosalind. She inhaled intensely and continued as if Rosalind had not said anything. She was not going to let the meeting descend into an irresolvable philosophic debate over the question of 'what is art.' 'Anyhow...what I see is some kind of combination of island-life charm with an artistic theme, and I seriously think that we can all work together really well. Right?' Jackie's positive question hung in dead air supported by doubtful looks.

'All in harmony...just like a family...half of us wanting the other half dead.' Thomas was highly amused by the negativity oozing from Rosalind. He sat lazily in his chair with his long legs crossed and his pint in his hand. People laughed nervously. Most of the people in the pub would have had no problem with the immediate removal of two of the people from around the table; in fact these two could have moved completely away from the island. Jackie shook her head in disbelief that Thomas would actually say such a thing out loud.

'We have eleven individual artists and one group of quilt makers. I think that is enough for our first tour. We just have to all put our heads together and do our best.' Jackie continued still hanging onto the possible positive outcome.

Caroline leant over to Rosalind and whispered loud enough for the nearest people to hear her. 'Good luck...this isn't exactly a Mensa meeting.' Rosalind nodded and let out a small shrill laugh. They both continued reading the brochures now and then showing something to the other. They no longer even tried to pretend that they were listening to Jackie.

'Okay. Now! We need to get down to business...unfortunately.' Jackie cleared her throat. It was time for the next item on her list. 'We should first choose a chair and then a secretary and a treasurer.'

'Well, why don't you be the chair? That just seems right to me, since you have gotten us all together here.' Russell suggested. 'Why would we even vote? Seems pretty natural to me that Jackie should hold the reins.' He glanced around the table and received supportive nods until his eyes met Rosalind's dark stare.

'But surely we must vote for the chair and not just have a shouting match like some kind of uncivilized tribe.' Rosalind barked in disgust.

'All right, all right, Rosalind. Hold your horses!' Russell said jovially, which drove Rosalind absolutely mad.

'Hold your horses,' she muttered under her breath. 'God, how I am truly living in the middle of nowhere.' She glared at Russell, who was not at all bothered by Rosalind's remarks. Her words had gone completely unnoticed by him.

'Who votes for Jackie to be the chair of this bunch?' Russell said and cleared his throat before lifting his tough weathered hand in the air.

People looked around, nodded, and followed Russell's example. They avoided Rosalind's sharp eyes scanning the room.

Nick stopped cleaning the glasses for a second. He found Rosalind's attitude amusing, and exactly what had been expected by one and all. 'Poor Jackie,' he thought and let his eyes rest for awhile on Jackie's face. There was determination behind her green eyes despite the bright red spots on her cheeks.

Reluctantly Caroline and Rosalind lifted their hands, casting their votes. They did so hesitantly and against their better judgement.

Russell rubbed his hands together with a newfound vigour. 'Well that wasn't that bad, now was it?' He smiled and slammed the table loudly with his fist. 'Off you go, Jackie, do your job, and tell us what to do. The stage is yours.' He spread his hands over the table and smiled encouragingly. It was a very priest-like gesture that was spoiled only by the final punctuation of a naughty wink.

Jackie breathed in deeply and exhaled the words, 'Thank you.' She now wanted to move fast. 'Who wants to be the secretary then…anybody?' She rammed her words together. She was longing to have the meeting done and to have her glass of whiskey at the bar, surrounded by people who truly cared for her.

Daisy Davidson lifted her hand hesitantly and spoke with a quiet voice that trembled slightly. 'I used to be a secretary before I retired, so I could do it.' She looked around the room, adding shyly, 'If you wish.' She clasped her hands tightly under the table, rubbing her thumbs together.

'I wish that very much, Daisy! All in favour?' Jackie gave a big supportive smile to Daisy.

Everybody lifted their hands, even Caroline and Rosalind, who were relieved to have escaped such a menial position as a secretary.

'Daisy, you are the secretary then, thank you.' Jackie squirmed in her seat as her eyes were going around the table looking for the next volunteer. 'The treasurer…anybody…?'

Thomas was going to say something, but Jackie cut him off before he was finished his throat clearing. 'No Thomas, not you… you still owe me money, if you remember?'

Thomas lifted his hands in the air and made a small gesture of disappointment. 'I'll buy you a pint after the meeting.' He finally said shaking his head sadly.

'Thanks. Very generous of you, Thomas.' Jackie smiled and then continued her hunt for a treasurer, 'Now then…who wants to be the treasurer? It will be fun…numbers…power, etcetera…Anybody…?' Her eyes looked around the table once more until they stopped at Rosalind. Jackie's eyebrows lifted slightly. A very pleasant thought had occurred to her. A devilish, happy thought that was worth trying out.

'Rosalind...how about it?' Jackie suggested with an impish coy smile. Nick noticed it and grinned. Jackie wasn't beaten yet. It reminded him of the ten-year-old Jackie who had fought with him on the beach, defending her sandcastle to the bitter end.

'Rosalind, what do you say?' Jackie asked. Her voice sounded cheerful, but it had an underlying naughtiness attached to it.

Rosalind was taken aback. 'Oh, no I couldn't.' She liked pointing out other people's mistakes, not taking on responsibility that could result in mistakes on her part.

Russell jumped in with amazing speed. 'All in favour for Rosalind?' His hand was jabbing the air, slicing it into millions of dust particles.

The vote of hands was unanimous. Jackie, with one side of her mouth rising higher than the other, looked at Rosalind. It was hard not to laugh at the sight of Rosalind's shocked face. Rosalind reluctantly nodded her acceptance, her long nose quivered and her thin lips, a mere line in her ashen face. This meeting really had not turned out the way she had envisioned.

'Well,' Jackie was smiling. She wanted to enjoy this moment as long as possible. 'We are all set then.' She stole a glance at Nick, who made a ridiculously exaggerated thumbs-up gesture. She buried her smile in her papers and reviewed her list while resisting the urge to burst into loud giggles. 'The timing of the tour—How about having the tour at the end of October?' Jackie suggested. 'Weather should still be nice and Christmas is just around the corner.'

Russell, as usual, jumped in first with his endless enthusiasm. 'October sounds good to me.' He bellowed and in his mind he declared the simple decision done. Sheridan's eyes wandered over a spot just above Russell's head and he cleared his throat ceremoniously.

'The date seems quite well suited for our needs. But we should consider alternatives as well, just to be sure that the decision we'll make will be the right one.' He tapped his round fingers against his protruding stomach. 'What are your thoughts on the subject, Rosalind?' He nodded his approval of Rosalind's future thoughts.

'Well,' Rosalind began, slowly fingering her necklace while rearranging her words in her mind. 'Luckily Alistair and his art are not tied to any specific time of the year; October could be acceptable, though further discussion will naturally be needed to avoid any mistakes that a hasty decision could cause, just as Sheridan so intelligently pointed out.' She closed her lips tightly around her pointy teeth and looked around the table challenging anybody to think otherwise. She was going to make the most of her position as a treasurer.

Caroline was examining her newly manicured nails. 'I do have another solo exhibition coming up in the end of November, but...' She gave a long, theatrical and thoughtful sigh. 'I guess October could be all right.' She didn't want to commit to October completely. She liked to keep all of her options open. Something better might come along.

Muriel talked for the first time. Jackie enjoyed her calm and kind voice after Caroline's sharp metallic clip. 'The bitchers and stitchers told me to say that any time is fine with them.'

Kenneth nodded his approval, and then returned to stare at his empty tea cup pondering if his sore throat was going to spoil his planned fishing trip tomorrow. He stole a quiet guarded glance at Janet who was occupied clearing the pilling off her pullover.

'It seems a good time of the year to me as well...sheep-wise, you know.' Janet said without raising her eyes. Caroline scrunched her nose at the thought of sheep having anything to do with a decision-making process that was supposed to evolve around art only.

Thomas yawned and tapped his flat stomach twice. 'October is fine with me...no problemos.' He took a long draft of his pint and turned to see if Nick was busy. It was definitely time for another beer, since this meeting seemed to be endless.

The rest of the tour members agreed and Jackie let out a big sigh of relief. She looked quickly at her list of topics and continued. 'We need to do a brochure and we need to find sponsors to pay for it all...'

Russell agreed and nodded his head vigorously and tapped the table loudly, which made Kenneth wake up from his fishing daydream. With heavy lids, he looked around the table and wondered what had been decided. The situation reminded him of the faculty meetings at his old school. Lots of talk prior to accomplishment. He stretched his legs and tried to swallow. The pain in his throat was worsening.

Nancy and Daisy kept their eyes on Jackie. Daisy was excited. She loved being busy and sometimes she found the quiet retirement days challenging even though she had her own art shop. But come January, even with the shop, all was quiet, except for the howling winter wind that found all the gaps in the house and forced its way in.

Alistair was deep in his own world. He happily let Rosalind take the lead in most things, without even bothering to listen. Many years with Rosalind had taught him that he would, in any case, be updated later at home. She would begin over the sound of the television, and eventually Alistair would have to resign the idea of actually hearing the news. Not that he would, in reality, be listening to Rosalind's account, but Alistair had also learned that it was far better to pretend to listen than to obviously not be interested. Rosalind only needed a few grunts and a few agreeing nods here and there, and she would be off again, analyzing and criticizing something else in great detail. Alistair had developed his coexistence with Rosalind over the years into an art of avoidance. He never did have to decide anything. And because Rosalind craved power and admiration, she had elevated Alistair's artistic talents onto a pedestal. This pleased Alistair, and even if not completely content about their situation, it allowed him to devote all of his time to his art. To fulfil her self-created characterization of Alistair, while he was working Rosalind did not dare to disturb the next Picasso in the making.

Thomas walked happily back from the bar with a fresh pint in his hands. He sat down and assumed his nonchalant listening position. Caroline followed him with her sharp eyes. She had heard his name mentioned many times by giggling girls and gossiping store clerks. She wondered if there was anything behind those stories about his alphabetical dating routine. His legs were very long indeed, and he hid well-developed muscles under his Che Guevara T-shirt. It was far more pleasant to think about what was under Thomas's clothes than to listen to Jackie going on about the studio tour. Carefully, she licked her lips and touched her hair.

'We need a nice and fancy and cheap brochure.' Jackie's voice interrupted Caroline's pleasurable thoughts. She shifted in her seat and fixed her short skirt.

'Well, because I seem to be the only educated, professional painter in this group...' Caroline said slowly still examining her skirt. 'I believe I should design the brochure.'

'What a fantastic idea! Isn't it, Alistair?' Rosalind yelped and pushed Alistair. Alistair looked around the table startled. He had absolutely no idea what he was being asked to agree to. 'Well...I guess...it's all right.' He looked at Rosalind and from the expression on her face he knew that his answer had been the correct one; he was once again allowed to go back to his own world of quiet dreams.

'Any objections?' Jackie asked quietly. There were none. 'All in favour?' The hands went up.

'You'll be in charge of the brochure then, Caroline.' Jackie said as she crossed one more item off her agenda.

'With pleasure.' Caroline said and smiled her toothy smile that was never truly happy or welcoming. Jackie always thought that she resembled a wolf just about to tear a piece off a newly killed prey. There was always an element of malice mixed with pleasure. 'And... uh...maybe Kenneth would be so kind as to take the photographs for the brochure?' Jackie suggested while observing Caroline, whose white predator smile had changed into a sudden gloomy frown.

Kenneth looked up from the brochure he was reading. He was startled. 'Uh...me?' He croaked and stared at Jackie.

'Yes, would you do that for us?' Jackie asked kindly while secretly enjoying the devastated look on Caroline's face.

'Well, uh...I guess it would be all right...Perhaps?' Kenneth was scratching his head now in confusion. He stirred uncomfortably in his seat. He wanted to watch birds, fish and spend time with Janet, not work with Caroline, who made him feel very nervous.

Caroline was staring at Kenneth as if he did not even belong to the same species. She leaned over to Rosalind and whispered with a voice dripping with irony. 'This is going to be so much fun.'

Rosalind nodded, covering with her hand a small, tight smile.

Suddenly Sheridan looked up from his notes. 'Since I edited the *Miniature Army World News*, may I offer my long experience and help writing the brochure? I particularly excel in proofreading.' His voice was very stern and matter-of-fact as he touched his moustache and cleared his throat.

Jackie stared at Sheridan in amazement. She was trying to think what the *Miniature Army World News* was. 'Sure…uh…Caroline?' She looked questioningly at Caroline.

'The more the merrier.' Caroline's voice was now icy, her face was hard as stone and she was not merry at all.

Jackie stared at her papers and slowly added Sheridan's name to the brochure group, along with Kenneth and Caroline's. It was just too good to be true. Caroline was now forced to work with the two people she liked the least. Not that she actually liked anybody, not even Rosalind—not really. Caroline and Rosalind's relationship was different. They needed each other to look down at the rest of the people on the island. Jackie knew exactly what Caroline thought of Kenneth. 'A bloody amateur nature photographer, ex-biology teacher, a bore,' Caroline would surely say. And then there was Sheridan. He was a well-known potter, but he was also pompous; and he did like to be very close, maybe too close, to Caroline's short skirts and her shapely legs.

'It hasn't been such a bad night after all,' Jackie thought and tried to hide her grin. 'Okay, next.' She continued, trying to sound serious. 'We need sponsors and who better get them than Thomas?'

Thomas looked up from his pint, which he had been happily drinking without any obligations attached to his name so far. 'Who? What? Me?' He stuttered.

'Yes. You!' Jackie said.

'Well…all right then. I'll collect the sponsors.' Thomas gave up before the war had even started. He knew when fighting would be useless. Better to preserve energy for something else.

Nick shouted behind his bar. 'I'll be happy to sponsor your tour. Just let me know how much and what you need from me.' He was drinking coffee, listening to the meeting and trying to ignore the chatter that was coming from the boy's corner.

'Great! Thanks, Nick. Write that down on your sponsor list, Thomas.' Jackie was all smiles.

'All right, Miss Chair…Any chance having another pint, Nick?' Thomas said and stirred uncomfortably in his seat.

'One for me too, if you would.' Russell yelled cheerfully.

Nick nodded and started pouring the pints. For a Monday night, business was good. Sheridan looked at Thomas disapprovingly. He did not approve of drinking beer during the meetings.

'Well, if Nicholas is going to be a sponsor, so surely we must ask Maximilian Woodland and his exceptional French restaurant, as well,' Rosalind said sharply, wrinkling her long thin nose and then added, 'I'm sure that more sophisticated people would like to have an alternative to this…this…pub food.' She pronounced *pub food* as if it were something entirely indigestible.

Jackie looked at Nick briefly but Nick wasn't at all insulted. Rather, he was highly amused by Rosalind's provocative words and happily anticipated her response when Pete's Fish and Chips, next door, became a sponsor, as well. He could not wait till next Monday night.

'Good idea, Rosalind. Why don't you go and talk with him.' Jackie said and, though Nick was laughing, she felt offended on his behalf by Rosalind's implied insult.

'Me?' shrieked Rosalind, 'I was under the impression that Thomas was taking care of all the sponsors.' She certainly would not go and beg for money for this disastrous tour. Her work was to be the treasurer. Her work was to assign things for other people to do and run about. She was the pointer and other people were the pointees.

'Yes, you, Rosalind, since you know him so well; Thomas has hardly even been to his restaurant.' Jackie returned to her papers, imagining the end of the meeting. Her ability to remain civil was being stretched and she was getting tired of Rosalind's sharp voice. 'And I'll talk to George from the hardware store, and I guess, I could ask Tim and John from the East End Bed and Breakfast.'

'What about the west end gays?' Thomas enquired innocently.

Everybody turned to look at him in embarrassed silence.

Thomas put his pint down and looked at the people staring at him. 'What? What did I say? Everybody calls them that...' Thomas was bewildered. He spread his hands in the air. 'The east end gays and the west end gays. That's what they are called, right?' Thomas tried to defend his words and make them sound less offensive, more politically correct. 'You know...' he added sheepishly hoping to make some kind of a point.

Jackie was aghast, 'Thomas...' She said and shook her head.

'But I cannot keep their names straight. Tim and Tom?' Thomas pleaded and stared at Jackie.

'No, Tim and John.' Jackie answered and tapped her pencil against the table.

'And they are the west end gays?' Russell asked.

'No, that's Tom and Kevin.' Jackie stared at the wall. Her mouth was a thin straight line.

'So Tim and Tom...no, no, wait.' Russell thought out loud, 'John!' He exclaimed merrily. 'Tim and John are the east end gays.' Russell was now concentrating hard in his efforts to put things straight in his mind.

'Yes...' Jackie's yes was a long and painful sigh.

'I can see now why you call them the east end and west end gays.' Russell nodded at Thomas. 'With names like that, who can keep them straight?'

'See, it just makes sense.' Thomas was trying to show with his hands that his nicknames weren't meant to be offensive; they were based on logic. He shook his hands in the air like a preacher.

'Now who's the writer chap, then?' Russell questioned.

'That's Kevin.' Thomas said brightly.

'And he was?' Russell looked at Thomas, waiting.

'East end gay? No, no...sorry. Kevin is a west end gay...that's right.' Thomas finally got the names correct and smiled cheerfully.

'And he has a dog...?'

'No, the east end gays have a dog.'

'Funny, I could have sworn that it was them west end gays.' Russell was rubbing his rough chin thoughtfully.

'They are really nice chaps.' Thomas said and had a sip of his beer.

'So it is then the east end gays who want me to paint their dog?'

'Most likely.' Thomas agreed, not entirely sure.

'What's the dog's name then?'

Jackie put her forehead onto the table in exhaustion. She had hoped the meeting would end brilliantly, without an incident. The meeting had not only fallen apart but had become politically incorrect. She didn't even bother looking in Rosalind's direction. She didn't want to die just yet. She felt Rosalind's venom even without staring into her piercing snake eyes. Thomas and Russell continued. 'Bristol, I think…or was it Brighton? I'm not really sure. Maybe it was Bristol Cream? Anyway, it was either a city or a drink and it started with B.' Thomas said brightly.

'Maybe it was Bailey's…or Ballantines?' suggested Russell helpfully staring at the shelves above the bar.

'Brussels…it could be Brussels or Bangkok? Or Berlin…? Yes I think it was Berlin.' Thomas thought out loud. 'Yes! It was Berlin.'

'Now that would be a ridiculous name for a dog,' exclaimed Russell, the dog connoisseur. 'Berlin? Can't be?'

Jackie stared at the two of them. Her head was pounding and she had a sharp pain just behind her eyes. 'Are we done talking at that end of the table?' Her voice was surprisingly threatening.

Russell and Thomas looked up at Jackie. They were disturbed and puzzled, but the look on Jackie's face pulled them back. Thomas straightened in his seat. 'Yes, Ma'am. We are done talking. Absolutely finito.' He pulled an invisible zipper across his lips.

'Good, so it is all sorted out then?' She was staring at them with a pair of unexpectedly vicious eyes.

'Yes?' Thomas and Russell answered together hesitantly.

Jackie sighed deeply, her narrowed eyes still on Thomas. Thomas fidgeted in his seat. 'I'll talk to all the B & Bs in the village.' Jackie said and then added. 'Now! How about a meeting next week? Same time, same place?' She looked around the table at all the nodding heads. With huge relief, Jackie blurted, 'Meeting adjourned.'

Scraping chair legs and scuffing feet joined the low rumble of people saying their goodbyes.

Thomas looked over the heads of the people in Jackie's direction. 'How about that pint I promised?' he smiled.

'I would love it, thanks.' Jackie pushed her hands through her hair, massaging her aching head. She leaned over her notes one last time, adding final suggestions and corrections for the next meeting.

Thomas brought the pint for Jackie while she was putting her papers back into her bag. She had the bag on her lap and was trying to slide the folder into it. Her eyes had sunk more deeply into her face. Thomas thought she looked exhausted.

Jackie took the pint and with a long sigh she had her first sip. She looked at Thomas questioningly. 'By the way, what is the *Miniature Army World News?*'

'Oh, it's a tin soldier army thing, you know?' Thomas lifted his shoulders up an inch; how else could one explain such a thing. 'Sheridan has a whole battalion in his basement.'

Jackie stared at Thomas a good long while and then shook her head in amazement. 'Really? Boy, we are quite a group.' She burst into tired, uncontrollable giggles.

Thomas laughed and tapped her on the shoulders. 'I warned you, remember, my love?' He sat down by Jackie and put his arm around her.

Caroline was sitting at the bar watching idly. She lit a cigarette, leaned back in her chair, and gave her shiny black hair a small shake, letting it then fall back on her pointy shoulders.

Sheridan was staring at Caroline—at her legs, well displayed in her short skirt. He scurried up to her with alarming speed for a plump man and offered to get them both drinks. Caroline lazily accepted. Sheridan's busy voice filled the air. He had a great many essential ideas for the artists' brochure, which, as he pointed out, came from his long experience being the editor of the *Miniature Army World News*. It would have been a great exaggeration to say that Caroline paid any attention to Sheridan's chatter. She mostly looked bored but entertained herself by keenly examining Thomas. Caroline exhaled her cigarette smoke into Sheridan's overly enthusiastic face.

'Would you believe that meeting! Revolting! So unprofessional!' Rosalind's voice began before the door of the pub closed behind Alistair as he followed her out. Her sharp voice trailed into the distance. 'Absolutely, the most horrid meeting I have ever, ever attended in my entire life.'

Russell moved to the bar. 'Now really, who would name their dog Berlin?' Jackie heard him question with a thunderous voice. 'Never heard anything as ridiculous in my life.'

Chapter 7

You Can't Go Home

Jackie tossed her knapsack onto the bed in her mother's guest room. She always stayed in this small room when she visited her mother and Robert. As soon as Jackie had left for university her mother had changed her old bedroom into a quilting room. After the quilting had fallen out of style, the room had been changed into a small gym and then into a yoga room. After that it became a meditation room with a small water fountain in the corner. It looked very pretty, Jackie thought as she quickly peeked into it on her way downstairs to join the rest of the family for drinks. The bamboo walls gave it a very tranquil feeling. Her mother's interior decorator Samuel was very good.

'Samuel is simply marvellous!' Her mother boasted as she handed Jackie a drink. 'He works wonders. He is so talented. You know that he is designing the wedding for Penny's daughter, Tracy. You remember I told you about the wedding?' Jackie nodded, although she had only a vague memory of her mother's mention of the upcoming wedding.

'You remember, now don't you?' Her mother enquired while stirring her gin and tonic.

'Oh, yes. I remember.' Jackie said quickly

'Yes. Tracy is marrying Charles. He is a banker.' Jackie's mother's voice had a dreamy edge to it as she spoke fondly of Charles, whom she had never met. 'Oh, look, here comes Andrew. He wanted to drop some papers off for Robert to sign. That young man works so hard. Robert simply could not live without him.' Her mother looked out the window, stretching her neck as far as it could stretch. 'Now remember, Jacqueline. Be nice and polite.'

'Yes, Mom.' Jackie felt like a five-year-old. She glanced over at Robert and wondered how he lived with her mother with such ease.

Andrew walked in holding a folder in his hands. Jackie looked at the clock, reckoning how many hours of torture lay ahead.

'Now, Jacqueline. Here is Andrew.' Her mother was all smiles. Her voice was unnaturally soft, even strangely giddy. She kept touching her hair and her smile was slightly distorted from so much trying.

Andrew gave the folder to Robert, who immediately disappeared to his office. Andrew sat down and Jackie's mother offered him a drink. The conversation crawled painfully forward. Her mother held it in her firm well-manicured hands and guided it embarrassingly toward subjects like weddings and christenings, couples and divorces.

Andrew smiled his pudgy smile, and Jackie stared at the paintings on the walls. She wondered why she came to visit her mother, since they didn't seem to have anything in common. Her mother tried to change her into something more like herself, meanwhile ignoring the real Jackie and her interests. The visits were pure guilt trips, she had concluded. Something that you had to endure, so you could say you were a good person, because good people were supposed to like their families.

'You will have to join the swimming club this year, Jacqueline. Andrew is a marvellous swimmer. Aren't you, Andrew?' Poor Andrew didn't even have time to answer the question before Jackie's mother moved on. 'And you play tennis as well? See, Jacqueline? Andrew plays tennis, just like Charles. You know. Tracy's fiancé, the banker. Did I tell you that Andrew's family used to own a castle? I'm sure I did. Where was it again?' Before Andrew could open his mouth, Jackie's mother had the answer. 'Oh, yes. Scotland. It was in

Scotland. Wasn't it?' Andrew nodded his head nervously and moved his feet.

'Marvellous place, Scotland, isn't it? We went there last year, Robert and I. You know how he loves to golf. Do you golf, Andrew? You must. All the young men golf these days. Golf and tennis, Jackie. Golf and tennis. I think Tracy is taking golf lessons as well. I'm quite sure Charles plays golf now and then. You know, being a banker and all.' Her mother's almost breathless voice marched energetically on.

Jackie leaned back in her chair and daydreamed. She needed to buy some more stains for her peppermills. She should try the red stain on the curly maple. Red would nicely pick up the patterns in the wood. The blue colour was a bit too dark and it tended to cover the grain rather than bring out the details. Yellow could be good as well, especially if it were the darker mustard colour.

Her mother's voice cut into her thoughts. Automatically Jackie nodded. A trait learned from her childhood. 'A castle.' She mumbled quickly before realizing that they had changed the subject. 'Oh...I mean...no, I haven't done scuba diving.' Her mother's eyes were burning a hole into Jackie's guilty heart. She hadn't even noticed that she had drifted off and lost the conversation. She had only just arrived at her mother's house, yet, already in her mind, she was beginning to leave.

Andrew finally gathered enough courage to say that he needed to go, and still Jackie's mother kept him standing in the doorway for another half hour. She waved after his car and then turned around, beaming. 'Andrew is driving a new Audi.' She could hardly breathe. 'Audi, Jackie. Silver Audi. Do you have any idea how much they are worth these days?'

'Good for him.' Jackie said. What could she say?

'No need to be sarcastic, Jacqueline.' Her mother snapped. 'You could do much worse than marry Andrew you know. You don't seem to be at all interested in him. I'm afraid that all my work to make this union between you and Andrew happen is wasted.' Her mother was cross. She stared at Jackie through burning eyes over her uplifted chin.

'Mom,' Jackie said calmly. 'I am not interested in Andrew. So please don't use your valuable time trying to make something work when it obviously cannot.'

'But…but he has a castle!' Her mother couldn't believe her ears. 'And a new silver Audi,' she added, stuttering slightly and holding onto the banister. 'A castle, Jacqueline, a castle!' She put her hand onto her heart. 'Imagine a wedding in a castle, Jacqueline. How Tracy would envy you. They are only getting married in the country club, you know.'

Jackie turned and went back into the living room where Robert was now sitting, puffing his pipe and reading the papers. Her mother ran after her.

'But you must. I simply cannot have Penny marrying her daughter off just like that to a banker when my daughter is still a spinster, for god's sake. And you don't even play tennis.' She slumped down in the chair. 'Robert say something, for god's sake.' She waved her hand in the air to get Robert's attention.

Robert looked up from his papers. He didn't like to be disturbed. 'Say what?' he asked and looked over his glasses at Jackie's mother who was panting for air. 'What would you like me to say?'

'Tell Jacqueline that Andrew is a good catch.'

'Why?' Robert simply did not follow Jackie's mother's mind.

'Because Penny's daughter is getting married to a banker and Andrew's family has a castle.'

Robert looked from Jackie to her mother, not knowing what to say. 'I'll be going to bed,' Robert said and left the room.

Jackie's mother looked at Jackie critically the next morning over the breakfast table. She sighed as she poured the coffee. 'If you would just take better care of yourself. Play tennis, instead of making those things, whatever you make. You'll never meet anybody there at your studio in that god awful island of yours. Even with the bridge, it's quite isolated. You don't come to see us often enough, Jacqueline. I could take you shopping, and we could go and join the tennis club together. I'm sure that Tracy's fiancé Charles would bring some banker friend of his with him, you know? He must know some single bankers. His portfolio is apparently marvellous. That's what Penny says, but you know she tends to exaggerate things to make herself look better. You should hear her going on and on about Charles in the tennis club. Charles this and Charles that. Well I hope you'll be invited to the wedding. You could meet some of the single bankers there.'

There was only so much listening Jackie could do. Robert was smart, she thought, watching him read his morning newspaper in peace. You couldn't even see his face from behind the paper. Jackie poured more coffee for herself.

'You know that too much coffee is bad for you, Jacqueline dear.' Her mother said. 'It has caffeine in it and it's bad for your skin. Penny read this article about skin management. And you are already twenty-nine years old.'

'Thirty-two.'

'What?'

'I'm thirty-two years old, Mom.'

'Oh, you sure? Well then…you better not drink too much coffee. It has all kinds of toxins in it. It is very bad for your skin.'

It was Saturday and she would go home on Sunday morning, early. Jackie poured milk into her coffee and tried to smile when she answered, 'Is that so? Interesting.'

Jackie managed to escape for a few hours to see Jill, who opened her front door with crying Nellie in her arms.

'Come in Jackie. Welcome to chaos,' Jill said and brushed her hair from her face where Nellie had pulled it out of her ponytail.

'Hi! You look great!' Jackie said and stepped over a pile of plastic toys lying in the middle of the narrow hallway.

'Liar!' Jill laughed and tried to stop Nellie pulling her shirt down with her strong toddler's arms. She began making coffee using only one hand till Jackie took over and told her to sit down.

'I'm trying to feed her, but she puts up a good fight every time and the food flies everywhere,' Jill said and put Nellie into her feeding chair. 'Here comes the train,' she said with forced energy, disguising her fatigue. Nellie pursed her lips together, determined not to let the mashed food touch the inside of her mouth. The spoonful of food landed on the bib and on Nellie's cheek as she pulled her face away at the last second. Jill grabbed a napkin to wipe off the stain but Nellie was too fast and grabbed the whole bowl of food and tipped it onto the table of her feeding chair. Jill stared at the mess silently, quickly wiping the table top before Nellie's little fists thumped into the spilled food. 'Mommy is so ready for you to go and have a nap, so ready.' She said and gave Nellie a spill-proof plastic cup.

Robbie walked in red faced from his run. He didn't even have a chance to say hello to Jackie when Jill lifted Nellie from her chair and handed her over to Robbie. 'Here you go, Robbie. She's all yours.'

Robbie eyed the mess in the kitchen and nodded, accepting his rescuer's role and walked into the bathroom with Nellie in his arms.

Jill poured a large cup of coffee for herself and then slumped onto a chair. 'My brain works only at half speed, so speak slowly,' she said to Jackie and wiped her hair from her face. 'How's your mom?' she asked.

'Normal…like always, which in fact is abnormal to most people.' Jackie answered and smiled hopelessly.

Jill laughed and threw her legs over the arm of the chair.

'She told me that I should not drink so much coffee, since it is not good for my complexion,' Jackie said. 'And she remembered my age incorrectly.'

'So all is normal?' Jill said and looked at her best friend sitting in her messy kitchen surrounded by mountains of dirty dishes on the tables and scattered toys on the floor.

'Yep, normal.' Jackie answered and started filling the dishwasher.

'You don't need to do that,' Jill protested feebly. 'But if you want to, go ahead. I have no energy for anything. That child never sleeps, or so it seems.' Jill drank her coffee and asked Jackie if her complexion was getting any worse. They were laughing when Robbie came into the room with clean Nellie holding onto his hand.

Jackie took her godchild into her arms and peered into those baby blue eyes of hers. Nellie's arms waved in the air for a while before they found Jackie's ears. Nellie held onto them firmly and squealed with delight. Jackie gave a big kiss on her soft red cheek.

Jackie spent a lovely morning with Jill, walking in the park pushing Nellie in her stroller. Max, Robbie's dog, which he had acquired while visiting Jackie the very first time in her new home on the island, was running around them trying to stretch the leash to its utmost limit. Robbie had promised to clean the kitchen while they were out. They walked in the park, had more coffee after Nellie fell asleep, compared their fading complexions, and laughed.

Reluctantly, Jackie left her friends and returned to her mother's house. The party that was supposed to be a small relaxed affair had turned out to be a large stress-inducing nightmare. The caterers were late and Jackie's hair was flat. There was a stain on the tablecloth, and Robert didn't seem to understand how much effort Jackie's mother had put into planning this party. He hid in the living room. Jackie was trying to comb her hair to please her mother, till her mother marched in and generously covered Jackie's hair, nose and mouth with hairspray. At this point, Jackie followed Bob's example and joined him in the living room where they each had a large glass of whiskey and sat together in the semi-darkness, listening to the dozens of feet frantically running around the house.

Despite the chaotic beginning, the party went well. The food was good, and it was served with fine French wines. Jackie met the Flemings and their son Jamie. She also met Tracy and Charles and Tracy's mother Penny. She danced one dance with Andrew and his clammy hands. She could see her mother's eyes light up as she began planning the future wedding. It had been a proper party, just like Jackie's mother had desired. Proper, no embarrassing incidents, nothing too extravagant, and nothing too frugal. It had been the perfect party.

Sunday morning Jackie woke up, had her breakfast, and blamed her business for her early departure. Her mother was reminiscing about last night's party and would have liked Jackie to stay a bit longer to review the excellence of the food, once again. Jackie declined kindly and stuffed the last of her clothes back into her bag. She kissed Bob and her mother goodbye and then walked the two blocks to her car. She was on her way back to her own life. She enjoyed her quiet drive while thinking how different lives can be in one family alone. She wondered what their lives would have been like if her father were alive.

Her contentment returned when she saw the ragged edge of the blue sea appear on the horizon. She shook off her sadness and savoured the vast wilderness stretching out in front of her—the bright blue skies and the fleeting white caps, the shrieking seagulls, and the forceful, ever present wind. She sang happily with the radio, tapping the steering wheel with her fingers.

The salty air smelled cold and free.

Chapter 8

Sponsors

The next day Jackie attacked her work relentlessly. Her long car drive home had given her renewed energy to make this dream of hers come true. No more hesitations, no more ifs and if nots. There was a lot of work ahead and she was happy to immerse herself in it.

She worked on her new designs all morning. She had her radio on and hummed along with songs. She mixed new stains, trying them on the different woods. The red stain worked exactly as she had imagined on the curly maple. The swirls became more distinct and, unlike the blue, which had darkened and flattened the natural patterns, the red allowed the wood grain to come forward.

She received small orders from two new galleries, making her grin from ear to ear. Energized, she began designing her webpage, playing with a look that mixed the cool industrial with the contemporary handmade.

After lunch, she and Felix took their usual walk together. She had planned visiting the possible studio sponsors, or victims, as Harriet liked to call them, in the late afternoon.

'I really do not like collecting money,' Jackie complained to herself as she rang the doorbell of the East End Bed and Breakfast, shifting her weight nervously from foot to foot.

Tim opened the door with a wide smile on his face. 'What a marvellous surprise! Come in, Jackie. Come in.' He ushered her busily in and then loudly called for John.

'Great!' John's voice came from the kitchen.

'You must come in and see the table in our breakfast room. It is simply divine.' Tim shepherded Jackie into the breakfast room.

The table Jackie had made for Tim and John was very large with French Provençal characteristics. It was slightly rustic with a modern edge and it had delicate carving on its sturdy legs. The table had been a welcome break from the daily routine of the making of small objects. It was one of her best pieces, and she was very proud of it. It was strange to see the finished product, created in her small, cramped workshop, standing in its spacious new home. The breakfast room had bright yellow walls and was filled with wonderful antiques and art. The room could have come straight from *Home and Garden* magazine. Jackie briefly thought about her own house and the pile of laundry sitting in the middle of her living room waiting to be sorted and ironed. Her latest home improvements included purchasing a new laundry basket made with durable vintage plastic.

'Isn't it gorgeous?' John walked into the breakfast room wiping his hands on a kitchen towel, followed by Berlin, their dog with the much discussed name. John was tall, with reddish hair set off perfectly by today's choice of orange out of his collection of much-loved brightly coloured shirts. His taste for colour counterbalanced Tim's love of neutrals.

'It looks great in this room, I must say.' Jackie agreed with all her heart, looking back at her table. She bent down to scratch behind Berlin's ears.

'You know, we are thinking about chairs.' Tim said looking meaningfully over the rim of his glasses.

'I have been playing with some ideas,' Jackie said, trying not to sound too pushy. She had been thinking about the chairs ever since she started working with the table design. She loved the idea of a total concept.

'Great! We'll come by one day to see the drawings.' Tim was glowing with excitement.

'Okay, now, come into the kitchen and I'll pour us some wine. You must taste this pie I made. I'm testing things. You see, Tim's parents are coming for a visit.' John winked and made a gesture with his hands as if slashing his throat. Tim shook his head theatrically, expressing his anxiety. He was slightly amused and, yes, worried. 'They are not so bad…' He said, trying to convince himself more than anybody else.

'See, the poor man is still in denial…we must love him even more for his good heart.' John pointed affectionately and touched his own heart briefly with his right hand before petting Tim's head mockingly.

Jackie and Tim sat down on the high chairs by the kitchen island and John poured the wine.

'Thank you, dear,' Tim said. 'To my darling family, hating the man of my life.'

John lifted his glass as well. 'Cheers!' He winked. 'To the wicked witch.'

'Cheers! To the wicked witch.' They all said loudly.

It was well known that Tim's parents were not too keen about John. Not that they minded their only son being gay, but they did mind that John was not wealthy. 'Now Elton John!' Tim's mother would exclaim. 'Now there's a catch.' She would cast a scornful look at John. 'Have you seen the size of his castle? His castle! Not a B & B, but a castle!' She would drone on and on during her visits.

John would often escape his humble B & B during these mandatory family visits. He would knock on Jackie's door—'In my desperate search for positive words and unconditional friendship'— were his exact words. 'And anyway Elton John is now married.' He would add with a frown. After an hour or so, he would return to the wicked witch and the witch's husband and to poor Tim, who would be as exasperated as John, but who wouldn't be able to escape the never ending litany of suggestions, kindly meant but savagely said.

'That was a long trip to buy milk,' the wicked witch would say. She suspected that something was not quite right and she would stare at John suspiciously with cold beady eyes. 'Well, I guess the distances are rather long here in the middle of nowhere.'

'How long this time?' Jackie asked sympathetically.

'Only the weekend. Thank god, if there is one.' John answered and drank some more wine.

'Umm…this is good.' Jackie looked at the wine bottle on the table.

'Isn't it? I just found it. It's Sicilian.' John said, happy that people agreed with his choice of wine. He turned the bottle around and read the label again.

Jackie thought this was as good a moment as any. She cleared her throat. 'I actually have something I need to ask you two,' she said quickly.

'Go ahead,' John answered and Tim nodded his head encouragingly.

They were ready to listen. Jackie inhaled deeply and then blurted. 'We are organizing an artists' studio tour for the end of October here on the island and we are printing a full colour brochure and—surprise, surprise—we are looking for sponsors. Would you two be interested?' She spread her hands in the air and then clasped them tightly together again.

Tim and John exchanged a look. Jackie waited and without knowing the outcome, held her breath. Then Tim spoke. 'Sure. October is not that busy a month for us, and we could use more paying customers…Right, John?'

'Yes. We'll be glad to be your sponsors. Anyhow it's the community spirit that keeps us all together.' John smiled.

'Well, that was easy.' Jackie sighed with a relief.

'Now about these chairs…' Tim began while John took the test pie out from the oven. Jackie was told to stay right where she was.

While Jackie was happily eating pie with John and Tim in their gorgeous kitchen, Rosalind was walking determinedly toward a large, beautifully restored red brick Victorian. She had spent more than her usual lengthy time on her hair and was pleased with its extra flair. She ran her hand carefully over it.

She had spared no hairspray while sculpting her hair into its helmet-like appearance. She walked through the wind with her head held high and her hair undisturbed. Rosalind loved meeting with Maximilian Woodland. He flirted shamelessly and his French accent brought red spots to Rosalind's cheeks. She had on her best casual clothes and had added an extra sprinkle of perfume between her breasts.

Anticipation made her pick up speed the last few metres to the grand entrance of the restaurant and hotel. The lobby was immaculate and everything breathed elegance. It was painted cream and sage with subtle golden accents and was lovely, although somewhat lacking in warmth. This was what attracted Rosalind to Maximilian's: distant, formal and exceedingly elegant.

Rosalind's shoes clicked on the stone floor and the echo carried the sound to the second floor. She walked to the reception desk and enquired after Maximilian Woodhouse. After being asked who's calling, she proudly answered, 'You can tell Maximilian that it is Rosalind McKay.'

'Of course,' the man behind the desk answered. 'I will call him immediately. Please do sit down. He'll be with you momentarily.'

Rosalind walked to a chair by the entrance and sat down. She felt so much at ease here that she even allowed herself the indulgence of marvelling at the decorative desserts on display in a tall aluminum tower with shiny curved glass doors.

The receptionist called the office speaking with his back turned to make sure that Rosalind couldn't hear him. 'Max, you are needed in the lobby. Please come soon. It's that McKay woman again.' He glanced nervously at Rosalind over his shoulder.

'Bloody hell.' The sound filled the receiver forcing the receptionist to hold it an inch away from his ear, covering it with his hand. 'When the fuck will you guys learn to smile and lie at the same time? How many times do I have to tell you to say that I'm not fucking in?'

'She is waiting,' the receptionist said with a strained voice and looked over his shoulder again. 'And she is looking at me. Please hurry.'

'Oh, for fuck's sake. Okay, I'll be there. Tell that savage bitch that her darling Max is coming right over.'

The receptionist turned to look at Rosalind once more. Rosalind raised her eyebrows questioningly and the receptionist nodded his head to let her know that Maximilian was on his way.

Maximilian cursed heavily in his private office as he slammed the phone down. He was a big man with a heavy gait. He stomped through the spotless kitchen tucking his shirt into his pants and opened the door to the reception area. Rosalind was patting her hair and staring at the desk. As soon as she saw Maximilian, she got up and a big smile spread across her hard face.

Maximilian walked to her extending his hand already and said, 'Bonjour, ma chère, Rosalind.'

'Bonjour, Maximilian.' smiled Rosalind. Rosalind loved speaking French, and she especially loved speaking French with Maximilian.

'What a surprise! How nice it is to see you again so soon,' Maximilian said with his deep accented voice and kissed Rosalind on her cheeks.

'Ooh Maximilian! You flatter me…and I like it.' Rosalind was as close to giggling as she could ever be.

'Why don't we sit down and have a cup of coffee.'

'Only if you have time. I hate to intrude.' Rosalind smiled and was more than willing to sit down and have a cup of coffee.

'For you…I have always time, mon chéri.' Max guided Rosalind into the restaurant. As they passed the reception desk he said to the receptionist, 'Frank, will you bring us two coffees. We'll be in the front room.'

'Yes, sir.'

Everything was very formal, just the way Rosalind would love the whole world to be. She was comfortably resting on the sturdy arm of Maximilian as he guided her through the doors into the front room.

'Now my dear, Rosalind. Did you enjoy your dinner here last week?' Maximilian asked, his voice resonating and smooth, easily conveying interest.

'I simply adore your culinary artistry, Maximilian, and Alistair appreciates your skill and execution. You know how hard it is to live here on this island. You, Maximilian, are our sole escape—our little piece of France right here on our doorstep.' Rosalind had become quite animated as she spoke. Needless to say, she never visited Honey's Parisian tearoom.

'I'm glad to hear that, Rosalind.' Max said politely. They sat down and Frank brought them coffee and then quickly disappeared again.

Maximilian crossed his legs and looked at his gold watch. He said with practised sincerity, 'I'm sorry to rush you, dear Rosalind, but unfortunately I have a staff meeting in five minutes.'

'Oh, I better be fast then, mustn't I?' She stirred her coffee. 'You might have heard about this studio tour Jacqueline Callaghan is organizing.' She stopped for a moment. 'We are looking for sponsors, and I do not know why I always need to volunteer to do most of the work.' She sighed deeply and looked into Maximilian's eyes. 'But you know how I am, Maximilian, don't you?'

'Yes, indeed I do, Rosalind.' Maximilian was drinking his coffee and keeping his eye on his watch. 'I know you so well.'

'So,' Rosalind continued full of vigour. 'Would you like to be a sponsor of our tour? It'll be in October. We are printing a full colour brochure and Caroline—you do know Caroline, don't you?' she asked suddenly, worried that Max might not know Caroline.

'Yes, I have met her once or twice, perhaps,' mumbled Maximilian.

'Well, she'll be doing the design for the brochure, so you can be absolutely sure that it will be magnificent.' She was about to continue, when Maximilian interrupted her. 'I would be honoured to be your sponsor, Rosalind.' He put his coffee cup down. 'I will make sure that Caroline gets our advertising pamphlet, so that she can see precisely what I would like to say about my restaurant and hotel.' He got up. 'Now I really must leave you dear Rosalind, as much I would like to stay here and chat with you, but...' He paused, pursed his lips, and said with a deep voice, 'Unfortunately, duty awaits.'

With these words he got up and offered his arm to Rosalind. 'I'll see Caroline about the details later. I have found that the message travels better when it is delivered to the right address to begin with.'

Rosalind straightened her jacket and let Maximilian walk her to the door. 'Thank you for the coffee, Maximilian.'

'Always a pleasure. I'll see you soon, ma chère.' Maximilian answered and closed the door.

Rosalind walked to her car feeling powerful. 'It is easy when you know what you are doing,' she said to herself. She felt good. She felt young again. She felt like a girl who had just returned home from a holiday to France where she had met Jean-Luc. Rosalind sighed and her voice trembled. 'Jean-Luc…'

Maximilian walked briskly back into his office and slammed the door closed.

Caroline was sitting on his desk, smoking a cigarette. 'Now, where were we?' she said and put her hand inside Maximilian's waistband. 'Talk French to me, you fat crème brûlée bastard.'

'Oh, you dirty bitch,' Maximilian moaned. 'Je t'aime! Je t'aime!'

The kitchen staff heard the key turn in the lock and they turned the sound of the radio up. Frank knew not to disturb his boss anymore today.

*   *   *

Jackie, feeling encouraged by her success with the East End Bed and Breakfast was about to make her way out to the West End B & B when the phone rang in the kitchen where she had forgotten it earlier while making lunch. 'Jacqueline Callaghan Furniture Design,' she answered, trying not to sound out of breath after rushing downstairs two steps at a time. It could be a gallery calling.

'Jackie. It is your mother.' She heard her mother's excited voice. Jackie sighed before she caught herself but luckily her mother was too thrilled to notice the disappointment in Jackie's voice.

'Guess, just guess, Jacqueline.' Her voice shrill and uneven.

'Guess what?' Jackie said and walked out into the garden to sit on a bench while her mother went on about something that should interest her

'I just spoke with Penny and they have set the wedding date and you'll be invited. Isn't that exciting? You'll have to come here for a visit over the weekend, and then you and I will go and buy new dresses and hats for the wedding. It is going to be absolutely divine! Like I said, you can meet some single men there.' Her mother had to stop to breath, and Jackie was able to add her few mumbled yeses into the otherwise one-sided conversation.

'Write this date down on your calendar, Jacqueline. The twenty-eighth of October. It is a Saturday.'

'Twenty-eighth of October,' Jackie repeated in her mind. 'That's the last weekend of October. Am I right?' She asked hesitantly from her mother.

'Yes, yes. The weather is still good, so that you can buy a nice pair of high heels.'

'But, Mom.' Jackie was holding her breath. 'I can't come. You see, the island is going to have its first studio tour that weekend.'

'So what?'

'I am part of that tour, Mom. I cannot come to Tracy's wedding. I'm sorry, but I can't.' Jackie bit her lip and waited for her mother's answer that came barking down the telephone lines, each word painted with anger and frustration.

'What do you mean you cannot come to the wedding? You must come to the wedding. I play bridge with Penny every Thursday.'

Jackie thought for awhile about the connection of bridge and weddings but decided not to ask her. She anticipated such a question would not be welcome.

'Who cares about your studio tour? There will be other tours and it's a small island, anyhow. Who would go there anyway? Nobody! Absolutely nobody! You are much better off to come to the wedding.'

'Mother, I can't. I promised to be part of this studio tour and I cannot cancel it. The whole island is involved with it. I cannot change my mind. Sorry, but I can't.'

'Oh, nonsense! What are you talking about? Of course you will come to the wedding. Why would you not come to the wedding?'

'Because of the studio tour. Because of my work. Because of my career,' Jackie said and sighed. Surprisingly, she was getting angry and her voice was edgy. She was having difficulty pronouncing her words correctly.

'Your career?' Her mother repeated. 'Oh, you mean your little peppermills and such. You call that a career?'

'Yes. That's exactly what I mean. "My little peppermills and such."'

'Well, I'll say.' Her mother breathed out her words as if exhaling.

'Mom. I need to go now.' Jackie's voice was extremely tense.

'Just remember to write that date onto your calendar. October twenty-eighth. We'll talk about the details later.'

Jackie pushed the off button on her phone so strongly that she almost hurt her finger. 'God damn it!' she cursed and then called Jill who was just changing Nellie's diaper.

'My mom is absolutely driving me crazy!' Jackie yelled into the phone before even telling Jill who was calling. 'She wants me to go to Tracy's wedding and not to do the studio tour.'

'But you must do the studio tour. It was your idea and all,' Jill said, lifting Nellie's legs with one hand and tilting her head so that the phone would not fall from between her chin and shoulder. 'Stay still!' she muttered to Nellie, who was kicking vigorously.

'Well that's what I said, but you know her. Did she listen? No! Of course not!'

Jill mumbled something while Jackie went on, venting her anger.

'Well?' Jackie finally said. 'What do you think? Your mother would never do that to you?'

'No, probably not, but she has been asking questions about my sex life.'

Jackie paused to ask herself if she had heard correctly what Jill had just said. 'Your sex life? But that's your sex life. Not hers.'

'That's what I think. But apparently she had read somewhere about how it is hard to continue to have a good sex life after having kids and so on. You know, being so tired all the time and carrying that extra weight from the pregnancy, wearing milk sodden shirts, and all. So she just wanted know how it is with Robbie and me. It was really a strange question, in the first place, but to hear it at lunch, when the twenty-something gorgeous waiter is standing right there with the big pepper grinder in his hands. I really didn't know what to say.'

Jackie began to laugh and Jill joined her while generously powdering Nellie's bottom. Nellie stuffed both of her fists into her mouth and gurgled at her mother's laughter.

After chatting with Jill, Jackie felt better and continued on with her original plan to visit Kevin and Tom at the West End B & B.

'My! It's Jackie. What a lovely surprise.' Kevin's face lit up and small dimples appeared at the corners of his mouth as he opened the door and saw Jackie standing on the large front porch.

'Hi Kevin,' Jackie said. 'You got a moment?'

'Come in, come in,' Kevin said and ushered Jackie in. 'Tom! Jackie is here.' Kevin's voice echoed in the large house.

Tom walked downstairs. He was a big man, built like a barn door, with a deep thundering voice. 'I'm glad to see you…any chance you came to ask us to sponsor the studio tour?'

Jackie stared at the two of them and uttered, 'Jesus, as a matter of fact I did. How did you know?'

Tom was laughing loudly. 'We went to visit Tim and John yesterday to see their gorgeous new table. Well, so little happens here, that of course we needed to exchange information about the people and things in the village.'

'Oh, so I don't need to tell you anything?'

'Not really, but please do come in and visit.' Tom smiled.

'Yes, yes, come into the kitchen. We just bought this new espresso maker and we are dying to try it out,' Kevin said, walking into the kitchen as he spoke.

A huge stainless steel espresso maker sat on the marble kitchen counter. The remains of a cardboard box were on the floor. Jackie had to step over the box to touch the shiny machine. 'Wow!' She marvelled. 'It is the size of a dog!' she said, genuinely impressed.

'Industrial strength espresso maker!' Tom proudly told her. 'Industrial strength,' he repeated.

'Here are the instructions, Jackie.' Kevin handed them over to Jackie. 'You read them to us and we'll make the coffee.'

Jackie grabbed the papers. 'Oh, all right.'

'And by the way—yes we would like to sponsor your tour.' Tom nodded and winked at Jackie.

'You boys really make my life so much easier, you know.' Jackie was smiling broadly.

'Don't say anything—you haven't gone through that instruction gibberish yet.' Kevin pointed to the thick booklet in Jackie's hands.

Jackie leafed through the instruction manual as she took off her jacket. 'Thank you for purchasing Espresso-the coffee maker for coffee lovers...It not only makes coffee, but it also changes the way you think about coffee...' She skipped half the booklet. 'Okay, how to make espresso...page 56.' She turned the pages. 'Here we go...'

*   *   *

Unlike Jackie, Thomas had put aside the task of getting sponsors for the tour as long as it was possible to do so. He was a master at the art of avoidance. In his hands it had become more a way of life than an occasional refusal to adhere to timelines. Finally, though, after receiving daily threatening messages on his answering machine from Jackie, he had decided that it was far better for his overall health to do as he was told.

He walked to the centre of the village, which would have been quite quick if not for the ladies who were gardening and wished to have a nice little chat with him. He obliged, of course, having never learned to say no to admiring women, regardless of their age.

Finally, after many weather laden conversations, he arrived at the village centre, which comprised the main street and the few cross streets. He popped into Honey's Parisian tearoom, whistling cheerfully as he opened the door.

'Oh, Thomas! Is that you?' A gleeful voice greeted him behind the mounds of cupcakes and cookies. The cinnamon and coffee smell encircled him as he walked across the floor.

'Yes, it's me, Miss Honey,' he said and bowed his head. 'And how are you today?'

'Oh you bad boy, I have not seen you for ages.' Miss Honey giggled and pinched Thomas's cheek.

'Sorry,' Thomas said and laughed, running his hand over the part of his face that Miss Honey had roughly treated.

'Now, which young lady are you dating at this moment?' Miss Honey asked curiously. 'Is it Jackie?' She stared at him expectantly with her gentle eyes.

'No, no, Miss Honey. We are just friends.' Thomas exclaimed and put his hands in his pockets. He wondered how many times people were going to ask him that same question.

'Pity—you two would make a lovely couple.' Miss Honey sighed and shook her head. 'You sure you are not dating her? You have been visiting her a lot lately.' She looked at Thomas skeptically. Thomas laughed and said once more that there was no truth in the gossip of him and Jackie dating.

'Pity. Now what can I do for you?' Miss Honey was wearing an Eiffel tower apron over her flowery dress and on her feet she had a pair of Nike elite running shoes. Just below the hem of her skirt you could see the faint line of the skin coloured knee-highs.

'You probably know about the studio tour we are organizing?' Thomas began. He knew that word about the studio tour had reached just about everybody's ears by the time the members of the artists' group returned home from their first meeting. Miss Honey nodded enthusiastically and Thomas continued. 'I'm here to ask you to sponsor us, so that we can advertise your lovely café in our brochure.'

'Of course, I'll sponsor you. Now have a cupcake. The brownies will be done in a minute or two. You just sit there and I'll get my money.' Miss Honey chatted happily and walked surprisingly quickly around her little café.

While Thomas was eating the cupcake, Miss Honey took the pan of steaming hot brownies out of the oven. 'Now how much is it?' she asked Thomas, and wiped her hands on her apron. The Eiffel tower in the middle of it began to suffer from handprint smog.

'Twenty-five for a small and thirty-five for a big ad,' Thomas managed to say between mouthfuls.

'All right. I'll go for the small one then,' Miss Honey said seriously. She took her purse from under the counter and counted the money carefully before handing it to Thomas. Thomas took a receipt book from his jacket pocket and asked Miss Honey if she had a business card that they could put in the brochure as well.

'Yes I do,' she said. 'Oh, the brownies!' She suddenly remembered. Her hands flew up in the air. 'You just wait here and I'll put a few into a bag for you.' She tapped Thomas gently on his back and scurried away again.

About half an hour later, after talking about his love life, his mother and his work, Thomas managed to leave Miss Honey's café. He had been saved by a ladies church group that visited Miss Honey's tearoom every Thursday. Thomas had smiled, shook hands and, with one wave of his long arm, he bid goodbye to the ladies. Just before the door closed behind him he heard his and Jackie's names mentioned. Gossiping was the village lifeline.

He shrugged his shoulders and walked into the book shop next door. The weather was rather cloudy and cool, so it was open. Thomas spent a pleasant half hour with Dan Finch. He didn't get any pastries, but he did walk away with a heavily discounted paperback after sharing his brownies with Dan.

Thomas paid a visit to all of the little food stores in town that afternoon and ate very well during those few hours. The more shops he visited, the more plastic bags he carried filled with things to eat later.

He stopped in front of Creations, Hillary's beauty salon and stared at the swirly golden letters painted on the window. Hilary was stealing a peek at him through the white lacy curtain. Her customer, curlers in her hair and a large plastic cape around her strong shoulders, quickly swivelled the pink chair around to see what was interesting Hilary. The look was not flattering for a woman of any age and the resemblance to a space alien was quite frightening. She blushed when she caught Thomas's handsome face peering in.

Her hand shot up but there was no hair to pat, only curlers and a strong scent of chemicals.

Hilary quickly checked her reflection in the mirror. With an expert touch, she straightened her bleached blond hair and added a new layer of lipstick on her already heavily lined lips before running to the door. Her high heels and tight skirt lent a certain awkwardness to her running style. Her movement was more upward than forward. She flung the door open with a huge smile on her red lips and slowly, tilting her head to one side, put her hands on her small waist.

'Hi, Thomas!' She sighed breathlessly and continued to smile widely, even when she spoke.

'Good morning, Hilary. You're looking absolutely stunning today,' Thomas replied shamelessly.

'Really?' Hilary was now beaming with pride. Her bracelets clicked together as she lifted her hand to touch her hair.

'Yes, really.'

Hilary giggled and turned to go back into her shop. Her hips were moving an extra inch as she walked slowly in, crossing her bright pink high-heeled pumps one with the other, zigzagging across the floor. Thomas happily witnessed this extra show, which was meant for his eyes, and followed her in. He was very pleased to get such a warm welcome. Being the advertising man wasn't half as bad as he had envisioned it to be.

The ladies in the shop all turned to look at Thomas and a sea of high voices filled the air, asking how he was and what has he been doing lately and if there was a girl in his life. There was a lot of commotion behind the lace curtain for a quiet Thursday afternoon. Jackie walked by the beauty salon and glanced absentmindedly through the window. She saw all the women swarming around Thomas and she couldn't help but laugh. 'Thomas, the happiest and luckiest of men,' she thought and called Felix to heel.

After an hour of uninterrupted attention paid to Thomas and an almost ruined perm for poor Mrs. Frost, Thomas came out of the beauty salon smiling happily. He had a lipstick mark on his cheek and his hair had been tousled so many times that by now it was mostly sticking up.

He walked down the street to Candles, Scents and More. Kathleen was delighted to see him. She had seen him stepping into Hilary's shop earlier and, after a quick telephone call to Mary Cullighan, she had found out about the studio tour sponsorship collection Thomas was conducting in the village. She had been waiting for him ever since, her cheque book ready by her cash register. She shook her head disapprovingly as she wiped off the red lipstick mark from his cheek. After another half an hour of inquiries into his personal life Thomas stepped out of the store and stopped briefly at the top of the steps to smell himself. Half a day spent going around the village visiting bakeries, beauty salons and potpourri stores had left their residue on his jacket and the concoction was quite strange. He smelled himself again and, with a nonchalant nod, accepted that the scent wasn't that bad after all and walked into Peter's Fish and Chips.

Peter sniffed the air suspiciously as Thomas walked in. 'Well, if it isn't Thomas Stockwell,' he bellowed. 'You owe me a fiver.'

'Ha haa,' laughed Thomas. 'Good one, Peter. But in fact you owe me ten.'

'Damn, is that so?' Peter scratched his balding head and stared at Thomas. For all he knew Thomas could be right; after all, the money had changed a great deal of hands that night accompanied by plenty of beer.

'Yep, never play darts with me. I warned you, didn't I? But tell you what, give me a big fish and chips and pay the rest later.'

'All right my man.' Peter chuckled. 'You are one mean man with the darts.'

'Yes, I am and now I'm starving.'

'You collecting money for the brochure?'

'Yes, how did you know?'

'Nick came by an hour ago. Had seen you going around the stores earlier.'

'Yeah—I am the head of the advertising committee.'

'Your head is full of shite, Thomas Stockwell.'

'That too—want to play darts tonight?'

'Can't afford to play with you anymore.'

'You can buy me a pint or two first.'

'All right.'

After half an hour Thomas stepped out from Peter's shop and sighed deeply. He rubbed his full stomach as he looked up and down the street.

Thomas walked very slowly to the next store, The Cozy Corner. A little while later Suzy walked him out. She too had called Mary Cullighan earlier and had waited for Thomas for well over an hour. She had applied lipstick three times already. Suzy was all smiles as she stopped outside her shop's door and leaned over the railing to wave goodbye. All she needed was a handkerchief in her hand, and she would have looked like a woman saying goodbye to her loved one on a platform of a train station.

Thomas also visited Mary's Flowers, the only place in the village that treated him with suspicion; but Mary suspected all the men, even when they bought flowers for their wives.

Thomas was looking at his list, satisfied with his achievements. His list was done. Then he stopped suddenly. He lifted his eyes to study the sign that hung from a bright brass chain over the main entrance of a tall majestic building. Thomas ran his hand slowly over his three day-old beard as his smile grew into a wide mischievous grin. He checked to see that no one was looking, not even Mary, and walked nonchalantly into the funeral home.

*   *   *

As Jackie stepped into the pub, she saw Thomas sitting at the bar talking animatedly to Nick. He was waving his arms in the air and Nick was clutching his stomach. They were both laughing uncontrollably.

Jackie sat down beside Thomas. 'So here you are!' She exclaimed, staring at him. 'I called your studio and there was no answer, so I thought to check if you were here and…here you are.'

Nick lifted an empty glass and Jackie nodded approvingly. 'Yes, please.' She turned back to Thomas. 'So did you get any sponsors?'

Thomas grinned wickedly and reached unhurriedly into his jacket pocket to take out the sponsor list. He opened the folded paper slowly and put it ceremoniously down in front of Jackie. With extremely exaggerated slow moves he carefully smoothed out the creases with his hands. Then he leaned back and took a long sip of his pint and waited for Jackie's reaction. Jackie eyed Thomas suspiciously. She picked up the list from the table and began going through it. She pouted but nodded approvingly at every name she read.

'Good...good...yes,' she mumbled. 'Uh...yes...Well done, Thomas.' She continued reading the last lines of the list when all of a sudden she stopped. She stared at the paper, frozen in shock, and then slowly lifted her eyes to look at Thomas. Thomas winked cheekily and waited. Jackie's mouth was slightly open as she turned her head back to look at the list she was holding. She swallowed and slowly read out loud the last name on the sponsor list. 'From Here To Eternity Funeral Parlour—what an earth?' Jackie's face was unreadable. She stared at Thomas, unable to speak. Her mouth was dry as she waited for some kind of clarification from him. Anything would do.

Thomas cleared his throat. 'Well, yes, they were quite happy to be one of the sponsors for our tour...and look...look.' He could hardly keep his face straight as he eagerly pointed to the list in front of Jackie. 'Look, they even wrote down the slogan they want to use in their ad.' He pointed to the slogan, jabbing his finger against the paper. 'Here, read that,' he said cheerfully, his voice quivering with laughter.

Jackie read the ad out loud. 'Everything for your last journey?' She put the paper down and stared in front of her for a while, expressionless. Then she looked at Thomas and Nick, who were both grinning, their wide smiles stretching from ear to ear.

'Brilliant, isn't it?' Thomas was on the edge of bursting out laughing. 'I say that is an advertising classic if I ever saw one.' He was grinning madly and Nick and he were both staring at Jackie. Jackie's face was completely blank as she looked at the two sniggering men in front of her. Thomas and Nick were holding their breath as they met Jackie's icy stare. All of a sudden Jackie began to laugh. The laughter burst out of her at an amazing volume and she slammed the list on to the bar and almost fell off her chair. Thomas and Nick stared at her and then they too burst out laughing, again. Thomas was cackling and holding his stomach.

'I wonder if that is classy enough for Rosalind?' Jackie muttered between hysterical giggles.

Nick and Thomas were laughing even louder than before at the thought of Rosalind. Nick was leaning against the bar wiping tears from his eyes and for a while looked almost grief stricken. Thomas was banging the bar with his fist, resting his slightly red face against the counter.

Jackie started hiccupping, but she could not stop laughing. As soon as her laughter would calm down, a vision of Rosalind reading the list came to her and the thought made her double-up with laughter once again.

The boys in the corner stared at the three of them and shook their heads. 'And they call us loud.' Jack Wilkinson muttered into his beer.

Chapter 9

Something Brewing

All the members of the studio tour were in the pub, gathered around the tables that Jackie had pushed together. The boys were at their favourite corner table, with their ears wide open, alert for juicy morsels of could-be-gossip material. The results of that night could fuel lively discussions around that table for a great many evenings to come.

Rosalind was sitting by Jackie as usual. She was emitting the newly acquired importance of a treasurer while reading the list of the confirmed sponsors, which Jackie had handed to her a few minutes earlier. Rosalind was surprised. She raised one of her thin eyebrows as she read the names. Thomas had indeed done a very good job at collecting sponsors. She could not complain, unfortunately. She really didn't like being in the position where she was unable to offer contradictory advice. 'Very well done,' she thought reluctantly as she kept reading. Suddenly Rosalind froze. Her eyes grew large and her thin mouth flew open. She gulped and closed her mouth, which began to look like a razor blade. A vein bulged on one side of her head.

Jackie was observing her secretly. Rosalind remained still awhile, then slowly lifted her majestic head and fixed her menacing eyes on Jackie. 'This is surely a very bad joke, Jacqueline.' Her voice was cold like a cracking tree branch on a bitter winter morning.

'What is a joke, Rosalind?' Jackie inquired innocently, but she was keeping her eyes steadily on the paper in front of her. She could not meet Thomas's eyes either, which were pinned on her. Neither could she look at Nick, who was leaning against the bar, watching intently. These days he loved owning a pub. There was never a dull moment. Monday nights had proven to be his most profitable night as the locals who had heard about the artists' group meetings filled the pub, eavesdropping on every word.

Nick, Thomas and Jackie had earlier been toying with the idea of making a bet on what Rosalind's reaction would be. Jackie had pointed out that Rosalind would unleash her icy anger on her no matter what—full frontal assault, heavy casualties, broken bones and blood loss. After that they had dropped the idea. Thomas had mentioned the excellent first aid kit Nick had in his office and the talk had turned to damage control.

Rosalind was shaking the piece of paper violently. Her eyes were burning with anger and embarrassment. 'This...this...' She could hardly speak.

'Oh, that...oh...no, Rosalind. It's not a joke. Far from it. From Here To Eternity Funeral Parlour wants to be one of our studio tour sponsors,' Jackie replied, keeping her voice surprisingly nonchalant.

'But...but, that is absolutely impossible!' Rosalind was stammering, her voice reaching the screaming point at the end of her sentence.

Thomas formed a cross with his hands to indicate to Nick that he should get the first aid kit ready. Nick shook his head and kept his eyes on Jackie. The boys by the window lifted their eyes from their drinks.

'Oh, no, Rosalind. It is *very possible*.' Jackie pronounced the words 'very possible' extremely slowly to make them more effective. She looked Rosalind straight in the eyes, which Thomas thought was the bravest thing he had ever seen anybody do. And then Jackie added, innocently enough, 'Personally I think Thomas did a great job getting all these sponsors.' She glanced at Thomas who was sitting in the corner with a pint in front of him. He was smiling broadly and scratched the back of his head with an indifferent theatrical gesture.

'It was tough, but I did it.' He finally said proudly and rolled his eyes.

'See Rosalind'—Jackie turned to look at Rosalind again—'the money from all of our sponsors pretty much covers the printing expenses of our studio tour brochure.'

'Well, yes...I can naturally see that as our treasurer, but...now, really...' Rosalind's voice was shaky as she stared at Jackie and then she slowly moved her eyes to stare at Thomas. Thomas was swollen with pride and he was casually smiling back at Rosalind.

'Don't you dare wink, Thomas,' Jackie thought just as he did so. Rosalind shivered with dislike.

Caroline was sitting beside Rosalind, idly watching Thomas with growing interest. She did not care about the funeral parlour sponsorship one way or the other. 'His smile is quite nice,' Caroline thought and gently bit her bottom lip. 'And so is his body.'

'Thank you, Thomas, once more.' Jackie's voice interrupted Caroline's delicate thoughts.

People clapped. Russell belted out 'Hurray,' and Thomas graciously accepted their congratulations by getting up and bowing slightly in every direction, grinning like a mad man in a toothpaste commercial.

After Thomas had sat down, Jackie brought the meeting back to business. 'I went to the hardware store and talked to George, and he said that he has odds and ends of plywood to give us for our signs—and did I mention?—He is giving them to us free of charge.'

'George is a good lad, I say.' Russell said and lifted his pint to cheer George. Thomas eagerly joined in.

'So I have them now in my studio and they are taking up a whole lot of space, which I don't have in the first place'—Jackie glanced around the table—'so why don't we paint them in the next couple of weeks? Nick has generously promised to store them for us after that. The pub has more storage space than I have, and this way it will all be done before we get really busy with the summer season.'

'Thanks, Nick. You are a good man.' Russell said, giving him another reason for a toast. Thomas followed his example enthusiastically. These meetings were great.

'Don't mention it.' Nick shook his head. 'I'm glad to be able to help.'

'So, we'll be painting the signs the last week of this month?' Jackie was asking but her words were more like a declaration than a question.

People looked at one another around the table and murmured a mutual *yes*. Daisy was dutifully writing everything down, and Sheridan was taking down his own memos, just in case there were differing stories. He would gladly be an expert witness.

Rosalind was still clearly upset with the funeral parlour sponsorship and did not join in the conversation. She sat rigidly on the edge of her chair and fumed. Alistair was absorbed with his own thoughts and agreed without even paying the slightest attention to what was being discussed. Russell was full of beans as always, slapping Thomas on his shoulders. Kenneth twiddled his thumbs and stared at a crack in the pub's ceiling.

Caroline said yes with her lazy occasionally honey-coated voice. The meeting did not really interest her, but she was curious about Thomas and, therefore, one must do unpleasant things to get what one really wants—according to her own philosophy.

'I think that is all for tonight.' Jackie said the words people had been waiting for.

Russell got up in a hurry. 'Good! I was starting to get mighty thirsty again.'

Thomas followed his lead. 'Mind if I join you at the bar?'

'Not at all.' Russell was rubbing his stomach. 'Kenneth, how's your cold? Need another tea with rum?' He turned to look at Kenneth, who was quietly getting up to leave. Kenneth hesitated. He was neither standing nor sitting, his hands rested tentatively on the edge of the table.

'Oh, come on, lad. Have a drink with us.' Russell's voice was blaring as he ushered Kenneth toward the bar.

'Well...I guess I could have a pint...maybe...' Kenneth pondered, not quite sure what he wanted to do.

'Great!' Thomas put his arm firmly around Kenneth and guided the quiet man cheerfully the rest of the way to the bar.

Harriet pushed herself up. 'I'm going to have a drink myself—ladies? What would you like to have?' The ladies glanced at their watches.

The TV program they all wanted to see was starting in an hour. They still had some time.

Janet got up to help Harriet with the drinks. She really quite enjoyed these meetings, apart from the needless, lengthy discussions.

They waited behind Russell and Thomas, who were getting their pints. Russell was in full swing and Thomas was doubled over with laughter.

Alistair was helping Rosalind with her jacket. 'Caroline! Will you join us for a drink at our house?' Rosalind enquired sharply.

Caroline turned slowly around. 'No, thank you, Rosalind. I have a few things which I need to discuss with Sheridan.'

'Oh?' Rosalind was startled. She had been surprised twice this evening, and she did not like surprises. 'Well'—she paused—'well, goodnight then.' She added decisively and walked to Alistair who was already holding the door open for her. Rosalind was not happy and she would tell Alistair all about it at home. Alistair shuddered as he let the door close behind him. His favourite TV show was starting in an hour and it seemed that he was going to miss it again.

'Goodnight!' hollered Jackie cheerfully and then turned to talk to Caroline. 'If you need any help with the brochure, I would be happy to…'

Caroline cut her off. 'No…it's all under control. Kenneth is taking the photos, and Sheridan has already offered his precious help rewriting some of the notes. I'm fine, thanks, but no thanks.' Her voice was cold and impersonal. It did not encourage a lengthy conversation.

'Oh, that's great then.' Jackie hesitated for a moment, but Caroline invited nothing further. She turned her back to Jackie and asked Sheridan, 'Would you like to join me for a drink?'

'I would be delighted.' Sheridan was stammering with delight.

They got up to go to the bar as Sheridan rested his eyes on Caroline's fine long legs. He brushed his moustache with his plump fingers and straightened his back.

Caroline positioned herself beside Thomas. Their hips touched and Thomas glanced at her. Caroline flashed her big, beautiful, yet tight-lipped smile. Unfortunately Sheridan managed to wedge his stout body between her and Thomas. Sheridan was very pleased. Caroline obviously needed his expertise and he was more than willing to tell her his numerous stories handling the misspellings and grammatical errors during his many prolific years with the *Miniature Army World News*. Oh, how it would make Caroline jump with laughter. He chuckled at the thought.

Russell was on a roll, helping the world by spreading Russell-ology. His loud voice gave everybody the opportunity to hear his medical reasoning behind the importance of good sex. 'Sex is good for your blood,' he lectured seriously. 'See, the problem with people with high blood pressure is that they don't have sex often enough.'

'Is that so?' Thomas asked, keeping a surprisingly straight face.

'Yes, you see with not enough sex, your blood pressure builds up and, hence, high blood pressure; but if your blood pressure is directed to the other parts of your body'—Russell winked—'it is released by the means of nature.' He took a long draw of his pint. 'And the same goes for cholesterol,' he added and knowingly smacked his lips together.

Thomas looked at Russell and emptied his pint. 'Amazing,' he said. 'Did you hear that Nick? Sex lowers your cholesterol levels, as well. That is simply amazing. I thought sex was purely recreational activity, when in fact it is a medicinal activity. Well, simply amazing information, Russell.'

Nick was trying not to burst out laughing and it took everything he had to control his voice. 'Yes, amazing indeed.' He turned toward Caroline and Sheridan and asked, 'and what would you two like to have?'

Caroline pursed her lips with distaste and tried to ignore Russell, who had gone on to describe the importance of having sex as a homeopathic remedy. 'Chamomile tea is nothing compared to good romping sex.' Russell declared. 'Have sex and then you'll sleep like a baby. No need for chamomile.'

Sheridan had not heard a word Russell had been saying. He had been too busy describing his responsibilities as an editor at the *Miniature Army World News* magazine. Caroline ordered gin and tonic and walked to a nearby table. Sadly for her, Sheridan followed right on her heels. Caroline sat down slowly, crossing her long legs and Sheridan brought out a large pile of brochures from his bag. He couldn't wait to go through them with Caroline.

Caroline already looked extremely bored, occasionally glancing at Thomas, who was in his element, listening and telling good stories at the bar, with a full pint in front of him. He patted Russell on his back and winked at Harriet, who blew him a kiss, and then laughingly shook her head.

Harriet and Janet returned to the table with their drinks. 'Here you go ladies.' Harriet said as she put the tray down on the table. She took a sip of her pint. 'I guess that's as close as we will ever get to seeing Rosalind speechless.'

The older ladies smiled mischievously behind their glasses of sherry. Kenneth, surprisingly, was still at the bar with Thomas and Russell. He seemed to be enjoying himself, though he remained quiet, with only an occasional nod here and there.

The boys in the corner were speaking busily in hushed tones, their heads bent together. Finally Jack Wilkinson hollered out to Nick.

'Nick, how much would you say we spend on average in your pub—let's say—monthly?' he inquired.

Nick looked up. 'I can't tell, since you never actually pay for your drinks yourself.'

'Well...ah, now.' Jack Wilkinson lifted his shoulders up and spread his hands at his sides.

'See, what you normally do is promise to cut everybody's lawn if they'll buy you a pint or two.' Nick explained.

'You're quite right, quite right. And as I recall, last year Sycamore got the third prize in the competition for the best-kept village on the island.' Jack Wilkinson corrected his posture proudly and straightened his imaginary tie.

'It would have been the first, but you drove over the flowerbeds in front of the church the night before judging'—Muriel joined the conversation from her table—'on your way home from the pub.'

'Very unfortunate incident.' Jack Wilkinson agreed solemnly.

'I'll say it was.' Muriel said sternly.

Jack Wilkinson turned back to his friends and they continued their discussion. Something was going on, but nobody had any idea what it could be.

The boys' daily life was a remarkably pre-arranged affair. No matter what happened during the day, they always ended up in the pub.

Nick looked at them wondering what would have caused such a burst of unexplained energy.

Rose, who spent as much time as Nick tending bar, returned from the kitchen. 'If they talk more than they drink, they are up to no good,' she stated grimly and started lifting the dirty glasses into the dishwasher eyeing the boys suspiciously. 'Just mark my words. You'll see.'

Chapter 10

One Dark Night

Postmaster Pam Johnson carried a big package from the back of the post office onto the front counter. She handed over some papers for Jack Wilkinson to sign. He grabbed the nearby pen eagerly and turned it restlessly between his bony arthritic fingers, while Pam Johnson had a closer look at the papers. The package was resting on the counter beside her elbow. Wilkinson's eyes were darting between the package and Pam Johnson's face.

'So,' Pam Johnson said slowly, rolling the word in her mouth unhurriedly. 'The sender is a company called Homemade and the receiver is'—she looked up from her papers and over the rim of her reading glasses—'Mr. Jack Wilkinson.' She puckered her lips and then stared at Jack Wilkinson suspiciously while tapping her fingers against the table. She was thinking. This was the second package Jack Wilkinson had received in ten years and the first one had been a mistake, meant for Jane Wilkinson—Jack's distant cousin on the other side of the island. Unfortunately, that package had contained a large order of women's undergarments. When Jack Wilkinson had opened Jane's package, he had found, amidst the red and black polyester lace, a letter, and it had not been from Jane's husband. One thing had naturally led to another and the whole affair had become public knowledge, just because of bad handwriting.

Pam Johnson was rightfully suspicious. She read the receiver's name again, and then with a long sigh she pointed with her painted fingernail to all of the three places where Jack was suppose to sign.

Jack Wilkinson wrote his name with urgency while he kept his eager eye on the big package resting on the counter.

Pam Johnson looked through the papers once more and, only after making sure that all was in order, pushed the package into Jack Wilkinson's waiting hands, visibly shaking with anticipation.

'Yes, thank you.' Pam Johnson looked on as Jack Wilkinson left in a hurry. His hasty words were still hanging in the air as he pushed the door open and stepped outside.

'You're welcome.' Pam Johnson muttered, when the post office door slammed loudly shut behind him, making the old window panes vibrate dangerously. She stretched her neck to see through the window onto the street. She wanted to know what Jack Wilkinson was doing. She reached for the phone on the counter. Mary Cullighan was number one on her speed dial.

Jack Wilkinson was tying the big package carefully into the small trailer behind his lawnmower. He checked the ropes by tugging at them hard and then began driving home at top speed, not all that fast.

Jack Wilkinson was on friendly terms with almost everybody in the village; he waved his hands constantly to the people he saw on the streets and cheerfully wished them *good morning*. He had somehow acquired the royal waving style while driving his lawn mower—his hand slightly and gracefully sideways in the air, like the Queen.

Soon after Jack Wilkinson got home Calvin, Glenn and Howard appeared, riding their bicycles feverishly. They bumped up and down the dirt road, stopping in front of Jack Wilkinson's rickety front steps, breathing heavily, and leaning over their handlebars. They carried the big parcel together into the house and Jack Wilkinson checked carefully that nobody had seen them before closing the door behind them. After a few hours they came out of the house rubbing their hands together joyfully. Their cheeks were flushed; their eyes gleamed; but whether this was the result of excitement or a few bottles of beer, was hard to tell.

This strange secretive activity happened quite often after that. Calvin, Glenn and Howard were seen bicycling through the village to Jack's house. The front door, which was never fully opened, closed very quickly behind them, showing in the gap, momentarily, Jack's long pointy nose.

A few weeks went by and then one day the boys came out of Jack's house smiling, keeping their hands deep in their pockets as they breathed in the clean country air. They seemed to be extremely happy and excited. They stood in front of Jack's house admiring the fair weather. Normally the boys would check the weather only on the way to the pub and on their way back home from the pub.

Jack Wilkinson rubbed his hands together vigorously. 'Well tomorrow is the day then, lads.'

Calvin agreed cheerfully. 'Yes indeed it is.'

'It is time to bottle the baby.' Howard chuckled.

'I'm getting mighty thirsty, lads. It has been hard work.' Glenn joined in, smacking his lips.

Jack Wilkinson banged his hands onto his stomach and sighed. 'All right, tomorrow, then?'

Glenn was getting ready to hop onto his bike. 'Yep, till tomorrow.'

'All right then. Bye!' Howard was right behind him.

'Bye!' Calvin tested his bell as he bicycled away with a big grin pasted on his weathered face.

The people in the village had been used to seeing the boys in the pub from late afternoon all the way to closing time. Without their presence, there was a void in the atmosphere. The balance had shifted.

The corner table sat empty, and when people walked in they still glanced in that direction, ready to greet them, exchange a few words and inquire after lawn mowing.

Jackie came into the pub and checked the boy's table as she walked by. She went to the bar and turned to look at the empty table again.

'Where on earth are they?' She asked Nick and nodded toward the table in the corner. 'Not that I miss them, but…' She didn't finish her sentence, only shrugged her shoulders. How could she explain in any other way how the boys' absenteeism was affecting her.

'The boys, you mean? I don't know. I haven't seen them for a while.' Nick stared at the empty table as well and shrugged his shoulders.

'It is like the Feng Shui has changed in here.' Jackie said.

Rose came to the bar and put her tray down loudly. 'Now we have only real paying customers in here.'

Muriel had heard the conversation from the nearby table. 'And the flowers in front of the church have actually grown back.'

'Well, there you go,' another older woman said thoughtfully. 'The pastor said he would be praying for a miracle before the annual church conference.'

'You are right, so he did. Didn't he?' Muriel was surprised.

All the old ladies nodded their heads and agreed. It was a miracle indeed.

George was standing by the bar and joined in the conversation. 'My wife is very happy because Jack Wilkinson has not been coming around the house every second day to cut the grass.' He took a sip of his pint.

'Now that you mention it. The village is actually greener these days,' Jackie thought out loud.

Pam Johnson had quickly spread the news about the package as soon as Jack Wilkinson had left. The last package addressed to Jack Wilkinson had brought no happiness to anybody—well apart from Mary Cullighan. It had been by far the most exciting and dramatic gossip Mary had ever laid her hands on. It had kept her busy for months. Nothing as important as that had ever happened on the island before.

'They are up to no good. Mark my word,' Rose said and, with a deep sigh rumbling in her motherly bosom, she went into the kitchen. Having been born and raised on the island, she knew.

The boys were admiring the results of their hard work. In front of them stood one plastic barrel full of red wine and one plastic barrel full of white wine. From the glow on their faces you would have thought that they were experiencing religious enlightenment, which they probably, in their own way, were. It was a wine epiphany. It was Genesis. Their eyes were shining and their hands never seemed to stop moving.

'Did you bring more bottles, Glenn?' Jack Wilkinson asked, his voice quivering with excitement and also with fear, because perhaps they didn't have enough bottles.

'Yes, yes. I took some of Ginny's juice bottles that she had stored up in the shed.'

Howard had poured some wine from the barrel into his glass and he was swirling it in his glass like an expert. 'Now taste the bouquet of this wine.' He nudged Jack on his arm and beamed with pride.

Jack took the offered glass and tasted it. He smacked his lips and assumed the gestures of a wine connoisseur. 'Floral with a hint of apple and pear, lingering taste, fresh and perhaps a bit acidic, but let it breath for a while and it'll be just dandy.'

The boys stared at Jack in amazement. Jack was no doubt the connoisseur of wines, and wasn't his cousin's name Marie. If that wasn't a sure sign of the French connection, nothing would be.

Calvin was eager to get his share. 'Pour me one too, will you Jack?' he said, rubbing his chin nervously.

'Coming right up.' Jack got a coffee mug from his cupboard and brought it to the 'bottling station.' He poured a generous drink for Calvin. Calvin took a sip and swished the wine around in his mouth like he had seen done on TV and then puckered up his lips and smacked them together thoughtfully. 'Yes, a bit sharp I might say, but nothing that half an hour can't fix.'

'What? You are going to wait half an hour to drink this glass of wine?' Howard was amazed. He had never heard Calvin talk like that.

'No! I'm not talking about waiting. I'm talking about drinking and letting it breath at the same time.' Calvin took another sip. 'Aren't I breathing?' he asked Howard with a nudge to his ribcage.

'I'm getting thirsty, boys. Pour me a drink will you?' Jack handed his coffee mug to Howard.

Howard chatted while he filled the mugs. 'Working hard can really get you thirsty. I might have another one myself.'

'Just don't drink Ginny's wine. Maybe if that woman would drink more, she would be happier and wouldn't nag at me so often,' Glenn reminded them, his crooked finger jabbing the air energetically.

'Wishful thinking.' Howard snickered and drank thirstily from his slightly stained coffee mug.

The boys cackled merrily. Ginny and the word happy were not normally mentioned in the same sentence. No. They were used to connecting her name with hail storms, lightning, hurricanes and other natural disasters.

The boys were filling the bottles. As soon as one of them filled a bottle, another one capped it and the third one poured more wine for all of them. To be fair, they rotated these important jobs.

As the night progressed the drunker the boys became. The rotation of duties became slower and sometimes two pairs of hands were needed to close the caps properly. It seemed that the boys had tasted more wine than they had bottled, which was altogether quite possible.

At ten o'clock, they were done. The boys were done; the bottling was as done as it possibly could be. Glenn glanced at his watch as he drained the rest of his Merlot and pulled on Calvin's sleeve. 'We better go home. It's bloody late.' Howard hiccupped and suggested a toast for the road. They had their last drink for the road, and then another last one, and to be on the safe side, they had yet another drink just for good luck, which they thought Glenn might need.

They eventually found their jackets and followed Jack to the front door. They had a hard time putting their jackets on, flapping the empty sleeves around like a flock of birds behind Jack, who was standing at the door, holding onto the doorframe with both hands.

It was very dark outside.

One by one they finally succeeded in dressing themselves. They stopped staggering momentarily and peered out into the darkness. The outside light was broken.

Glenn had a good hold of Jack's shoulder. 'It is bloody dark out!' He blurted and swayed between Jack and the doorframe.

Howard closed his eyes and then opened them wide to see better. When that didn't work, he squinted his eyes and, when he still couldn't see anything, he began the whole process again. 'Blimey, lads. Have I gone blind?' he asked with his one eye closed, cocking his head from side to side.

'Have you got a flashlight, Jack?' Glenn grabbed Jack's arm with both hands and held onto it while his knees were slowly giving in.

'I have one, but it doesn't have any batteries.' Jack was still holding onto the doorframe with both hands with Glenn now desperately hanging onto his sleeve. Slowly Jack's body began bending toward Glenn, so much so, that eventually, much to Glenn's surprise, his knees touched the ground.

'Don't worry boys. I've got a dynamo on my bike. I'll go first and you two follow me—all right?' Calvin straightened himself, focused his eyes and took a few more seconds to tell his body to move forward.

Glenn staggered up and put his arm around Jack, tapping his shoulder.

They were all swaying in the doorway, squinting and trying to see where their bicycles were and where, exactly, the road was. Calvin finally pushed through the crowd and stood on the front steps swaying. 'Where the hell are our bloody bikes, lads?'.

'You know. I haven't the foggiest idea.' Glenn had moved forward and now he leaned over Calvin's shoulder to see better. They both supported each other as they kept staring into the darkness. 'No bloody idea.'

'Where is the road then?' Calvin asked.

Jack pointed his wavering finger into the darkness. Howard was leaning against the doorframe behind Jack. He had finally stopped blinking his eyes and was having a small rest. 'You really should invest in a porch light, Jack,' he said.

'I had one once, but it burned out three years ago. Those things never last.'

'You got that right.' Calvin agreed seriously.

'All righty then lads,' said Glenn. 'I'll go and find the bikes. Hold Ginny's wine for me, will you?' He shoved a plastic bag with two bottles of wine into Calvin's hands and disappeared into the dark night.

The plastic bag seemed to make Calvin lopsided and he stood in front of the steps in the dim light holding onto the bag, which was almost touching the ground. Suddenly they heard the sound of Glenn bumping into something metallic and after that a whole lot of curses came from the darkness.

'Jesus! Mother of god!' All was quiet for a second and then they heard Glenn's voice again. 'Bloody hell! I found the buggers.' Calvin looked into the darkness. 'Where are you?'

From the dark night came Glenn's voice. 'Right here.'

'Where?'

'Right here, damn it. Just follow my voice.'

Calvin and Howard began walking unsteadily and hesitantly toward the sound of Glenn's voice. They soon disappeared into the darkness as well. Jack was left standing on the shaky front steps. He stared into the black night unable to see anything.

Calvin stopped. He could not find Glenn. 'Keep talking then.' He shouted into the dark night.

'Shut up.' Came the answer from the darkness.

'You shut up,' bellowed Howard back.

'But he can't shut up, can he? If he does, we will never find him.' Calvin slurred into Howard's ear.

'I talk and you shut up,' Glenn shouted from somewhere.

Both Howard and Calvin bellowed, 'Oh, shut up!'

'Gladly lads.'

Calvin and Howard now bumped into the bikes.

A duet of curse words were heard coming out of the darkness, accompanied by the sound of Ginny's wine bottles dangerously clanging together.

'Careful with them bottles, lads.' Glenn warned the boys.

'Yes, yes.' Howard agreed.

The boys had gotten hold of their bikes. Calvin had managed to switch on his dynamo and, as he walked his bike, the light came on.

Jack watched the little light swirl as Calvin walked drunkenly from side to side on the road.

'Bon voyage, lads.' Jack Wilkinson waved his hand into the darkness.

'Goodnight to you, too.' Glenn wished, slurring.

Calvin and Howard both hollered their goodbyes into the dark and otherwise quiet night.

'Ready to go lads?' Calvin asked.

Glenn nodded and Howard got the feeling that he was in the army. 'Ready, sir, when you are.'

They hopped on their bikes with some difficulty and began following Calvin's bike and its little dynamo light weaving a crooked path in front of them.

The white plastic bag swung dangerously on Glenn's handlebar, forcing his bike to steer to the right. The road ahead was bumpy, scattered with small potholes, lit only by the tiny dynamo-powered light.

The inevitable happened. They hit a pothole on top of the hill.

'Damn!' Calvin yelled struggling to keep his bike straight.

'Jesus bloody Christ!' Howard cursed loudly.

'Bloody hell! Watch the road, damn it.' Glenn barked.

'What?' Calvin could not hear what the boys were saying. 'What did you say?'

'Watch the bloody road, I said.' Glenn growled.

'What? I can't hear you.' Calvin looked back into the darkness behind him. He couldn't see anything. He stopped his bike, so that he could hear where the boys were and what they were saying. The little dynamo light went out at the same time and then—all was black, pitch black, blacker than black.

First to come down the little hill was Howard, who smashed full speed into Calvin. A second later came Glenn and smashed into Howard's rear end.

The dark night was filled with the sounds of crashing bikes and wine bottles and painful yells accompanied by very loud and profane cursing.

'Augh…bloody, god damn, shit!' Calvin screeched.

'Augh! My foot! My foot! The god-damn wine is gone.' Glenn howled first because of the pain and then because he, to his horror, realized that Ginny's wine was gone.

'Augh! Watch out! My leg! Jesus! Get off my frigging leg!' Howard bawled.

'Jesus mother of god! The wine!' Glenn screamed.

'I can't move,' Howard cried.

'Bloody hell!' Calvin howled.

Suddenly from afar, came the sound of a car approaching. The humming of the engine cut into the night. The car lights came closer and closer along the bumpy country road, and then the car stopped, its brakes screeching to a halt. The boys were lying in the middle of the road in the spotlight of the car. They were frozen, like deer caught in headlights—mesmerized. They blinked their eyes uselessly in the ray of bright light from the head lamps and continued to stare at the car, seeing nothing.

Glenn suddenly thought about heaven and wondered if he was dead. But he hadn't seen the blue light, yet, so he waited.

The car, as it happened, was a police car. The police officer stared motionless at the bizarre scene in front of him. His face completely white from the shock of such a horrifying surprise lying in front of him in the middle of the normally deserted road. He was clutching the steering wheel with both hands. His knuckles drained of colour. As he began to decipher what he was seeing, the absurdity began to strike him: a pile of bicycles and a pile of older men, all smashed together in the middle of an empty country road between vast fields of hay and corn.

None of the boys could get up. Their legs were stuck under their bicycles and they were, of course, completely and utterly drunk. Glenn was covered in red wine and it made him look injured.

The police officer continued to stare at the sight in front of him. Finally he came to life; he exhaled, turned off the car, opened the door and stepped out. The boys were staring at him—a tall, dark figure in front of bright lights. Glenn thought about the pearly gates of heaven and wondered what Saint Peter was going to say.

The police officer walked slowly toward the pile of disoriented, drunk men.

'Good evening, boys.'

'Oh hello, Scottie.' Glenn grinned. He was relieved that it wasn't Saint Peter after all. 'How are you?' He was trying to be charming and casual while lying in a heap of bent metal and broken glass.

'You could have gotten yourselves killed,' the officer said sternly, still shocked by the thought of almost killing three almost innocent men.

'That would have made my wife a really happy woman.'

All the boys started to laugh hysterically.

The police officer stood in front of the cackling men. He did not find the situation funny. 'Are you all right? Glenn, are you hurt?' he asked.

'No, no, I'm all right, but my foot is not.'

'But you're bleeding?'

Glenn then noticed that he was covered in red wine. He was amazed to see the red stains covering his clothes. He touched himself all over to be sure that everything was all right—that all of his bits and pieces were still there and breathing. 'Bloody hell! I smashed Ginny's wine,' he said as the hard reality sank in.

The boys started to laugh again.

The police officer shook his head in disbelief. 'Okay, boys. Why don't I drive you home?'

'That is very kind of you, Scottie.' Calvin said.

Scottie walked beside the tangled pile of men and bicycles and began sorting them out by lifting the bikes and helping the men get onto their shaking feet. He pulled Calvin up and supported him with his one arm.

Calvin leaned on him heavily. He was trying to whisper something, but miscalculated the strength of his own voice and ended up yelling. 'Just promise me one thing, son. Don't tell your mom.' He tried to put his finger in front of his lips as he made the shh-sound.

'Dad, I promise I won't. But if she finds out, she'll be mad, and Loraine doesn't want you to stay with us for weeks at a time anymore.' Scottie looked at his dad and tried to stay away from the warm smell of alcohol that surrounded him.

'She won't find out. I promise.' Calvin wanted to tap his son on his back, but, again, misjudged, and ended up waving his hand in the air as he began walking unsteadily toward the police car.

Scottie bent down to pick up Calvin's bicycle. 'You can come back for your bikes tomorrow.' He put all three bikes beside the road next to the ditch. 'Now, in you go.' Scottie held the door of the police car open.

The boys got in. Glenn in the front seat and Howard and Calvin in the back. Glenn was pleased to be sitting with Scottie in the front. 'Nice car you got here, Scottie.'

'Do not touch anything.' Scottie's voice was surprisingly threatening as he turned the car around. 'I'll drive first to your house, Glenn.'

'All right, that'll be fine, Scottie.'

Howard chuckled in the backseat. 'Fancy me driving in a police car.'

They drove a short distance and arrived at Glenn's house. The lights were off, which made Glenn feel a bit more optimistic about his situation.

'This your house, Glenn?' Scottie asked.

'I really can't tell. I've lost my glasses.' He was looking through the car window, squinting his eyes, his nose almost touching the glass. 'Is there a large, angry woman at the window?' He asked.

'Be brave, Glenn.' Calvin tapped Glenn's shoulder.

'Life is short and then you die.' Howard added philosophically and smacked his lips together knowingly.

Glenn sighed deeply. 'I just don't fancy it being this particular night.'

'Off you go Glenn and goodnight.' Scottie leaned over to open the car door.

Glenn hesitated for a moment. The car was warm and there were no hostile females around. Life could be good, but then again, reality is reality. He stepped out and started limping unsteadily toward the house. Suddenly the front door of his house opened and in the bright ray of light was a big woman's silhouette.

The silhouette spoke with a thunderous voice. 'Is that you, Glenn?'

Glenn's face lost all of the colour drinking had earlier brought to it. 'Yes, dear,' he stammered.

'Did the police bring you home?' The silhouette barked into the night.

'Scottie gave us a ride.' He tried to sound casually cheerful. Maybe all was not lost yet.

'Goodnight.' Scottie closed the car door quickly and drove away, spraying gravel as he sped down the road.

'What did he do this time?' The woman silhouette in the doorway yelled at the police car but the car had already driven beyond hearing distance.

As they were driving away, the two drunken boys in the backseat watched through the rear window at the sight of a big woman and a very small fragile limping man.

They turned around and stared straight ahead at the road.

'It might have been better for him to spend a night in jail.' Calvin suggested.

'I think you are right.' Howard sighed.

They were thinking of how lucky they were not to be Glenn just now. They smiled blissfully, thanking their good luck at not being married to Ginny, but then the thought of what their own wives might say entered their drunken minds. This thought brought a deep silence into the backseat of the police car.

Chapter 11

Signs and Signs

The pub was filled and the boys were back at their regular table. They had miraculously survived the wine making adventure and were, as would be expected, the object of much interest. Naturally the boys obliged and eagerly gave a detailed description of their escapades during that dark and special night.

Glenn had a pair of crutches leaning against the back of his chair and his glasses had been hastily taped together. He was drinking his pint leisurely, happily clarifying the information about his ankle. 'No. it's not broken. It's just a twisted ankle…nothing serious. The doctor said I would be up and running in no time at all.'

The word running sent the rest of the boys into rowdy laughter.

'Yes, running away from that wife of yours, I bet.' Jack blurted and snickered, almost tipping over his glass of beer.

'He was like a lamb before being sacrificed,' declared Calvin.

'Yes, begging for his life,' uttered Howard and then they all rolled over with laughter while Glenn coolly observed the situation, pushed his glasses further up his nose and took a long, long quiet draw of his beer.

Russell was fascinated by their story and he wanted to know how big Ginny actually was.

Calvin got up to mimic Glenn begging for his life in front of a giant. Russell and the boys, apart from Glenn, laughed at the sight.

Glenn took another sip from his pint, propped his glasses up again and then asked, innocently enough, 'And how is that guest room at Loraine's, Calvin?'

'Well...' was all Calvin could mutter and then he rose quickly to go and buy another pint at the bar.

It was Glenn's turn to laugh. 'I bet Loraine does not put her best china on the table for Calvin.' Then he got up and limped over to the bar to give a friendly tap on Calvin's stooped shoulders.

Rose was behind the bar cleaning the counter when Jackie and Nick came in with their hands filled with paint cans and brushes.

Jackie put her bags on the floor. The cans clanked and Rose lifted her eyebrows.

'Are you sure, Nick, that this is a good idea?' Jackie asked with a worried voice. 'You know, paints mixed with what will most likely be a large quantity of alcohol?'

Nick shrugged his shoulders. 'I think it will be all right.'

'I brought some paper with me; I'll cover everything with it and promise to clean any mess we make.'

'Sounds fair to me.' Nick smiled. He glanced at the clock on the wall. It was almost time for work.

Rose winked at Nick quickly and beckoned him to come to the bar. She looked more serious than normal. Nick wondered why the strange secrecy and walked slowly to her, glaring at her suspiciously.

Rose bent to whisper in a barely audible voice, keeping her eyes on Jackie. 'Nick,' she said. 'Denise just called.'

Jackie was looking at the two of them. She was used to seeing Nick cheerful and relaxed, so when she saw the dramatic change of expression on his face, it came as a shock. Nick's face drained of all its colour. The happy relaxed expression was gone and she was looking at a hard stone face with angry unapproachable eyes. Nick mumbled something to Rose and then stormed into his office. The door behind him closed harder than usual.

'What was that about?' Jackie innocently asked Rose.

'Oh, nothing,' Rose answered too quickly for the answer to be true. 'Just some mistake in orders we made today.' Rose looked critically at the glass she had started to clean, rubbing it vigorously. 'Too many sacks of potatoes, that's all.'

Jackie stared at her awhile, trying to find clues, but Rose turned her back to her and busied herself with the icemaker.

It was none of Jackie's business, of course, but naturally she wondered what could have happened. She had lived long enough on the island to recognize a story in the making.

Nick had helped Jackie to cut and paint the plywood sheets earlier in the week, and today they had loaded them into their cars, to be brought later to the pub. It had been very nice of Nick to help her, especially on his day off. They had lazily been sitting in the sun by the wall, protected from the wind and doubled over with laughter remembering the summers Jackie had spent on the island as a child. They had chatted more than they had worked but neither one of them had pointed it out.

Nick had been very relaxed and he had been whistling cheerfully while carrying the heavy signs.

Rose would not tell Jackie anything, so she went back to her car to bring in the roll of paper to cover the tables.

When she came back in, Nick had come out from his office.

'Is everything all right with the order?' she couldn't help asking.

Nick looked puzzled as he looked at her. Rose quickly jumped in—'The order about the potatoes that the phone call was about.' She nudged Nick.

'Oh! That order!' Nick exclaimed, acting surprised so badly that it almost made Jackie laugh. 'Yes. Everything was straightened out. The potato order is under control.' He continued scrambling for words and staring at Rose.

'Anything I can help you with, Jackie?' He asked, just to change the subject.

'No, no, thanks. You have done enough already. Especially on your day off.' Jackie said and began covering the floor and the tables with the paper. Nick disappeared back into the office, and Jackie could hear him talking on the phone again. And he was not talking about potatoes. Rose went to close the door that Nick had left ajar by accident.

The boys were sitting at their normal place. Jackie overheard their discussion while she spread the paper on top of the tables.

'I bet it was that Denise who called,' Jack Wilkinson said, nodding his head knowingly.

'How so?' asked Howard.

'Well every time that devil calls, Nick looks like he is going to be sick.'

'Uh. Why's that?' Calvin put a word in.

'Well, let me see. I think she owes Nick some money and she hasn't paid it back yet.'

'Was it the house they bought together and she's still living there?' Glenn asked.

'Yeah, something like that. I don't know the particulars, because that Rose there guards Nick's personal life like a mother wolf, and she refuses to say anything about it, no matter what I do to make her break the silence.'

'Yes, she truly treats him like her own son, doesn't she?' Calvin said.

'Yes, she does.' Jack agreed vigorously. 'But I gather the story goes something like this: Denise lives in their house and she hasn't paid him for his half yet, and that has brought financial troubles on him, you know. Owning a house there and owning the pub here. Double loan payments and so on.'

Jack's knowledgeable words reached Jackie's ears and she almost stopped working. She was so glued to what the boys were talking about. Nick had a past and an ex-girlfriend, could be ex-wife and a house in town, or ex-house in town. Jackie was intrigued. Nick had never ever mentioned anything about it, not even a hint, but then again she had not talked about her past either. Somehow it just didn't matter. What was past, was past, but she was still interested in what had happened between Nick and this Denise. She couldn't help it. She quickly glanced at Nick who had come out from his office and was talking to Rose in hushed tones. Nick was now calm but Rose was beginning to look angry.

'Give me the number and I'll call her.' Jackie heard her say with a strained voice. Nick muttered 'no' and said that everything was being sorted out.

'Yes, sorted out to benefit her, I bet.' Rose said harshly. 'I guess she wanted another six months rent free again! That blood sucking smiling witch!'

Nick shrugged his shoulders and walked back to the office pulling his hair with both hands. Rose stood in the bar fuming; Jack Wilkinson winked to the boys, and then asked, innocently enough. 'Was it Denise who called?'

Rose looked up sharply. 'It's none of your bloody business.' She said and tossed the rag into the sink with the force of anger. She then followed Nick into the office, slamming the door closed behind her.

Jack winked knowingly at the boys, and they all murmured into their pints: 'Yep, Denise. Nobody else makes her act like that.'

Despite the closed door the boys and Jackie heard angry voices coming from the office. They heard someone dialling the phone, and then Nick's hushed voice and Rose's harsh voice, booming over the telephone conversation, giving instructions on what to say.

Jackie continued to arrange her things waiting for Nick to emerge from the office. She had set everything in its place by the time Nick came out, his face flushed and his hair sticking out where he had run his fingers through it.

'Is this all right for you?' Jackie asked him and pointed to the tables covered with thick brown paper.

'Looks good and secure.' Nick answered. He was almost back to his cheerful self again. 'Need any help?' He managed a small apologetic smile.

'No, thanks. I'm fine.' Jackie said and stuck the last bit of tape onto the paper and stepped back to see if any part of the table was not covered.

She was setting the paintbrushes, paint cans, sponges and templates on top of the papered tables when Russell walked in.

'Good evening, ladies.' He hollered merrily.

'Hello, Russell. Ready to work?' Jackie cheerfully answered.

'Yes, yes, but first I need a pint.' Russell walked straight to the bar and ordered his pint. 'As you know I am a thirsty fellow.'

Russell was blissfully drinking his pint when Thomas walked in with a young girl who was dressed in tight jeans and a short jacket with pink pompoms. Thomas was all smiles. The grin on his face stretched from one cheek to the other. He put his hand protectively behind the girl's back and ushered her in. Jackie turned around and yelled, 'Thomas! Did you bring the other signs?'

Thomas looked up, concentrating hard, trying to think back to the time before the pink pompoms and tight jeans. 'Sorry, Master Jackie, I forgot.' He ran his fingers through his unruly hair and smiled apologetically, though he was not sorry at all. He was too happily busy with the pompom girl.

Thomas was eager to help her to take her jacket off. He was in fact looking forward to helping her to get her jacket off. The tight jeans promised a tight top. He wasn't disappointed as he witnessed the marvellous strength of spandex. It had a lovely translucent effect, stretching to the extreme the words that were printed on the front of the T-shirt.

'Ginger here offered to come and help us with the painting. She is really handy with her brush.' He said proudly as he stared at the glittery words on Ginger's T-shirt: 'Fun starts here.'

'Well, that's great news! Now, Thomas, could you get those damn signs in, so that we can get on with this work.' Jackie barked at him.

Thomas looked at her, smiled and offered a salute with the added effect of hitting his heels together. 'Right away, Captain Jacqueline.' Thomas scampered out the door to retrieve the neglected signs, and Ginger bid him goodbye with small wrist movements and giggles. Nick wondered if she was old enough to drink legally. Jackie stared and cursed and waited for the rest of the signs.

Russell was nodding approvingly at Ginger. 'Fancy a pint?' he asked jovially, but Ginger politely declined Russell's offer and mentioned something about Thomas buying her a coke and Bacardi later on. 'I don't drink beer.' She explained. 'Too many calories, you know. It goes straight to my hips.'

Thomas came back in with some signs under his arm. He put them on the floor, bent to give Ginger's cheek a kiss, and then went out again to get the rest of the signs, while Russell vehemently argued that a bit of meat on a woman was attractive.

Nancy, Daisy and Muriel greeted everybody with warm smiles and with a few well-placed questions they found out that Ginger was Hilary's little sister. She was visiting her for a few weeks and she was old enough to drink, which made Nick breath a little easier. Ginger was going to be a beautician and planned to work with Hillary after her graduation.

The pub slowly filled with the rest of the members of the artists' group.

Rosalind pinched her nose disapprovingly at the sight of Harriet drinking beer. 'Maybe you should have one too, Rosalind,' Harriet suggested merrily, though not in a totally friendly manner. 'You might even become a human with feelings and all.' Harriet's voice was undeniably loud, so everybody in the pub heard.

Rosalind's face was stern as she walked past the bar to go and sit with Alistair and Sheridan.

Caroline was leaning against the bar, chatting with Nick about martinis and the right way to mix them. She amused herself by eavesdropping on Ginger and the older ladies. It gave her some kind of entertainment, considering that she found all the members of the studio tour ridiculous.

Jackie looked around her. It was time to start the painting project. Now she only needed to get the other people to start—and finish—the project. She rubbed her hands energetically and finally slapped them together loudly. 'Okay, people. Let's get on with it, shall we?' She cleared her voice and continued. 'Nick and I spray-painted these signs two days ago, so all we need now is to stencil in the words. Simple, fast and fun. Right?' She looked around to see if there were any enthusiastic faces in the crowd.

Ginger was still standing in the corner where Thomas had left her earlier. She was getting slightly tired of the older ladies. She had not come here to chat with grandmothers about skin care. She pulled on her T-shirt and quickly slipped her hand under it to fix the straps of her bra. She was ready for Thomas to come and buy her a drink.

Calvin was puffing his cigarette nearby which made Rosalind pinch her nose. 'I do wish, Jacqueline, that we could have chosen a better place for this painting night.' She spoke loudly and waved her hands in front of her.

Jackie did her best to ignore Rosalind but it didn't stop the comments from coming. 'You do know how sensitive Alistair's sinuses are to cigarette smoke?' Rosalind turned to look at her husband, expecting to receive a confirming nod, but instead, Alistair had walked to the bar to order a gin and tonic for himself. Rosalind was left to disapprove of everything by herself, which she was completely capable of doing.

Jackie's thoughts were not with Rosalind and she certainly was not concerned about Alistair's sinuses. She was desperately trying to get people interested in the painting project. That was the reason they had come to the pub in the first place. 'Let's divide into groups, shall we?' She asked with a forced smile pasted on her face. 'Here are the letter templates.' She lifted a stack of letter templates up and showed them to everybody. 'And Nancy has sorted the paints out.' Her voice was hesitant despite her best effort. 'So, let's start, why don't we? No time like the present!' She let out a small laugh that was supposed to sound positive.

Just then Russell walked up to Jackie and surprised her by grabbing her by the arm. 'My girl, you can't start working straight away. You must have a pint with us first. That's an order!'

Jackie stared at Russell and tried to say something, but Russell was fast and Jackie was briskly swept away by him. A few seconds later she found herself holding a full pint in her hands at the bar.

Russell was very busy and animated as he organized drinks for everybody. He handed a pint to Janet and Harriet, accompanied by an exaggerated wink and a smirk. Alistair got a strong pat on the back, and Ginger's short T-shirt got special acknowledgment, followed by an approving nod to Thomas. Jackie tried to walk away from the bar with a pint in her hand, but more people came to get drinks and in the end she was stuck at the bar, sandwiched tightly between Russell and Thomas. Everyone was merry and Jackie was patted many times on her back and congratulated for getting the group together.

Ginger was giggling at anything Thomas said, and Russell was just about to start his geriatric sex talk, when Jackie finally managed to squeeze through the tight crowd and walk to the painting tables in the middle of the room. She cleared her throat loudly and determinately—'Okay, let's start now, shall we?' But even she wasn't sure if she would ever get the full attention of the merry group with drinks, despite her earlier fortitude.

People turned slowly around to look at her and Jackie used this semi attention and began passing the letter templates out. She quickly pressed them into the hands that were not holding a drink and ushered the resisting crowd to move toward the different work areas.

Russell was ordering Jackie another pint. 'No thank you, Russell. I don't need another one. I still have this pint.' She pointed to her half full pint at the table. 'Remember to put the word *studio* first and under it you put the word *tour*.' She yelled over the hum of voices that were wondering what was to be done first.

'Let me know when you are done with that pint and I'll get you another,' Russell hollered. 'I'm here to take care of our little leader.' He had a wide grin on his slightly flushed face.

'Thank you, Russell. Very kind of you.' Jackie pointed once more to the signs, this time jabbing her finger in their direction. 'How about painting some signs?' She added with a phoney cheerfulness in her voice. To her great relief people finally started picking up the brushes. Slowly, very slowly, they began stencilling the words.

Sheridan brought Jackie a gin and tonic. 'Oh, thank you, Sheridan. How very nice of you.' She took the offered drink, and glanced at her half full pint on the table.

'Oh...it's nothing...drinks for the troops. It's a social event and not a meeting. Drinks are good for teambuilding.' Sheridan waved his hand in front of him and then returned to his table.

Thomas was chatting with Ginger in the corner and her giggles were more like background music than responses to Thomas's amusing self-reflecting stories. Once in a while Thomas got up and went to the bar to get refills. He happily divided his time between painting and Ginger, and once in awhile he helped Ginger paint by teaching her how to hold the paintbrush correctly. Jackie rolled her eyes at the sight and muttered 'Jesus' to no one particular.

Russell chatted loudly and he made sure that everyone had a pint in front of them. He kept checking on Jackie's progress with the drinks.

Caroline smoked a cigarette and chatted with Alistair in one corner of the cramped pub. Alistair seemed happy enough with his gin and tonic. Rosalind was not in his immediate vicinity, which allowed him the freedom to speak his own mind.

Rosalind and Sheridan were together in the far corner of the pub where they were both talking, though neither of them was listening. Their words bounced off the other, barely even touching the surface. The word dialog did not apply. The level of their voices rose as the non-conversation progressed—the fight of the titans.

Jackie found this strange competition amusing and kept looking at the two of them waiting for the actual exchange of words to commence. Thomas sailed by with two drinks in his hands.

'It's amazing'—he said quickly—'how those two can be at it for hours and have absolutely no clue what the other one has said.' He pointed to Sheridan and Rosalind and was off again whistling cheerfully. The older ladies were admiring Ginger's pompoms and Ginger quietly wished them to go far, far away, especially when she saw Thomas walking toward her with the drinks, trying to avoid spilling them while squeezing through the crowd.

Harriet talked loudly about the dog shows she had participated in with Winston, and Janet listened quietly beside her. The talk changed to sheep dogs, and then Harriet needed a refill.

Alistair ordered another gin and tonic, and Russell gave a compliment to Ginger regarding the length of her shirt. 'Now there is nothing wrong in showing your body, in my mind at least. God gave you this body, so I say, celebrate it.' He drew an hourglass shape in the air with his hands and then left with a pint in his hands, humming happily.

Jackie was slapped on her back many times and congratulated on her great idea of the studio tour. People kept bringing her drinks. The whole thing acquired a pattern: pat on the back, kind words and a new drink.

Jackie muttered her thanks and took another sip of beer, wine, sherry or gin and tonic. There had been an awful lot of people to congratulate her.

Russell walked to the table where Rosalind was admiring the sign she had finally finished with Sheridan. Her face revealed a slight pleasure, quickly gone when she noticed Russell standing next to her, rocking back and forth on his heels and toes.

Russell was oblivious to the icy welcome he received. He casually draped his hand over Rosalind's shoulders and then patted her arm thoughtfully. It was time for Doctor Russell's advice. 'Now you seem a bit tense, Rosalind. But don't worry. Old Russell will tell you what you need to do to relax.' He smiled cheerfully into Rosalind's anxious face and continued. 'All you need is a good roll in the hay with that husband of yours.' He squeezed Rosalind comradely. 'My wife is so relaxed. Before we got married she suffered from terrible headaches…What are they called now…them terrible headaches?'—Russell paused, trying to find the correct word—'ah… migraines…that's it! Migraines.' He smiled broadly. 'But since our wedding night, no migraines ever since, soooo.' Russell was winking at Rosalind and thrusting his hips back and forth.

Rosalind was dumbfounded. She stared at Russell, disgust spreading over her white stony face. She held onto her glass of dry white wine with trembling hands. She was rigid. Russell winked and smiled as if he had just done Rosalind the greatest favour of her life.

Alistair stared at Russell for a moment. He had, as had most of those in the pub, heard every word of Russell's advice to Rosalind. The only person who was completely oblivious of the events was Sheridan. He had not heard anything, as he had made it a habit never to listen to anybody. He took a sip from his gin and tonic in a soldier-like manner and began lecturing Alistair about the sorry state of fine arts today, punching his finger into Alistair's arm to emphasize his point. Alistair pondered for a while if he should say anything at all, when Russell patted his back and walked briskly back to the bar. Alistair turned, avoiding Rosalind's fierce eyes and pretended to continue paying attention to Sheridan's never-ending lecture while rubbing his sore arm.

Jackie stared at Russell and then again at Rosalind. She looked around and walked to the bar to talk to Nick.

'How is it going, Jackie?' Nick asked and smiled.

Jackie scratched her head, 'Good, I guess?' She was starting to get a bit tipsy just like the rest of the group. 'Did I just hear Russell giving sex advice to Rosalind?' she finally asked and looked questioningly into Nick eyes.

'I think we all did.' Nick smirked.

'That's what I thought.' She walked back to the table where she had been working. She placed the stencils on the board and pushed them firmly against the board while painting in the letters. Her fingers were already stained from the paints and once in awhile the stencils got stuck to her hands. By this time she was having some small difficulty placing the letter stencils in a straight line on the board. She was concentrating hard, biting her bottom lip ever so lightly. Nick smiled and thought that possibly the outcome might not quite follow the original plan.

Finally, things were beginning to wind down. Jack, Glenn, Howard and Calvin were in deep discussion with Russell. Russell was waving his hands in an animated way and the boys were listening carefully, once in awhile grunting their approval.

Some of the finished signs were leaning against the wall. Nancy, Daisy and Muriel were tidying up before going home. Jackie was trying to get the last bits and pieces together. It all seemed to take much longer than she had anticipated, but then again, she had drunk more than she had expected. 'Maybe it wasn't entirely my fault.' She was trying to convince herself.

Thomas helped Ginger to get into her tiny jacket. Then he waved his hand and at the same time guided Ginger out the door holding his other hand over the small of her back. Ginger giggled and leaned closer to Thomas, who didn't mind it at all. 'Goodnight to you all and happy Christmas.' Thomas hollered.

Ginger found this very funny and started laughing even louder and leaned closer to Thomas, wrapping her arm around him.

Rosalind pinched her nose disapprovingly and looked at Alistair, wanting him to hurry getting their jackets. Alistair had been secretly drinking quite a few gin and tonics during the night, and he walked very carefully and very slowly while carrying their jackets in the crook of his arm. Rosalind was sober and she stood rigidly by the door. She wasn't the beacon of light to guide you safely into the harbour; she was the rock you tried desperately to avoid hitting.

Alistair hiccupped while he helped Rosalind with her jacket; her eyes scrutinized him briefly, before she turned her back on him.

Caroline was talking with Sheridan at the bar. She was slowly smoking a cigarette and Sheridan was repeating himself for the thousandth time. 'The state of the art nowadays...' His voice lingered in the air and was slightly slurred, but his finger was still jabbing the air energetically. At some point in the evening, he had tried to touch Caroline's arm, but had been warned off by a menacing look that even Sheridan understood well enough, despite his drunken state of mind.

Nick poured a few new pints and handed them over to Russell.

Russell walked like a sea captain, as with great agility he made his way stepping sideways on springy feet. He stopped in front of Jackie and handed her one of the pints.

'Here you go girl. It will put hair on your chest.'

'Oh, thank you, but please Russell, seriously, no more pints after this.' Jackie pleaded as she accepted, again, the 'last pint of the night.' 'How can I say no,' she said to herself. Her thoughts were starting to swim slowly around in her head. Relaxed thoughts aimed at nothing, just going round and round and round.

Russell went back to the bar and took a few more pints to the table where the boys were sitting. 'Now where were we...oh yes! Let me tell you about that picnic spot I found with my missus. It has very soft and smooth grass...you know.' He winked again and the boys hummed together approvingly and leaned eagerly over their pints to listen to Russell's stories

Jackie began cleaning the work area. She put the signs against the wall, trying to keep the wet paints from touching the wall or the other signs. Kenneth, with slow and exaggerated movements, was quietly helping her. Finally he straightened his long body and tried to focus his eyes, looking for Jackie's face in the fog. 'Well, Jackie, I'll be off now.' He stated and walked unsteadily toward the front door.

Jackie took a sip of her pint, the one Russell had just brought for her. She had one last look at the signs and then put the paint cans and cleaned brushes into plastic bags, making sure there were no spills anywhere. She set the bags by the signs and then walked to the bar, just as Nick rang the bell for last call.

'I better be going home as well. Russell said that drinking gives you a hairy chest, and right now I'm about as hairy as Sean Connery.' She grinned drunkenly and leaned against the bar.

'Uh, interesting, though a very disturbing thought,' Nick said and studied Jackie more closely. Jackie laughed and put her sweater on.

'I'll come back tomorrow morning to clean up the mess.' Jackie promised and let her eyes rest on Nick a little longer than usual. He really isn't a bad looking man, really. 'No, in fact,' Jackie thought, 'he is quite a handsome man, quite a handsome man indeed.' She smiled and finished her drink.

'Sure, no problem,' Nick said. 'Goodnight, Sean Connery. See you in the morning.'

Jackie walked out of the pub and stopped on the doorstep to breathe in the fresh air and admire the clear night sky. She glanced down beside her and there, by the wall, was Kenneth. He was sitting down on the ground and leaning his back against the old stone wall. At first, Jackie merely thought he had fallen asleep. It was a very strange place to sleep, but you never know what people themselves consider strange. Maybe it was perfectly normal for biology teachers, she thought. Finally, she understood. The quiet man had passed out.

'Kenneth! Kenneth?' Jackie called him, trying to wake him up. She bent down slowly and gave him a nudge on the arm. While she was down, Jackie realized that maybe she should not have drunk that last pint. She had to lean her one hand against the doorframe and her other hand on Kenneth's shoulder to steady herself while she willed her body to straighten up. She gave a small tap on Kenneth's shoulder.

He did not budge. Jackie pondered this awhile and admired the night sky again. Finally after an ineffective search for Orion in the sky, she turned around and walked back into the pub. She stopped at the threshold.

'Kenneth needs a bit of help outside. I think he has passed out.' She blurted, and then she smiled for absolutely no reason at all.

Everybody stared at her.

'Has he really?' Russell yelled.

'Yes, he's out like a rock.' Jackie steadied herself on to the doorframe and then suddenly giggled. She had no idea why she was laughing.

Russell, the boys and Nick hurried out.

They all stood there by the front door and stared at Kenneth, who looked like a man just having a casual afternoon nap in the middle of the night, in a flower bed by the pub's front door.

Jack Wilkinson nudged him on his shoulder, but nothing happened. Kenneth remained unmoved.

'He sure is a quiet drunk.' Calvin scratched the stubble on his chin.

'And a tall drunk, too.' Howard said and put his hat on.

Jack Wilkinson was about to say something, when Nick cut him off. 'No, you are not going to drive Kenneth home with your lawnmower.'

'But, the fresh air would do him good.' Jack Wilkinson protested loudly looking for the key in his pant pockets.

'No!' Nick said again. 'Definitely not.'

Jack sighed with a heavy disappointment and stood once more in silence staring at Kenneth.

Finally Nick spoke. 'Well, I'll go and get the car.' He went back into the empty pub to get his keys. On his way out he locked the front door and then went behind the house to get his car. Russell offered his help.

The boys were trying to get a hold of Kenneth's legs and arms to lift him up, but they failed. Kenneth fell silently down onto the ground. Jackie was observing all of this and leaning her back against the closed door. Her legs were tired. She began to giggle. It was the hysterical, exhausted late night giggle powered by excessive amounts of alcohol. The boys looked at her for a second, and then tried again to tug Kenneth's arm. The flowers were crushed flat in the flower bed. This all made Jackie laugh even more. She slid down to the ground, her knees almost touching her chin.

'Laugh away girl, maybe that will wake him up,' Russell said.

Nick parked his car in front of the pub and opened the back door. He looked at Jackie, who was still giggling sitting down at the doorstep and wiping the tears from her eyes. He smiled. It was not a dull night.

All of the men tried to grab Kenneth again and shove him onto the backseat of the car. Kenneth was a tall man with very long legs that kept unfolding and sticking out of the car before they were even able to close the door.

Jackie found this exceptionally amusing. She walked slowly to the other side of the car, climbed into the car and held Kenneth's knees bent as the men were trying to close the door. Jackie almost fell on top of him and she thought this was extraordinarily hilarious as well. She then got stuck between the seats and laughed even more.

'She sure is a happy girl.' Russell said to Nick and nudged his arm.

'Yes, she is.' Nick murmured and looked at Jackie who tried to turn around in the car.

Finally they got Kenneth pushed far enough into the car, so that they were able to close the door. It took a little while longer for Jackie to come out from the other side of the car. She seemed to have too many feet that got stuck in strange places and her arms were of no use either.

Nick helped her, pulling her by her hand. Finally she more fell out of the car than stepped out. She bumped into Nick and grinned merrily while she looked up into his eyes. 'Such lovely eyes,' she thought and leaned on him happily.

'Should I drive you home as well?' Nick asked and held onto Jackie, who found it a strangely comfortable place to be. She was trying to remember if she knew the colour of Nick's eyes.

'No, no. The fresh air will do me good.' Jackie smiled and snuggled into the crook of Nick's arm. It was a lovely place to be. She could stay there much longer. She could stay there for good, actually. The thought swam through her somewhat cloudy mind and it scared her.

'You're sure?' Nick was concerned. He held her tight, making sure that she did not fall.

'Positive…' Jackie slowly recommenced her balance and leaned away from Nick.

'Really?' Nick asked again wanting to make sure that everything was fine.

'Yes, yes.' She did her best to stand up straight. She put her hand on his chest and tapped him gently. 'You go and take the tall man home.' Her head was suddenly clearer.

Nick hesitated. He wasn't sure what to do, when Jackie said, 'I am all right and your car is full anyway.'

'All right then.' Nick sighed and straightened Jackie's jacket. He let his hand rest a while longer on her arm. Jackie swayed slightly, looking at the many buttons on Nick's shirt. She tried to focus, so that she could count them. Five or six…maybe more.

Nick looked at Jackie one last time just to make sure that she was all right, and then he got in on the driver's seat and Russell dropped down beside him on the passenger's side.

'Goodnight everybody.' Russell waved his hand in the royal manner and chuckled.

Jackie and the boys were watching them as they drove away and then, they too wished each other goodnight and began the long winding walk home, that felt longer than it actually was.

Later that night, on his way back home, Nick drove by Jackie's house. He slowed his car a little to have a look to make sure that she had gotten home safely. Jackie's bedroom light was on. He saw Felix's silhouette in the middle of the lit window frame. Otherwise her house was dark.

He smiled at the thought of Jackie's hairy chest and drove on.

Chapter 12

Recovery and Restoration

The next morning was as beautiful as a morning could be. The sun was shining brightly from the clear blue sky making the shadows sharp. The birds were singing as Jackie dragged her feet, which she felt were made from cement, slowly toward the pub. She tried to shield her eyes from the dazzling sunshine and cursed quietly that she had forgotten her hat. She also cursed her cheap sunglasses which let the sunlight leak in from the sides. She also wanted to curse the loud birds, but ran out of energy; her mouth was dry and bitter tasting.

Her eyes seemed to have grown hairs inside them and her forehead felt as if it were made from an ice block, slowly and painfully melting away.

She said good morning to people who walked by, but once they had passed, the expression on her face revealed the pain the effort had caused.

She stepped carefully into the pub, cursed the creaking front door and nodded very quietly to Nick.

'Good morning! How are you and your extremely hairy chest this morning?' Nick enquired loudly with a shameless grin on his face. 'Jesus mother of god, please don't shout or I will have to leave and go to Honey's Parisian tearoom instead.' Jackie sat gingerly on the barstool and slowly laid her pounding head against the tabletop, which was nice and cool against her hot, parched skin.

Nick was laughing, 'No, don't go to the tearoom. You might scare the old ladies. You know, being so hairy and all.'

'Please. Could I just have a cup of coffee, please.' Jackie's voice ascended weakly from under her folded arms. 'I didn't drink any at home because, honestly, I couldn't bend down to find the coffee can,' she explained feebly and remembered her pathetic attempt to get the coffee can from the bottom shelf of the cupboard. She grimaced. It had felt like a heavy brick had landed against her forehead when she had lowered her head past her knees. 'Mission impossible,' she had said as she had slowly straightened up and leaned against her cupboards, defeated. How many times had she promised not to drink that last drink? The road to hell was indeed paved with good intentions. Her old teacher's wise words echoed in her throbbing head.

'Well at least I don't have a new puppy.' Jackie attempted a smile, but the effort sent a flashing pain through her head and she gave up. Felix had been happy enough digging in the garden this morning. She would try to take him for a walk later in the afternoon.

Nick walked behind the bar and took a big mug from the shelf. He filled it with strong black coffee while watching Jackie. He tried not to laugh too loudly. 'Poor Jackie,' he thought as he took the milk out of the fridge.

'Did you get Kenneth back home all right?' Jackie asked.

'Yeah, Russell and I carried him into the house and dropped him off onto his sofa. For a skinny man, he sure weighs a lot.'

'That was very nice of you, Nick.'

Nick handed Jackie the coffee, which Jackie more than gratefully accepted. 'Bless you, Nicholas Matthew O'Neill.'

'Customer relations. I have to help my hairy regulars.' Nick smiled and shrugged his shoulders.

Jackie took a long, slow drink and sighed deeply as the hot liquid warmed her insides and brought her back to life. The block of ice on her forehead began to melt and she felt her whole face relax.

'Thank you, you saved my totally unworthy and extremely painful life.'

Nick leaned both his elbows on the table, his eyes on Jackie. He had something on his mind, but he could not decide if this was the right moment.

'You had quite a night last night,' he finally said. His words falling sparsely from his lips, each word separated by a momentary pause.

Jackie looked up through her throbbing existence into Nick's sympathetic eyes. 'Yeah, people gave me drinks here and there. Oh god! Way too many of them.' Then a happy thought swam slowly into Jackie's pain-filled head. 'But luckily we got our work done.' She congratulated herself that now she could cross one more item off from her momentous to-do list. The list appeared to be never ending. 'Would the studio tour ever be a reality?' She sighed deeply.

Nick looked at her and mumbled something sympathetically, slowly straightened himself and grunted. 'Well—I had a look at those signs this morning.' He paused and thought about how to say what he intended to say. He shifted his weight from foot to foot, buried his hands deep in his pockets and finally added grudgingly, 'and you might have a little wee problem.' Nick rubbed his chin. 'I think.' He didn't like to be the messenger of bad news. He walked out from behind the bar, trying to avoid Jackie's shocked eyes, now glued to him.

Jackie felt as if she was in a very, very bad dream where huge boats sink and innocent people die by the thousands. Her throbbing skull had stopped pulling apart, but now her whole body was cold. She shivered in anguish.

Nick walked hesitantly to the pile of signs and Jackie followed him as though in a trance.

'What do mean…wwwha…whha…what kind of problem?' Fright made her rasp.

'This kind.' Nick lifted one sign and tentatively turned it around.

Jackie stared at the sign for a very long time. She was trying to see and at the same time trying to ignore the evidence in front of her. She was still hoping to avoid a catastrophe.

On top of the sign was the word *Studio* and below *Tour* stencilled upside down.

She drew her breath in sharply, giving her stomach a jolt. Her heart skipped a beat.

'Or maybe this kind.' Nick continued and picked up another sign to show her. This time both of the words were the right way up, but they pointed down toward the right-hand corner of the sign, like little steps leading down from an Italian medieval hill-top town.

'Or it could be as bad as this one.' Nick lifted up the third sign and turned it toward Jackie. The words were in the wrong order—*Tour Studio*—and there were handprints all around its edges.

Jackie could not talk. Her hands were feeling for a chair. Her knees felt weak. She sat down and cupped her head in her hands, leaning her elbows on her shaky knees. Nick looked at her, hesitated a moment, but then carried on. 'And then we have couple of these.' He lifted up a sign. It said *Stuoid Tuor*.

'There are quite interesting new words in here, actually,' he added as an afterthought. He glanced at the pile while holding the sign up, and then, at the sight of Jackie's ghostly face, he thought maybe he better say nothing more.

Jackie was devastated. She could hardly move her lips to speak. 'Are…are they all like this?' She finally asked with a small voice that did not seem to belong to her.

'No, no; there are a few good ones.' Nick was trying to sound optimistic. It was a feeble try, but he meant well.

'Oh my god.' Jackie sighed and held her aching head with both hands.

She leaned her head against her knees for a long time, or so it seemed to Nick, who was standing helplessly by the wrecked signs. Finally Jackie lifted her head and looked up. There was resignation and determination in her eyes. Her face was hard, and Nick thought that Rosalind might have found her match in fortitude.

Jackie got up. 'Well, I'm already feeling beyond crappy, so I might as well go through them all right now.' Her voice was flat. She finished her coffee in one swallow and then, holding her hands on her hips, walked to the pile by the wall. She picked up the first sign and, with Nick's help, she began going through them. They divided the signs into two piles: good and bad. There could have been a third pile dedicated to the ones beyond help, but unfortunately she needed them all. All the mistakes would have to be fixed, even if it meant that she'd have to prime them once more and begin from scratch. This time she would do them herself in her studio. She would definitely not paint them in the pub, and she would definitely paint them without Russell's heart warming help.

'Thank God we did not paint any arrows!' Jackie suddenly blurted out and a few giggles escaped from her lips.

Nick looked at her for a moment as if he had misheard her, but then he too burst out laughing. The ridiculous thought of the multiple mistakes that arrows offered was too much.

'Ahh...my head hurts,' Jackie moaned between her hysterical giggles. This whole idea of the studio tour began, again, to feel doomed, but instead of creeping desperation grabbing a hold of her, Jackie felt that the power to control the tour's future was so far beyond her that she could do nothing but laugh. 'There was no way the tour would ever succeed,' she thought, and this very thought made her laugh again. She must have been a fool to even think that she could handle this bunch of people.

Nick put his hand on Jackie's shoulder and pulled her slightly toward him. 'Don't worry. I'll help you fix them all.' He said half laughing and half speaking.

Jackie was wiping the tears from her eyes. 'Thanks Nick. I really appreciate your help.' She looked up at Nick and smiled the best she could without hurting her aching head.

'No problem. Any time.' Nick fixed a loose strand of Jackie's hair and smiled. Jackie experienced a strange, inexplicable feeling in her stomach, but she wasn't sure if it was the hangover or something else.

Puzzled by this sudden, but not unwelcome feeling of closeness, Jackie accepted Nick's offer for late breakfast before carrying the disastrous signs together into Jackie's workshop. They primed the signs again with the little bit of white paint that still lingered in the bottom of the paint cans.

Jackie wiped her hair from her face. 'I guess I should have done the whole job myself from the beginning, but I thought that a group activity, like last night's event, would bring the group closer together and make the future meetings slightly easier.' She sighed as she looked at the still wet boards lined up against the wall, loosening her ponytail to tie it back again, catching the stubborn missing strands.

'The idea of the group activity *was* a good one. Everybody enjoyed themselves. Never mind the sign disaster,' Nick said, wanting somehow to make Jackie feel better.

'Well, I have to admit it was fun watching Rosalind get advice from Russell!' Jackie laughed.

'Yes, I think you all would agree on that—even maybe Alistair,' Nick said, smiling, as he washed the paint brushes in the sink. 'So you have succeeded in creating a sort of a cohesive group,' he added positively and squeezed more white paint off the brush. He watched as the white pigment became lighter and lighter in the running water till there was only clear water. He turned off the tap and put the brushes upside down in a metal tin sitting on the shelf above the sink.

'Well,' he said, not knowing what else to say. 'We are done, for now at least,' he finally added and wiped his hands on a towel. He leaned against the sink and watched Jackie taping together some of the more roughly used templates. Her mouth was in a thin line, twisting slightly as the tape got stuck to her fingers. Unsaid curse words hung in the air.

Jackie glanced up and smiled. 'Yes I think you are right.' Then she looked at the poorly fixed stencil that would have to do. 'Thanks for your help, Nick. I can do the stencilling later on tonight myself.' Not that she didn't want Nick's help. He was very nice to have around, but she didn't want him to think she was using him. 'There's not so much to do anymore.'

Nick nodded reluctantly. He had no objections to helping Jackie with the signs. Actually, he had rather enjoyed their late morning together.

He glanced at his watch and to his dismay realized that it was time for him to go to the pub. Rose was going to the dentist and he had promised to fill in for her. Most of the time he liked owning a pub, but at times like these he would have liked a more normal schedule. He needed some time off.

'I'll be off.' He grunted and put his jacket slowly on. 'I need to go back to the pub.'

Jackie watched him walk out to the garden and scratch behind Felix's ear before opening the gate and walking away to the pub. All of a sudden she felt alone. She absentmindedly fingered the battered templates before slowly returning to her workshop. She put the templates beside the boards. She would paint the words later, but now she would have to get to work. She had received a large order for peppermills and salt grinders. There was not a lot of time to produce them all and she would have to work many late nights. First she would have to turn the peppermill and saltshaker shapes. Then she would have to drill the spaces for the grinding mechanisms. Each single peppermill took a lot of time as it went through each various and difficult stage in woodturning. The sanding stage held mixed feelings for her; on one hand, it was her least favourite part. The dust always made her cough and sneeze, despite the mask she wore. But at the same time, it meant that the work was almost done. After that she would have to stain the finished peppermills and salt grinders.

On bad days Jackie wondered why she did this kind of work for a living. It would be much easier to work for somebody else. On good days, though, she would not change a thing. On those days she loved it all: the smell of sawdust, the sound of the lathe, the empty, silent studio in the morning when anything was possible. It still made her mad when people wondered why her peppermills were more expensive than the mass-produced ones they could easily buy from a department store.

She set a piece of wood into the lathe, adjusting it carefully before beginning her work. Today was going to be easier than most days. The new gallery had ordered simple forms—slightly tapered cylinders with some patterns, and she had already done the needed diagonal inlays. Now she would just have to make the shapes.

Jackie enjoyed the planning, the stage others might have thought of as tedious. She loved finding ways to work more efficiently and with less cost—cost always being present, hiding in the dust, making itself known without a word.

'How to make beautiful things as cheaply as possible? Where was that fine line between a compromise and selling your soul? That is the most interesting question every designer is forced to ask at some point,' Jackie thought as she worked. She enjoyed being by herself in her workshop, nestled in the quiet of her own imagination while the radio played in the background, connecting her to the outside world.

She worked late into the evening, catching up on those hours she had spent lying in bed suffering from the effects of the previous night's sign-painting venture.

She set the almost ready peppermills on the table and rechecked the list of colours the gallery had ordered. She would need to mix more yellow, and she would need to order more grinder parts. She could make the whole order in one week, but she would have to work around the clock. The faster she shipped the order, the faster she would get her payment. She wrote her tomorrow's to-do list on her information board, looked at the work she had done today and then went to call Felix. It was long past time for his evening walk.

The village was quiet as she and Felix walked down the streets to the beach near the yacht club. The wind was blowing from the sea. Jackie looked at the beach and laughed at Felix who was frolicking in the sand, smelling and investigating, preparing to dig a hole for no particular reason.

By the time she left the beach, with Felix disapproving of her decision, John was by his worm machine filling the coke cans with the results of his digging in his wife's garden. Cybil hated him digging in her garden, so John was forced to do it secretly when she was at her quilting club at the church. If questioned, he would blame her dog for the deep holes between the flowers. That bloody mutt got more sausages than he did anyway. John waved his hand and bellowed his greetings into the windy late evening. He was going fishing tomorrow, for sure. The weather forecast had promised a sun filled day.

Jackie got home and only then did she remember the signs in her studio. They would have to wait. She was going to have a sandwich for dinner and then lie comfortably on the sofa with her tired feet up on a pillow. She was going to drink tea and try to find something decent to watch on the TV, something that didn't have dying people, dead people, sick people or murders-in-making.

'Mission impossible,' she thought as she clicked the remote's buttons. 'Just like the studio tour.'

Chapter 13

Lazarus

The pub was fairly empty. Nick was, as always, behind the bar; wiping the counters, filling the pints and trying to keep Rose's well-meant advice beyond his earshot. It was a normal, quiet, after-lunch afternoon in the middle of the week. Suddenly Jack Wilkinson stormed into the pub. He looked shocked, his face was ashen and his eyes sank more deeply than usual into his thin weathered face.

'I need a glass of scotch, Nick.' He croaked and stretched his hand across the bar while leaning onto the counter heavily.

'Are you all right?' Nick asked and looked at Jack at the same time as he took out the glass and the bottle. He poured him a large drink. If Jack could not talk, the matter must be very serious.

'You all right, Jack?' Howard and Calvin walked quickly to the bar from their official corner table. They leaned against the bar holding onto their pints with their rough hands and waited patiently for Jack to tell them what had happened.

Jack took a huge gulp of his scotch and coughed as the strong liquid burned his insides. Everybody anxiously waited. It was not normal for Jack to behave like this. Jack paused for a moment and let the scotch settle. The deep lines of skin enveloped his forehead as he closed his eyes collecting his thoughts.

'You will never guess what I just heard,' he said, and then took another swig from his drink before delivering his news. 'That damn Glenn has dropped dead!'

The pub became silent as the news sank in. The air was heavy and everybody's eyes were on Jack Wilkinson and his sad, wrinkled face.

Nick was first to break the unnatural stillness. 'What? That can't be right,' he whispered in shock. 'I just saw him here last night and he seemed all right then.'

'That's right,' Howard blurted, jabbing his finger toward the floor. 'He was right here with us as always. Wasn't he, Calvin?' He turned to Calvin to have his words seconded.

'Sure was.' Calvin agreed and nodded his head strongly. His eyes looked suddenly wet.

The two old boys were shaking their heads and looking into their pints. Their best mate Glenn dead. That couldn't be, could it?

'What happened?' Nick had to ask it because nobody else did.

All heads turned toward the bar. Everybody was listening in stunned silence.

'Heart attack.'

'Who told you?' Nick was astounded.

Jack took another big gulp of his scotch. 'I was at the hardware store looking for some nails, when I overheard Mrs. Cullighan talking to Bridget—you know, the girl at the till, the redhead…you know… the one with…' He made some gestures with his hands suggesting a very well-formed bosom.

The boys agreed with this very vital piece of information and nodded their heads again, encouraging him to go on with his story.

'And as you all know, Mrs. Cullighan knows first who is dead, because she always makes the wreaths for funerals.'

The boys agreed again, bobbing their heads up and down. Yes, everybody knew Mrs. Cullighan, whether they liked it or not.

Nick looked at Jack and shook his head slightly, remembering the stories Mrs. Cullighan had started when he and Denise had separated.

'Nothing escapes that woman's ears.' Calvin stammered remembering the time when the story of his drinking had reached his wife's ears, helped on by Mrs. Cullighan. Loraine's sofa bed hadn't been that comfortable. His back still bothered him because of those two weeks he had spent sleeping on it in his son's house. And that Loraine was not a bunch of roses either.

'Nope, nothing.' Howard mumbled having been in the exact same situation as Calvin. His ears had rung for days afterwards. No wonder his wife sang in the church choir. She did have an extremely strong and high voice. 'The angels in heaven for sure have gotten a good preview of her and her booming voice,' he thought and put his hands into his pockets trying to find a handkerchief amongst the nuts and bolts.

Just about then, the door opened and in walked Jackie. 'Hi Nick! Hi Boys! What's up?' She hollered cheerfully, tossed her jacket on the back of a chair and sat down.

'Glenn's dead. Heart attack.' Jack blurted and then stared at the wall behind the bar. His eyes were misty.

Howard and Calvin were shaking their heads in unison, eyes on their pints.

'My god! That's awful! When did it happen?' Jackie's eyes opened wide as she stared at the heartbreaking sight of these three men in front of her.

'Last night. The ambulance came but he was already dead by then.' Jack was getting into the heavy details now.

Howard and Calvin shook their heads. Calvin coughed a couple of times. Howard blew his nose noisily into an old handkerchief, wiping the tears quickly from his cheeks as he carefully patted his reddening nose.

These old childhood friends were trying to be brave. 'That is just awful. I saw him only yesterday here in the pub. He seemed all right.' Jackie said, trying to make some kind of comforting conversation.

'Sure did. Talked even about politics and cursed his wife as always.' Jack remembered. 'The same as always. Same as always.' He added sadly.

'Oh, poor Ginny! We should send her flowers.' Jackie suddenly realized.

'I'll pitch in.' Nick offered and took some money out of the till.

Jack scratched his beard and glanced at Howard and Calvin beside him, 'How about it boys? Some flowers for Ginny?'

Calvin and Howard nodded their heads yet again. They seemed to have lost all their ability to speak and they could only communicate by nodding or shaking their heads. All three put their hands in their pockets.

The other grief stricken customers reached into their pockets as well and came over to the bar. It was a small village, after all and one person's grief was everybody's grief.

The boys were given kind words as if they were the joint widow of Glenn Wright. They received many pats on their backs and the money was given to Jackie to purchase flowers for Ginny, Glenn's much feared wife.

Everybody talked about Glenn and what a nice fellow he had been. Many stories were told: some true, some exaggerated and some totally false, spiced up with a couple of pints. These included the one about Glenn and the former Miss Universe and a secret, passion-filled love affair that took place in Mexico in the sixties. Glenn's name was mentioned in every single sentence that was uttered in the pub that afternoon.

Jack, Howard and Calvin were remembering the old times and the nearly deadly run-ins with Glenn's wife Ginny. It was time to map his life and their fifty-odd years together as 'the boys.' Now they were going to be the boys minus one. It wouldn't be the same without Glenn.

Jackie put the money into her pocket and slipped off her chair. 'I'll go to Mrs. Cullighan's and get something nice,' she told the sad crowd.

Nick looked at her quickly and asked if she was coming back later that night. As soon as he said it, he regretted it.

'Yes, I think I might pop in for a few minutes later on, if you want.'

Nick sighed happily and then added in haste, 'It's not necessary. I mean if you have something else, but…Good. Okay, see you tonight then.' Afraid that he had said too much, he hastily turned around. All Jackie could see was his back.

'Okay,' she said to Nick's back, shrugged her shoulders and walked out the door.

Mrs. Cullighan's Flower Shop was down the street from the pub. In fact just about everything in the village was down the street from the pub. If you were given instructions how to find your way somewhere in the village, you most likely would to be told, 'You can't miss it. It's just down the street from the pub.' That was the official saying. 'No worries. It's just down the street from the pub. Five minutes, tops.'

There was also the Bermuda triangle of information right in the centre of the village; the post office, the church and then the infamous Mrs. Cullighan's Flower shop.

Jackie opened the flower shop's door and walked into a small shop filled with floral aromas: lilies, roses, carnations and tulips. Behind the counter was a middle-aged woman in a bright floral dress. She was wrapping flowers and talking busily to a woman across the counter.

They were obviously gossiping; the other woman was leaning into Mrs. Cullighan to make sure she did not miss a single vital word of what was known as The Truth.

Jackie could hear Mrs. Cullighan's authoritative voice: '…found him dead…right there on the floor.'

The other woman gasped and her hand flew up to cover her lips, which uttered in horror, 'No!' Pam Johnson was clearly shocked and she pulled away from the counter, and then leaned in again to hear more gruesome details.

'Yes. He was dead all right,' said Mrs. Cullighan and nodded her head knowingly. She smacked her lips and let the information sink in before she continued with the great pleasure of a person who happens to be the first to deliver bad news. Mrs. Cullighan never got tired of that feeling.

'Poor Ginny! She has suffered a lot and'—Mrs. Cullighan tightened the string with a skilful yank—'now this.' Her voice had that perfect pitch of sadness and sympathy.

'Yes,' agreed Pam Johnson enthusiastically. 'Wasn't she in the hospital last year? What was it again?' She tried to remember, but Mrs. Cullighan was faster.

'Hysterectomy.' She declared knowingly.

'That's right and she did have some complications, didn't she?'

'Yes. The poor woman. She did. Awful time. She almost died you know.'

The two women suddenly noticed that Jackie was within earshot and quickly straightened up, ending their conversation.

Mrs. Cullighan cleared her throat in a well-practised manner and made a hush-hush gesture, giving Pam Johnson a last knowing nod. 'I'll tell you later,' the nod seemed to say. Mrs. Cullighan looked up at Jackie and greeted her with a smile. 'Good afternoon, Jacqueline. How are you?'

Jackie was smiling. She knew that she and all the minor details of her life would be discussed as well. 'Good, good and you?' She answered.

Mrs. Cullighan gave a theatrical sigh, and with an equally theatrical gesture, wiped her hand across her forehead. 'Same old, same old. You know.'

She quickly finished wrapping the bouquet of flowers. Pam would come back later and then they could talk some more about poor Ginny and, perhaps, about Jackie and that artists' group of hers.

When the door closed behind Pam Johnson, Mrs. Cullighan turned toward Jackie. 'Poor woman. Her mother has been ill for weeks and the doctors don't know what's wrong with her. Talk about modern medicine. I told her to fix her a nice cup of chamomile tea with honey. That's what I do when the weather gets the worst of me. Chamomile tea and cod liver oil and her mother will be on her two feet in no time at all. That's what I told her.'

Jackie was trying hard not to smile, because she knew that Pam Johnson's mother was 93 years old and she had been in a wheelchair for the last five years. It seemed very unlikely that she would ever be on her two feet again.

'And what can I get for you, Jackie?' Mrs. Cullighan's sharp voice cut into Jackie's thoughts.

'Oh, I need to send some flowers to Ginny Wright.' She pulled the handful of bills and coins out of her pocket and dropped them on the counter.

'Ah, yes! Poor Ginny. Horrible thing, just horrible.' Mrs. Cullighan said with a voice filled with exactly the right amount of sympathy, a talent acquired from many years of practice.

'Yes it is. It is sad.' Jackie agreed. 'This is from all the people at the pub.' She pointed at the pile of money before beginning to count it.

'So what kind of bouquet would you like me to make?' Mrs. Cullighan's sharp eyes glanced over the organized stack of bills on the counter.

'I don't know. I will trust your better judgment, Mrs. Cullighan. You're the expert.' Jackie was shamelessly flattering Mrs. Cullighan.

Mrs. Cullighan was very pleased by her words, and she busied herself with the flowers. She picked up some greenery from one vase and added it to the flowers already in her hand. Mrs. Cullighan loved when she was told that she knew what was the best. She, of course, knew what was the best for everybody, and she had told so to many of her customers. Still, she appreciated when this was acknowledged. She fixed one unruly freesia among the white roses and then added some steel grass. She held the bouquet at arm's length and studied it critically. A few more sprigs of steel grass and it would be perfect.

Jackie was choosing a card from the display by the counter.

'The pens are beside the cash register, dear.' Mrs. Cullighan's voice interrupted Jackie's thoughts.

'Oh, thanks.' Jackie picked up a traditional flowery card with a golden border and began writing the condolences.

The door was opened with a loud bang and Mrs. Cullighan's teenage son stomped in. 'Hi, Mom!' He hollered and then saw that he had brought in a pile of sand with his shoes, again.

Jackie looked up from the card she was writing. 'Hi, Steven.' She smiled to him. Steven only nodded shyly. He looked everywhere except at Jackie's face.

'Steven! After you have eaten your snack, I have a delivery for you to make.' Mrs. Cullighan said loudly as Steven disappeared into the back of the shop. 'Steven does all my deliveries. You keep the children busy; you keep them out of trouble. That's what I have always said.' Mrs. Cullighan spoke proudly of her son with her distinctive know-it-all edge.

Steven made a face in the kitchen and opened the fridge. He was starving.

Mrs. Cullighan had finished the bouquet and was admiring the results. It can be said with honesty that she was the best admirer of her own work. It gave her as much pleasure as passing on newly overheard information.

'Thank you Mrs. Cullighan.' Jackie said. 'That is a beautiful bouquet!

You have a way with colours,' she added and gave the card to Mrs. Cullighan to place in the bouquet.

Mrs. Cullighan was pleased to hear compliments and she smiled, keeping her mouth closed. Only the corners of her mouth moved up slightly, giving just a hint that she might be happy. 'Thank you, Jackie. I'll send Steven to take these to Ginny.'

After Jackie left, Steven came back into the store holding a sandwich in his hands.

'I need you to deliver this to Ginny Wright?' Mrs. Cullighan told Steven. Then, sniffing the air, she abruptly grabbed her son's arm and pulled him closer. She looked him straight in the eyes. 'Have you been smoking?' Steven tried to pull away but in vain. His mother was surprisingly strong.

'Of course not, Mom. It's the other kids. I would never smoke. You know that.'

Mrs. Cullighan looked at her son suspiciously, but then decided to let him go. Steven shoved the rest of the sandwich into his mouth and shook his jacket sleeve to straighten the crease created by his mother's strong fingers. With the other hand he smoothed his short hair. He grabbed the bouquet and walked out of the shop. He was cursing his mother silently when he picked up his bike. Early experience had taught him to swear inaudibly. He put the flowers into the big delivery basket on the back of his bike and slowly bicycled through the village. The Wright's house was just down the street from the pub.

Steven was hoping to get a glance of Hilary as he bicycled past her beauty parlour. He got his hair trimmed often and he loved the attention Hilary gave him. He loved especially when she fluffed his hair back and forth with her fingers and cooed. 'You little devil. You'll be a lady killer one day with those long eyelashes of yours.' Yes, Steven's hair was the shortest in his class. He twisted his neck for one last look before turning onto a small country road.

The hilly road bent around an old oak tree before reaching the flat fields where Glenn and Ginny's house stood. It was easy cycling down the steep road, but coming back was going to be hard work.

Steven hopped off his bike and leaned it against the fencepost. He walked to the front door of the house and knocked, hearing the dogs barking inside and a woman's robust voice telling them to bugger off.

Ginny Wright opened the door. She was a big, heavy woman with a very stern face that seldom smiled, because, according to her, there wasn't much to smile about. Her mouth remained a thin, sharp line even as she spoke.

'Flowers for you, ma'am.' Steven said loudly. At first Ginny stared blankly at Steven and then slowly her eyes recognized the large flower bouquet that he was waving in front of her face. Distractedly, she took the flowers. She was completely bewildered.

Steven left swiftly, hopping back onto his bike. Somehow he didn't feel like staying. After his mother, Ginny Wright was perhaps the next scariest woman on the island.

Ginny was still standing at the door holding the flower bouquet in her big rough working hands. She picked up the card that had been tucked into the bouquet, closed the door and went into the kitchen. She put the flowers on the table, slowly opened the envelope and read out loud.

'Our deepest sympathies for the loss of your husband. He will be truly missed. You are in our thoughts…' She stopped in mid sentence and stared. Her anger began to rise inside her like a big steam engine ready to start its journey.

She read the card slowly once more, her eyes narrowing with fury. With her other hand she grabbed the bouquet and stormed out of the kitchen and out the back door into the garden where Glenn was sitting beside a compost heap, shovel by his side. He was peacefully smoking a cigarette, watching the plume of smoke disappear into the sky. 'Lovely blue sky,' he thought as he puffed.

When he heard Ginny's heavy footsteps, he quickly threw the cigarette into the compost heap, grabbed his shovel and was struggling to his feet as she arrived.

Ginny's shrill voice cut the air. 'What's this? Some kind of a joke from your useless friends at the pub!' She shook the flowers violently.

Glenn truly had no idea what his wife was talking about. He knew that the boys would never punish him so savagely that they would send a joke of any kind to his wife. 'What is what, dear?' he enquired with a soft voice. He wiped the imaginary pearls of sweat from his forehead and looked at his wife.

'These flowers!' Ginny screamed and shoved the bouquet closer to his face.

'What about them?' He looked at the flowers. 'Why would someone send you flowers?' Glenn asked gently. He was as puzzled as his wife.

'Your friends think that you are dead.'

'They do what?' Glenn exclaimed. His shovel dropped from his hands.

'They think you're dead.' Ginny screeched and the flowers danced dangerously in the air.

'They do?' Glenn stared at Ginny in complete amazement.

'Yes.' Ginny spoke now slowly, leaning dangerously toward Glenn's frail figure.

'Well, I'll be darned. Me, dead?' Glenn looked at himself, stretched his fingers and started to find the idea of him being dead extremely funny.

That was it. Ginny let go of her anger. She was like a big, monstrous volcano that had been collecting strength and was now ready to burst with a magnificent lava flow. The first words that she spat out, made Glenn jump. He stared at Ginny with the look of an old wet dog on his weathered face.

'The only bloody time you arrange to send me flowers, is when your friends think you're dead.' Ginny's voice was as strong as she looked. It thundered over the tranquil landscape, sending the birds in the nearby bush flying, chirping loudly as they passed over Ginny's greying head.

'Did I get flowers on my birthday? NO!'

'Did I get flowers on our bloody anniversary? NO!'

'Did I get flowers on Mother's day? NO!'

'When do I get flowers? When?'

She had to stop to breathe and then she bellowed out the last words.

'I get flowers when the whole goddamn village thinks you are DEAD!' She stopped for a second and then roared with all her might.

'You useless piece of skin! GET OUT!'

It was as if Glen had been waiting for this moment to come. He adjusted his loose pants by pulling them up by the belt and, for a small frail man, he ran surprisingly swiftly to his bike, which was in front of the house leaning against the wall already pointing toward the pub.

He could still hear Ginny wailing behind the house.

'You useless piece of skin...USELESS. USELESS I SAY, USELESS!'

Glenn started bicycling toward the village. From previous experience he knew it would be worthwhile to stay away from his home, for at least the next six hours or so. Luckily he knew just the place to go. He peddled by the old twisty oak tree that stood majestically by the road. Steven was sitting underneath it, resting his back comfortably against its thick trunk. His bike was lying beside him in the shade provided by the large braches of the old tree. He looked very relaxed and contented as he smoked his joint.

Steven looked up when he heard Glenn passing by on his old rattling bike. His eyes followed the speedy little dead man bicycling up the hill almost as fast as Steven had done on his way down the hill to the farm a while earlier. Steven could not believe his eyes.

When Glenn had disappeared behind a curb, Steven turned his head slowly around and studied his joint for a good long time, before he took another long unhurried drag and muttered to himself. 'Wow, cool stuff, man.'

By now the pub was full of people mourning the loss of Glenn Wright and toasting his memory. 'Poor Glenn. He was a grand lad,' Howard said with a heavy, shaken voice. His wrinkled handkerchief was sticking out of his pocket.

'He'll sure be missed.' Jack patted Howard's back comfortingly.

'Here's to Glenn!' George from the hardware store proposed.

'Hear hear, to Glenn!' the mixed voices filled the air.

'I'll get the next round.' Someone offered.

People lifted their pints to cheer again. A wave of the sound of glasses touching went round the pub.

Glenn opened the door and stepped into the pub. He was somewhat breathless after bicycling so fast up that hill. At the sound of the door opening, everybody turned to look. When they saw Glenn wheezing by the door, all voices stopped as if cut with a knife. People froze in their very places. They were still holding their pints in midair; their mouths hung open; their eyes stuck on Glenn's slight figure by the door.

Nick was the first person to recover from the shock. 'Glenn?' he muttered, utterly confused.

Jackie stared at Glenn as well. 'What on earth?' she managed to say.

Glenn staggered to the bar. 'Give me a pint, will you, Nick? That crazy wife of mine is at it again.' He leaned against the counter as if beaten. Jackie gave him more room, continuing to stare in amazement.

Jack, Howard and Calvin approached Glenn slowly. They were quite drunk already having toasted Glenn's memory all afternoon. From their previous beer-drinking knowledge they knew not to trust their vision one hundred percent at the present time.

'Bloody hell! Is that you, Glenn? We thought you were dead.' Jack Wilkinson blurted out and poked him hard just to make sure.

Glenn was drinking his beer as if he was dying of thirst. He wiped the froth from his mouth and looked at the 'boys.' He rubbed his arm where Jack Wilkinson had punched him. 'It's me all right. I escaped from one of Ginny's fits again. Lord that woman is scary!' He took another grand sip and then looked at the boys again.

'But we heard you were dead. Heart attack and all.' Howard whispered, his eyes as round as plates.

'Naah.' Glenn was laughing.

'We thought you were dead.' Calvin's voice was slurred.

'Why is that?' Glenn was utterly surprised.

Nick was looking at the four of them. He was happy to find Glenn alive and well, and he was also amused by the strange situation caused by Glenn's sudden resurrection. People were crowding around Glenn.

It was an amazing sight: the ought-to-be-dead man drinking a pint.

Nick cleared his throat. 'Jack here told us that he heard at the hardware store that you were dead.'

'Me, dead? I'll be darned.' Glenn stopped for a second, pursed his lips and considered the options. 'Well...I guess I would have been if my wife had gotten her big hands around my neck.' He chuckled at the thought.

'Have a pint on me, Glenn. Glad to have you back, Lazarus.' George from the hardware store came around and slapped Glenn's bony shoulders.

Nick poured another pint for Glenn. 'Here you go, Lazarus,' he said and winked.

'Thanks. It's sure good to be back.' Glenn laughed widely, showing his missing tooth. He drank the offered pints cheerfully. People came to talk with him. They gave him a pat on the back and welcomed him back to the world of the living. Many offered him pints to celebrate his return to life.

'I'll be darned if it isn't Glenn Wright. Have a pint on me, old boy.' And so another pint was being poured for Glenn.

'Hey Lazarus, tell us how does it feel to be back with us ordinary folks?' A man across the room yelled.

'Grand, just grand.' Glenn beamed.

'How were the heavenly gates?' the man continued.

'Looked just like the doors to this pub.' Glenn lifted his almost empty pint and made a toast as he spoke.

The pastor came to the bar to buy himself a drink. He glanced at Glenn and then turned back to Nick as he took his money out of his pocket to pay for his beer. 'Pour Lazarus another pint on me, will you Nick?' the pastor said quietly. 'It's not often that we have such a religious incident in this village.'

'Sure thing.' Nick said and grinned.

'To Glenn! The Lazarus of Sycamore!' Their slightly slurred voices roared into the night. Somewhere near the end of the night Glenn leaned over to Jack and tried to whisper something, but because he was so drunk his whisper turned into a hissing yell and was heard in every corner of the pub.

'This is the best wake a man can have.'

At the bar Jackie turned to Nick and asked as she put her empty glass down. 'I wonder who died then?'

Nick rubbed his chin and said, 'I really don't know.'

'Strange?' Jackie shook her head and got up, Nick's hand managing to brush hers as he picked up her empty glass, their eyes briefly meeting. She wished everybody goodnight. It had been a wake to remember.

The celebration continued till closing time, when all the blissfully drunken men were politely asked to leave the pub.

'I'm sorry lads, but it is time to go home,' Nick said loudly over the noise. The men finished their last drinks and the celebration party exited two or three at the same time, and for a while there was a blockage at the door. Finally everyone was outside. The light from the pub illuminated the men from behind as they stood in front of the door trying to get used to the dark blue light of the night.

One by one they zipped up their jackets, put their hats on and bid goodnight to the rest of the group, crisscrossing across the narrow road, grateful that Mary Cullighan was already fast asleep. In the end the boys were the only ones standing in front of the pub, swaying back and forth, keeping their hands in their pockets.

'Damn good wake, I say.' Glenn uttered with his one eye closed.

They all nodded their heads in unison and admired the night sky.

The next morning, Nick was reading the local newspaper in the pub with a cup of coffee steaming in front of him. He leafed through the national pages and then glanced at the social notices, second only in detail to Mary Cullighan's notices. 'Waste of perfectly good of paper,' Nick thought and turned the page. He came to the obituaries and something caught his eye. He paused to straighten out the paper and then leaned in to see the article better.

'Gwen Right dies at home in her sleep at 89. She was a well respected and loved teacher at the Sycamore Primary School where she worked tirelessly for 35 years. She leaves behind her niece Annabelle Right and her family.

'The funeral was held on 24th of June at the Sycamore Presbyterian Church.'

Nick turned slowly to look at the calendar on the wall. The red day marker was on top of the 26th of June. 'Damn! I wonder if anybody went?' Nick rubbed his chin and felt guilty.

Miss Gwen Right had been his teacher as well. She might have been more respected and feared than loved, but nevertheless she had relentlessly hammered the times tables into the heads of Sycamoreans for those 35 years. 'Even Nelson could do better than that,' he remembered Miss Gwen once snapping at him. Nelson was her cat and the class always thought of him as their competitor.

Needless to say, the class always lost and Nelson, a fat tabby who never attended any classes, excelled.

'Nelson, the bloody Einstein.' Nick smiled, and wondered, again, if anybody had gone to the memorial service.

Chapter 14

Oil and Water

Jackie had successfully guided another studio tour meeting to the end. Harriet had not publicly attacked Rosalind and Russell had not talked about his sex life any more than usual. All in all, everything seemed, finally, to be going in the right direction.

She organized her miscellaneous papers into one large pile and tapped the heap against the table to make its corners even. Luckily nobody had anything to add and Jackie gladly declared the meeting over and almost smiled.

'That's it then. Meeting adjourned. I'll call the reporter and, hopefully, I'll get him to come here to write a story about us for the newspaper.'

Rosalind cut in. 'Remember to take him to Maximilian's for lunch.'

'I'll do my best.' Jackie's answers to Rosalind had become automatic. Say something, but keep it very vague and say it like you mean it. That was the best way to keep Rosalind contented and, at the same time, guarantee peace and happiness for the rest of the group.

Russell tapped his hands loudly against his stomach. 'Good. I'm mighty thirsty. How about a pint, lads?'

All the men murmured yes and walked together to the bar. Nick was already filling pints for them. Even Kenneth was joining them at the bar. He still didn't say much, but he seemed to enjoy the company.

Jackie put her neatly organized papers into her bag and walked to the bar.

She was buying herself a drink when Caroline sat down beside her.

'Two martinis, would you be so kind, Nick.' Caroline said coolly. The sweet scent of her perfume drifted toward Jackie.

'That Thomas is gorgeous, don't you think?' she murmured. 'Almost edible.' She took a long drag of her cigarette and then blew the smoke in Thomas's direction.

Jackie was not quite sure what Caroline was after. She didn't know how to respond to such a question, if it even was a question. 'It depends what you like, I guess.' She finally said, suspicious of this sudden act of friendliness by Caroline.

'I'm going to seduce him and then I'm going to use him till there is nothing left of him.' Caroline took another long, slow drag of her cigarette and continued to gaze at Thomas. She blew a circle of smoke through her beautifully lined, thin lips and narrowed her cool eyes as she let them rest on Thomas's perfect body.

Jackie almost choked on her pint, but succeeded in composing herself enough to be able to say with relative calm, 'Well—uh—good luck.' She walked away from the bar to the table where Tim and John, Tom and Kevin were sitting.

Caroline finished her cigarette and then casually picked up the two martinis. She walked slowly toward Thomas, who always welcomed female company, especially if the company fancied him and came with a drink.

Jackie was sitting a few tables away from Thomas. Caroline stopped in front of her for a few seconds and said to Jackie, perhaps just to show Thomas that she too got along with his best friend, 'If you need anything, just come by my house Jackie. My door is always open.'

Jackie was surprised. 'Okay, thank you.' She said and then added, 'As a matter of fact I need to ask you something about the broch…'

Caroline was not in reality listening. She had set her eyes and her pearly smile on Thomas already. She cut Jackie off in the middle of her sentence—'Yes…uh…anytime, whenever'—and then she walked toward Thomas with softly swaying hips.

Tim and John, Tom and Kevin were admiring Caroline as she walked seductively to Thomas's table, nonchalantly handed him the other martini and then sat down, elegantly crossing her long legs in her very short black skirt. She tossed her dark voluminous hair back and leaned over to Thomas.

'Ahh!' Tim admired. 'She is going to eat him, poor boy.'

'He looks pretty happy to me.' Jackie grunted and made a face.

'It is so exciting to see predators in action,' Kevin said.

'…in their natural habitat…' Tom added laughing.

'…showing off their well-practised hunting skills.' John had acquired the monotonous voice of a nature-film narrator.

Tim chuckled and rubbed his hands together in excitement. 'This is going to be so much fun to see—better than *Natural Geographic* on the Nature Channel. I think I'll be needing another drink.'

Caroline had moved a bit closer to Thomas. She was smiling at every word he uttered. Thomas was surprised by this sudden attention and was flattered by it, clearly enjoying her beautiful legs as they got closer and closer to him. Caroline took out a cigarette and waited for Thomas to light it for her.

Kevin marvelled at this and murmured, 'Uh….classic style of seduction! How marvellous! Textbook material. Next comes tossing of the hair and the bosom display.'

Caroline put her hand on Thomas's leg, tossed her hair and laughed showing all of her pearly white teeth while straightening her back, just so that her well-formed bosom jutted slightly forward.

'Ah, what did I say?' Kevin cried.

'Poor Thomas,' was all Jackie could say as she watched Caroline beginning to devour Thomas alive.

It was raining heavily, when Jackie got out of her car a few days later in front of Caroline's house. She ran quickly across the long front yard, trying to avoid the deep puddles that had formed overnight. She knocked on the front door. The rain was falling so hard that she could hardly hear anything but the rain beating against the walls, window panes and the old tin roof. She knocked again, this time louder than before and waited. There was no answer, so Jackie did what everybody in the countryside does and pushed the door handle down. As expected the door wasn't locked. It opened quietly and Jackie walked into the hallway looking slightly apologetic and called out softly.

'Hello, anybody home!' She listened for an answer, but heard nothing but the rain and the howling wind.

The kitchen door was open to the hallway and Jackie was about to holler her greetings again, when those words died on her lips.

What she saw was Thomas casually closing the fridge with a well-practised heel kick. He was completely naked and he was holding two cold bottles of beer in his hands. His back was turned toward Jackie so, luckily, he didn't see her standing there in the hallway, her mouth frozen in a silent scream. Her breathing seemed unusually loud, and she could hear her heart bumping rapidly in her chest. Her forehead was suddenly cold with sweat.

'Why did I come in?' she kept asking herself. 'Shit! Shit! Shit!' She wished she could suddenly, by some bizarre miracle, master the art of being invisible or very, very small.

Thomas whistled happily as he walked away from the fridge. He took a sip from one of the beer bottles, cursed cheerfully when the foam dripped from his lips to his chest and then hollered loudly into the other room,

'Here's a cold beer for my sex goddess. To my wicked Venus of Sycamore. To my dirty, dirty wicked witch! Your Tommy-boy is coming back for more!'

Jackie backed out of the house quietly. She really didn't want to hear Caroline's answer to the wicked Venus name. No, because then she would never, ever be able to have a chat with Thomas again without thinking about the name Caroline had given him. No, she didn't want to hear anything anymore, or see and or even think about it. The dirty wicked witch had been quite enough. She ran to her car through the pouring rain, getting her shoes and her pant legs completely wet.

'Well, she said her door is always open and so it was.' Jackie mumbled to herself as she reached her car and yanked the door open. She sat in her car, totally drenched. The pounding rain had made the front seat wet during the brief time the door had been open. Jackie sat uncomfortably on the wet seat and gave a last look to the house. Then she suddenly smiled mischievously. 'I wonder if there will be anything left of poor old Thomas.'

Jackie heard from Caroline by phone a week later. Jackie thought she sounded tired; she seemed to speak in a slightly more languorous manner than usual.

'Jackie. It's Caroline.'

'Hi, Caroline. How are you?'

'Fine. Listen. The brochure is done.'

'Good.'

'You need to come and pick up the disk from my house.'

'Oh...'

'I have done my share. More than my share, actually. Working with non-professionals is a drag.'

'Oh...'

'I'll leave the disk in my mailbox for you, in case I'm not home. Bye!' Caroline hung up.

'What the f...' Jackie yelled into the air and slammed the phone down. Then she picked it up again and dialled a number.

'Rosalind! It's Jackie. How are you? About the brochures...'

After that Jackie did not manage to get a word in edgewise during the whole conversation. The red patches on her cheeks grew larger and her hands started to tremble with barely controlled anger. In the end she slammed down the receiver, yelled 'bye!' into the thin air and then walked in circles cursing madly, before grabbing her car keys and stomping out the door into the continuing heavy rain.

She kicked the garbage can on her way out to the car and with the pain throbbing in her foot, she found herself wishing she had someone with whom she could share her ups and downs. This thought made her feel even more miserable. 'Great. Just great!' She mumbled as she watched the windshield wipers fighting the continuing downpour. 'And I need a new set of windshield wipers.' She grumbled in her fury as Caroline lived quite far from Jackie's house. 'Great! Bloody fantastic. Fucking great! God damn! Shit!' She muttered under her breath and then forced a smile on her face as she greeted Mr. Johnson through the window. There was no need to be rude to him. He hadn't done anything. She rolled down the window just a bit.

'I'm fine.' She answered to his polite enquiries that came from under a very large umbrella. 'Busy as always.' She would need to call the newspaper as well. There was no end to things she needed to do. She cursed once more under her breath and said goodbye to Mr. Johnson, who thought that Jackie was the nicest person ever. It was always a pleasure to chat with her. Such a nice girl. He continued his walk in the rain as Jackie sped off with her car toward Caroline's house. 'Twenty-four hours a day didn't seemed to be enough,' Jackie thought while driving through mud, drizzle, cow droppings and gravel.

Rose, who worked for Nick, was a big bodied older woman with a good sense of humour. She had had a few rough patches in her life, but she had never let them dampen her spirits. She had a loud voice, large mouth and arms that were as big as any man's; she was obeyed immediately and unquestioningly by anybody who came into the pub. She had a keen interest in Nick's life and treated him as her younger brother.

It was a quiet night. The rain had kept most of the daily customers away and Nick was slowly filling a couple of pints, while Rose was cleaning the counter; she could not sit still.

Suddenly she stopped wiping and gave Nick a long, questioning look before opening her mouth. 'So how is it, Nick? When are you going to get yourself a woman?'

Nick looked up completely surprised by Rose's straightforward question. 'What kind of talk is that?' He stuttered and felt the hot flush of blood reddening his face.

'Straight talk, the kind you men like—or so you say.' Rose said and then she grew frustrated. 'Oh…come on Nick. It's been three years since Denise left with half of your money.'

'Thanks for the kind reminder, Rose. Truly appreciated.' Nick began to sulk. There was no need for anybody to remind him of that time of his life.

'No need to be hostile, dear. Just thinking what's good for you,' said Rose and studied Nick's face.

Nick looked at her grumpily. 'Yeah, right…'

'Now come on, Nick. Seriously. Where are you going to find a woman for yourself? Not in this pub, I say.' She paused and then sighed deeply. 'Well, just look around.' Most of the people present were men. 'Well what do you see? The same old. The only suitable women for you here are Jackie and Caroline. And frankly that Caroline woman scares the hell out of me, and from what I have heard, she truly uses men to the end. Maximilian is recovering from a slipped disk and Thomas is apparently totally exhausted and they only met a week ago.'

'Well, I'm not interested in Caroline!' Nick blurted out and immediately realized what he had said; his face flushed an even deeper shade of red.

Rose looked at Nick in a motherly way. 'It's time to make a move, Nick.' She said in a gentle voice.

Nick looked as if he had taken a bite of something strange and he didn't know whether he liked it or not.

Exactly at the same time the door opened and Jackie stomped in.

'There's your chance, old boy.' Rose gave a nudge to Nick's elbow and walked away winking shamelessly.

Nick muttered to himself, 'Damn women.'

Jackie greeted Nick. She seemed cross and the rain had soaked her from head to toe.

Nick stammered, 'Oh, hi Jackie, how's it going?' But luckily Jackie did not see his reddening face, nor hear the strain in his voice.

'Don't even ask.' Jackie barked and put down her bag with a loud and angry bang. She took her rain jacket off and hung it on the back of a chair beside her. 'Could I have a cup of coffee, Nick?'

'Sure, of course.'

'Thanks.'

Jackie leaned closer to Nick and shook her head sadly. 'I think, that one day that Rosalind is going to drive me absolutely stark raving mad.'

Nick handed the coffee to Jackie. 'How come?'

'It seems that I have to drive to the city tomorrow to take the brochure designs to the printer.' Jackie added a generous heap of sugar into her coffee and then grabbed her bag and pulled out a folder that had papers and a computer disk in it. 'I just got these from Caroline. In fact, I had to drive all the way there to pick them up.' She shook the file in her hand. 'Rosalind is apparently too busy to go to the city herself, and of course Caroline will not go because she has already done her share...so I have to go. And as we all know, I have nothing better to do—damn!' She spread her hands up in the air and let them fall down again. 'I just got a new order and I'm swamped with work and now this.' She crossed her hands on the table and looked suddenly very tired. 'The last thing I want to do is just that—drive in this weather all by myself.' She turned her head to look out the window. The heavy rain was falling down, battering the windowpanes, and the wind was starting to pick up. The temperature had fallen, and the summer with endless sun shine was now just a hopeful wish.

Nick was both confused and eager. He was working on finding the right words to say, but rejected them all. Finally at the sight of Rose glaring at him across the room and shaking her hands vigorously, he decided to speak. He gulped deeply, gathered his strength and said to Jackie. 'Why don't I come with you?'

Jackie was drinking her coffee. She stopped with the cup on her lips and looked questioningly at Nick. She was genuinely surprised. It had never occurred to her to ask Nick to come along. She had always assumed that he was too busy with the pub to get away at all.

'I mean…just to keep you company. And, and…it would be nice to visit the city for a change…uh…if you don't mind, of course.' Nick stammered as he spoke too fast, too eagerly, too readily.

Jackie stared at him. She was happy at the thought, but mostly she was utterly astonished.

'That would be great! But what about the pub?' She drank the last sip of her coffee and stared at Nick.

'Rose can take care of the pub for one day with no problem.' Nick was getting excited. His suggestion hadn't been turned down. Maybe Rose was right and he should move on from the bitter memory of Denise.

'Okay then. I'll pick you up at 7 a.m. Or is that too early for you?' Jackie was putting her rain jacket on. 'Are you closing tonight?'

'No, no seven is fine with me.' Nick spoke rapidly as if not to lose the momentum and his sudden courage.

'See you tomorrow morning, then. Bye!' Jackie turned and left the pub clonking awkwardly in her heavy rain boots. Nick stood behind the counter looking quite happy and a little lost in his own thoughts.

Rose came back to the bar to find out what had passed between the two of them. 'What are you smiling about?' She asked raising her eyebrows.

'Oh, nothing.' Nick paused for a second. 'Rose you wouldn't mind minding the bar by yourself tomorrow…uh…now would you?' he finally asked awkwardly, looking everywhere except at Rose, who was standing right in front of him with her big hands resting on her wide hips.

'No, of course not.' An all-knowing smile spread over Rose's face. 'You did ask her out! Well, I'll be darned! You are having a date with Jackie Callaghan!' She squealed with delight and clapped her hands together. Rose was smiling broadly, victoriously and mischievously.

'A date?' Nick felt extremely awkward. 'Nooo…no, no, no…I'm just going to keep her company when she is going to the printer to get the studio tour brochures. You see, the weather is really bad for driving and…I…and…uh…I thought…' There were many different levels of panic fighting for first place in Nick's mind. The words made him perspire cold, heavy, anxious pearls of sweat. His face felt frozen.

Rose started laughing heartily and shook her head sympathetically.

Nick stopped muttering and filled up a pint and then put it down on the table absentmindedly. 'Date! Definitely not!' He was talking more to himself than to Rose.

'Whatever you say, Nick, but I smell a date.' Rose spoke with a voice that almost sang with laughter and sympathy. She wiped her big farm-girl hands on her apron and smiled. It was a big knowing smile that illuminated her big round, honest face. 'Definitely a date.' She winked and walked away.

Nick stared in front of him not seeing anything and then wiped the counter again, inattentively. He was thinking, but he was not quite sure what exactly.

Jack Wilkinson strolled casually to the bar and leaned his elbow on the side of the counter. He lifted up the rim of his hat and stared at Nick's face for a long time. 'Now what's this I hear? You going on a date with the Callaghan girl?' He licked his teeth and smacked his lips.

Nick looked up completely surprised and a new panic began to seep into his thoughts. 'It's not a date!' He muttered and shook his head forcefully. He looked at Rose, who was across the room in deep conversation with the ladies club from the church. Nick was now yelling. 'Rose what the hell are you telling to all these people?'

Rose waved her hand from across the pub and smiled. 'I didn't think it was a top secret.'

'It is a not a secret and it is not a date!' Nick defended himself without much hope.

Jack Wilkinson was still leaning against the bar and thinking way back to his own, accident-prone youth. He had acquired the air of a scholar.

'Let me tell you about these Callaghan women.'

Nick looked at him in deep agony and, for the first time in his life, he truly wanted to be somewhere else than in this pub on this small island. He wanted to be somewhere where nobody knew his name or recognized his face. He wanted to drink a bottle of beer without a dozen church ladies watching over him and keeping track of how many beers he had had already. He wanted to be somewhere where he could go to the pharmacy without people beginning to speculate as to what was wrong with him.

Jack Wilkinson's words brought him back from his miserable thoughts to reality and to the very same people he wanted to get away from.

'Your granddad used to go out with Jackie's grandmother, Evelyn.'

Nick had to interrupt him. 'What! For god's sake, I'm not going to go out with Jackie.'

But Jack Wilkinson was not listening; he was settling into his storytelling mode. 'And your dad tried to go out with Jackie's mother, Betty—sorry, Belinda, as she is known now—anyway, he got a lovely black eye for a souvenir; now, I don't know the particulars, but, well, you see—we all grew up together.' He paused and nodded his head, remembering his childhood adventures with the boys. 'And me... well, all I wanted was a wee kiss from pretty Betty and what did I get...' Jack stopped for a theatrical pause. 'The thing I got was this crooked nose...my only lasting memory of the beautiful Betty... ah!' He pointed to his nose and nodded knowingly. 'So if I were you, I would be careful. You just never know about those Callaghan girls. O'Neills and Callaghans have never ever mixed before, though, they have tried for three generations. They are like oil and water. No mixing no matter how hard you try.' Jack Wilkinson finished off his pint and grabbed the new pint that Nick had just poured and winked. 'So if you feel like kissing her, I suggest, from personal experience, to ask first...Politely, I might add.'

With these useful words, heavily laden with wisdom, he walked back to his corner table. He had a quick word with Glenn, Howard and Calvin. All of them looked at Nick and nodded knowingly. Jack pointed again to his nose and Howard put his thumbs up and grinned.

Rose came back to the bar smiling widely. 'I know it's not a date, but what are you going to wear?' She asked Nick, who was still fuming.

Nick stared at her as if she was speaking a completely different language. He had no idea what she was talking about. 'Wear? What you mean, wear? Wear? The same clothes I normally put on in the morning—a shirt, pants, perhaps a jacket. What the hell are you talking about?' Nick was losing it now.

Muriel walked slowly across the room and stopped in front of the bar on her way to the ladies room. 'We girls in the Bitch and Stitch Club think, that the two of you would make a wonderful couple...and I would wear something blue, if I were you.'

Nick looked in the direction of the Bitch and Stitch Club and all those lovely church ladies nodded their heads and smiled gently, murmuring their approval. Blue was definitely Nick's colour. They knew it, because he had his mother's eyes, the exact same hue of light blue.

Nick stared straight ahead of him and then turned slowly to face Rose. 'What is this? Should I just put a notice on the board or something?'

'No use doing that, dear. This whole pub is a notice board.'

Nick was glaring at her; from the look in his eyes you could tell he was preparing himself for a slow, painful descent into the fiery pits of hell.

Nick left Rose to close the pub. He had had enough. He went home and sat in his kitchen staring at the tea kettle, waiting for its whistle as it came to a boil. He had very mixed feelings and he didn't like it. Nick was a man who liked clear things, orderly things, facts and not estimates. Not that he would say no to an adventure, but he certainly did not like these unclear feelings that were romping in his head and chest cavity right now. He had a knot in his stomach, which he knew would go away with time, but while it was there he was feeling very ill at ease.

He hated to admit it, but maybe Rose had been right. It was time to move on, away from Denise and the pain and disarray she had caused. 'What if it happens again?' He asked himself and then he hated what his thoughts made him look like. An adult man afraid of getting hurt. Not at all what he had thought he would become when he was a little boy playing by the sea, throwing rocks into the water and diving off the cliffs.

'Maybe this is it,' he thought. 'I have come to the end of the road and now it is time to take another road. Shit!' The tea kettle whistled but Nick just let it go on, remaining at the table, motionlessly staring at the wall, lost in his miserable thoughts.

It had been hell with Denise, he admitted looking back. It hadn't been that bad in the beginning and he had just sort of grown used to the steady unhappiness and had thought of it as normal. He had been comparing his state of misery today to the state of misery from the day before and then it hadn't seemed that bad. Now when he looked back, he couldn't believe that he had been in that relationship for so many years.

'Only Rosalind can be bitchier than Denise,' Rose had said many times. 'And you wouldn't go out with her, now would you?'

Rose had never liked Denise, not that Denise had ever regarded Rose with warm feelings, either.

'You are a good man, Nick; why do you need somebody continuously telling you otherwise, for god's sake.' Rose had kept saying.

Denise had left him in the end. She had packed her things and moved back to the city and in with Gary, who had an office and a lumbar-supporting chair instead of a cramped room in the back of the pub with files all around and a chair that had seen a better decade. Somehow Nick's office had been the last on Nick's to-do list. He had fixed the kitchen first and then all the other things that had been neglected far too long over the years. Somehow the office was the last and it still remained so. Denise had talked about an antique desk and a leather chair. 'To make a clear line between the employees and the employer,' she had said and then she had looked at Rose menacingly, the way only Denise could.

It hadn't been nice with Denise, but nevertheless, it had been a relationship. Nick got up to take the kettle off the stove. He made tea and then wandered upstairs to see what there was for him to wear tomorrow.

He opened the closet and then glanced at the dirty laundry pile on the floor. Rephrasing his earlier question, he asked himself, 'Was there anything *clean* to wear?' Nick stood in front of the open closet, took a sip of his tea and muttered, 'Shit, what am I doing?'

The closet was messy; all you could see was piled up underwear that had been stuffed onto the shelf; pullovers that had once been folded but as the space had become tight, they had been pushed on top of each other to make more space; there were plaid shirts in different colours hanging from the hangers. Here and there was a lonely sock. Nick had solved his ongoing battle with disappearing socks by buying forty pairs of identical socks. He had reasoned that that way he never had to find a pair ever again. Any sock would do.

'What to wear? What to wear?' He mumbled and then repeated all of those things that people had said to him at the pub. 'Blue?'

He took a shirt out and looked at it closely. It was wrinkled and it was obviously very old.

'Perhaps another one?' He looked at another similar shirt in a similar condition as the earlier one. He grunted and pulled out another shirt but it was in exactly the same condition as the previous two. Then he remembered that he had bought ten similar shirts at the same time as the socks from the same store. It might be a good time to go and do another shopping trip, he thought. He threw the shirts on his bed and so began Nick's desperate search for a good shirt.

He held a white shirt against himself studying its wrinkles and then caught a glimpse of himself in the bathroom's small mirror. 'Good god, I look like I'm going to a funeral.' He threw the shirt on the bed on top of the other ones he had rejected earlier and scratched his head. He took a sip of tea and pulled another shirt out of the closet.

The pile of clothes on the bed was slowly getting bigger than the pile of clothes that were left in the closet. Nick was experiencing a completely new level of frustration.

In the end he held a light coloured plaid shirt in one hand and a blue pullover in the other. There were no more shirts in the closet and the bed was covered with rejects.

'This is it then.' Nick sighed and shook his head in defeat. He put the shirt and the pullover back into the closet and then looked at his watch. It is well past midnight. He grabbed all of the rejected shirts from his bed and dropped them into a huge pile at the bottom of his closet and pushed the door closed, using his shoulder and his foot to get it locked.

He had trouble falling asleep that night. He told himself to stop thinking about things, but as soon as he closed his eyes Denise and Jackie merged into one disastrous person with Rose looming in the background. He tossed and turned kicking his blankets off. Then he got cold and pulled the blankets back on. He fixed the pillows, pounding them with his fist to make them softer.

At one o'clock he gave up and went downstairs to watch some past midnight TV. From experience he knew to take his alarm clock with him and set it on the table by the sofa. Nothing would put Nick to sleep as fast as the calm replay of a golf tournament, where the sportscaster's most heightened excitement would include a mellow, 'Oh, my! Did you see that? What an incredibly well-placed putt.' The answer invariably would include an equally mellow, 'Yes I did. Very well done indeed. Goodness gracious me! He is on fire tonight.'

Nick was asleep in fifteen minutes after a few very well played greens.

Jackie had driven slowly home. She had forgotten to curse at the windshield wipers, which were not functioning properly forcing her to bend her head slightly to the right to be able to see out past the smudged line left by the wipers. She was deep in her uneasy thoughts.

She parked the car in front of her gate and admired her small house for awhile before getting out. Even in the rain it looked beautiful. She loved her home. Every inch of it. She loved how it looked and smelled and how the footsteps echoed in the rooms and hallways.

Jackie opened the front door and clomped into her house. She threw her keys onto the hallway table and let her bag fall on the floor. She thought about the brochure design disk inside her bag and suddenly she had an urge to kick it, but she liked her bag too much and she, unfortunately, needed the disk.

She was too poor to be able to show her true feelings. The thought made her smile. I'm so poor that I even have to be nice to Rosalind. Though Jill would call it being politically correct. That sounded much better.

Felix and Oscar came to meet her. By the look of him, Oscar had slept all day. Smart cat. Why venture outside in this weather? He stretched lazily in front of her and offered his back to be scratched. Jackie forced Felix outside for his night run in the yard and got the towel ready to dry him off when he got back a few minutes later soaking wet, paws covered with mud. She dried him with the towel and then walked into the kitchen to get food for the animals. She slowly made herself a sandwich and leafed through an old magazine while eating in the kitchen. She did the few dishes and listened to the clock ticking on the wall. It was such a quiet night, despite the rain mercilessly beating on the house. She wandered aimlessly from room to room, thinking absentmindedly about cleaning, before picking up the phone.

She had to call Jill. She hoped it wasn't too late.

Jill was giving a bath to Nellie. Jackie could hear the splashing water and the delighted squeals echoing in the tiled bathroom.

'What do you mean, you might be going on a date?' Jill said, her voice muffled against the receiver. 'Either you are or you're not. No Nellie! Do not pull mommy's hair, no...No!' There was a silence and then the happy splashing sounds continued once again. 'So where were we?' Jill asked. 'Who's this could be date-man?'

'He's the owner of the pub, Nick. You remember him?' Jackie said and bit her lip anxiously.

'Aha, him?' Jill suddenly remembered. 'He was quite handsome, wasn't he? That weathered outdoors Marlborough-man face, without the Marlboroughs.'

'Yes…he doesn't smoke. Thank god.' Jackie mumbled and blushed. She was happy Jill could not see her face, or else she would have erupted into laughter and started acting as if they were teenagers, saying things like 'You like him' or 'Have you kissed yet?' Or something equally silly that would make Jackie laugh and then she would have to admit that, yes she had once or maybe twice noticed that Nick was a handsome man.

'So are you going on a date with him?' Jill enquired.

'Well…' Jackie hesitated. 'It's not a date, at least, I don't think so.'

'Hmm…did he ask you out or what?' Jill questioned.

'Not really, you see…' Jackie began to describe the details of her conversation with Nick to Jill, who was getting her shirt completely wet by Nellie's bathwater.

'He sounds like a nice man,' Jill said in the end and then she added. 'He obviously likes you and wants to help you and, my god, Jackie, let him. He seems polite and considerate.' Jill paused for a moment. 'A complete opposite to that sleazebag Chris.'

'Oh please, don't bring Chris into this. I know as well as you do that he was a mistake.' Jackie cried and really tried not to think about Chris.

'Mistake…I would call him *the* major mistake and an extremely bad musician.' Jill added helpfully. 'Remember his John Lennon imitation?'

'Oh, good god,' howled Jackie. 'Don't say anymore about it, please.'

'Has he paid back the money he owed you?' Jill continued. 'Of course not. What am I thinking?' She answered her own question.

'Hurt me when I'm down, thank you for being my best friend, Jill.'

'That's what friends are for. Just wanted to remind you that when you meet a nice, good looking man, who has a job…he has a job, right?' Jill paused. 'Please tell me he has a job?' Jill prayed on the other end of the line.

'He has a job. He owns the local pub, remember?'

'Oh, yes. Thank god! For a minute I thought you were going to say, that he is an aspiring forty-something musician, who has not yet broken into the global music market.'

'Please, Jill!' Jackie begged. She felt her face blushing again.

'Just wanted to bring a little perspective to the situation, that's all...Now then...'

'What? Don't make me do the list again, Jill. Please don't!'

'Do the list Jackie!' Jill's voice was determined.

Jackie grunted on the other end of the line and she reluctantly began, because Jill, her best friend, was right and was truly on her side no matter what. 'Okay, just because I want to be nice to you. Not because I need to.'

Jill snorted and mimicked laughing sounds. 'Start! What men do we NOT want?'

'Men, who live with their mom.' Jackie started reluctantly.

'And...'

'Men who are forty-something, look tragically hip and have no job but have pretended to be artists, musicians, etcetera for the last twenty-five years.'

'And...'

'And men who wear white leather shoes and or any kind of burgundy clothing.'

'Excellent!' gasped Jill. 'Did you hear that, Nellie, your godmother Jackie is a very smart woman.'

Jackie laughed. She could not help herself.

'By the way, I saw Chris the other day.' Jill suddenly said.

Jackie felt unexpectedly very strange. 'You did?'

'Yes. He said he was very close to getting a record deal but that the guy at the record company had no taste and that they don't take any risks anymore and sign artists like him. I can't exactly say out loud what he called the man at the record label, because I have my very young daughter right here with me, but you get the idea—right?'

Jackie sighed. Jill was so right. She had chosen, although she had not consciously chosen. It had merely happened that, somehow, through some incredibly twisted act of fate most of her boyfriends had been scum and Chris had been a particularly bad one—the ultimate good looking looser.

'I heard you, Jill. Don't worry. I am an adult now and I have learned my lesson.'

'Good girl! Now what are you going to wear?'

Jackie got suddenly very cold. She had not even thought about what she was supposed to wear. 'I don't know…god, Jill. I have no idea. I haven't thought that far.'

'Don't worry. You've got that black jacket that I forced you to buy last time we went shopping, right?'

'Yeah…'

'Good…any jeans which are clean and hip and not full of sawdust with screws in their pockets?'

'I think so…'

'Excellent…white T-shirt and a pullover and you'll be set.' Jill beamed. 'And that scarf I gave you for Christmas.'

'Okay, mother…'

'Got nice underwear?'

'Lord! Why did I call you?'

'Because you love me and I love you and we are best friends and you are the godmother of my child.' Jill went on. 'And, by the way, Robert says hi.'

'Say hi to Robbie as well,' Jackie said. Jackie could hear him in the background. 'Tell Jackie to fall in love with a man who owns a sailboat. I need a holiday.'

'Jackie,' Jill said. 'Robbie here wants to learn to sail, so any chance that this Nick has a sailboat?'

'I'll let you know, and say thanks to Robbie for being so thoughtful and wishing me all the best.'

Jill laughed and said, 'Robbie, Jackie calls you a selfish eejit.'

'Send her my love as well,' was his answer.

'Jackie, sorry to say but I need to put Nellie to bed.'

'Oh, no problem. I'll see you next weekend and give kisses to Nellie for me'

'I will. And by the way. I expect a full report by tomorrow night.' Jill giggled as she yelled her goodbyes.

Jackie put the phone down slowly. She didn't move for awhile. She sat on the sofa thinking about her past mistakes. It wasn't pleasant. 'Chris—god, why did I go out with him?' She thought and stared at the opposite wall where the old wallpaper had begun to bubble at the seams.

'I better paint this house,' she said looking at the faded wall. 'And start a completely new life.' She got up and inspected the wall more closely, flicking the edge of the wallpaper up and peaking at another layer of old wallpaper—it was something sage green with peacocks. 'Yes, it needs painting.' She bit her lip. 'Perhaps I'll paint it terracotta.'

Jackie couldn't help going over the details of her relationship with Chris and the misery he had brought to her life with his unhappiness and his total lack of talent. Yes, he had the looks of a rock star, but he might as well have been playing bongo drums instead of guitar. They had never ending arguments at the end of their relationship where Chris accused her of having no faith in him and his music. Jackie had felt guilty because it was so close to the truth. But when he had said that she was a middle class artist wannabe, she had finally exploded and left. Especially since Chris had not complained while he had enjoyed the benefits of her middle class designer income.

'Anyhow, this is my new life, and I will start it with a terracotta coloured living room.' She looked around the room; 'Yes, any change is a good change and a step further away from the old me.'

She went back to the kitchen and made herself a cup of tea, and then climbed upstairs to find the clothes Jill had suggested. She put her teacup on her bedside table while she looked through her closet. Luckily she had a clean pair of not so bad jeans and a brand new white T-shirt. Even the pullover had been nicely folded away. She pulled out the black jacket from the closet and she was done. It had been less painful than she had assumed. A good sign.

She smiled, set her alarm clock and turned off the lights.

Chapter 15

The City

The next morning arrived filled with beautiful sounds of the busy birds in the nearby bush. The horrible cold rain was gone and the air was crisp and damp with the promise of a warmer afternoon.

Nick walked onto the street and into the damp and misty morning sunshine. He looked around to see if there was any sign of Jackie yet.

A car drove slowly by. Howard's smiling face peered out the window and he slowed his car down just enough to be able to wink and then point to his nose with an emphasis on nodding his head sideways as if somebody had planted a very well aimed hit on it.

Nick shook his head in disbelief. Luckily, he had decided not to let anything spoil his mood, which was optimistically excited. He hadn't felt this way for a long time. 'This is strange,' he thought, inhaling deeply while admiring the clear sky.

Nick looked at his watch and then glanced down the street again. He wasn't worried that she wouldn't come. No, if there was a person, who would always keep her word, it would be Jackie. Nick put his hands in his pockets and waited. He looked at Mary Cullighan's flower-shop window across the street. Between roses and lilies, he saw Mary's flushed face staring at him. She was already talking on her phone. 'My, my,' thought Nick, just as he saw Jackie's car driving toward him, and he felt a sudden happiness going all the way through him. His reaction scared him. He hadn't expected such a strong response to seeing her.

Jackie stopped her car in front of him. She leaned over to unlock the door. Her hair fell over her face and Nick noticed a bracelet on her wrist.

Nick opened the door and peaked in. 'Good morning,' he said, throwing his bag on the backseat and sitting down beside Jackie.

'Sorry I'm a bit late,' Jackie said. 'I took Felix to Harriet's. Did you wait long?'

'No, not at all. Well, long enough for Mary Cullighan to watch me intently.' Nick stole a look at Jackie. She looked different.

'Oh, good god! That woman never rests.' Jackie shook her head and looked at Mary's flowers. Mary Cullighan was still talking animatedly on her phone, and pretending to fix flowers in the window display, while staring at the two of them sitting in the car. 'Let's go,' Jackie said and waved goodbye to Mary.

'She does look different,' Nick said to himself and tried to look at Jackie without her knowing.

Jackie had done what Jill had told her. She actually felt quite good about herself. The jacket felt comfortable and the round brush had not become stuck in her hair in the morning while she had been drying it.

They sat quietly, staring at the road ahead of them, neither one of them knowing what to say. The atmosphere was beginning to feel a bit awkward.

Nick tried to open up a conversation. 'It's a nice morning.' He said and then cursed silently. 'What a bloody fantastic opening, so original, so interesting.'

'Yes, it is.' Jackie replied and looked at the blue sky.

They continued travelling quietly. Jackie's eyes were on the road that followed the rocky seashore.

Nick looked at her profile and then decided to jump head first into unknown territory. 'What the hell,' he thought and said, 'You look nice.'

Jackie was surprised to hear such a compliment. She looked at him quickly. 'Thanks.' She was quiet for a second or two and then glanced at him hastily. 'So do you. Blue suits you.'

Nick looked happy. The old ladies had been right. He relaxed a little and straightened his legs. 'Did you know, that your grandmother and my grandfather used to go out together and that your mom gave my dad a black eye and that she also gave Jack Wilkinson his famous crooked nose?'

Jackie was stunned. Her mother in a fist fight. She looked at Nick to see if he was joking, and then she looked back at the road. 'Really?' She asked with a skeptical tone in her voice.

'Yes, really. Jack Wilkinson told me last night in the pub.'

'That is unbelievable. I did not know my mother was capable of doing anything but being pretty and proper. That is shocking.'

'Jack also told me not to try to kiss you.' Nick added quickly and then regretted before the last word had even escaped his lips. 'I mean that's why your mom gave him a hook on the nose and, well… nobody knows why my granddad had a black eye but they suspect…' Nick stammered. 'So, anyway Jack told me to be careful with the Callaghan women.' Nick began sweating uncomfortably. He clasped his hands together and said nothing more.

Jackie started to laugh. First quietly but then her laughter began to grow and grow. 'Oh, my god! Can you just imagine it?' she howled.

Nick stared at her.

'I mean, just think about it. Jack Wilkinson trying to kiss my mom or, actually, Jack Wilkinson trying to kiss anybody.'

Nick began laughing as well. Jackie was wiping tears from her eyes with the underside of her hand. She was trying to stop laughing and concentrate on driving, but then she burst into loud giggles again. 'Oh, my god. I didn't think that Jack could have a romantic side to him.' She said and shook her head. 'I have never seen him with a woman, come to think of it.' She ran her finger under her eyes and looked at Nick.

'You're right.' Nick agreed. He furrowed his brow and tried to think of the past. Jack Wilkinson had never ever been seen with a woman. He came to the pub and then he left the pub to cut somebody's lawn, but inevitably he always returned to the pub, alone.

'Gosh, I still can't believe it. My mom hitting somebody.' Her mother didn't even want to shake hands with people with certain accents and dialects.

'I remember my grandfather talking about your grandmother.' Nick said and looked at her.

'Really? What did he say?'

'He never told me about the black eye, though, just that they went to school together and that she was a very pretty girl with a very fierce temper. Every time he talked about her, he would mention the Callaghan girls and their bad temper.'

Jackie sighed. 'Well yes, who else would whack poor old Jack on the nose or give a black eye to your grandfather than us Callaghan girls.'

They laughed again. It was a relaxed, happy, easy laugh.

'My grandmother was a very lovely woman, though you better not cross her.' She looked sad for a while. Nick glanced at her and then looked at the road again. 'You spent every summer with your grandmother here in the village.' He said.

'I did and I loved it. I could not wait to come here when the summer began and smell the ocean.' She looked happy but kept her eyes on the road.

Nick rubbed his chin, 'I think that you once almost punched me on my nose, come to think of it.'

'I did?' Jackie turned around sharply. Her eyes were big with disbelief.

'Yeah, remember we were on the beach and I guess I broke your sandcastle or something.'

'Was that before our swing fight or after?'

'After, I think.'

'Ahh! I remember it now. Lord, I was mad.' Jackie was grinning at the memory and her eyes filled with laughter again.

'Yeah, you sent me running all around the beach cursing as badly as a nine-year-old kid from the city could do.'

'That sounds like me all right. My granny used to tell me all the time that I should try to control my temper and watch my language and then she would drop something in the kitchen and curse like a sailor.'

Nick laughed and Jackie smiled, savouring the memory. 'I also think that I had a small crush on you, as well,' she added.

Nick stared at her. 'You did?'

'Oh, yes. Why else would I try to hurt you?'

'Uh huh, I forgot about the romantic side of nine year olds.'

'Yes, but I did get your attention, didn't I?' Jackie asked and looked at him, then quickly averted her eyes back onto the road.

'Yes, you did.' Nick laughed. 'And I got to be a really fast runner by the end of the summer. Next school year I won all the short distance competitions.'

Jackie laughed and ran her hand through her hair.

'So why did you come back? I mean, you have always lived in the city...and...' Nick asked and then suddenly thought that it could be a sensitive subject and left the end of the question to float in the air.

'My granny left me her house after she died, and I had just lost my job and didn't know what to do next. And then I thought, why not have a change of life and have a home and a studio in the same place. Start a business and then one thing led to another...'

Nick waited for her to finish the sentence. Jackie was quiet for awhile. The thought of Chris had suddenly swum into her head and she was trying to shake it off. 'Anyhow, I always loved the village and the sea.' Jackie said quickly and gripped the steering wheel harder than needed. 'And it was time for me to move away from the city.'

'It is a nice place.' Nick was relieved that Jackie had not been upset about him asking a personal question.

They both stared at the road, lost in the jungle of the past.

'What about you?' Jackie asked after a while.

'Me? Well.' Nick stalled. 'Uh, after my dad died I came here to help my mother with the pub,' he began hesitantly, glancing at Jackie. 'Then she died and I thought, why not, it might be more interesting than being a history teacher in high school. Though sometimes I wonder, especially when the time seems to stand still and I hear Jack and Glenn tell the same old stories for the fiftieth time.'

Jackie glanced at Nick. 'So you were a history teacher?' She was surprised. Somehow she had never thought of Nick as anything but a pub owner.

'Yes.'

'Interesting.'

'Yes and no.'

'How so?'

'Well, I didn't take into my calculations that I don't like teenagers.'

Jackie looked at him, and Nick shrugged his shoulders and grinned sheepishly. 'Wouldn't you say that that is a fault in a teacher?' He then asked.

'One might say so.' Jackie was amused.

'I don't like being the disciplinary person and teaching is fifty percent that, and the fact is that some people don't want to learn. But I did enjoy the summer holidays.' Nick explained making sure that he said something positive, as well. He didn't want to come across as a complainer and the teaching hadn't been that bad. Especially the summer holidays. He looked out the car window at the passing landscape and tried to think about when was the last time he had had a long holiday.

Jackie glanced at Nick quickly. 'I'm happy you came along to keep me company,' she said.

'Good, I'm happy too.' Nick got into a more comfortable position stretching his legs.

The atmosphere in the old station wagon had changed.

'I hope you don't mind, but I promised to drop some peppermills and saltshakers off to one of my galleries.' She suddenly asked Nick and nodded toward the backseat.

'Oh, that's what the package is back there,' Nick said and turned to look at a parcel in the back seat. 'No, of course I don't mind.'

'Great,' Jackie answered. 'I just thought since I'm in town and, well, I could save some money if I delivered them myself instead of shipping them. The owner is an old friend of mine and it's not that far from the printer's, either.'

'No, I don't mind at all.' Nick smiled. He was going to enjoy his free day with Jackie. Anything was going to be fine with him as long as it did not involve serving beer and cleaning counters. He was not going to think about the pub. Nick put his hands behind his neck and began to enjoy the drive.

Jackie smiled and put some music on, turning the volume low enough for them to be able to talk.

Nick asked Jackie about her art school studies and her work. Jackie asked Nick about the pub and his work as a teacher.

Nick told her about the many strange events that had taken place in the pub, and once he almost blurted out about Denise but managed to pull the words back in time and hide them under a coughing spell.

Jackie grew animated as she talked about art and design and her sudden discovery of woodworking. 'Oh you should have seen my mother's face when I told her that I was going to change my economics studies to art. I truly thought she would have a stroke.'

Jackie remembered that moment well. Her mother's face had turned ashen, and then her cheeks had acquired bright red spots, and from her distorted mouth had come an awkward sub-human shriek. Jackie shivered at the memory. Luckily there had been a bottle of cognac nearby, both for Jackie's mother and for Jackie.

Jackie's step-dad had quickly disappeared from the room talking something about a conference call to the States. It had been a horrible day. A day that Jackie didn't want to think too much about. Luckily she had met Jill in the art school and Jill being an ex-finance minister's daughter had quickly changed Jackie's mother's view of art schools. Instead of being a bloody waste of time amongst hippies and whatnots, the art school had changed overnight into a bohemian rhapsody, where all sorts of useful connections could be made.

'She was against art?' Nick asked.

'No. Not against art itself. For her art is a status symbol, but she strongly did not want me to become a woodworker—oh no. Painter perhaps, yes, a bohemian painter with Yves Saint Laurent pant suit and friends in high places. Champagne lunches and fashionable art exhibition openings in a fashionable part of the city, oh yes. But a woodworker, no, definitely not. Machinery and tools are really not quite chic enough for her.'

'Why is that?' Nick was curious.

'I guess the main reason was and still is that woodworking does not buy you a new BMW.'

'Neither does a pub.' Nick sighed. 'It doesn't buy you an Audi either.' He added as an afterthought.

'And I guess woodworking is more like work and less like champagne lunches.' Jackie shrugged her shoulders. '…and somehow it might be easier for my mom while she is golfing to talk about a daughter who is a painter. Woodworking just doesn't go well with my mother's circles. I am the accessory that doesn't match.' Jackie smiled.

Without the constant criticism, Jackie thought, they might have nothing to keep them together. Quite strange how some relationships existed plainly on negativity with not even a chance to change that. Luckily Jackie had grown a thick skin with the help and love of her grandmother.

After necessary stops for gas and water, they arrived at the printing shop. Jackie and Nick both went into the office. Colin who owned the business was an old friend of Jackie's. He had promised to print the brochure for Jackie as a favour with a very generous discount. His wife was extremely pleased about their new peppermill-saltshaker set that Jackie had sent them to thank him for his goodwill. Jackie leaned against the table and waited for Colin to finish his phone call. Colin gestured for Jackie and Nick to sit down while talking animatedly on the phone about an unpaid bill. Jackie took the brochure design and the CD out of her bag and looked around her. The smell of new paper and printing ink hung heavily in the office.

Colin slammed the phone down. 'Bloody mess! Why can't people just pay their bills on time without me having to call after them?' He cursed and rubbed his forehead. 'Hi there, Jackie. Sorry about that, but it just makes me so mad.' He fumed. 'I keep my end of the bloody deal and I'm stupid enough to expect that the customer would do the same thing, but no !'

'No problem. I have done a couple of those calls myself lately. Nothing can make you more upset than going through invoices and realizing that you don't have enough money.'

'Yeah. Bloody blood sucking bastards.' Colin sighed sadly and shook his head. 'Anyhow. Did you bring the designs? I thought you were sending somebody else—Caroline was it?'

'Change of plans, I'm afraid.' Jackie grunted still mad at Caroline and Rosalind. Though travelling with Nick had been very nice.

'Oh, by the way this is my friend Nick.' She turned around to introduce Nick to Colin.

'Nice to meet you, Nick.' Colin extended his hand.

'Same here.' Nick smiled and shook hands with him.

'Nick came to keep me company,' Jackie explained and then wondered why an earth did she have to explain to Colin why Nick had come. 'Explain less,' she told herself. 'Anyhow, here's the design for the brochure,' she added quickly and pointed to the papers on the table. 'Caroline did some changes since we talked last, but nothing major. It should be no problem, I hope.' She added, crossing her fingers for good luck.

'Okay. Let's have a look.' Colin said and popped the disk into the computer.

'There's some coffee in the kitchen if you want some,' he hollered to Nick.

'Thanks. A cup of coffee would be great.' Nick answered and walked into the kitchen. 'Would you like me to bring you some as well?'

'Yes, thank you,' Jackie answered.

'No thanks. I had mine already. I made a fresh pot for you guys.' Colin said as he studied the new brochure designs. 'Uh huh, I think we will be okay with the changes.' He mumbled to Jackie while leaning his hand against his cheek, staring at the screen.

Nick opened and closed the doors in the small office kitchen until he located the sugar tin on a shelf.

Colin mumbled something about colour separation, glossy paper opposed to matte paper and then scratched his head absentmindedly. Jackie and Nick waited for him to say something else, but Colin was lost in thought, swivelling from side to side in his office chair. He looked at the clock on the wall then ran his hand over his two-day-old beard and tapped his foot against the floor. He was still thinking, counting the hours.

'Okay, I'll tell you what. What time is it now?' He glanced at the clock again just to make sure and then drummed his fingers against the table. He was full of nervous energy. 'Okay. Come back after six.' Colin slammed his hands on the table and got up.

'Great!' Jackie exclaimed.

'I think I'll be able to do them today as a favour. I'm going to tweak my timetable a bit for you, but if all hell breaks loose, I'll give you a call. Okay?'

'Fantastic. Love you Colin.' Jackie laughed. Maybe the tour would be a success. If everything from this moment on would go without problems, then they would be on schedule. They could start advertising the tour and they could distribute the brochures all through the summer. Jackie felt good and for the first time she was quite optimistic about the tour. She felt light.

'Thank you so much. You just made me the happiest woman in the world.'

Colin looked at her first, and then he winked in Nick's direction. 'Well, I don't think I did that much. Don't you have this chap here for that job?' He looked at Nick teasingly. Nick stared at him and then he busied himself by taking the coffee cups back into the kitchen before his face reached its reddest stage.

Jackie glanced at the disappearing Nick and suppressed a giggle. Colin was spreading his hands in an innocent gesture. 'What? What did I say?' He had a huge grin on his unshaven face.

When Nick came finally out of the kitchen Jackie grabbed his arm and guided him out the door. 'See you at six, then Colin.'

Colin waved his hand and was already walking to the back of his printing shop with the CD and the papers when Jackie turned around. 'Hey, do you mind if we leave my car here? I was going to hop on the bus and not worry about parking.'

'Sure, no problem.' Colin answered in a way that you could not really tell if he had been listening to you or not.

'Thanks.' Jackie yelled into the already empty office and closed the front door.

Jackie and Nick were at the top of the steps, staring straight ahead of them waiting for the right words to say to each other. It felt like they were given an extra holiday. One full day to spend doing things they wanted to do far away from the normal routine of life. It was a guilty but extremely pleasurable feeling. Almost comparable to the feeling of skipping school and enjoying the first bright rays of shy spring sunshine while eating rapidly melting ice cream. Jackie was so happy that Nick had come along with her. She looked at him and grinned from ear to ear.

'Well…we have quite a few hours to kill. What should we do?' She broke the slightly uncomfortable silence.

'I don't know about you, but I would love to have another cup of coffee and something to eat. I didn't have time to make any breakfast this morning.'

'Sounds good to me and I know just the place,' Jackie said and pulled Nick's arm. 'Let me just grab those peppermills from the car.'

She went to the car and got the package out. Nick offered to carry it for her. It wasn't heavy, but Jackie happily handed it over as they hopped on the bus and drove to the centre. It was still very early in the morning and the city was just beginning to wake up. It was busy already, but the busyness was still masked by the mist from the previous night. The early morning stillness hung there like dew, soon to be gone and forgotten, replaced by pulsing energy and the loud sounds of organized chaos.

Jackie and Nick walked along the river to a cosy café that Jackie knew. They sat at a table by the window and ordered coffee and croissants. They watched people walking busily by, glancing nervously at their watches and then quickening their pace. The hectic scenery made Nick and Jackie enjoy their slow morning even more.

Jackie found herself thinking how much she knew about Nick's everyday life, but how little she knew about Nick: the person behind his everyday life.

She knew that he worked too much, lived behind the pub, owned a beat-up car just like her, made good coffee and had a great sense of humour. She did not know, though, what he was like, what he liked to do, what music he listened to and what his favourite pastime was.

'Do you have a sail boat?' She found herself suddenly asking.

Nick looked up from his cup of coffee. 'Yes.'

'When do you have time to go sailing?' Bloody Robbie, she cursed silently and wondered how it was possible to be having two conversations simultaneously in one's mind. 'You're always in the pub it seems.' She added quickly.

'I try to take time off as much I can, here and there. I would go crazy if I would only stay in the pub.'

'Uh huh.' Jackie agreed.

'I could take you sailing, if you would like to.' Nick offered amiably.

'That would be great. I'd like that.' Suddenly she was feeling coy and disliked herself for it. She looked at their empty cups and plates and hastily said, 'Well, should we go? I think the gallery has just opened and we could go and drop the peppermills off and then we can do whatever we want to.'

'Sure, if you wish. I'll just pay the bill.'

'No, I'll pay.'

'No, Jackie. You drove, I'll get this.'

'But...' Jackie didn't go much further with her protests as Nick got a hold of the bill and wouldn't hear anymore about it. Jackie caught herself looking at him more often than usual. He was a handsome man, but unlike Thomas, he didn't know it and therefore it seemed more intriguing.

Nick paid the bill and they walked slowly down the street looking into the shop window displays. Jackie pointed at some mannequins and laughed. 'I can see myself wearing that one while working in the studio.'

Nick laughed as well. 'You might get those puffy sleeves caught in the lathe but the lacy underskirt is a must.'

'The dress would be handy to sweep up the wood chips from the floor.'

Nick looked closer to have a better look at the dress. 'A broom might be a cheaper solution.' He said with his eyes suddenly wide at the sight of all the zeros at the end of the price tag.

'Jesus,' Jackie said when she saw what Nick was pointing at. 'There is no way I can afford to be fashionable.'

'You look very nice today, very fashionable in an artist sort of way.' Nick said and looked at Jackie pleasantly.

Jackie was surprised and hid the new awkward feeling with nervous laughter and brushed the compliment away with a nonchalant gesture, but inside she did feel quite different. Now it was Nick's turn to feel coy and he studied the sky for a moment longer than needed; he was not really *that* interested in airplanes or hot air balloons.

They walked down the street together. They were close to each other in the way friends walk together, not the same way couples walk, sharing the same air and space, considering their bodies as one. Jackie and Nick kept a distance: my air, your air, my space, your space, my side of the sidewalk, your side of the sidewalk. If they would accidentally bump into each other it would be followed by a flow of apologies and quickly parting hands.

They arrived at the gallery. The golden letters above the window said New Dimensions. It was owned by Jill's mother Helen: a busy, fashionable young sixty year old. It was a vast beautiful space and Jackie was happy with the success of her designs in the gallery.

Helen treated Jackie as her second daughter. She pried into her personal life with as much vigour as she pried into Jill's.

Helen was behind her office table; her hair impeccably combed and sprayed. Her nails were clicking on her keyboard and her new Hermes scarf was casually tied around her slender neck.

'Hi, Helen.' Jackie hollered cheerfully as she walked into the gallery, while Nick held the door open for her.

'Oh, there you are.' Helen looked over her gold-rimmed glasses and came out from behind her desk to land three kisses on Jackie's cheeks. One, two and a third one back on the right cheek. 'I was in Russia last week and they always kiss three times,' Helen said and then took Nick's hand into hers.

Her numerous bracelets clanged together as her hand went downward. 'Nice to meet you,' she said. Her piercing black eyes were studying Nick's features. 'I'm Helen Highbury.'

'Good morning. I'm Nicholas O'Neill. Nice to meet you, too,' said Nick and smiled his broad and warm smile. Despite Helen's hawk-like appearance, he liked her.

'Well,' Helen said slowly and then turned around, casually adding that Jill had called her last night. Then she mentioned something about a report, the deeper meaning of which was totally lost on Nick, but which made Jackie blush slightly and study her shoes. Helen smiled mischievously and stared at Nick again.

Jackie put the parcel on the table. 'I brought you the new colour combinations.' she said. 'I hope you'll like them.'

'I'm sure I will. The other ones have been selling very well. I am very pleased with them.' Helen replied and fingered the invoice Jackie had given her.

'Great,' Jackie said. It had been awkward at first dealing with Helen. Jackie had felt that Helen had been doing her a favour by ordering her peppermills because she was her daughter's best friend; but Helen had bluntly said 'business is business and friendship is friendship.' And if they don't sell she would not reorder: 'No hard feelings, no harm done. Dinner on Sunday at 5 p.m., starting with drinks. Be on time.'

Jackie had also seen the other side of Helen which she had not seen before. Helen truly meant business and she did not take fools slightly. She was direct up to the point of being rude, but luckily

Jackie's product had proven to be one of the best sellers in New Dimensions.

Helen followed Jackie into the storage room and switched on the light. 'Is this the man Jill called me about?' She asked and pinched Jackie's arm.

All Jackie could do was to say something that started with a 'hm,' and then she felt her cheeks getting hot again.

'I thought so. Jill told me to spy on you two and call her back later.'

'She told me to give her the report tonight.' Jackie laughed and started peeling off the wrapping paper around her peppermills.

Helen put the recycling bin near her and pointed to the shelves on Jackie's right. 'Just put them there. Zoë will put them on display later,' she said as she disappeared back to the gallery to write a cheque for Jackie.

Jackie could hear Nick and Helen talking in the gallery. She was happy to be alone for awhile in the dark storage room to collect her strength and get rid of her embarrassing burning hot cheeks.

When she returned to the gallery she found Helen telling Nick about her favourite new designers. Helen turned to look at Jackie and smiled again. 'Thank you, Jackie,' Helen said, and then added, 'I'm thinking about doing an exhibition about a living space—new interior artists of the year. The visionaries. Putting beauty and function back together.' She looked at Jackie questioningly. 'What do you think?'

'Sounds great,' Jackie said.

'Good. I'll sign you up for the show then. I need new things, new designs, new colours. Go crazy and invent something spectacularly exciting for me, won't you?'

'Thanks Helen.' Jackie was all smiles. Exhibition meant income. Exhibition meant being able to pay the bills without tears. Exhibition also meant a nice night out drinking champagne, but mostly nowadays, it meant new tires for the car and an extra bottle of wine on Fridays.

'No problem. Just be as brilliant as always,' Helen said and started energetically bossing around Zoë, a twenty-something art student dressed in black.

They left the gallery and Jackie felt Helen's cheque warming her pocket nicely. This month would not look too bad in the books, she hoped. She had received quite a few wholesale orders. There would be more breathing space. There would be time to rest a little and enjoy the sunshine. They walked aimlessly, chatting casually about this and that when, unexpectedly, they found themselves in front of the art museum. Jackie remembered that there was an exhibition of French Impressionists on. And, oddly enough, there wasn't the customary unimaginably long line of art lovers waiting to get in.

'Let's go here.' Jackie said, her eyes brightened by the anticipation. She already had Nick's hand in her firm grip and she was pulling him to follow her.

Nick didn't seem to need much encouragement to visit the art museum. He laughed happily and they joined the small group of people in the line that steadily disappeared through the heavy wooden doors.

They walked slowly in a line to the ticket counter. Jackie saw Nick taking his wallet out.

'No,' she said determinedly, pushing Nick's wallet away. 'It is my turn to pay.'

'No. I will pay,' said Nick, and he was already taking the bills out of his wallet when Jackie hissed, 'Definitely not,' and fought her way in. She had to push through Nick's already outstretched hands, and then she planted herself firmly between him and the cashier. Nick tried in vain to push his hand through but Jackie spread her elbows over the counter and smiled victoriously at the cashier. 'Two tickets, please.'

The cashier stared at them numbly. She had heavily lined lips, which were slightly parted as if she had allergies that caused her to breathe through her nose. The look on her face said that she had seen two people foolishly in love before, though she herself had never experienced it and, therefore, she felt it was a highly over rated experience.

Reluctantly she took the money from Jackie, her plump fingers extended with long red fake nails. As she dropped the change on the counter her nails clicked against the table top and the sound echoed through the hall.

Jackie took the change, the two tickets and, with a wide triumphant grin, handed Nick his ticket.

Nick looked at the ceiling and shook his head slightly. A big beautiful smile spread over his face and he guided Jackie through the door by placing his hand over the small of her back. Jackie felt the warmth of his hand and suddenly she was aware of how she was breathing. They walked up the main stairway and entered the first room.

Immediately they were surrounded by beautiful, soft colours and the playful light of the paintings. The lush landscapes and the garden scenes welcomed them with their harmonious hues, intertwining light into deeper shades. Orange sunsets met late night drinkers in cafes, and children in white dresses played in gardens, while the ballet dancers in pink tulle skirts practised in grand opera halls. Jackie and Nick dodged the tour groups and weaved through the small gatherings of people trying to get closer to the paintings.

A few times Jackie grabbed Nick by his sleeve and pulled him to see a very special painting that she adored. Nick allowed himself be guided and smiled.

He let her tell him all that she knew about the Impressionists. Jackie pointed to particular parts in the paintings and drew lines in the air with her hands explaining about the composition and the importance of the light. She was clearly in her element as she talked about art.

Nick enjoyed watching her growing animation. He had always enjoyed visiting museums. There was something special about the dull echo that went around the large rooms and the way people tried to talk quietly, but, still, somehow the vast space multiplied their hushed voices and in certain corners you could follow a conversation from across the room quite effortlessly. They spied an art history student giving a lecture to her obviously bored girlfriend and Nick helped a few older ladies up the steps. They were asked to join the ladies church group tour of the exhibition, but they declined the kind offer politely, preferring to be alone.

They spent a wonderful two hours leisurely walking through the exhibition. The distance between them as they walked was growing smaller and once in a while their shoulders brushed together. The awkwardness was gradually disappearing.

When they were leaving Nick helped Jackie to put on her jacket. His hand lingered slightly longer than necessary on her shoulder.

Jackie found herself wishing that his hand would have stayed there after he pulled it hastily back and then casually buried both his hands in his pockets. He stared at the empty uneventful sky once more.

They walked for awhile around the busy fast-moving streets before deciding to have a very late lunch in a small quaint Italian restaurant with red and white tablecloths and Chianti-bottle candleholders. Jackie demanded to pay for the lunch but Nick shook his head adamantly and sighed—'Callaghan girls'—and then pushed her hand gently but firmly down and said softly. 'I insist.'

He looked at Jackie seriously. There was no arguing with him. Jackie leaned deeper into her seat and let him pay.

She looked at his hands, his forearms and his face—lips, nose— and then she nearly had a fit when she found herself thinking about how it would be to kiss him. She drank the rest of the wine from her glass and stared at the tablecloth. It had been a long time since she had had a leisurely lunch, never mind having a lunch with a man she wanted to kiss. She didn't like the uneasy feeling she was experiencing.

Nick held the door open. Jackie flung her handbag over her shoulder and thought that she could easily get used to being treated this way. Chris had never done anything for her and she had never expected it from him either.

They walked around the city aimlessly, wandering along the streets looking at the curiosities not found in the village of Sycamore.

Finally they walked by Helen's art gallery again and saw that Zoë had indeed changed the whole presentation in the window. Jackie's just delivered peppermills and salt grinders were there in the centre of the display. Helen waved at them through the window and continued talking on the phone while putting a pen behind her ear.

Jackie basked in the happy light of her small success and grabbed Nick's arm squeezing it without even noticing herself doing it.

It had been a wonderful day, one of those rare days that had begun normally and then, by some magic touch, had changed into a perfect, long and blissful day.

They were sitting in a café having coffee when Jackie's cell phone rang. She rustled through her purse mumbling as she pushed aside her wallet, hair brush, lipstick and a scarf that she thought she had lost a week ago. 'Ahh,' she exclaimed when she was finally holding her phone in her hand, looking at the name that was flashing on the display. 'It's Colin.' She greeted him excitedly and then smiled. 'We'll be there in half an hour or so. Great! Thanks a million.'

She looked up at Nick and explained. 'Colin is just finishing, so we can head back and go pick up the brochures. There's no rush though, he said. He'll be working late tonight.'

Nick felt strangely disappointed. He had enjoyed his time with Jackie in town and was now reluctant to leave their perfect day behind.

Colin had five boxes waiting for them on the counter in his ink-smelling, somewhat rundown office. He had left a few brochure samples out for Jackie and Nick.

'Looks very good!' Nick said honestly as he turned the flat, crisp, odd smelling pages. In the brochure the village looked very touristy and very appealing.

'Fantastic job, Colin!' Jackie sighed in relief and then thanked him profusely. The brochure was so beautiful—perfect—her dream of the studio tour seemed almost plausible now. 'Thank you, Colin.' Jackie exclaimed once more, and then again studied the brochure in her hands. She nudged Nick's arm. 'Look at your pub. It looks such a friendly place to visit.'

Nick turned the pages and admired Jackie's studio article. 'The photo of your gallery is fantastic. It looks very professional.'

Jackie smiled and lovingly stroked the boxes, which now held the possibility of a brighter future.

'I'm happy you like them and if you need more, just let me know.' Colin said and tapped the calculator buttons with his thick ink stained finger, while mumbling something about discounts and favours and pints in the pub and so forth before settling on the final price.

Jackie happily paid for the brochures and Nick began carrying the boxes to their car. Jackie thanked Colin one more time. She felt light and festive. She could now cross one more item off from her never ending to-do list.

'No problem.' Colin shrugged his shoulders and then added, a half-smile spreading over his face, 'By the way, you have quite interesting B & Bs in your village.'

Jackie stared at him apprehensively. She knew they had a very nice selection of bed and breakfasts in the village, but nothing out of the ordinary. 'Yes we do,' she finally said, eyeing him warily. Maybe Colin was just paying a compliment. 'You should come for the tour.'

Colin winked. 'I might. Thanks for the invitation.'

'See you in Sycamore then.' Jackie turned around to leave. She waved her hand as she went out the door, folding the receipt in half and stuffing it into her jacket pocket. She would have to remember to give it to Rosalind.

Nick was putting the last box into the car. He straightened his back and closed the trunk. He looked at Jackie while playing with the car keys in his hands, flipping the long end of the string from one side to the other.

'Why don't I drive us home?' He didn't wait for the answer but went and opened the passenger door for Jackie. She got in and sat down. She was not going to argue. Jackie didn't like driving in the twilight, so it was all right for her if Nick insisted on driving. Nick smiled and closed the door and then walked around the car and got in. He adjusted the seat and mirror. Jackie looked at him. 'Thank you for driving, Nick.' She said and got comfortable in her passenger seat. Funny, she had never sat in that seat before; she had always been the driver.

'No problem. I'm glad to drive.' Nick was happy to deal with the distractions brought on by driving in rush hour.

They had had such a wonderful time and now the day was ending and they were on their way back home. While he concentrated on driving, the beautiful day still stayed intact in his mind.

They commented about the rush hour traffic and compared it to the evening pint runs in Sycamore. Small talk and small smiles, trying to make the pleasant day last a bit longer.

Suddenly Jackie heard the familiar sound of her cell phone. She found it in the bottom of her purse after a few seconds of frantic search. 'Damn,' she said without even thinking and then added as if her explanation would help Nick understand the unfathomable things that made up her life.

'It's my mom.'

Nick glanced at her. Jackie sat holding her cell phone between her hands, deciding whether she should answer or not. Which choice would cause more problems than the other? Which choice would have less troublesome consequences? 'If I don't answer, she'll be mad. If I answer, I'll go crazy.' She muttered her questions into the air expecting no answers. In the end she pressed the little green button on her phone and said with a very unnaturally cheerful voice, 'Hi, Mom.' After those two words she remained silent for almost the whole conversation. Once in a while she began to say something just to be cut off a second later.

Nick followed her unsuccessful attempts to have a conversation with slightly amused interest.

Finally Jackie was quick enough. She didn't miss her chance this time.

'Mom! We are going into the tunnel.'

Nick looked at the road in front of him. It was a straight highway with no tunnels, hills or mountains or any other natural or unnatural obstructions.

'I'm going to lose the signal soon, Mom.'

This time even Nick heard Jackie's mother's voice echoing from the phone and filling the tiny car. 'Now really, Jackie.' A minor disappointment was attached to the words. 'There are no tunnels on that road. What an earth are you talking about?'

Jackie stared at the ceiling of her car and could not find words. Nick was trying to hold his laughter. He stared at the highway with great concentration.

'Well, whatever,' Jackie's mother's slightly annoyed answer cut the air. 'Anyhow,' she continued. 'We are expecting you for a Sunday lunch.'

There was a very strange pause and Jackie's mother's voice altered. 'Andrew is coming. Did I mention that?' The last question was an ill attempt to sound casual, because Jackie's mother was anything but casual.

Jackie narrowed her eyes. Nick forgot to laugh. He found himself wanting to know everything there was to know about this mysterious Andrew.

Jackie's mouth was a straight angry line when she finally spoke. 'Mom. No you did not mention that. And...' She didn't have the slightest chance of finishing her sentence.

'Oh, no I did mention it. I'm sure of that and wear something nice, won't you darling? Something feminine. Skirt would be a nice change. Oh, I've got to go. Tony is here for my Italian lesson. I want to travel to Firenze this summer. Ciao, ciao, bella!'

And she was off.

Jackie stared at the road in front of her. She angrily tossed the cell phone into her bag with more force than was needed.

'Who's Andrew?' Nick had to ask against his own better judgment. He knew that he would sound jealous, which was true. He was very jealous and he needed to know.

'Oh, Jesus!' Jackie blurted. Her voice didn't sound happy at the thought of Andrew, which made Nick excessively happy.

'What, he's Jesus.' He said jovially.

'Oh god,' Jackie sighed.

'Going up the ladder. No wonder your mother wants you to have lunch with him.'

'Oh, shut up.' Jackie rolled her eyes, but, somehow, she started to feel better.

'So?' Nick glanced at Jackie questioningly.

'How much time do we have?' Jackie asked.

'Another hour at least.'

'Okay, it's a long story with no meaning or sense, and it is full of unimportant, uninteresting details.'

'Go ahead. Love to hear.'

Jackie smiled and then began telling the Andrew saga.

'My mother has always wanted me to marry well, which means to marry money and a position. Preferably those two together, which would in turn, obviously, lead to important connections. Andrew is my stepfather's business partner's son. He is nice and that just about tells everything there is to tell about him. He has money, lots of it. He has connections and his great-great grandfather was sir something-or-other and there apparently was a castle at one point, a fact which my mother never forgets to mention when speaking about Andrew.'

Jackie took a deep breath. 'So Andrew fills my mother's dream of the perfect son-in-law. Except I don't want him and I have no idea what it is that he wants. Probably a new Aston Martin, but he definitely does not want me.' Jackie sighed. 'So therefore these lunches are painful experiences. They are torturous affairs and...' Jackie ran out of breath and negative words.

'He wears white shoes and when he eats he makes the most good awful smacking sounds I have ever heard and my mother always puts me to sit by him. At the end of the lunch, I'm ready to kill him.'

'So you don't like him.' Nick was feeling good.

'I can't say that I hate him, because I don't.'

Jackie paused trying to find the right words. 'He is...he is...he's like a smelly dog that cannot help the fact that he smells, but you don't hate the dog because he smells.'

Nick raised his eyebrows and laughter started to build up inside him.

'You know, a nice but smelly dog.' Jackie added, not really knowing if she should talk more or not.

Nick burst out laughing. 'What a description.' He roared.

'Well.' Jackie blushed. She felt guilty. It was not a very nice description, she had to admit, but her slightly cruel portrayal explained Andrew perfectly. '...well you asked.' She said accusingly, sulking on her seat.

'So what kind of dog am I then?' Nick smiled invitingly.

'I'm not going to say anything anymore.' Jackie folded her arms in front of her and the corners of her lips dropped into a tight, straight line.

'Oh, but you must.' Nick said.

'I'm not going to say anything.' Jackie's hands remained folded against her chest. She observed with ever growing passion the passing monotonous scenery along the highway.

'Maybe I'm a poodle?' Nick suggested trying to pull Jackie in. 'Or I could be one of those hairless dogs,' he continued jovially.

'Definitely not the hairless,' Jackie said and glanced at his forearms.

'So a poodle, then.' He set his bait innocently.

'Not a poodle, though you do have curly hair.'

Nick waited.

'Maybe you could be...' Jackie laughed at her own thought and only after a couple of giggles was she able to add, '...you could be a basset hound.'

Nick rolled his eyes and exclaimed. 'I don't have big ears!'

'Whatever you say.' Jackie grinned. She was enjoying this and she was fighting back the urge to laugh at the sight of Nick checking the size of his ears in the rearview mirror.

'They are a perfectly normal size.' He declared. 'Very normal ears.'

'Maybe you are a dachshund then.'

'And now I have bloody short legs as well.' Nick glanced at his legs quickly.

Jackie began to laugh. Tears rolled down her cheeks and she was unable to stop the hysterical giggles that came out through her closed lips.

'I know what you are Jacqueline Callaghan,' Nick declared seriously. 'You are a bloody terrier, who never lets go after they get a good grip on things. That's what you are, a terrier.' He paused and then exhaled the words. 'A bloody nosy, annoying terrier.'

Jackie had a fit of hysterical laughter erupting from her again. She couldn't help it. She laughed even more than earlier. Nick looked at her and then a smile appeared at the corners of his mouth. 'A bloody terrier,' he repeated and slightly nudged Jackie on her shoulder.

'Basset hound.' Jackie snorted.

'Terrier.'

'Basset hound.' Jackie nudged him back.

They were like nine year olds again, playing you-are am-not game.

A sound happiness had settled into Jackie. She didn't know how to describe it, but she decided to enjoy the feeling to the fullest.

Nick drove on, but once in awhile he would look at Jackie and shake his head, which made Jackie laugh out loud again.

Both of them seemed to know that something extraordinarily good had just happened between them. It was too fragile to talk about. The best way was to tread casually around this newly found connection and gently follow its course.

It was dark when they drove into the village. Nick parked the car in front of Jackie's house.

'We can drive to your house first and then I'll just drive back home.' Jackie suggested.

'That's all right. It's a nice night, I can walk. Don't worry.' He put the keys into his pocket and got out.

'Where do you want to put the brochures?' Nick asked as he was ready to open the back of the car.

'Just leave them there. We'll have a meeting the day after tomorrow and I can just bring them straight to the pub.'

'Okay.' Nick stood by Jackie's car dangling the car keys between his fingers. He was looking at the car, Jackie's house, the street that led to his pub. He even looked at the flower bushes by Jackie's house. Everywhere but Jackie. Somehow he just could not look into those green eyes.

'Well...' he finally managed, when Jackie blurted at the same time. 'Do you want to come in and have a glass of wine with me?'

Nick answered very quickly. Too fast for his own liking, but he could not help it. 'That would be nice. Thanks.'

They walked up to her house and as Jackie was looking for her keys Nick felt that he had been there before. So familiar and so exhausting. So much anticipation and nervousness.

Nick pushed the door open. Jackie flicked on the light. They walked into the kitchen stepping over magazines and shoes. Jackie took out a bottle of wine and two glasses.

'Please, ignore the mess.' She said and pointed to the sink full of dishes.

'I really don't see anything mess like.' Nick looked around and over the dishes and the table filled with pencils and sketch pads. Jackie quickly pushed the papers aside and put the pencils into a jar. They lingered in the kitchen and Jackie opened the bottle of wine. She handed a glass to Nick and an odd complicated silence followed. It was a silence out of which the next thing was unknown.

Finally they clicked their glasses together and Jackie said with an unnatural perkiness. 'To the brochures and to our great day!'

'To our great day!' Nick repeated slowly, looking at Jackie intently.

He moved closer, as if to kiss her, when the kitchen door suddenly flew open and Thomas stomped in. Nick and Jackie both froze in their positions. Thomas was stunned and could only stare at the two of them with his mouth open.

'Shit! I didn't know you were here, Nick. I just came to borrow Jackie's tools.' He stammered.

Nick and Jackie moved quickly apart from each other. Hands to their sides, the untouched wine almost spilling over the rim of the glass.

'Oh. Okay, then...they are in the studio.' Jackie finally managed to say. Her eyes were darting between Nick and Thomas.

Nick took the first sip of his wine. He tasted nothing. Thomas stood by the door, his mouth still wide open, moving his feet on the threshold.

'No need to help me.' Thomas finally said. 'I'll find them myself. Continue…whatever you were doing.' He turned around and went out the door laughing jovially.

Nick looked at Jackie and then moved closer to her. Jackie was ready to kiss him this time, when Thomas put his head in the door again.

'Where's the key to the studio?' He grunted and stared at the wall behind Jackie and Nick, pretending not to see them at all.

Jackie and Nick withdrew again and Nick took a long sip of his wine as if nothing was going on between him and Jackie, and he was merely there to share a glass of wine amongst good friends.

'Where it always is—under the board on the wall beside the door.' Jackie's eyes were burning with anguish as she stared at Thomas.

'Nope, not there.' Thomas leaned against the door frame and scratched his rough jaw.

'Yes it is. Just go and look.'

'Okay, but I'm telling you it's not there.' He went out again, spreading his hands above his head in mute protest.

Both Jackie and Nick knew that this time Thomas was going to pop into the kitchen again. They leaned against the kitchen counter and drank their wine in silence, looking at each other, wanting it to be but knowing that the moment was not meant for them.

Thomas returned in a couple of minutes banging his feet loudly against the steps announcing his approach this time. 'Not there, just like I said.' He yelled from the door into the kitchen. 'Can I come in or are you two doing something?' Thomas asked innocently enough and then tried not to laugh out loud.

'I think you'd better go and help him.' Nick said as he drained the last of his wine.

'But…uh…' Jackie muttered and looked like a helpless woman in a b-movie who is just about to wring her hands in distress before an evil man kidnaps her or a strange exotic animal attacks her tent in the middle of a desert. It was going to end disastrously, no matter what. Somebody was going to devour something; a helpless woman, lost hopes, almost-there-kisses…something.

'I'll see you later.' Nick said and moved closer to the kitchen door. 'Thank you for the lovely day.' He put the car keys on the table.

'Me too. I had a very, very nice time.' Jackie said slowly, cursing the word nice that came so often out of her mouth. It had been more than nice. It had been the nicest day that she had ever spent with Nick and she wanted more of the same.

'Bye!' Nick said as he disappeared into the darkness.

'Bye!' Jackie whispered. She remained still for awhile, leaning against the counter, staring at the closed door. She rubbed her face with her hands, grunted and then opened the old kitchen door with one aggressive push, turning her burning eyes to Thomas, who was lingering in the garden path between the house and the studio, kicking stones and keeping his hands in his pockets.

'And you needed the bloody wrench just at this very moment!' Jackie hissed at him.

Thomas pushed his hands deeper into his pants' pockets. He was staring at his feet. 'I'm sorry. I didn't know Nick was here with you.'

'And you just couldn't leave when you saw us? Now could you?' Jackie asked. She was still fuming. She had wanted that kiss and now, when it was not possible, she wanted it even more than ever.

'Well that would have just looked plain awkward.' Thomas shrugged his shoulders.

'Oh yeah and this isn't awkward at all…now where the hell is that bloody key?' Jackie stomped to the studio door and started looking for the key. It had fallen on the ground between the flowers.

Jackie picked it up and ceremoniously dangled it in the air in front of Thomas's face. Thomas whispered sorry and waited for Jackie to open the door.

She switched on the light and let Thomas in.

The studio floor was covered in sawdust as always and Thomas kicked it around and was just about to mention the mess to Jackie, but then thought twice about it and decided to say nothing. Which, considering the situation, was probably the right thing to do.

Jackie had a huge selection of tools all arranged on the shelves on the wall, each tool with its specific place.

Thomas pointed silently to the wrench he had come for and Jackie picked it up, but before giving it to Thomas, she wanted to hear him say something.

'Okay, okay, you horrid tool goddess. I will return this wrench to you in the same condition as it is now or let the tool gods strike me down dead.'

Jackie nodded gravely and let Thomas have the wrench. 'All right then.' She said grumpily.

On his way out Thomas stopped at the door and grinned wickedly at Jackie. 'And so does the passionate romance begin between the steadfast pub owner and the innocent woodworker...?'

'Not funny!' Jackie interrupted Thomas sharply. 'Now get out AND I want my wrench back unharmed tomorrow morning early— or I will have to rip off your arms.'

'I will, I will.' Thomas muttered and under his breath he added, 'Jesus, mother of god, she's a bit touchy for a woman in love.'

Thomas left and Jackie returned to the kitchen and finished the glass of wine she had earlier left on the counter when the evening had still been full of promises.

She sighed and looked out the window into the dark night. Her reflection visible in the window against its dark frame. She was holding onto her empty wine glass, turning it absentmindedly in her hand.

It had started to rain again. No silver linings there.

Chapter 16

Brochure!

The late night soft rain had changed overnight into a downpour, falling from the dull, dark grey sky. It was not the light happy rain that promises a humid sunshine filled afternoon. It was rain that offered you an opportunity to study each raindrop individually as it fell solidly onto the soaked, marshy ground. It was rain which made you automatically think of Noah and his ark and all the undone cleaning projects in the house.

Jackie tried to work. She sat in her studio staring at the empty white papers in front of her, her pencil ready, well sharpened, but her thoughts were running wild. She had organized the gallery and she had dusted the display shelves. It was almost an impossible job to try to keep the gallery dust free. 'Well, it was impossible,' she had said to no one as she had looked at her dirty dust rag. She checked her supplies in the storage room and made a list of materials she would need to order. She wanted to make something very different for the new show Jill's mother had talked about. She fiddled with her pen, stretched her arms and was staring at the still empty drawing paper admiring its fine grain when she heard heavy footsteps at the door. Her heart jumped and then got caught in her throat, where she could very clearly hear its panicky beat.

She waited for what seemed like an eternity. The door flung open and Thomas stormed in, stomping his muddy boots and cursing the rain drops that had found their way down his neck despite the umbrella.

'Good morning!' He hollered happily, and then cursed the rain again, shaking his wet head like a dog.

'Here is your wrench,' he said slowly, wanting to emphasize the fact that he was bringing the borrowed property back on time. 'I have brought it back, as promised.' He said and bowed his wet head.

Jackie stared at him. Right now she hardly cared for the return of her wrench, whereas normally she would have acted surprised, and then she and Thomas would have engaged in horrifying mockery of one another.

'Thanks,' she said slowly and put the wrench back in its own place in the studio.

'Well…' Thomas was waiting for her to say something more.

Jackie sighed and occupied herself staring at the tool box on the floor.

'Hmm.' Thomas sighed and a small knowing smile appeared on his face. 'Our Jackie is truly in love.' Thomas was grinning shamelessly now. 'Oh, my my.'

'Oh, shut up.' The thought that this was perhaps love was so shocking that Jackie could not think of anything else to say. She stared at Thomas with a horrified look on her face and more or less threw Thomas out of her studio. She heard him laughing as he walked down the muddy garden path. Jackie tried to work but in the end she locked the studio and went into her house. She sat in the kitchen listening to the rain and the old clock on the wall, ticking away the time.

It was a very long, rain filled, miserable afternoon during which time Jackie first ate all the sweets she was able to find in the kitchen cupboards till she felt sick. After that she changed to salty snacks, which in turn enabled her to eat the rest of the sweets. She admired the strange plastic taste of wine gums and tried to think of a reason why she liked them. Her thoughts were going round and round, never quite reaching a happy conclusion. She detested the strange feeling of waiting for something to happen, but strangely not knowing exactly what.

Nevertheless she waited for that something to happen. She waited for that somebody to stop by or call. She waited and while she waited she continued the cleaning she had started earlier in her gallery, extending the nervous energy into her house. Not that she wanted to clean her house, but it was the only occupation she could perform while her thoughts were scattered in millions of directions.

The sound of her phone interrupted her monotonous existence. Her heart missed a beat as she answered the phone waiting to hear Nick's low voice.

'Buon giorno, carissima.' She heard her mother's sharp metallic voice instead. 'Come stai?' Her mother continued, obviously very happy to have a chance to impress somebody with her newly acquired ability to speak rudimentary Italian.

'Bene, grazie,' Jackie answered swallowing her disappointment.

'Yes, yes,' her mother's harsh voice travelled through the airways. 'Robert and I are definitely going to spend a summer in Firenze and enjoy the beautiful vast landscapes of Toscana.'

'Good...' Jackie answered preparing herself for a lengthy explanation while she began dusting her bookshelf.

'I would love to visit Rome as well, but your stepfather's sister's refusal to agree to my plans is making our travel planning very hard indeed. Some people are so disagreeable. She has no knowledge of Italian, and therefore I believe I should be the one to make the plans, since I will be the primary translator anyway. Don't you agree?'

Jackie looked at the books lying in front of her on the floor. She picked up one and began leafing through the pages paying more attention to the pictures of the paintings than to her mother's travel plans.

'I would love to buy an olive orchard while we are in Toscana.'

Jackie murmured something that could be taken any way a person listening would like to interpret it. Not that her mother was actually listening to her responses at all. In her mind, she was already picking the first harvest from her olive orchard.

'Anyway'—Jackie's mother interrupted her own train of thought—'I was just calling to remind you about the Sunday lunch. Dress nicely and for god's sake wear stockings. Ciao bella!' And she was off, leaving Jackie listening to the rhythmic beep of her own phone.

Jackie put the books back into their places in the now clean bookshelf and went to make herself some more tea. The cold rainy day was beginning to make her feel chilled. She let Felix out and then one minute later he ran right back in with his tail under his body, looking at Jackie, asking quietly—why on earth did she think he would like to go out in that weather. He shook himself dry before Jackie had a chance to cover him with an old towel. Mud drops were everywhere on the floor and some even on the wall. The afternoon slowly rolled on. Nothing happened, nobody came. The old clock ticked away the time and Jackie felt anxious.

She finally finished cleaning her house and found herself standing on top of the basement stairs staring into the darkness with a cup of tea in her hand. She flicked on the lights and walked down. The basement was a historical collection of things stored from the past quarter of a century. Amazing what you cannot throw away, Jackie thought as she stared at a pair of old rubber boots in the corner. 'Who the hell in their family had such enormous feet?' She asked herself as she pushed the boots aside. The basement had to wait; she would rather do the laundry right now—after another cup of tea.

There was nothing worse than being alone when there was no other choice. Most of the time Jackie didn't mind being on her own, but those were the times when she had chosen the loneliness and she filled that time happily with her work. She was too busy to notice any kind of a void, but when time stood still and the only sound in the house was the dog's nails scraping against the floor boards, then she noticed the ever present emptiness. This unwelcome, threatening solitude was hard to live with. It bode of more days like this in the future. There was no choosing to be done with this isolation. It was her only option when everybody else was busy with their own lives and people in it. Even being angry at Chris would have been welcome, she thought, compared to this futile feeling. At least I would have somebody in the house to be mad at and to yell at.

Sadness hung above the house like the rain, beating Jackie down with its heavy clouds.

Jackie called Jill later that night. Jill sounded very tired as she answered the phone and Jackie felt guilty for calling so late. 'I'm sorry, Jill. Did I wake you up?' She asked apologetically.

'No, that's fine. It would have been Nellie anyway, if it would not have been you. That child never sleeps. I swear she is Rosemary's baby, and I'm losing my brain cells at an alarming speed. I think I've become one of those women with a vacant stare. When someone brings me coffee, I've already forgotten that I asked for it!'

Jackie heard a baby cry in the background.

'Like I said,' Jill said. 'It would have been Nellie if it weren't you.'

'Sorry.' Jackie whispered into the phone. She felt terrible to have bothered Jill.

'I'll just take the phone with me. Hold on, hold on. Yes, Nellie, I'm coming.'

Jackie waited till Jill had Nellie in her arms and she was comfortably resting in her rocking chair.

'So how was your non-date with the respectable man.?' Jill asked.

'Fine. My non-date was fine and you can tell Robbie that he indeed has a sail boat.'

'Great. Robbie will love him like the brother he never had.'

'I knew he would.' Jackie laughed. 'Anyhow I had a lovely time with him.'

'Good and....'

'And what?' Jackie asked defensively.

'And what did you do?'

'Went for breakfast and late lunch. Visited a museum....' Jackie began.

'Yes, yes...any kissing?' Jill interrupted. 'I want some real action here, Jackie. Not Harlequin-romance hand holding. I want some Arnold Schwarzenegger hasta-la–vista-baby action. I'm a mother with sagging boobs and track pants. I need some information from the other world. Any kissing?'

Jackie felt her face getting hotter and a strange feeling was moving in the pit of her stomach.

•

'Well…' Jill's voice cut through Jackie's baffled thoughts.

'Well, we tried to kiss. If that's what you want to know.'

'Well, yes. What do you mean you tried to kiss? Did you kiss or not?'

'No…' Jackie bit her bottom lip.

'So what happened?'

'Thomas walked in to borrow a wrench.'

'No! A man came into your house to borrow a tool when you were making out with another man.'

'I'm afraid so.'

'You know that sounds very strange.'

'I know.'

'Poor Jackie.' Jill was trying not to laugh.

'Don't laugh at me.' Jackie mumbled.

'I'm trying not to. Actually I can't because Nellie fell asleep again.'

'Give her a kiss for me. You better go to bed as well.' Jackie said.

'Okay, I will. I'll call you tomorrow and I'll tell Robbie the happy news about the sailboat.'

'Goodnight.'

'Bye.'

Jackie put the phone down and thought about 'the almost kiss' that had happened in her kitchen earlier. It would have been very nice if Thomas hadn't arrived at that very moment. Who knows what would have happened then.

*   *   *

Jackie could smell the newly printed paper as she walked into the pub, carrying one of the cardboard boxes filled with the studio tour brochures. The wind had blown yesterday's menacing rain clouds away and the afternoon had arrived with shy sunshine, a fair promise of good weather to come.

Russell, Thomas and Kenneth were already at the bar having a pint. Russell was in the midst of his favourite topic.

Nick looked up at Jackie and smiled, a careful, private smile, meant to be shared with only her.

'Hi, Jackie.' Nick's voice was calm. His voice was as tranquil as the surface of a lake with nothing hiding under the water: no secrets, hidden feelings, rocks, shipwrecks, nothing. It was a very casual greeting.

'Hi, Nick. How are you?' Jackie's answer was equally bare of emotion, to her own surprise, disguising all the feelings rampaging through her veins. 'Good, good. You need help with those boxes?' A kind offer which any good friend would propose in a similar situation.

'Actually, yes. I have four more boxes in the car.' Both of them glanced at the door and the possibility of being alone even for a few seconds.

Nick came eagerly out from behind the bar, but unfortunately Russell was faster. 'I'll carry them for you, girl.' He hollered and finished the rest of his beer in one quick swig. 'Just pour me another one, will you Nick.'

A slight disappointment flashed across Nick's face. Thomas was staring at both of them with a wide open knowing smirk spreading over his face. He sat there at the bar, smiling and swivelling in his chair, obviously following the two of them closely.

Jackie put the box down at the meeting table. She looked at Nick across the room and then walked toward the door with Russell, kicking Thomas's chair on the way out.

'I'm always ready to help you ladies.' Russell chatted as they walked to the car.

'Well, thank you Sir Russell.'

Russell chuckled. 'At your service, m'lady.' He attempted a bow.

They came back in, each carrying two boxes and set them on the table. Russell was looking at the brochure, which was taped on the top of the box. 'Looks darn good to me,' he said. 'Bloody fantastic job.'

Jackie opened up one of the boxes with a pocketknife she had with her.

Thomas looked at her and then turned to Nick deciding to amuse himself a bit, while he waited for the meeting to start. 'You better be careful, old pal. She carries a knife with her.'

Nick ignored Thomas.

'I like a lady with a little danger in her.' Russell chuckled and fixed his pants by pulling them up by the thick belt.

Jackie admired the clean, neat, tightly packed stacks of brochures. She let her hand wander gently on top of them—smooth, shiny new paper. She took a few of them out of the box and then walked to the bar to give them to Nick.

Nick smelled them. 'Ahh, I love that newly printed paper smell,' he said. 'I'll hand them out for you…to real customers.' Nick quickly glanced at the boys in the corner, who were playing rock, paper, scissors about whose turn it was to buy a round.

Jackie smiled as her eyes followed Nick's. 'Thanks, Nick.'

'It's nothing. You want coffee?'

'Love to.' She sat down at the bar. She was still smiling as she waited for her coffee. It was good to see Nick again. She had missed him yesterday. Strange to miss somebody who lives only a few hundred yards from your house.

The men at the bar were studying the brochures they had snatched from Nick's hands. They were sipping their beers and admiring the colourful brochure cover. Thomas looked up at Jackie. 'This is really good, you know.'

'Yes, I think Caroline really did a wonderful job.' Jackie grinned.

The studio tour project had reached an important landmark. Jackie was almost beginning to get excited about its approach. Looking at the brochures made it all feel more real.

Thomas shook the brochure open in a stiff ceremonial manner and winked at Jackie.

Jackie drank her coffee. Nick stole a couple of careful glances at her. Luckily for them the others were absorbed in the reading of the brochure; they paid no attention to Nick and Jackie, otherwise, by nightfall, there would have been rapidly spreading rumours about their quickly approaching wedding.

Suddenly Thomas froze. He stared at the open page in front of him and then very slowly he lifted his eyes to look at Jackie.

'Um…Jackie you haven't by any chance read the brochure yet?' Thomas's voice was very tentative, as if walking on thin ice.

Jackie smiled happily, 'Well, I leafed through it, but no, I haven't read it in detail yet. Why?'

Thomas was quiet for awhile before answering. 'Well, you better read through the B & B directory then…' He couldn't finish his sentence.

Jackie gave a suspicious glance at Thomas and then grabbed the paper from his hands. She read the listings of the B & Bs; her face turned a sickly colour. She bit her bottom lip as she put the brochure down with trembling hands. Jackie felt all the hairs on her scalp rising and her blood pumping all the way down to her fingertips. She stared into the distance and with a faint voice she slowly moaned, 'Oh, dear god!'

Nick's eyes were darting between her and Thomas, who had started to giggle hysterically, wiping the corners of his eyes with his hands.

'What is it this time?' Nick asked Jackie, whose shoulders now slumped as she sat at the bar next to giggling Thomas. Nick took the brochure and Thomas helpfully pointed to the part that had created these two entirely different reactions.

Nick read out loud. 'East End Gay's Bed and Breakfast, lovely, historic place to spend a luxurious weekend…' He stopped in the middle of the sentence as the words he was reading hung in the dead air of the pub. He looked up at Jackie. He couldn't believe what he was reading.

Jackie lifted her limp hand and waved it in the air. There was no hope for the tour. It had all drained away in a matter of seconds. There would be no tour. There could not be a tour. There would be nothing. 'Go on. Read the other one as well,' she said with a voice void of strength and the earlier optimism.

Nick hesitated, but Jackie's hand was still waving impatiently in the air telling him to go ahead. He cleared his throat and read aloud,

'West End Gay's B & B.' Nick paused and lifted his eyes from the brochure. 'Holy shit'—the words flew out of his mouth—'how could this have happened?'

Jackie's voice was weak. 'I have no clue. Sheridan was the proofreader; he was supposed to have the experience.' Her last words were a faint whisper.

Meanwhile Russell had taken the brochure and was reading the two advertisements in question. 'Blimey me, those names have really stuck, haven't they? My, my.'

Thomas leaned back in his chair. 'Now this is why I never ever take any responsibility.' He stated and drank his beer casually, happy not to have been the cause of the problem.

Jackie stared at Nick without seeing him clearly. 'Jesus mother of god, what are we going to do?' She wrung her hands in the air.

Nick took her cold, shaking hands into his own warm hands and held them tightly together. He looked into her dazed eyes and said slowly. 'I think that you better talk with Tim and Tom'—and here he faltered though he tried so very much not to—'no, Tom and Kevin…no…Tim and John…no.' He paused and then cursed under his breath. 'Damn.' And continued, 'with both East End and West End boys, before you start handing these brochures out.'

Jackie's eyes grew wide. 'You're right…oh…shit!' Her last words were spoken with a long deep sigh, which held doom and destruction and blame. She closed her eyes tightly. 'Shit, shit, shit.'

The door to the pub opened and everybody at the bar turned their heads to look. Thomas was the first to recognise who it was. 'Here comes Sheridan now,' he announced cheerfully and took a long sip of his beer to hide his face and the big grin that had flashed over it. Thomas found the situation quite hilarious, but had enough sense to keep it to himself.

Jackie looked at Sheridan, who was briskly walking toward her. She felt sick to her stomach. Thomas absentmindedly tapped her shoulders, while keeping his eyes on Sheridan's portly figure. He was going to observe very closely how Sheridan acted in his self defence. In the middle of this tragic incident there might be a very good opportunity to laugh at Sheridan, he thought. 'And that was always fun.'

'Good evening everybody!' Sheridan bellowed his greetings and let his hands wander across his large firm midriff, playing with his vest's brass buttons.

Jackie had the crumpled brochure in her limp hand. She didn't realize that she had been holding onto it so tightly. Sheridan saw it as he marched toward the bar.

'Are those the new brochures?' He asked. 'Splendid! Let me see.' He was puffing with eager anticipation.

Jackie handed one of the brochures to him. Her face was very grim and her voice solemn. The words fell out of her dry mouth one by one.

'Sheridan, we…have…a…little…problem.'

Sheridan looked up from the brochure he had been admiring proudly. 'Problem? It looks perfectly good to me. What is the problem?' He was genuinely puzzled and stared at Jackie from under his bushy eyebrows.

Thomas helpfully decided to shed some light on the matter. 'Just have a look at the bed and breakfast listings over there on the right-hand side, if you would, please.' He leaned over eagerly to point out the specific part of the brochure, barely hiding the obvious pleasure he was having in doing so.

Sheridan stared at Thomas. He was very suspicious; Thomas had never, even once, during their acquaintance offered any kind of help.

Slowly he took his reading glasses out from his vest's breast pocket and put them on his nose, giving Thomas one more puzzled look over the rim of his glasses. He gradually lowered his eyes and began reading the listings in front of him. He went through the list alphabetically, mumbling his endorsements here and there.

Suddenly his whole body became tense and rigid. The brochure began shaking in his firm grip. He felt for a chair behind him with a trembling hand and sat down, his legs buckling under his mighty weight. He stared in front of him and spoke with a fragile voice.

'Well…well…I'll be darned. I never, um…I mean…terrible… uh…' He took a handkerchief out of his pocket and wiped his forehead and neck. He was suddenly perspiring heavily. 'Well…' He patted his forehead again. 'I mean that's what we all call them, right?' His pathetic question hung hopelessly in the air.

'Privately, yes, but not publicly in print.' Jackie said quietly.

'Oh, my…oh my…It never struck me to correct it…I never actually noticed it even…Well, otherwise I would naturally have corrected it, but I never…I never even realized.' He stared at Jackie and desolately shook his head. Then he paused for a second and turned slowly to Nick. 'Would you please give me a whisky. Oh, my. Make it a double, will you?' He tapped his neck and forehead with his handkerchief once more. Suddenly he had realized the magnitude of his mistake. Sheridan stared straight ahead. He couldn't fathom that he had made a mistake. He, Sheridan Remington Watson, who was in charge of the proofreading had failed to recognize a mistake, maybe for the first time in his entire life.

Nick gave him the whisky and Sheridan drank half of it in one gulp. He sighed deeply as he felt it burn in his throat and then the fiery warmth of the whisky settled in.

Thomas ordered himself another beer. He felt entitled to it since Sheridan was already drinking whiskey.

Jackie cleared her throat. 'Look, it's almost time for the meeting to start.' She stared at Sheridan who was not there at all. 'So we will all have to think what on earth we are going to do.' She paused and then plunged on. 'We have no more money to reprint the brochure and we cannot erase the mistake from the existing brochures either. There's only so much liquid paper can do.'

Nick was looking at Jackie and trying to think of a way to help her out of this trouble. Russell and Thomas were listening to Jackie, drinking their pints and mumbling their halfhearted support. Sheridan had crossed his hands and was resting them on top of his considerably large middle. He continued to stare at the bare wall of the pub, deep in the world of self-doubt and pity.

The front door opened and people started trickling in for the meeting. Jackie got up. 'Okay, give me all of the brochures. I better get ready for some tongue lashing.' She walked to her usual place at the end of the table. She still had no idea how to start the meeting. What could she possibly say? 'Dear all. We have fucked up the brochure.' It didn't sound too good.

When Rosalind arrived, she noted with utter surprise Sheridan's presence at the bar with Thomas, Kenneth and Russell. She pursed her lips, raised her eyebrows and waited for some kind of recognition from him. When Sheridan didn't move from his hunched position to greet her, Rosalind turned away and walked briskly after Caroline and Alistair to the meeting table. 'How very inappropriate of him.' She muttered quietly.

Rosalind sat down under Jackie's watchful eyes. She mumbled something about Sheridan to Caroline and Alistair. They all turned to look at him at the bar.

Caroline shrugged her shoulders and then she saw the brochures in front of Jackie. She reached forward, lazily grabbing one, barely hiding her obvious pleasure. Seeing the results of one's work was always pleasing. She didn't say a word and didn't need to; Rosalind already had the brochure in her eager hands and was bursting with compliments.

'Absolutely fabulous work, Caroline. It is as good as it could be— you know—considering the company and all.' She nudged Alistair's elbow. 'Quite good, quite good,' he mumbled before turning back to his own deep meditation.

Caroline nodded, a slight quiver of her nose revealing her pride.

Muriel walked to the table with Daisy and Nancy in tow. 'Oh, the brochures have arrived. How exciting!' She said cheerfully.

Daisy was turning one in her fingers. 'Really pretty,' she said shyly.

'Well, thank you.' Caroline spoke mockingly. Pretty was not a word she associated with.

'It looks astonishing, Caroline. It really does,' Nancy said softly. Caroline acknowledged by lifting an eyebrow, the subtlety of which was lost when Russell walked to the table and clapped Caroline on the back sending her lurching forward under the impact.

Sheridan was drinking another double whisky at the bar. He had not uttered a word to anybody yet, his square back was facing the crowd, while his shoulders were bent around his whisky glass; he was holding on to it tightly.

'Good evening, people.' Harriet bellowed as she stomped in with Janet. Kenneth glanced at Janet, took another sip of his pint and walked to the table to seat himself beside her.

Jackie noticed but had no time to ponder its sweetness. Doom was too close; the fiery pit of hell was going to be opened at any moment and she was to be the first one down. Finally she let out a long sigh. 'Okay. We better start then.' She looked around the table at the people excitedly turning the shiny pages of the brochure. 'As you have noticed, we have the new brochures.' She paused, creating an unintended theatrical pause as she collected her strength. 'Yes, they are beautiful, but we have a small problem.'

People's expressions changed. To their eyes everything looked fantastic.

Rosalind's eyes followed her thin nose and finally rested on Jackie. 'What kind of problem? If I may ask?'

By now Jackie was beyond fearing Rosalind. This newest development had given her a new extra thick skin. 'Look under the bed and breakfasts and then tell me what are we going to do. And let me point out that any, *any* brilliant ideas will be truly appreciated.'

People tried to find the bed and breakfast section as quickly as possible. There was a burst of feverish activity. Otherwise, the pub was quiet.

Suddenly a sharp intake of breath drawn in between teeth came from Rosalind. 'How can this be?' She spat. 'Jackie, why did you not correct this dreadful mistake at once? This is absolutely unacceptable negligence on your part.'

Jackie was about to answer when Sheridan strolled over from the bar. He had the half-full glass of whisky in his hand as he slumped down heavily on a chair, putting his glass on the table with more force than was needed. The whiskey whirled treacherously, almost overflowing. 'Because it was my bloody mistake—my mistake and nobody else's; that's why. So blame me and not her.' He blurted, his words slurring slightly.

Rosalind stared at him and then quickly tried to take back her hurtful words. 'Oh. Well. It is quite understandable. It could have happen to anybody.' She stuttered finding suitable words as she went along.

Jackie, mouth set in a thin, straight line, eyes fuming in anger, stared at Rosalind. Rosalind averted her eyes and turned to Caroline, who, completely taken aback by this bizarre incident, was trying not to laugh.

Jackie relaxed her stare and let her eyes wander around the table. 'Any thoughts—what can we do to fix this?'

People glanced around, hoping that someone else had a solution. The air was thick with scattered thoughts but nothing materialized. Muriel, Nancy and Daisy looked worried, feeling deep sympathy for Jackie.

'Rosalind knows, as our treasurer, that we have no money left for a reprint—what to do?' Jackie let her words fall into the dazed atmosphere.

Russell fidgeted in his seat before he spoke. 'Well. I see only one way to solve this problem. We need these brochures and we cannot print them again—right?' He looked at Jackie quickly. 'So,' Russell continued. 'What's left is to talk to those boys and see if they will let us distribute the brochures as planned despite the mistake.' He looked around the table and his eyes were met by blank faces. 'They seem like very nice chaps with a good sense of humour. I am sure they would understand the situation.' He added hopefully, spreading his hands in the air.

'And I guess it is me who has to go and talk to them.' Jackie blew air between her pursed lips. Her head was pounding with sudden pain.

The whisky had gotten to Sheridan's head and he felt brave enough to face anything. 'I'll come with you. It is only fair. I must face my troops.'

'I believe it is better if I go alone,' Jackie responded softly. She slid a couple of brochures into her bag, closed the flap and then glanced at Sheridan. 'You could check the website, though, and fix the mistake in there.'

Sheridan concentrated very hard to look dignified. 'Yes, yes… Copy that. I'll do that immediately.' He had two red spots on his cheeks and his lips had acquired a dark purplish tint.

'And give me that website address, because I'm going to a dog show with Winston tomorrow,' Harriet said loudly, and then all hell broke loose.

'A dog show?' Rosalind exclaimed in a sharp sneering voice. 'You certainly are not going to drag my husband's reputation into a bloody country dog show.' Rosalind looked as if she could actually die; others, on the other hand, seemed to consider the dog show and the publicity it offered a good thing, especially if it irritated Rosalind this much.

'A dog show?' Caroline spat out. 'Oh, dear god help us.'

Jackie thought that she might as well leave immediately, abandoning the fighting and the dog show for the volunteers. 'All right then. Meeting adjourned. I'll let you all know what happens with the brochure.'

Sheridan slurred, 'Damn good of you to go and face the fire.' He had slightly watery eyes.

Jackie patted his shoulder. 'Yeah…right…goodnight.' She slung her bag over her shoulder and walked out of the pub under Nick's watchful eyes while Rosalind's rant continued. She was fair in her fury. That had to be said about her. She declared her disgust evenly toward everybody: dogs, cats, rodents and bad artists alike.

Sheridan got up on his wavering legs and gave Caroline a friendly pat on her shoulder. The whiskey made him more sociable than usual. He was in touch with his rampantly running feelings. Nothing better than a good disaster to make you appreciate the few good things in life. 'Damn good looking brochure, though. Keep up the good work.'

Caroline stared up at him. She was more than surprised and didn't quite know what to say to. Sheridan wandered back to the bar for another whiskey, leaving Caroline sitting by the table looking awkward. She didn't know who to loathe more: Sheridan and his gullible mistake or Harriet who was going to drag her reputation as a serious artist into the gutter with the dog show.

Jackie left the loud, hostile atmosphere of the pub and walked out into the quiet night. She could still hear Sheridan's voice congratulating people for having such a fine young woman as Jackie as their chairman. Rosalind's high pitched seething voice carried through the door into the still night as well, but Jackie walked briskly away from it. She already felt bad enough.

Jackie walked slowly through the village counting her steps. She wished to have the disaster resolved one way or another, but at the same time she wanted to delay the inevitable and continue to pretend that the world could be a happy, orderly place, where people loved each other and all those other heavenly things that could never exist in a real life.

'Crap,' Jackie cursed as she stopped in front of the West End B & B. She kicked a tiny pebble with her shoe, her hands deep in her pockets. Pearls of cold sweat were beginning to form on her forehead and she felt as though multiple small arms were tightly squeezing her body. She took a deep fragmented breath, hesitated for a moment more and finally knocked reluctantly on the handsome door. As she listened to the approaching steps, her heart curled into a tight, hard unwinding knot in her chest.

Tom opened the door. He was his cheerful self, as always, and Jackie felt every bit of her courage fall away in front of this kind man.

'Jackie. Good to see you. Come in.' Tom hollered happily and ushered her into the house. Jackie stepped in and stood on the doormat mumbling half to herself and half to Tom. 'I don't know if you will think that nicely of me afterwards.'

Tom looked at her face. He was surprised by the lack of Jackie's usual positive attitude. He raised his eyebrows with a puzzled look: 'Why on earth not?'

'We have a tiny wee problem.' Jackie narrowed her eyes as if in pain when she spoke. 'Well, actually it is a huge, horrible, *horrible* problem.'

'Problem? Well, good that I have Tim and John here—we can all help. Come into the kitchen. Everything will be fine; don't worry, Jackie. We'll fix you up.' Tom put a brotherly arm around Jackie's slumped shoulders. 'Tim and John brought this fabulous wine from Chile with them. We'll pour you a glass and then you can tell us all about it.' Tom began walking into the kitchen, gently holding onto Jackie's hand, pulling her along with him. 'It has this wonderful vanilla undertone.'

'Kevin's not here?' Jackie interrupted him.

'No, he isn't. He went to visit his mom. He'll be back tomorrow, though. But don't worry. I'm sure the three of us will be able to help you.'

'Oh...' was all Jackie could say as she stumbled forward. Her legs felt heavy. She did not know if she could make it all the way to the kitchen.

Tim and John were there sitting by the marble counter drinking wine. They smiled when they saw Jackie.

'Oh, hello Jackie.' Tim greeted her cheerfully and lifted his glass. 'Perfect timing, dear.'

'What a nice surprise.' John declared with a welcoming grin on his friendly face.

'Yes, a surprise definitely.' Jackie tried to smile. It felt like a mask had been stretched tightly over her face. The uncomfortable sensation made her head ache. Jackie sat down clumsily. She wasn't sure if she should bury her head under her arms and let out a loud cry or should she sit like a soldier, very upright and blurt out the bad news all in one go. The easiest solution would be to pretend that the mistake had never happened.

'Jackie says she has a small problem.' Tom said while he took a new wine glass out of the cupboard.

'Well then, have some wine first and then you can tell us all about it.' Tim said. He paused and then added slowly, tilting his head to the right as he spoke. 'Is it about men?' He suggested slyly; after all, nobody was immune to the gossip that circulated around the village.

The three men studied Jackie's face for clues.

'Nick, perhaps?' Tim suggested with a knowing smile, letting his words fall very slowly.

'What?' Jackie lifted her head with a jerk. 'Nick? No!' Jackie stared at the three laughing men and repeated herself, though her last *no* was more of a question than a definite denial. 'Nick? No?'

'Too bad.' Tim sighed. 'I really wanted to hear some new hot island gossip.' He shrugged his shoulders but he had the kind of knowing grin on his face that made Jackie feel uncomfortable.

Tim poured Jackie some wine and Jackie took the brochures slowly out of her bag. Her hands were trembling and her palms were damp. She closed her eyes and then inhaled deeply. Her voice faltered when she spoke. 'I...I...I don't even know where to begin. I am so, so, so, *so* sorry. I got these the day before yesterday.' Jackie handed the brochures to the boys and then took a long sip of her wine.

Tom turned the brochure in his hands. 'But it looks simply marvellous?' He declared. 'Great colours. Very modern layout. Not bad at all.' He looked up at Jackie questioningly. 'What is it? What is the problem?'

Jackie let out a long and painful sigh. 'Looks good, yes...but... but...uh...just have a look at the B & B listings, then you will see what I mean.' She took another long sip of her wine and stared at the boys, studying their faces for reactions. She wanted to see their exact responses very clearly.

Tim, John and Tom glanced at each other, raised their eyebrows and then opened the brochure. They began looking for the problem, reading the listings line by line. Nobody said a word for awhile. Jackie held her breath and bit her bottom lip. Seconds were like hours. She could hear her own heartbeat.

Then they found it. There was a sudden jerk of the head, sharp, deep inhale of air, clicking of tongues and a few words for dear Jesus.

Tom recovered first. 'Oh. I see now what you mean.' His words hung in the air, going neither here nor there.

Tim managed to utter breathlessly, 'Ahh.' And then he looked at John, who cleared his throat longer than was needed. 'Well, that certainly is interesting.' And then he too ran out of things to say and just blew air out from between his lips, letting the brochure fall slowly onto the table.

The kitchen remained terrifyingly quiet. They all stared at the brochure on the table between them. It lay there open with its brightly coloured pictures of smiling artists at work. The antique clock on the wall ticked. The tap faintly dripped. Tom pushed his glass with his fingertips. The wide foot of the wine glass scraped against the table's cold marble top. A car drove by.

Jackie couldn't take the dreadful silence any longer. 'I am so, *so* sorry…and…and now we have no more money to do a reprint…and…oh god!' She was pulling her hair and her face was flushed. 'I'll give you all of your money back of course. Hundred percent refund—I know that it will not make it any better, but…I have no idea what else to do.'

She looked so devastated and was so obviously on the verge of hot wretched tears that Tim, John and Tom could not help but feel sorry for her.

'Well—' It was a very long *well*-word. Jackie held her breath waiting for Tom to continue. He sighed deeply while running his hand through his hair. 'Well…all our customers know that we are gay. Right?' Tom looked at Tim and John, who nodded in agreement. Tom continued. 'It is quite obvious, now isn't it? And most of our customers are gay anyway…so that doesn't matter. But, the thing is…' He took a sip of his wine, composing the words in his mind, trying to organize them into a coherent sentence. Jackie stared at him, wanting to hear the rest.

Tom cleared his throat. 'See Kevin has not come out yet—not to his mother at least, or to the rest of his relatives, come to think of it.'

'What? Oh, shit! Fuck!' Jackie yelled. 'Sorry.' Jackie covered her mouth after realizing that she had cursed out loud. 'But?' She stared at Tom in silence not knowing how to put her thoughts into words; she swallowed, mumbled and then tried again. 'But…how does he explain the fact that you live with him? If I may ask?' She added.

'You know that Kevin is a writer, right?' Tom said, starting from the beginning.

'Yes...?' Jackie answered quickly. Tim and John were nodding their heads. They knew the story already.

'Well...to his mother I am his secretary and research assistant.' Tom said and took a slow, unhurried sip of wine.

'Oh, I see.' But she did not see. Jackie stared at Tom, unable to say anything remotely more intelligent. She waited impatiently for him to tell more.

'I have been his secretary for nearly twenty years now. Gosh, how the time flies.' Tom said with a gentle smile and saluted those wonderful almost-twenty years with his glass of wine. They had been very good years.

Tim and John joined his salutation. They clicked their glasses together while Jackie stared at the table trying to understand it all.

'So as long as we can keep it out of his mother's eyes, it should be all right,' Tom said and looked at Tim and John, asking for their opinion.

'Yes, I think so.' John agreed and thought about the slim possibility the cover-up offered

'Yes, I think it should be all right.' Tim agreed. 'We should be able to hold on for a couple of days.

'We just have to clarify to his dear mother that the meaning of our name is that we are a very jolly place—we could be the West End Jolly B & B.' Tom said.

Tim and John snorted and then laughed mimicking being happy.

'We are such jolly men, aren't we?' Tim said and clicked his glass against Tom's and John's.

'She is 86 years old. She might buy it. And if it all comes down to a fine line, I can always misplace her reading glasses for a couple of days.' Tom suggested.

'It might work?' Tim and John agreed. With a lot of planning and meticulous preparations, it might just work.

Jackie sat there and looked at these three lovely men in front of her. She had such an immense affection and appreciation for them. The relief she felt was so enormous that at first she could not find words to express her gratitude. They could have just as easily behaved in the complete opposite way, which they would have been entirely entitled to.

'Oh, god!' she sighed. 'You're all so nice. I don't know what to say. I was so worried. So, *so* worried.' She shook her head. 'Thank you. You're the best neighbours a person could ever ask for.' She sighed and suddenly she felt light, 'Oh, my god. You don't know how horrible I felt before.' Jackie sat there, hardly able to lift her hand. The sudden relief had made her weak.

Tim looked at her. 'Have some more wine and we'll plan our keep-Kevin's-mother-misinformed-a-bit-longer strategy together.'

He refilled the glasses and all four bent their heads together and began seriously contemplating the marvellous effects of white-out.

Chapter 17

In The News

'Well, I'll be darned. Artists here on this island? Well I'll be.' This was the response Jackie got when she finally managed to get through to the editor of the local newspaper. It didn't bode particularly well, but it was more than she had been able to get from any of the other many calls she had put out. The editor then called for somebody in the office named Bob to get his big fat lazy ass into his office ASAP. Jackie did not care how fat Bob's ass was or if he got into the office ASAP. The only thing she cared about was that she had an appointment with a reporter that very afternoon.

Jackie had prepared her little commercial pep-talk earlier and she had spent some time trying to control the stubborn curls in her hair just in case there would be photos. For some reason her mother had the island newspaper delivered to her house and Jackie didn't want the coming Sunday lunch to begin with a cleverly placed innocent observation on her bad hair. She glanced in the mirror to check that all was in order: no sudden dirt on her face, no visible sawdust and lipstick on the lips only. She grabbed the brochures and the biographies of the studio tour artists from the hall table and walked quickly the short distance to the pub where she had arranged to meet the reporter.

She recognized him immediately when she walked in. He was the only unfamiliar man sitting at the bar. He had shoulder-length greasy hair that might have been fashionable in the 80s. He had round metal-rimmed glasses that fell down his short, stout nose. He was wearing a yellow shirt with a wrinkled collar that was left open, so that his thick golden necklace could be clearly seen amongst his bushy chest hair. His worn out Iron Maiden leather jacket was hanging from the back of the chair. And he did indeed have a fat ass.

He looked like a man who would rather be writing that famous novel than be interviewing a woman about her little studio tour in a little village in the middle of nowhere. For the time being though, he was working for the island newspaper while the novel was still in its infancy, saved on his computer where it had been lying dormant for the last five years.

He was chatting with Rose when Jackie came to introduce herself.

'Hello! You must be Bob Waters?' She said cheerfully.

'Yes and you must be Jacqueline Callaghan.' Bob Waters lifted his eyes slowly to look at Jackie's face, and then added sarcastically, 'I presume.'

'Nice to meet you.' Jackie put her hand out to shake the reporter's, but he ignored it completely and instead ran his fingers through his greasy hair. Suddenly Jackie was happy that she had not shaken his hand.

Bob Waters cast his eyes around the pub. 'Great pub you have here.'

Jackie was just about to answer, when Jack Wilkinson casually strolled into the pub and yelled to Rose with his raspy voice, 'Why aren't you cheerful like all those barmaids in them movies?' He walked over to Jackie and Bob Waters and then leaned against the bar, acting like he owned the bar and at least half of downtown New York.

'I would be cheerful if I didn't have to look at your ugly face every day.' Rose grunted back with venom, but filled his pint all the same.

'Tsk, tsk, aren't we touchy?' Jack Wilkinson grinned and pushed his hat off his face with his thumb.

'Touch this you old goat.' Rose shook her big farm-girl fist in front of Jack Wilkinson's face. Jack winked and adjusted the collar on his—as Jackie suddenly noticed—new shirt. Jackie leaned over to look at Jack Wilkinson more closely.

He did wear a new shirt and a new hat. His shoes were polished and he was wearing suspenders. Jack walked away gallantly, his thumb hooked around one strap of his new suspenders. He flashed a big smile in Jackie's direction, showing the missing tooth on the left side of his mouth.

Jackie leaned over the counter and asked Rose quietly, 'What's up with Jack?'

Rose whispered back, 'He heard about the reporter and he wanted to make a sophisticated impression.' Rose could hardly keep her mouth straight. 'Sophisticated?' She giggled. 'Those are two words that do not go together: Jack Wilkinson and sophistication.' Rose was laughing uncontrollably now. 'And I thought I would never see the day when Jack Wilkinson would be wearing aftershave and suspenders.' Rose wiped the tears from her eyes with her big hand and glanced in Jack's direction before bursting again into rowdy laughter.

Jackie turned to look at Jack Wilkinson sitting comfortably at his corner table. He had crossed his legs and on his knee he balanced a new green felt hat with a feather stuck inside the decorative band. Jackie turned back to look at Rose, who rolled her eyes and shook her head. 'I know, the hat is too much,' she whispered.

Jackie cleared her throat to get Bob Waters's attention. Bob turned around slowly. He hated being interrupted by people who wanted something from him. He looked Jackie up and down. Yes, she was definitely not his type. He had a sip of his beer and studied the people in the pub, particularly Jack Wilkinson, who he thought was a wealthy, eccentric landowner.

'We have a lot of colourful characters here in the village.' Jackie tried to laugh, but her laugh was the nervous kind of laughter that dies out before it has even properly started. She wanted this interview to go well.

'So it seems.' Bob Waters let the words roll off his tongue rather than use any energy to speak. 'Who is that man?' He asked Jackie and pointed in Jack Wilkinson's direction.

'He? Um…well…He is Jack Wilkinson—the village personality.' She said feebly. How would anybody describe Jack Wilkinson? She made an effort to sound cheerful as she tried to divert the reporter's interest from Jack Wilkinson back to the main subject: the studio tour. She took a few brochures out from her bag and put them on the table in front of the reporter. 'Here is our studio tour brochure fresh from the printer's office. It has all the information you will need about the tour and the participating artists.'

'Thanks.' Bob Waters answered absentmindedly, staring at Jack Wilkinson stretching his suspenders.

Jackie pulled out the separate artists biographies as well. 'And here is some more information about the studio tour artists.' She felt like yanking Bob Waters's sleeve to get his attention. 'Would you like me to show you around the village, and we could maybe visit some of the studios, as well?' Jackie got up hoping that Bob Waters would follow her example and forget all about Jack Wilkinson—the village personality extraordinaire.

'All right.' Bob Waters finished off his pint and, without so much as a quick glance, stuffed the brochure and the biographies into his bag. He put his camera strap around his thick neck and got up slowly.

'Bye, Rose. Say hi to Nick, will you?' Jackie said. 'Where is he, by the way?' Jackie had suddenly realized that this was the first time she could remember that Nick wasn't behind the counter. It felt strange and she didn't know which feeling felt stranger: her asking after Nick or her feeling oddly lonely for him not being there. Luckily, Rose didn't flinch.

'He went to fix something on his sailboat but he should be back in a couple of hours.'

'Oh, all right. Bye for now.' Jackie led the reporter out of the pub under Rose's watchful eyes.

Bob Waters bumped immediately into Jack Wilkinson's riding lawnmower parked right in front of the pub. He stopped and pointed at it with his plump, hairy hand. 'What is that doing here?'

Jackie sighed and grabbed the reporter's arm and tried pulling him away. 'It is Jack Wilkinson's...we should start first at Sheridan Watson's gallery and...' She began walking toward Sheridan's house, but the reporter was standing still, staring at the rusting lawnmower parked in front of the pub. He was mesmerized.

'So this Jack Wilkinson drives to the pub with his lawnmower?'

Jackie sighed even louder than before. She had now given up any hope of having her way with the reporter. 'Yes, I'm afraid he does.' She answered flatly and stared at the rooftops and counted to ten, very slowly.

'Interesting, very interesting.' Bob Waters murmured with a sweaty, lazy voice and took his notebook out from his pocket to write down a few lines. An idea was beginning to develop in his mind, much to Jackie's sorrow if she would have known. He licked his finger and turned to a new blank page in his notebook, which until now had merely held the grocery lists for his mother.

He continued to write while they walked slowly toward Sheridan's gallery. Key words: riding lawn tractor, pub, beautiful full-bodied barmaid and an irritating female customer with brochures.

The reporter turned around to have one more look at the lawnmower, but Jackie quickened her pace, firmly grabbed his shabby jacket's sleeve and pulled hard. Bob Waters had to take a few fast steps to catch up with her. He managed to stuff his notebook back into his breast pocket while scurrying after Jackie, reminding himself to add the word 'very' in front of his description of Jackie. He really didn't like women who had an agenda and who were striding to achieve. They made him feel small.

In the pub the boys looked out the window; Glenn stretched his neck to be able to see Jackie, who was just knocking on Sheridan's door, reporter in tow. He was wiping his sweaty brow with his hand when Sheridan opened the front door, the boys snickered thinking of the thunderous marching music filling the air.

Bob Waters stared at the rotund man in a safari outfit in front of him. He couldn't hear anything Sheridan was saying. He heard only deafening horns. Maybe this Sycamore village would not be as boring as he had earlier thought.

They marched into the house following Sheridan's stout figure and, thankfully, Sheridan turned the music off and then turned on his heels to face Bob Waters. Sheridan was beaming, almost glowing—a reporter in his house. This was something special.

Jackie looked around the room, suddenly aware of what had not been there earlier. Bob Waters saw it too. They both stared at the wall their mouths dropping open; Sheridan wrapped his thumbs inside his belt and bellowed. 'Oh, yes. Ernest Hemingway and I share the same birthday and, if I may add,' he paused, cleared his throat and continued, 'and our mutual love for Africa.'

Jackie stared at the huge stuffed lion's head looking down at them with its shiny yellow glass eyes. Its mouth was frozen in a huge roar, revealing the sharp white canine teeth. Her knees felt weak. Bob Waters had gotten over his initial shock remarkably fast. He pulled out his pen and a notebook and began writing feverously. He might not be the best reporter in the world but even he noticed a good story when its big yellow glass eyes were staring straight down into his own.

As they walked toward Sheridan's studio Jackie pulled him over and hissed in to his ear, 'Where the hell did you get that god awful lion's head? And what the hell is this Ernest Hemingway stuff?'

Sheridan stared at Jackie blankly and rubbed his ear.

'Don't tell me that you have been to Africa.' Jackie warned and squeezed his arm more strongly than she intended. Sheridan whimpered and brushed his safari shirt's sleeve with a discontented grunt. 'I just ironed it,' he hissed back.

Jackie stared at him and narrowed her eyes.

'Well, I was surfing on the net and I happened to check that eBay everybody's talking about.' Sheridan explained.

'Please don't.' Jackie begged and shook her head.

'Oh, yes, fascinating stuff and very reasonably priced, if I may add.'

'No,' cried Jackie when she stepped into the gallery and saw the zebra carpet and African hunting spears.

'As I said, Africa fascinates me.' Sheridan boasted loudly and lit his pipe with his new camping matches.

Bob Waters was now sure that visiting this village would not be a waste of his precious time. There may have even been a slight smile on his otherwise unfriendly, sweaty ruddy face.

Jackie worked very hard that afternoon, taking the reporter to visit all of the studios and galleries on the tour. She had managed to yank the reporter out just as Sheridan had tried to begin a new long-winded monologue about his famous adventures in the African wild. She had restrained herself quite admirable and had not strangled Rosalind after she had pointed out the inadequacies of the studio tour organization, which would have certainly ruined the planned tour had it not been for her, Rosalind McKay, the highly regarded financial officer of the organization. Luckily, she had noticed these mistakes and had managed to intervene in time.

Kenneth had actually talked and, surprisingly, Russell had not talked so much. Nancy and Daisy had offered just baked warm muffins and Thomas had, unexpectedly, remembered correctly the time of the interview. Caroline had been wearing a tight black mini skirt, which had made Bob Waters speechless. The skirt's length or the lack of it, had convinced him to think very favourably of the studio tour.

All in all the day had been quite successful despite the little Africa–Ernest Hemingway detour. Therefore, when Jackie walked toward the pub in the early evening to see if Nick had come back, she felt that the future might even have a slight pink tint to it, like a beautiful evening sky that promises fair weather in the morning. She strolled into the pub, and then stopped, her earlier cheerfulness quickly draining away. The reporter, his yellow shirt fallen further open, sat comfortably with Jack Wilkinson and the boys at their corner table. He had obviously enjoyed quite a few pints and was listening to Jack Wilkinson telling one of his many tales that may or may not be true.

Bob Waters laughed heartily and banged his hand against the table. Jackie heard him say, 'I can't believe it. I just can't believe it! And then what happened?'

'Well, he came running out of the house and…' Jack Wilkinson lowered his voice to a whisper, which was followed closely by a sudden burst of laughter from the reporter and the boys.

Jackie stumbled to the bar where Nick was waiting for her. She leaned over the counter and hissed, nodding her head toward the snickering reporter.

'Why is he still here? I dropped him off hours ago. He said he had all the information he needed for the story.'

'Well,' Nick paused and thought about how to say the following as delicately as possible. 'Well, he came back here and Jack took him for a spin on his lawnmower.'

Jackie stared at Nick. She felt sick. 'What! He did what?' She did not realize before the words left her lips that she was yelling.

Nick avoided looking directly in Jackie's eyes when he spoke again. 'They went for a drive on Jack's lawnmower. I did try to stop him, but…'

Jackie's mouth was open and she closed it and then opened it again but no words came out. She rested her head on the bar. Nick could barely hear her distressed whisper through her folded arms. 'Oh, shite…all is lost.'

Nick patted her arm. He didn't know what else he could do or say. He had tried to stop Jack Wilkinson, but there hadn't been much he had been able to do.

Bob Waters left the boys' table and, somewhat unsteadily, walked to the bar. 'Thanks man. Your pub is an absolute gem.' He slammed his hand heavily against the counter as he spoke. Bob Waters had new ideas and a new story was already forming in his mind. He was on top of his game and the beer tasted good. He rapped the edge of the bar with his stubby fingers and whistled. He glanced beside him and saw Jackie slumping on her chair in the midst of her misery. 'Oh, hi there.' He said coolly and then turned his head to see his own reflection in the mirror on the wall behind the bar. He looked like a writer, he thought, and then he smiled approvingly at his own image.

'You still here?' Jackie yanked her head up and stared at the reporter who was finger combing his hair. She was trying to sound positive and she was trying hard not to bite the reporter's head off. Bob Waters was completely oblivious to Jackie's aggressive feelings. As far as he was concerned, all the women in the world wanted him, even the types like Jackie, therefore he didn't treat any of them nicely. Plenty of berries in the bush, as he often said. Jackie wasn't his type anyway. He had seen it immediately. He thought that Jackie was far too tall for him and a bit too pushy. Two traits in women he didn't much care about.

'Yep.' He scratched his stomach slowly. 'I came down here for a pint and could not resist the temptation to have a spin on the lawnmower. Quite a village! Quite a village! I've got some great stories out of that old professor over there.'

'What? What professor?' Jackie jerked her head around.

Bob Waters pointed to Jack Wilkinson, who had been drinking steadily all afternoon, since, to keep them talking, the reporter had been buying him and the lads more than a few pints each. Jack's new hat was on the table surrounded by empty glasses. Its feather was broken in two.

Jackie words froze in her mouth, 'Jack Wilkinson…?'

'Yes, that's the one.' Bob Waters chuckled and gave a loud tap on his full stomach. 'The eccentric professor.' He sighed merrily. 'Well I better be off now, I got some real first-class stuff for the article. Good stuff. I'll send you a copy of the paper when the story comes out.'

The reporter left with surprisingly springy steps and waved his hand to the boys as he walked out. He was completely unaware of how devastated Jackie was by his words. Jackie held her head with both hands.

Jack Wilkinson walked slowly to the bar. Jackie looked at him. There was an odd mixture of venom and desperation in her eyes.

'Professor Jack Wilkinson,' she said slowly pronouncing every single syllable separately.

Jack Wilkinson took an unlit pipe out of his mouth. 'Yes?'

'What the hell kind of professor are you?' Jackie blurted crossly.

'Psychology, my dear,' said Jack Wilkinson with his newly acquired academic voice. 'Human mind. The small little intricacies that make us what we are as humans. Very fascinating.' He pointed his pipe at Nick, who began filling a pint for him. 'Great chap that Bob.' Jack Wilkinson smacked his lips together thoughtfully. 'Great chap!'

'I bet he was. I heard you took him for a ride on your lawnmower.' Jackie croaked.

'Yep. Bob said he had never been on one, so I took him for a little spin around the village. Showed him the sights and all.'

'And what did you tell him?' Jackie's voice was raspy with fear.

Jack Wilkinson grabbed his pint. 'Oh, this and that—you know—the normal stuff.'

And that was the moment when Jacqueline Victoria Callaghan lost it.

'No! No. I really don't know. Could you specify your normal to me, so that I can compare it to my normal—because I seriously think that your normal and my normal aren't exactly the same!' Jackie was breathing hard. Her mouth was a thin line and her cheeks had two bright red spots on them. She had yelled and her words had been spat out in fury.

The pub had fallen quiet. Nick was frozen in his spot and Jack Wilkinson stared at Jackie with fear. Perhaps not everything had gone well for him and his new look today. Jackie had never ever lashed out like this before. Never. Perhaps the stories about the Callaghan women had been right all along. He covered his nose with his hand for safety's sake.

'Well, stuff...you know...' Jack Wilkinson stuttered. 'Like the doctor running around naked after he was found in a car with the nurse doing...you know ... well...I told him that I have never seen a man run so fast in my life, but then again, he was the school champion when we grew up and his son is pretty fast too. At least that's what I heard. I think he won the 100 metre race this year at the school sporting event. I think it was him. Or, wait! It could have been the other one. What's his name again? The tall skinny boy...'

Jackie stared at him for a long time and then all the anger left her and was replaced by misery and despair. 'Oh, my god! This is not good. This is not good. My god. The tour is ruined.'

Jack Wilkinson moved nervously from foot to foot. Jackie suddenly started up again. 'And that's your normal everyday chitchat? Oh my god!' She leaned her head against her hands and then covered her eyes with her palms. She was trying to breathe normally.

Jack Wilkinson put his arm on her back and carefully patted her shoulders. He was trying to cheer her up. 'Who was it that said that any publicity is good publicity?'

'Jack, you are hardly a PR person.' Jackie mumbled and glared at him, shaking her head.

The TV in the corner had been on all the time. All of a sudden Harriet's loud voice pierced the air. She was saying thank you with her best polite voice.

All the people turned their heads toward the TV, and sure enough, Harriet was there with Winston in her arms, filling every inch of the screen. She was glowing with pride. Winston had a bow tied around his neck. You could not see the interviewer, but you could hear his voice.

'Well congratulations, Miss Grey. Your dog Winston won today the Best in Show prize. How do you feel?'

'I couldn't be happier.' Harriet was almost giddy.

'I heard, that you have been doing dog shows quite a long time, haven't you?'

'Yes I have, though this is the very first time my Winston here has won the overall prize.' Harriet had to stop and breathe. 'He has, of course, won many other prizes during his competitive career, but not the best in show.' She beamed at the camera. Her cheeks were flushed and her lipstick was slightly rubbed off in one corner.

'He is a quite a dog.'

'Yes he is. Aren't you, Winston?' She lovingly fluffed the fur on top of his head.

'I've also heard that you are quite a painter as well.'

'Yes I am. I paint porcelain and as a matter of fact, the last weekend in October my home village Sycamore will be hosting its first studio tour event in its entire history.'

'Well, that's cert...' The interviewer tried to say something but Harriet's booming voice was not to be stopped.

'You can click online and then type sycamorestudiotour.com.' She was speaking very slowly so that the viewers would be able to write the address down. 'We have painters, glassblowers, potters and quilters and...' Harriet was staring right into the camera as if hypnotized by it.

This time the interviewer succeeded in cutting Harriet off. 'Well, thank you so much for your time and congratulations once more.'

'Thank you.' Harriet hugged Winston and smiled at the camera once more before it moved away from her and focused on the interviewer.

The eager, young reporter turned around to face the camera. 'That's all from the national dog show. And now back to the studio.'

When the riot exploded in the pub, the newscaster was already beginning a story about a car bomb in the Middle East, but nobody paid any attention to the news anymore. Everybody in the pub was talking at the same time. The pints were lifted high and there was a lot of commotion in the room. Harriet had become Sycamore's first TV personality.

'Next step a reality show,' somebody shouted.

Jackie turned to look at Nick and she grinned blissfully. 'Harriet...she is wonderful! Isn't she?' She sighed.

'Yes, she is.' Nick was laughing out loud. He knew that this TV appearance by Harriet had saved the otherwise disastrous day. Jackie began laughing. Nick patted her back gently; he didn't know how else to show his support. A hug would have given away his feelings and a kiss never even came to his mind. So he awkwardly patted Jackie on her back for the second time.

On her way home from the pub, Jackie walked to Harriet's house, only a few doors down from hers. She wrote her a short note: 'Thank you and congratulations!' She dropped it into Harriet's mailbox and whistled happily as she walked the rest of the way home, listening to the faint party sounds that carried from the pub as people celebrated the new celebrity status of Sycamore.

Mary Cullighan's flower shop was going to be busy tomorrow.

*　　　*　　　*

The Sunday lunch at her mother's house had gone surprisingly well. Jackie had snuck into the city earlier staying the whole weekend at Jill's. She had enjoyed being with Nellie, who took pleasure in everything. Hiding behind a coffee cup sent her into gurgling laughter. Jill and Jackie had also managed to go out to the movies alone, leaving moaning Robert home with Nellie. He didn't mind actually. The moaning was mainly to ensure him a quiet Sunday afternoon filled with soccer.

Jackie and Jill had also gone to visit Helen, Jill's mom, who had given Jackie the final information about the upcoming show. It had been a nice weekend. Even Andrew had been reasonable and that was more than Jackie could have ever hoped for. Jackie had needed this small break. For such a long time, now, her life had been filled with studio tour plans and long hours working alone in her workshop. This weekend left her feeling energized despite the lack of sleep and the vast quantities of wine.

She returned to the island late Sunday night to find that she had no food in the house. She ate some crackers and cheese from the back of the fridge and wrote a shopping list for the next day.

Monday morning on her way to the general store, Jackie chose a short cut that took her to the back of the store, right where the loading docks were situated. This way was only a bit shorter but Felix could run free and Jackie liked walking through the narrow pathways behind the houses. She hopped over a few rocks, admired the well kept gardens and then put Felix on the leash and walked along the fence that led to the back of the store.

A car with a rolled down window was parked next to the building behind a huge oak tree. Once in a while a hand came out and shook the ashes off a cigarette. Jackie walked beside the car ready to greet whomever it was in the car—it was inconceivable in a small village like Sycamore that the person would be unknown to her.

The long thin hand belonged to Alistair.

'Oh, hello, Alistair,' Jackie said and peered into the car. Felix barked and wagged his tail. Jackie had surprised Alistair, terribly. He didn't know about the shortcut and he had thought himself to be completely invisible by the loading docks. Some ashes from the cigarette fell onto his lap and he began franticly slapping his trousers to stop the hot ash from burning a hole into them. When Alistair finally looked up at Jackie his hands were trembling. He tried to collect his dignity. 'Oh, hello Jacqueline.'

Alistair did not know what to do with the cigarette. Should he throw it out or should he continue smoking? His hand was hanging out of the window, still holding the cigarette. The smoke from it circled upwards toward Jackie.

Jackie grinned mischievously. She was surprised to have caught Alistair smoking secretly behind the store. It was a once in a lifetime opportunity and she decided to get all the entertainment she possibly could out of the situation.

'Nice day isn't it?' She spoke slowly, leaving the tone open, inviting a long and leisurely conversation.

'Yes. It is a nice day.' Alistair grunted and looked nervous and extremely irritated. The cigarette remained in his hand as if it was not even there.

'Yes. I think it is the nicest day we have had all week. Don't you agree, Alistair?'

'Yes…' Alistair was eyeing Jackie suspiciously.

'Yesterday was a bit on the cold side, wouldn't you say so?' Jackie chatted on.

'Yes.' Alistair's answer was very grumpy. He didn't like to chitchat about weather, in the first place, and second, he wanted to finish his cigarette. Only the good lord knew how much he needed nicotine to be able to live with Rosalind.

Jackie almost burst into loud laughter at the sight of the squirming Alistair, but she succeeded in controlling herself and was able to continue her innocent, aimless chatter. 'Are you waiting for Rosalind? Is she in the store?' She asked with a straight face.

Alistair could not take it anymore. The cigarette was starting to burn his fingers. 'For god's sake, Jacqueline. Yes I do smoke, whenever I can...so there, I confess. Happy now?' He threw the cigarette away and stared right into Jackie's eyes; 'But...um...please do not tell Rosalind. She would make my life even more miserable than it already is.' He turned angrily to stare at the steering wheel, now avoiding Jackie's eyes.

Jackie was having the laugh of her life and she purposely wanted to keep Alistair squirming a while longer. 'Alistair, but what about your sinuses?' Jackie pretended to be very concerned.

'Oh, the fuck with my sinuses. Just don't say a word to Rosalind.' He started the car glancing grumpily at Jackie.

'Don't worry. Your secret is safe with me.' Jackie grinned as Alistair drove to the parking area in the front of the store.

Jackie tied Felix onto a post outside the store and told him to be good.

She had a big smile on her face as she walked into the store and grabbed the shopping basket by the door. She hollered her greetings to the cashier. 'Good morning, Stella. How are you today?'

'Oh, good morning, Jackie. Could not be better.'

'Glad to hear that.' Jackie started walking down the aisle when Stella turned around on her small squeaky seat by the cash register and hollered after her. 'Oh, by the way. Today's newspaper has the studio tour article in it.'

Jackie stopped, turned and galloped to the cash register where she grabbed the newspaper from the rack. She feverishly leafed through it, biting her bottom lip in anticipation. All of a sudden she froze.

Jackie opened the paper a little more to see the article better. She stared at the page in front of her and two red spots appeared on her otherwise white face. Jackie closed her eyes and then looked to the heavens above. 'Oh, why! Why! Why!'

Stella got up on her chair and looked over Jackie's shoulder. 'I think that's a pretty good picture of Jack Wilkinson. I don't think you could take a better photo than that of that old goat.'

The article had a large photo of Jack Wilkinson smiling broadly and standing beside his lawnmower in front of the pub. In his one hand he was holding his new pipe while the other stretched his new suspenders. He had pushed his hat to the back of his head. The title of the article was 'Sycamore's own eccentric storyteller tells it all.'

Jackie began reading the article. She mumbled something inaudible as she skipped through it as fast as she could. Suddenly she came to a standstill. There was still a small flicker of a positive outcome. 'Here he mentions the studio tour,' she said quickly and read on, her expression changing from curious to desperate. 'Five lousy lines…all my work and…five lousy lines.' Her voice was rising. 'Damn! That bloody Jack Wilkinson! I could kill him right now.'

Rosalind walked to the cash register and heard Jackie's last words. 'Oh, you saw the article too.' Rosalind's voice was nonchalant with a hint of pleasure anticipating the words that she had not yet uttered. She was saving her 'I told you so' for her next sentence. Rosalind smiled haughtily at Jackie.

Jackie turned around to face Rosalind. She was talking extremely slowly, trying to control her temper and to give fair warning to Rosalind. 'For the love of your life Rosalind, I would not say another word to me because I'm truly, *truly* in a bad mood.'

Rosalind was about to say something sarcastic as usual, when Stella spoke to her as she began processing her groceries. 'If I were you, Rosalind, I would keep that mouth of yours closed today.'

Rosalind turned sharply around to look at Stella. She was clearly shocked to hear such words coming from a woman who sat behind the cash register most of the time. 'I thought you were in customer service.' She uttered, her words smeared with scorn.

'Yes, deluxe customer service and you don't seem to have the membership card with you today.' Stella spoke calmly, raising her eyebrows only slightly to show that she really did not care if she had been rude to Rosalind.

Rosalind stared at her sourly, but she couldn't find anything to say. She paid for her shopping in brooding silence and went out to where Alistair was waiting for her, standing outside in the wind trying to get rid of the faint cigarette smell that clung to his clothes.

Stella turned around to look at Jackie and then got up from her chair behind the cash register. She walked to Jackie and gave her a motherly pat on her back. 'The tour will be all right, Jackie. Don't worry. Everything will turn out fine. I'm happy to help with whatever I can.'

'Thanks Stella.' Jackie was still holding the crumpled paper in her fists.

'And if you still want to give a good beating to Jack Wilkinson, I'm glad to help you there as well, because the last time he cut my lawn, he also cut my precious peonies.' Stella's wide and friendly face was smiling gently and Jackie could not help but smile back.

'Thanks, Stella. You're a gem.'

Stella gave Jackie another big motherly squeeze and sighed. 'I know.'

Chapter 18

Hot Thomas

It was almost time to finish the meeting and Jackie was putting her papers in order. She wanted to go home as soon as possible to see if the new colour for her peppermills had dried without problems. She had painted a few different wood samples just before the meeting and they had still been wet when she left the house.

Harriet got up whispering loudly to Jackie. 'I'll be back in a minute.' She pointed meaningfully toward the bathrooms.

Jackie nodded and then said, 'I think we are almost done here. Is there anything else?' She paused and tried to avoid looking at Rosalind, because she knew that, if given a chance to speak freely, Rosalind would do so and the meeting would never come to an end.

Rosalind lifted her thin diamond adorned hand half way and cleared her throat. Everybody around the table sighed and dropped their heads in defeat.

Jackie tried to avoid saying the words she had long ago learned to hate: 'Yes, Rosalind.' She wondered if she would ever be able to think of Rosalind positively.

Rosalind sat erect on the edge of her chair, her legs crossed and a pen ready in her hands. 'Well'—she tapped the pencil twice against the table, before continuing—'I would like to solve the problem about the town hall for once and for all.'

Jackie stared at her for a while. 'Do we have a problem with the town hall?' She was as puzzled as everybody else around the table, since nobody had mentioned there being any problem with the town hall before.

'What if somebody wants to purchase something at the town hall studio tour exhibit? Who's going to take the money? What about receipts? Change?' Rosalind asked, looking victoriously around the room. She had thought of something vital these other members had not.

'Any thoughts...anyone at all?' Jackie was sitting deep in her chair, her hands folded across her chest. She was looking around the table for somebody to offer a solution, so that they all could go home.

Muriel was the first. 'Well. There is a bank machine down the street. People could always walk there and then come back with the right amount of money.'

'That's a good idea!' Russell exclaimed and banged the table with both of his hands. 'What do you say? Problem solved. Good.' Russell was eager to go and have a pint but Rosalind's piercing voice stopped him in his tracks.

'We cannot just tell people to walk to the bank machine and then walk all the way back carrying large sums of money with them. It is not at all professional. Quite unacceptable. Even *you* must recognize that.' Rosalind efficiently put an end to that suggestion like a chef with a sharp knife cutting off the unwanted ends of a cucumber.

'What if a customer would like to purchase a high-end item and use their credit card. A bank machine would not be a solution then, now would it?' Rosalind lifted her chin and cast a look around the table.

'I would take a cheque. Problem solved and I need a pint, girl.' Russell spoke speedily, hardly breathing between his words. He started to get up from his chair for the second time. He looked at Jackie hoping that she would put an end to this painful torture.

'You would take a cheque?' Rosalind couldn't believe her ears. 'A cheque!' Her voice was sharp as she spat her words out.

'Well, heck yes, why not? Now who else wants to have a pint?' Russell was up and going. He was not going to be stopped this time—he hoped.

'But, what about credit cards? Does no one at this table belong to the modern world? Really, now. Who would be daft enough to have a business and have no credit card processing machine in their studio?' Rosalind laughed. She found it hilarious.

Everybody in the pub was now staring at her in glum silence.

Rosalind did not let go. 'Well? Who does not own a credit card machine? Hands up!'

Slowly Russell, Nancy, Daisy, Muriel, Janet, Kenneth and Sheridan lifted their hesitant hands into the air.

Right at this moment Harriet came back from the bathroom. She had not heard the question. She only saw the many hesitant hands up in the air and the shy unhappy looks on people's faces. 'What are we voting for? Ah, I know. Who has Rosalind driven crazy so far? In that case...' She rubbed her big hands excitedly together. 'I'm in.'

'Well...uh...well.' Rosalind was shocked and couldn't say anything, maybe for the first time in her life. Not even Sheridan ran a proper business.

People slowly put their hands down. They were looking at each other and around the room, but they were all avoiding Rosalind's eyes. Russell was miming a pint to Nick, drawing air pictures with his hands.

Rosalind breathed through her long, thin nose. It quivered. She turned toward Alistair for support. 'What are your thoughts on the subject, Alistair?' Her voice was rising, so much so that her voice by the end of her sentence was a shrill shriek, leaving Alistair's name echoing in the room.

Alistair slowly lifted his eyes toward Rosalind and looked at her hesitantly. 'I don't know Rosalind.' He paused for a moment and then something flickered in his eyes, something lifelike that hadn't been there for a long time. He rubbed his chin thoughtfully and added, 'Maybe I should just give you a good roll in the hay.'

Rosalind stared at him with an astonished look, not quite believing that she had heard him correctly. Her eyes grew wide and her face began to change hues, from white to a strong, glowing red colour.

The rest of the group was exceptionally quiet. Not even Russell could think of anything to say. They all stared at Alistair and Rosalind. Their eyes were darting between the two, waiting for one of them to say something.

Suddenly Kenneth began to laugh. Nobody had ever heard him laugh out loud, so the event in itself took everybody by surprise. No one would ever forget it either, because Kenneth's laugh was an extraordinary combination of a mule neighing and an old door with rusty hinges slowly being opened and closed. His laugh effortlessly filled the dead air in the pub. People turned to stare at Kenneth instead of Rosalind. First nobody could say or do anything, but then slowly, very slowly, laughter began to grow and then it evolved into a huge, loud and hysterical hilarity.

Through the noise Alistair spoke to Rosalind. 'What do think, dear. Shall we go?' He got up and offered his hand to Rosalind who was still unable to speak or get up for that matter.

Alistair looked expectantly at Jackie.

'The meeting is adjourned.' Jackie managed to get out. Kenneth's laughter had knocked all the sense out of her.

Alistair took a hold of Rosalind's arm and guided her out of the pub. Rosalind had not uttered a word since Alistair's sentence and she followed him as if in a trance.

The laughter seemed to have no end to it. It only quieted down enough for people to wipe the tears from their eyes. Then Kenneth would neigh and the laughter would start again, roaring to reach new never before achieved heights.

You could hear Russell's keen voice over the crowd. 'That's exactly what I have been telling him to do.' Russell was talking to no one in particular, jabbing his finger in the air like a preacher.

'Well I'll be darned.' Thomas was rubbing his hair with his hands.

Nick was behind the bar. He was leaning on the counter with one hand and wiping his eyes with the other. His stomach was beginning to ache from so much laughter.

The ladies were giggling softly. 'Well, that was certainly something else,' Nancy exclaimed.

'I never thought Alistair would have balls quite big enough to silence her.' Harriet stated. Daisy and Nancy murmured a few more oh my-mys.

'Oh my god, my stomach is hurting.' Jackie wailed. She was grinning while holding her sides with both hands.

'I wonder whose barn they are going to.' Janet's voice calmly cut through the commotion, her question asked in such a serious manner that people paused for a second to consider it. Then the laughter started anew, louder than ever.

People walked over to the bar to order drinks. If there was a date to remember, it was today and it needed to be celebrated. Rosalind had been silenced. It was a remarkable day.

Nick was filling pints and pouring wine. He was grinning and once in a while he chuckled at the thought of Rosalind's shocked face. Russell banged the bar with his fist. 'I have to say this. I really have to say this: That Alistair is a brave man. Yes indeed, he is.'

Thomas posed in front of the bar, one hand on the bar and one hand holding a full pint in the air. 'Here's to Alistair.' He lifted his pint even higher into the air and then grinned shamelessly. Others joined him and raised their glasses to make a toast to Alistair.

Thomas bellowed, 'To Alistair the Brave.' And the people followed his example. 'To Alistair the Brave.'

The loud happy voices travelled through the late summer air.

*   *   *

The last month before the studio tour went by even faster than people could have thought possible. Over the summer, tourists came, visited the studios, ate lunches and dinners and marvelled at the little village. All of the studios and businesses on the island were giving out the studio tour brochures to their customers, inviting them to attend. They were kind, but ferocious, reminding the tourists to bring friends and family. Sheridan's website was also attracting interest, which, at the meetings, enabled him to boast endlessly on the number of visitors.

When Jackie wasn't selling in her gallery, she was in her studio making more peppermills and salt grinders. She turned Christmas tree peppermills and snow men salt grinders with her lathe solely for the upcoming festive season.

As it was the first studio tour she had ever done, it was difficult to estimate how many items she needed to make for it. Over the summer season, she had been making notes about which peppermills and saltshakers had been the fastest selling designs. Therefore she knew which were her best sellers and she had doubled the number of those in her storage. She also felt the pressure of the upcoming exhibition. She was dividing her time between production work and the purely experimental work for Helen's gallery. She wanted to create something unique, spectacularly different.

For weeks, she had been playing with different material combinations. She wanted the natural grain of the wood to stand out against the cold surface of metal and plastic. She had been drawing ultra modern architecturally inspired designs, creating her own cityscape of tall pepper grinders and saltshakers. She was very excited about her new designs and she felt confident when she scrutinized the finished prototypes in front of her. There were only a few minor adjustments to make, but on the whole she was optimistic that they would be well received. Jackie knew from past experience that, in the end, it was the sales that counted the most. An interesting new design that does not sell does not pay the mortgage. It was the typical designer's dilemma: how to create something functional, experimental, original, aesthetically pleasing and, most importantly, very saleable. It was this often contradictory challenge that had lured Jackie into the design world in the first place, and she tried to keep that in mind when she fell into bed exhausted and full of doubt at midnight, suddenly remembering that she had forgotten to return her mother's phone call.

Jackie worked long days. She had gotten into a routine of waking up at six in the morning and, since turning the wood was tiring, she did that first. In the afternoons she stained her peppermills and then assembled those she had stained the day before. Her life was structured but hectic; she could hear the invisible clock ticking in the background, announcing the fast approaching studio tour weekend.

Jackie's social life was almost non-existent, and if Nick hadn't visited her regularly, she would easily have become a hermit quite unintentionally, purely a result of the great workload. Jackie was always happy to see Nick; that strange, yet now-familiar feeling she had whenever she saw him walking slowly up her garden path was beginning to be less frightening.

Unfortunately they were seldom alone for long—there was always someone. Tourists wandered in or Harriet burst into the studio dragging Nick away to do a handyman's job in her house. Or there was Thomas, who had an uncanny ability to pop in to borrow things at just the moment when, by some miracle, Nick and Jackie had managed to steal a private moment.

All the studios were busy preparing for the Big Event. Already in August Sheridan had started making small clay angels. He was saving money to go on a safari in late December to explore, in more detail, his newly found connection with Ernest Hemingway. Jackie was already horrified imagining what he would bring back from his travels that he hadn't already purchased from eBay. The pub had set up a betting sheet for his return. Malaria was number one on the list of unwanted souvenirs.

Janet knitted Christmassy pullovers and Thomas had been blowing Christmas ornaments for two months. He preferred blowing big plates and vases, but as he said, 'The gas company does not care what I make as long as I pay my frigging bill on time.'

Nancy was having trouble keeping Christmas wreaths in stock— much to her surprise, they were selling even in the height of summer. Kenneth had enough snowy photos to make Christmas cards and Daisy painted everything she had with Christmas themes. She hoped that nobody would notice the strong resemblance between the Santa Claus and her husband.

Pam Johnson had bought a Christmas mail box from Daisy and had proudly put it up by her gate. Rosalind lived across the street and the reindeer-themed mail box drove her to the verge of a nervous breakdown, which of course made Pam Johnson appreciate it even more.

Maximilian was already fully booked for the weekend and was planning a jazz concert in his hotel on the Saturday night. He preferred classical music, but he knew that jazz would make people order more drinks than Debussy. He was, after all, a very good business man.

Almost all of the bed and breakfasts in the village were fully booked for the studio tour weekend and John was planning to organize fishing trips; he thought that there would be many husbands who would be far happier fishing than carrying shopping bags for their wives.

The boys kept reasonably quiet and talked about their past achievements more than made new ones, but it was all put to the benefit of the exceptionally warm weather that kept Jack busy cutting the grass and Glenn tilling his garden under the watchful eye of his wife.

Not a day went by without somebody mentioning the upcoming studio tour. It was all people could think about and argue about. The pub was filled in the evenings with heated speculations about the tour. There were running bets on the number of visitors, and on the weather and, in case of rain, the amount of rainfall.

Finally, all those months of planning came to an end and, somehow, Friday, the day before the studio tour weekend, arrived and panic, rightfully so, was in full bloom.

All the participants, volunteers and even a few outside spectators were in the town hall transforming it into the studio tour's information centre. The old building echoed with excited voices and busy footsteps. Jackie had wanted this done on Thursday, but the town hall had been booked for the girl scouts' monthly meeting. Everything, therefore had to be done on Friday.

The long tables were pushed alongside the walls. Their sturdy legs screeched against the old floor, sending dust flying in the air. The large information table was to be placed in the middle of the big room so that visitors would be able to walk around it and, at the same time, they could admire the display of the artists' work along the walls. Muriel had proudly organized the information into categories; food and drink, local interests, hotels and bed and breakfasts and, finally, the artists' studios and galleries.

Rosalind had had a heated conversation about the difference between fine dining and pub food. She had demanded a different section under the title of fine restaurants and had even suggested that the word *gourmet* be used to add a flamboyant feeling to the tour. 'A more cultured touch,' Rosalind had explained with a slightly irritated and tired voice.

This conversation had only come to an end when Honey from Honey's Parisian Tea Room had arrived with her business cards and demanded to know if Rosalind liked her tea room lunches or not. Rosalind had answered her question with a long explanation about the difference between caramelized onions and plain fried ones. Honey had taken this for a while and then she had told Rosalind, in an icy voice, that her presence in her tea room would no longer be welcome. Honey dropped her business cards on the table, turned on her flat rubber heels and left. Muriel had kept her short and snappy Food and Drink heading under Rosalind's glaring eyes and flared nostrils.

Muriel sighed and she mumbled something about adults behaving like children; the disagreements had already begun the night before at the meeting in the pub.

The group had had an intense discussion about the colour of the tablecloth that was going to be used for all of the displays. It had made Muriel shake her head in disbelief. She had finally broken into the dispute about multicolour versus white by saying that the church had a large selection of natural white tablecloths used normally for church bazaars and other activities and she would, herself, bring the tablecloths to the town hall; 'Surely'—she had interrupted Rosalind's skeptical response—'the pastor would not mind lending them to the studio tour organization at all.' This had finally closed the argument and the meeting had gone forward and a new item on the agenda had been found to create a fresh never-ending debate.

Muriel personally brought the tablecloths with her to the town hall on that Friday morning and she tut-tutted when Rosalind approached her. This made Rosalind complain about the country folk to Alistair, but Alistair was too busy arranging his table and he had no time to join in on Rosalind's tirade. When Rosalind moved away from Alistair's table, obviously displeased with his lukewarm welcome, he snuck behind the town hall for a cigarette, where he peacefully admired the dramatic view of the sea for half an hour.

Despite it all, Jackie was happy. She was gathering together the last loose ends, pleased that the group had come this far with the tour. It was a pure miracle, she thought.

Sheridan had bought himself a beige safari vest with millions of little pockets. He had also started to grow a beard to match his newly found fascination with Ernest Hemingway. He had his business cards in one of his vest's pockets; his cell phone was in another pocket along with a pair of scissors, markers, pen knife, some tape and a dusting cloth. Stella and Muriel watched him with growing interest. Stella found Sheridan's strange patting of his pockets fascinating. She even thought about calling Sheridan's cell phone just to see if he could find it. Muriel said that that was just too mean, but she had a laugh anyway.

Sheridan was meticulously arranging his display, turning a teapot an inch to the right and then stepping back to study the overall impact from afar. He pondered the matter seriously and then stepped forward again to make another adjustment.

Rose could not help herself and chuckled out loud as she walked by on her way out to go to work at the pub. She was going to give Nick the latest progress report on the town hall.

Sheridan looked up and shook his head and then bent forward to adjust his precious teapot again. He opened his cardboard box and took out two teacups and began arranging these into his display, which naturally affected the current position of the teapot.

Muriel observed Sheridan from her quilting table. She shook her head and nudged Stella's arm. 'With this speed he'll be done sometime next week.'

Jackie had set up her table with her peppermills and salt grinders. She had also brought with her drawings of her furniture designs and large professional-quality photos of the finished products. She laid them down on the table creating a colourful background. She stepped backward and inspected her display. She wanted her display to jump out and entice people with its curves and blasts of energetic colours not normally associated with wood products. It looked as good as it was going to get, she thought as she laid down two more peppermills on top of her drawings. She was very happy with her new colour combinations and styles. The future design show had given her creativity the much needed energy boost.

The island's Bitch and Stitch Club was busy. They had filled the town hall with their cheerful laughter and chatter as soon as they had walked through the door. They brought cookies and cakes with them and then busied themselves making tea and coffee for everyone.

An older Bitch and Stitch Club member was balancing dangerously on a rickety stepladder. She was trying to straighten a quilt on a wall while another elderly woman was holding onto the ladder. A few metres away from them stood another woman who gave loud instructions to the woman hanging on for dear life on top of the stepladder.

Jackie could hear her calling, 'To the left…no, no more to the right, to the left again.' Then she squinted her eyes and continued. 'No, a bit more to the left. Yes! That's it!' She finally declared with a shrill excited voice. The woman hanging on the ladder shook her head slowly and asked with a tired shaky voice, 'Are you absolutely sure, Ethel?'

'For god's sake, Ethel, let Judith came down before she breaks her neck,' Harriet boomed and stomped to the two women standing by the ladder. 'Let me hold that for you and you come down this very minute, Judith.'

Harriet grabbed the ladder from Helen, who was very pleased to let go. Her hand and arms were tired. Judith climbed shakily down, but Ethel folded her arms across her large bosom and pursed her lips, staring at Harriet disapprovingly.

'Now, now, Ethel,' said Harriet. 'Don't you start pouting there. The quilt looks fantastic and nobody is dead.' With these words Harriet walked away with the old ladder under her arm.

Judith tried to suppress a smile behind her hand. She grabbed Ethel and Helen by the arm and suggested that they should go and see if they needed to make more tea. Ethel was still upset and she glared at the quilt hanging on the wall. It was not straight. The right side was still lower than the left side.

Russell had already put his table in order and was happily chatting with Nancy and Daisy, who were glad to have him hanging around. His presence guaranteed Rosalind's absence, even if it meant listening to Russell's never-ending odd life stories. Still, a far better option than being viciously attacked by Rosalind.

Once in a while Jack Wilkinson put his head in the door and inquired after the progress. He also offered his and the rest of the boys' help, but this was firmly and kindly refused. Jack left, determined to find a way for the boys to help.

But first he needed a pint.

Caroline walked into the town hall, letting the heavy oak door slam shut loudly behind her. She stood by the door with a few large paintings under the crook of her long willowy arms while looking at the busy scene in front of her. It was hard to know what she was thinking behind her motionless face. She carried the paintings, wrapped in thick paper, carefully as she went to Muriel to ask where she should hang them.

Muriel checked her list and pointed to the place by the wall beside Sheridan.

Caroline stared at her display area critically and then shrugged her bony shoulders and walked slowly to her table. She had hoped for a much better space by the end wall of the room, far away from the others and with a direct view from the front doors.

Sheridan was still dissatisfied with his display. He tapped his stomach and adjusted the teapot once more. 'What do think,

Caroline?' He asked her and sighed so deeply that he made his orderly moustache stir.

'It's fine,' Caroline answered shortly without even looking at Sheridan's display.

Sheridan was still pondering over the teapot and cups when Caroline pulled out one of her paintings from under the brown paper cover.

It was a very large painting, almost life size. Caroline put the painting on top of the long table, carefully leaning it against the wall. Muriel's tablecloth formed deep pleats against the frame.

Sheridan looked over his shoulder at the painting and then let out a loud sharp shriek dropping the teacup he had been holding in his hands on the floor. It shattered into millions of pieces by his feet with a crash that echoed noisily through the hall. Everyone turned around, wondering what had caused the loud crash. As they did so, they saw the painting that Sheridan was gawking at, his mouth hanging open like a trap.

The room came to a standstill. Nobody said a word. Nobody moved. The room was filled with silent shock and withheld breaths. The only sound was that of an irritating fly buzzing aimlessly around the room, bumping against the bright windowpanes in its futile attempt to find fresh air.

Russell was the first person to break the unnatural silence by bellowing deafeningly, 'Sweet Jesus!'

Janet put her hand over her mouth and Kenneth plainly stared at the painting. Ethel put the teapot carefully down on the nearby table and Judith held tenuously onto the tea tray she was carrying in front of her. The evenly laid teacups rattled as she tried to catch her breath.

Sheridan's face was reddening into an ugly purplish hue. He stared at the painting without being able to utter a word. Only his moustache quivered as he exhaled heavily.

Rosalind marched toward Caroline pushing the group of shocked, elderly women aside and stood in front of the painting for a while before declaring it to be, 'a masterpiece of playful colours and harmonious shadows.'

'He has been playing, that's for sure,' Stella snorted and Harriet agreed by chuckling loudly, shaking her head, unable to believe what she saw with her very own eyes.

Suddenly the main door of the town hall opened and Thomas backed sideways into to the room carrying a large box in his arms. 'Good afternoon, ladies and gentlemen,' he hollered happily over his shoulder as he held the door open with his right foot.

People turned slowly to watch him as he set his box on the nearby table. They stared at him, eyes wide, unsaid words stuck in their throats.

Thomas whistled nonchalantly. He tore the thick tape from his box and squashed it into a big tight ball. He tossed the ball into the waste basket by the front door. It went in. He happily rubbed his hands together and spun around completely unaware of the unnatural silence in the room and the mute apprehension his entrance had caused.

Thomas bobbed his head along with his tune and stared at the people questioningly. He was still whistling cheerfully, when from the corner of his eye he caught a glimpse of Caroline's painting, leaning against the wall.

Thomas's happy whistling ended abruptly. He stared at the painting and turned deathly pale, as if somebody had just hit him violently in the abdomen. His face went from white to ashen. He stared at the painting for a long time without being able to utter a word. He could hardly even blink his eyes.

The painting was a very large realistic depiction of Thomas standing, his back turned toward the viewer, in front of an open fridge. He was casually leaning his right arm on top of the fridge door and he was completely and utterly naked. The light from the fridge enhanced his beautifully toned body, creating a golden halo around the masculine lines. He looked like a perfectly proportioned Greek god, who just happened to be looking for a can of beer from the fridge in a house that obviously belonged to Caroline.

Thomas was in deep painful shock. His eyes were glued to the painting. Not even a moan escaped from his dry lips. The air surrounding him was dead, thick; he could not move or talk.

The older ladies were staring at Thomas, silently comparing Thomas in the painting to Thomas in real life. Thomas was a beautiful man, there was no denying that. A very, very beautiful man, with or without clothes.

Caroline moved out from behind the tight group of women and walked across the room to him. 'Well, what do you think?' She asked her question nonchalantly and as always she spoke slowly, drawing out the words to give them more momentum and meaning.

Thomas blinked his sore eyes and uttered with a hoarse voice that didn't seem to belong to him, 'I think I need a drink.' He turned around unsteadily and staggered out the door.

Caroline watched him go. She seemed slightly amused. 'I think he likes it,' she said indifferently and then walked back to her pile of paintings and began to unwrap another. All the women in the town hall walked toward Caroline and formed a tight circle around her.

Muriel was the first one to speak. 'Any more lovely paintings, Caroline?' She asked innocently.

The rest of the older women mumbled something similar, that they too would love to see more of her lovely, lovely, lovely paintings.

Jackie was watching the situation from behind the information table. She felt sorry for Thomas, but she was also extremely amused by the commotion Thomas's painted nakedness had caused amongst the older and usually calm ladies.

'Poor Thomas.' She sighed sympathetically. 'Even he does not deserve this.' And then she tried to think of ways she could comfort Thomas, but she couldn't find any. What could you say to a young man whose beautifully painted naked, almost life size, body was hanging in the town hall in front of admiring retirees?

Chapter 19

Signs of Things to Come

After Thomas stepped out of the town hall, he stood motionless on top of the old stone steps. He tried to think of what had just happened, but he found it extremely hard to breathe. He felt light headed and he wanted to sit down and put his head between his legs.

Jack Wilkinson and the boys strolled leisurely across the street. They stopped in front of him and asked cheerfully how the studio tour was getting along. Thomas looked at them but was unable to answer their jolly greetings. He could not speak. The boys rolled their heads at Thomas's strange behaviour and then pushed the door to the town hall open and went in. They had come to investigate.

Thomas's mouth was dry as he slumped toward the pub across the street. He sat down at the bar in front of Nick's surprised eyes. Thomas usually entered the pub with loud salutations. This was not like him at all. Nick silently poured him a pint and watched him drink. He was waiting for Thomas to explain, when Jack Wilkinson bounced into the pub, the rest of the boys in tow. They had run across the street as fast as they could. Their faces were flushed with excitement and they were grinning like small mad men.

They spotted Thomas sitting at the bar. 'Bloody fantastic,' Jack Wilkinson said and slapped him on the back. 'Great painter that girl of yours, old boy.' Thomas grimaced as Jack Wilkinson's words caused a new level of unexplainable pain deep in his chest cavity. He quietly drank his beer. He said nothing. He didn't even bother to lift his head to look at Jack Wilkinson, who was sniggering beside him like a teenager.

Glenn murmured something like 'my, my' and grinned gleefully. Howard and Calvin smiled and claimed their appreciation for the fine painting. 'Darn good painting, almost like a real photograph.'

Nick was at a loss. He thrust his long arms forward. 'What? What? What has happened now?' He asked, his hands shaking rhythmically in the air with each word.

Russell strolled leisurely into the bar and slapped Thomas on his broad shoulders. 'Good day, you all. My, my, my, my, there are some handsome paintings there at the town hall. I have not seen the old ladies so excited for years.'

Nick still remained uninformed. 'Would somebody please tell me what has happened?' He shouted at no one particular.

Rose walked into the pub with surprisingly springy steps. 'What a wonderful sight for my sore old eyes!' She declared and walked behind Thomas trying to have a good look at his body which at the moment was sadly slouching over his pint of beer. Rose was imagining his shirt and pants away. 'That lucky Caroline,' she mumbled somewhat bitterly.

This time Nick yelled, 'What the hell has happened? Somebody say something, anything, for god's sake?' He looked at everybody in the pub, waiting to hear some kind of explanation from someone.

The boys sniggered, nudged each other, but said nothing. Rose rolled her eyes and Russell cleared his throat and then pointed in Thomas's direction. Nick stared at Thomas willing him to say something.

Thomas looked up with his expressionless eyes. 'Caroline has painted a painting,' he began in a battered voice, but Rose couldn't contain herself and chimed in. 'A loooo-vely painting, if I may say so. It has our handsome Thomas here in it and'—she paused and took a deep theatrical breath before continuing—'And he is naked, and I mean butt naked, no clothes at all, nothing, totally naked in front of a fridge looking for a can of beer after a wild session of sex.

The sex part is my conclusion, but why would he be in her kitchen butt naked otherwise.' Rose snorted and stared at Thomas eagerly, waiting for him to verify her conclusions.

Thomas glanced at her: the look was not a pleasant one. Rose wasn't bothered by that at all; she laughed loudly and then jovially added, 'I was just asking.'

'Oh,' was all Nick was able to say. He didn't quite know where to look, what to think and he had absolutely no idea what to say. He stood there behind the bar shifting his weight from one foot to the other, desperately thinking of something to say to poor Thomas.

'Yes,' Thomas muttered and stared at Nick with sad, desolate eyes. 'And now, I'm hanging on the town hall wall...butt naked, just like our Rose here so courteously explained.' Thomas lifted his hands in the air and then let them fall. The magnitude of it all was unexplainable.

'I'm telling you what; this man is a gift for us ladies.' Rose chuckled behind the bar.

There hadn't been so much commotion in the village since the doctor took a midnight spin around the village after being caught with the nurse. The pellet gun his wife had been holding in her delicate hands made it impossible for him to sit down comfortably for quite some time. His wife later said in a police report that she was aiming to shoot his front, but the swine ran too fast making his white behind the only available target.

Thomas grimaced and leaned closer to his pint of beer.

'I think he might be a bit sensitive about the painting.' Nick frowned and tried to hush up Rose.

'You don't say?' Russell was stunned. 'If my arse would be thirty years younger, I wouldn't mind having it hang in the town hall.'

'I don't know if people would like to see your arse up on the wall, Russell,' Jack Wilkinson blurted and all of the boys started laughing.

'It might be too hairy,' Glenn snorted, which caused the boys to laugh even harder.

Nick gestured to the boys from behind the bar to stop talking about arses. 'The usuals, boys?' He asked loudly his voice cutting through the snickering laughter.

'No, not yet.' Jack Wilkinson declared and wiped the tears away from his old wrinkled eyes. 'We are men on a mission.' He added proudly and held on to his jacket front with both hands. 'We came here to get those studio tour signs. We will put them out on the roads to lead all the visitors to the right town. I have my trailer set up behind my vehicle and we boys are ready to go and get busy. You know, community effort and all that sort of thing.' Jack put his hands to rest on his hips. The boys nodded proudly standing right behind him in line.

Nick stared suspiciously at the boys for awhile. 'Does Jackie approve of this?' He asked them. Somehow this just did not sound right.

'She would, if she would happen to know anything about it.' Jack Wilkinson grunted and rubbed his belly.

'You mean to tell me, that you haven't told her? Asked her?' Nick stared at the boys skeptically. He couldn't believe his ears.

'Minor detail, son.' Jack Wilkinson cleared his throat and shook his shoulders. 'Minor detail.'

'I really think you should talk with Jackie first, before you do anything.' Nick sounded very stern and worried, but the boys took no notice. They were feeling proud, good and helpful, and for men such as they, those feelings were not so easy to come by. Therefore when there was a chance, they naturally wanted to make the most of it.

Thomas drank the rest of his pint and got up. There wasn't that usual springiness in his step. He looked like a man with chronic back pain who had grown used to it.

'I was given the job of putting those road signs out, but I guess I could use some help.' His voice was far from his normal happy tone. 'And I really want to stay as far away as possible from that town hall right now.' He glanced silently across the street through the pub window and grimaced. The front door of the town hall was very busy. Many people who were not part of the studio tour were hastily going in and out. Thomas bit his lip and sighed deeply. 'So? You coming?' He looked at the boys questioningly.

'Yeah' was the united answer and then the boys followed Thomas to the storeroom behind the bar.

The boys were busy and helpful and Thomas was grumpy and exceptionally quiet. The world seemed to have turned upside down. Russell looked questioningly at Nick, gesturing slightly with his big bushy head toward the storage room. Nick nodded in agreement and then quickly turned toward Rose, who was wrapping forks and knives into napkins.

'Rose, would you mind looking after the pub for a while? I better go and help the boys and Thomas to put up the road signs.'

'No, not at all. Go!' Rose shook her hand in the air, already shooing him away. Nick grabbed his jacket from his office and handed the keys to Rose mentioning the three o'clock delivery and a slight change in the menu.

Rose tutted and shouted, 'Go!' waving a handful of forks in the air.

The boys and Thomas came out from the storeroom carrying the signs. Rose leaned over the bar to check out Thomas's behind as he walked by. Nick shook his head at Rose trying to prevent her from saying anything about the painting. Rose just smiled cheerfully and clicked her tongue approvingly.

Nick wasn't sure but he thought he heard Rose mumble 'yummy' under her breath. 'Poor Thomas,' he thought.

Russell looked at the boys and then the pile of signs. 'I'll come with you.' He offered his help to Nick.

'Thanks, Russell.' Nick was putting his jacket on. 'Because I have this strange feeling that without us no roads will lead to Sycamore.' He mumbled to himself, finally finding the sleeve that had turned inside out. He was able to quickly grab the signs that Jack Wilkinson dropped without even noticing.

Howard carried signs under his arm and banged them loudly against the doorframe. It took some time for him to sort out the unruly signs, but finally he negotiated the door. 'That damn door is too small,' he cursed.

Calvin dropped one sign and the corner landed heavily on his toes. This unfortunate event was followed by a litany of foul words that made even Rose shout out her objection to hearing such language. Glenn happily carried only a hammer in his big hands. He whistled cheerfully which made Calvin glare at him, his toe still pulsing with pain.

'How come you have only a hammer in your bloody hands?' He demanded to know, holding his foot in the air.

'What? Are you saying that we won't need a hammer?' Glenn quickly answered back.

'No. Of course we need a bloody hammer.' Calvin snapped gruffly.

'So what's your problem then?' Glenn asked lifting his shoulders up one inch in an exaggerated manner.

Calvin couldn't find an answer fast enough and Glenn walked casually by swinging the hammer by its handle.

'Watch out that you don't put somebody's eye out.' Calvin complained loudly through a grumpy frown. There was a dent in his shoe that he could not get out.

Glenn just snorted and walked out to the tractor trailer and tossed the hammer in, much to Jack Wilkinson's dismay.

Nick shook his head slowly. He felt like hollering to Rose that his trip might take a bit longer than originally planned. This was not going to end well, he thought, as he piled the rest of the signs into the back of his car.

They set out. Russell, Thomas and Nick driving in one direction and the boys in the other. Nick looked at the lawnmower clunking down the street with its rusty trailer in tow. He was convinced that people arriving from the south side of the village would never be able to find their way.

Nick drove past the only alcohol store in the village and Thomas lifted his hand in the air and told him to stop. Nick steered the car to the side and Thomas leapt out and disappeared into the store. A few minutes later he came out holding a bottle of whiskey. The two cash register girls were giggling inside the store as they stretched their necks to get a better look at Thomas through the window. They too had obviously heard about the painting.

Thomas climbed back into the car and closed the car door with a loud bang. 'How fast does the bloody news spread in this town?' He asked and frowned at the girls in the window.

'Pretty fast, I reckon.' Nick answered shrugging his shoulders.

Russell agreed and compared the speed of gossip to a 100 metre relay in an Olympic field. 'The gossip in this village is like Ben Johnson on steroids: fast and hard to believe true.'

Thomas opened the whiskey bottle and offered it to Nick. Nick shook his head and started the car. Russell said that he would wait till he was back at the pub and gently pushed the bottle away.

Thomas took a long sorrowful sip from his bottle and settled into a gloomy, brooding mood.

They drove in silence through the long winding roads between the vast fields. Once in a while they had a clear view of the sea. Nick never got tired of looking at the rolling waves and gushing white caps hitting the endless rugged shoreline. He drove with the window open. The wind blasted in, ruffling his hair and making his eyes water. Russell whistled and enjoyed the view as well; Thomas kept his eyes on the middle of the road and steadily sipped his whiskey.

They came to the first crossroad and Nick pulled the car onto the rocky edge of the road. He and Russell got out and hammered the first sign into the ground. Thomas remained silent in the front seat of the car. The more signs Nick and Russell put up, the more drunk and miserable Thomas got. Russell tut-tutted and hammered yet another sign into the hard ground. He glanced at Thomas's sad drunken figure in the car.

'I mean...who the hell understands these women? Do you, Nick?' Thomas inquired. 'Do you, Nick?' He repeated his question, his words slurring ever so slightly.

'I can't say I do, Thomas.' Nick said and took out another sign from the back of his car.

'What about you, Russell?' Thomas was talking louder than needed, his voice rising with each word he uttered, so that by the end of his question, Russell's name was a deafening yell.

'Women, no problem. I keep my woman happy by giving her the old Russell treatment every day, and you know what that is.' Russell explained proudly and winked.

'Yeah, but she doesn't go around and paint frigging pictures of your arse, now does she?' Thomas's pointed out.

'I can't say she does. I wouldn't mind posing though.' Russell chuckled at the thought.

'Frigging hell!' Thomas groaned, leaned back in the front seat and stared lifelessly at the beige ceiling of the car.

By the time Nick and Russell were pounding the last sign into the ground beside the main road, Thomas was quite drunk and was having a vivid conversation with himself. He argued and swished his bottle around. At one point he pointed his finger up into the air and then aimed it back at himself. 'Never, never…never trust a woman… again.'

Nick and Russell finished hammering. They straightened up and then stood silently by the edge of the deserted road, watching Thomas in the car. The countryside was quiet, only the whistling wind in the trees accompanied Thomas's sorrowful monologue. Nick put his hands in his pockets and looked at Russell. 'Well, what do you say? We'd better take him home.'

'Yeah. Poor chap. It's hard to get your ass kicked, artistically speaking.' Russell shook his head and they walked together back to the car. Thomas took another swig from the bottle.

As Nick sat in the driver's seat he said to Thomas, 'We better take you home, don't you think?'

'All right. You can take my painted arse home, I guess.' Thomas slurred.

'You know, she could have painted a full frontal portrait—so having only your arse up on the wall is not that bad, actually.' Russell suggested helpfully from the backseat. He was sitting in the middle and leaning his elbows on the backs of the front seats, his grey head bobbing up and down.

'You never know what she has in her storage room, just waiting to be revealed. You just never know.' Thomas moaned and shook his head miserably.

Nick and Russell pondered this in silence; finally Russell said, 'Well in that case, have another drink.'

Thomas lifted the bottle up to salute Russell and took a long sorrowful swig as Nick turned the car around.

On their way back to the village, Nick saw the first of many studio tour signs which the boys had haphazardly hammered into the ground. It was pointing completely in the wrong direction and was already rapidly falling down. Nick sighed and stopped the car.

'Russell, hand me the hammer will you?' He got out of the car. 'Bloody Jack Wilkinson and the boys. I know they mean well, but…' he muttered as he hammered the sign deeper into the hard ground after turning it to point in the right direction.

The people driving from the south side of the island would now be able to find the village.

After repairing the rest of the signs the boys had tried to put up, they arrived at Thomas's house. As they manoeuvred him out of the car, Thomas moaned and cursed Caroline. He also told Russell and Nick that they were his best friends and that men understood each other better than any woman ever could. He put his arms around Nick and Russell and repeated his appreciation for their masculine companionship. Nick and Russell smiled sympathetically and agreed with everything he said. Russell patted Thomas's back and muttered 'yes, yes,' every so often.

Suddenly a man appeared from behind a large tree. He pointed a wavering finger at Thomas and muttered, 'You, you…you have slept with my angel…you.'

Nick and Russell almost let go of Thomas in their surprise. Maximilian Woodhouse was standing in front of them in his pristine white chef's jacket. Before they could stop him Maximilian punched Thomas, then let out a deafening howl as he covered his fist with his other hand.

Thomas yelled 'Fuck!' and held his stomach and all Nick and Russell could do in their astonishment was to stare at the two men in front of them.

'You slept with my darling little Caroline.' Maximilian wailed and held his hand. 'And she painted your arse. Your arse and not mine.'

Thomas said nothing; his mind was not capable at this time of concentrating on two things at the same time. He stared at Maximilian trying to focus his eyes so that he would only see one man in a white jacket yelling at him.

'I have been educated in Paris, France, in one of the finest culinary schools in the world and she, she chooses to paint your uncultured country arse and not mine.' Maximilian let out a deep sorrowful howl.

Thomas rolled his head, counting the large white men dancing in front of him.

'Do you cook for her?' Maximilian bawled and stomped his foot, almost in tears.

Thomas mumbled something about a drink and held onto his whiskey bottle for dear life.

'I cook, I make her delicate crème brulée, coq au vin. I give her everything and you? And you...' Maximilian cried out, unable to finish his sentence. The thought of Thomas and Caroline together was too much.

Nick had had enough. 'Okay. I think it would be better if you two talked this over tomorrow. Now is not a good time. I'll take Thomas inside and then we'll take you home, Max.' He nodded to Russell. 'Take Max to the car, will you?'

Russell stared at Maximilian who was now crying uncontrollably. Finally, Russell grabbed onto Maximilian's starched sleeve and led him to the car, mumbling something about nutters and madcaps.

Nick got the key out of Thomas's pocket and opened the front door. He walked Thomas into his apartment above the studio and set him down on the sofa in the living room. He pried the whiskey bottle from his fingers, took off his shoes and threw a blanket over him.

'Thanks, lads. I'll be fine.' Thomas muttered half asleep waving his hand in the air until finally it fell to the floor and stayed there motionless.

Nick stood by him for a few seconds and then decided he would be all right. There wasn't much else he could do for a drunken man who had first been humiliated and then beaten. Nick left lights on in the bathroom and in the kitchen and then returned to the car.

Max was howling in the front seat. Russell was standing by the car stretching his hands toward the sky in despair. 'I can't shut him up!' he yelled over the wailing, covering his ears with both hands. 'The bloody man won't stop crying.'

Nick got into the car and tried to talk to Max, but all Max wanted to do was to declare his undying love for Caroline in between his sorrowful sobs. Nick turned around to look at Russell sitting in the back seat, but Russell just covered his ears again and told him to start the bloody car.

By the time they reached Maximilian's restaurant, Russell was begging to be allowed to kill Max by throwing him out of the moving vehicle. Max's loud sniffling had driven Russell to the edge. Nick parked near the staff entrance and went to ring the bell. Frank opened the door and stood in the doorway listening to Maximilian's moans and Russell's menacing yells coming from the car. Nick just shook his head. There was no point explaining anything.

Nick and Russell guided Maximilian in and all Frank could say was, 'Mon dieu,' and then he scurried off to get a cold compress and a pot of strong coffee. They were fully booked for dinner.

Nick and Russell wasted no time in leaving. As they drove past the brightly lit restaurant, Russell suddenly furrowed his brow. He looked at Nick. 'I thought that chap was French. What happened to his accent?' Their simple night had turned into something very strange.

Jack Wilkinson's lawnmower was already parked in its normal place when Nick and Russell returned to the pub. The traffic to the town hall had not diminished. People were going in and coming out carrying parcels and boxes in their arms. The town hall resembled a very busy anthill.

After parking his car, Nick walked toward the pub and Russell was already heading off to the town hall.

'I'll go and see if I can help them ladies in there, and I guess, I better take Thomas's stuff out of the box as well.' Russell said and put his hands in his pockets, pointing his head toward the hall.

Nick and Russell had made an unspoken agreement not to mention the Thomas–Maximilian episode to anybody. They thought some things were better left alone.

Nick stared at the town hall trying to catch a glimpse of Jackie. He spotted her through the brightly lit windows scratching her head frantically with one hand and with the other pointing toward the tables. Janet, carrying empty brochure boxes, was approaching her. Jackie turned around and began immediately walking toward Janet, grabbing yet another empty box from a table and disappearing into the back room.

Nick returned to the pub where Rose was busily working. The boys were already there sitting comfortably at their corner table drinking celebratory pints. According to them, their trip had been very successful—despite that the hammer had been lost for good. Everything seemed to be back to normal.

Chapter 20

Show Time

Jackie woke up early on Saturday morning, and the first thing she did was to look out her bedroom window. She had been reading the weather forecasts religiously for the last two weeks. A downpour on the opening day would have been disastrous for the studio tour.

She smiled when she saw the bright blue sky and the colourful autumn leaves rustling in a gentle breeze. It could not have been a more beautiful day. No rain, no sudden hurricanes, no other natural disasters. 'Maybe the gods are smiling on me after all,' she thought peacefully and got up. She felt the warm thrill of anticipation.

When Nick woke up, he did the exact same thing. He looked out his window and as he saw the bright blue sky, he fell back into his bed smiling, folding his hands under his head. He decided to give himself an extra five minutes to stay in his warm bed before beginning the long day. He breathed in deeply, stared at the ceiling and started making a list in his mind of all the things he needed to do before opening the pub.

Thomas, on the other hand, woke up on his couch and immediately felt the severe pulsing pain in his head. He thought his forehead was going to crack in half at any second from the slashing, icy cold pain just above his eyebrows. He smacked his lips together carefully and realized that his mouth was extremely dry. Slowly he pulled himself up, not entirely sure if his body could be asked to perform such a task under the circumstances. Finally he was sitting on the edge of the sofa leaning his head in his hands. He was the very image of acute pain. He could have made an excellent advertisement for a migraine medicine, if his pain had not have been so obviously related to alcohol consumption and hangover.

'Jesus, my eyes have grown hair inside them,' Thomas mumbled to himself and closed his sore eyes again. He was in the process of trying to collect enough strength to be able to walk all the way to the kitchen. He wanted and needed to drink a litre of apple juice alongside a handful of aspirins. Luckily for Thomas, the pain in his head had taken his mind off Caroline and the painting.

Jackie was in her kitchen standing by the window looking out onto her garden. She glanced at her watch and then quickly drank the remains of her coffee, grabbed a piece of toast from the table and walked out to her studio. She flicked on the lights and for a brief moment admired her well-organized gallery. She had worked late for many nights just to get the gallery to be at its best for this morning. The studio tour sign was leaning against the wall by the door. She stuffed the last bite of the crumbling toast into her mouth and picked up the sign and a hammer. She walked out her gate and hammered the sign deep enough into the ground to withstand the wind that blew in from the sea in the afternoons.

An older man walked by with his dog. He was taking small, hesitant steps on the uneven pavement. The weeds and flowers had won the battle and now they pushed their delicate shoots gloriously through the rough concrete, lifting it here and there. The man's dog turned his face to look up at him. It was trying its best to walk as slowly as the old man. Once in a while the dog would run ahead, then, once its curiosity was satisfied and its territory marked, it would sit down to wait.

The old man lifted his hat. Jackie noticed that his hands were shaking. 'I see that you are getting ready for the tour, Jacqueline.'

'Yes I am, Mr. Todd. Will you go for the tour yourself?'

'My daughter is coming here for the weekend and we will do the tour together.'

'That's nice.'

'See, I can't drive anymore and my legs are not what they used to be.'

His dog was sitting by him, waiting patiently and thumping its tail against the pavement. 'Good luck for your tour, Jacqueline,' the old man said.

'Thank you, Mr. Todd.' Jackie smiled and added, 'We need all the luck we can get.'

The man carefully inspected Jackie's sign, put his hat back on and walked on.

Jackie stepped onto the sidewalk and looked in both directions. She saw Sheridan putting out his sign in the distance and on the other side, she saw Harriet putting out hers. Winston was running around Harriet's feet and when Felix saw that, he wanted to dash off to Harriet's house. Jackie held him by his collar and pushed him back into the garden. Poor Felix would have to be in the house most of the day.

In the village centre, Muriel opened the church hall's heavy double doors. The cool morning sun was shining brightly. The women standing on the front steps created elongated shadows that moved into the church hall with them. The voices of the women soon filled the quiet space as the long curtains were pulled open and the lights were switched on.

Muriel put the studio tour sign outside, right beside the tall front doors.

Stella, the cashier from the general store, was walking down the street toward the town hall and waved her hand to Muriel. 'You girls all ready?' She shouted cheerfully, dangling from her hand a big ring filled with keys.

'As ready as we can ever be.' Muriel pulled her cardigan tighter around herself. The morning air was still a bit cold and damp. She turned to call for Linda. 'Linda! Stella is here to open the doors to the town hall!'

'I'm coming.' An old woman with stiff yellowy hair hurried to the door and greeted Stella with an excited smile.

They walked together to the town hall. Stella found the right key and after a gentle push and a tough yank, the old door opened.

'Nice of you to help us, Stella,' said Linda.

'Nah, it's nothing.' Stella grunted and flicked on the lights.

She stared at Caroline's painting of Thomas and smiled. She did not mind tending to the information centre at all. She preferred Caroline's paintings to Russell's. 'Seen enough dogs in my life,' she had said to Jackie. 'Don't need them on my walls.'

Linda brought out a sign for the Studio Tour Information Centre and placed it on the sidewalk in front of the town hall's old stone steps and then she quickly disappeared inside again. She needed to put the sandwiches she had made for her and Stella into the fridge. She suspected that there would not be enough time to have an official lunch break. She flicked on the tea kettle and took the tea bags out from her purse.

Tim and John were preparing breakfast for a full house of overnight guests in their East End Bed and Breakfast. Tim was cooking in the warm kitchen and John brought out plates full of sizzling bacon and fried eggs. He had on a pristine blue and white striped apron. The overnight quests were sitting at the breakfast table and they were all drinking tea or coffee while studying the studio tour brochures and planning where to begin their tour.

At Maximilian's French Restaurant, Maximilian Woodland was yelling in his kitchen. 'Get those fucking trays ready or are you a complete moron?' He ground his teeth together in agony. His kitchen character was completely different from his non-kitchen character and somehow his French accent always disappeared as he ranted about the poor quality of the tomatoes. His staff rolled their eyes but kept quiet. They knew better than to say anything. The hotel was fully booked and both the lunch and dinner were going to be hectic. In fact, Frank had been telling people who called in to make a reservation, that they were unfortunately full, but that they would be more than happy to make a reservation for them for the following weekend.

Max had to admit that Jackie had done well for the island, even though he did not approve of some of the choices she and the group had made. Somehow, though, these opinions were not so important at the moment. He had had a long discussion with Rosalind about the quality of the tour. He had agreed that, yes indeed, the painted postal boxes were an absolute embarrassment, but he could hardly care about it now when his hotel was fully booked. Had it been otherwise, then yes, naturally, the postal boxes would have had to carry the weight of being the single reason why the tour was not successful. But now, he just wanted to get the fucking lunch preparations under way.

Outside, an elderly man drove by in a bright green car. He squeezed the steering wheel with both hands and glared at his wife who was reading the map. She calmly told him that there should be an intersection coming soon, when they suddenly saw the studio tour sign on the side of the road.

The wife looked at her husband. 'See, darling. It seems that I CAN read a map after all.'

The husband grunted, but did not utter a word in response. His wife folded her map neatly away, and tucked it inside the pocket of the car door. They drove to the village in a heavy silence. Behind them, other early arrivers were turning off the highway and following the signs to the village of Sycamore.

Alistair saw the green car as it passed, while Rosalind was organizing his biographic notes in the studio. She was almost humming as she leafed through Alistair's plentiful merits. 'They are arriving already,' Alistair pointed out to Rosalind and then quickly disappeared behind the studio to have a cigarette before the crowds would come to interrupt his day.

Janet was carrying two tea mugs into the barn, which had been converted into a gallery for the time being. Kenneth was hanging the last of his photographs on the walls. He turned at the sound of Janet's footsteps. She handed him his tea.

They looked slowly around the barn and Janet spoke as if making a statement rather than beginning a conversation. 'Looks good.'

'Sure does.' Kenneth didn't go for a lengthy answer either and they both had a sip of their tea. Enough said. The steam rose from their cups as they continued inspecting the barn in silence.

Nancy was hanging a new wreath on her front door. Her mudroom had been converted into a small gallery. The walls were covered with different sizes and styles of wreaths. Her hands were trembling slightly as she hung the Christmas wreath. She straightened the bells and the red bow and then stepped back a few feet to make sure that the wreath was straight, and she almost tripped. She put her hand to her chest as if to tell her heart to stop beating so fast. She blew air through her lips and closed her eyes for a second. She hadn't been this busy for years.

'Oh, no,' she exclaimed when she saw her flower pots by the door. 'I forgot to water them,' she muttered in disbelief and scurried off to the garden shed to fill the watering can, only to remember afterwards that she was still wearing her terrycloth house slippers.

Caroline was smoking a cigarette and lounging on the corner of her worktable, swinging her long leg idly up and down while dangling her shoe from her toes. She was studying her paintings. There were many paintings of Thomas and also some smaller landscapes and still lifes. Some of the paintings were hanging on the walls, but there were also many in piles leaning casually against the wall. She had had a very productive autumn. Thomas had been exceptionally good for her artistic flow.

She blew the smoke through her thin lips and fixed one stray hair back behind her ear. She pushed the end of the cigarette into the overflowing ashtray on the table and let her legs fall to the ground with a sharp click from her heels.

Daisy was straightening the little painted jewellery boxes in her gallery for the fifth time that morning. As soon as she moved one box, she would move the other box next to it and then the others beside the others, until she had changed the whole display. She stood in the middle of her gallery biting her lip, wondering if the display had in fact been better before. Small pearls of sweat were forming on her greying hairline and she wiped them off with a trembling hand.

'I really need to stop this,' she mumbled. 'But I just need to move this little thing here.' She reached in to move the photo frame and as she was leaning over the display, she instinctively straightened the painted rolling pins.

Her gallery was full of wooden cutting boards with pictures of herbs painted on them. Daisy had identified each herb by writing their French name elegantly underneath them. She also had breadboxes with roosters and serving trays with roses. Her much cursed and loved mailboxes painted with garden motifs, sailboats and Christmas themes were right by the front door.

Too bad for Rosalind, but Daisy truly loved her mailboxes and she knew that the mailman was happy with them as well. He had said many times to Daisy that his daily rounds in the village became much more interesting after Daisy started selling them.

The door opened and Daisy's husband carefully peeked in. 'I made some tea if you wish to have some,' he said softly.

'I'll have it in a minute, just after I sort these out,' Daisy said and she straightened the few rolling pins again.

Dennis left quietly and went back to reading his newspaper in the kitchen. The radio was playing swing music and the early morning smell of toast was still lingering in the air.

Russell was hugging his wife in the kitchen while she was trying to make a cup of tea. Jane shooed him away agitatedly and then turned to face him. 'Now, really Russell. We ought to get ready for the tour. Get the dogs in and lock them into the bedroom, will you?'

Russell sighed and walked out of the kitchen. He was standing in the doorway staring at the road, whistling for the dogs.

Jane could hear the happy yelping sound as the dogs ran to Russell. He flung the kitchen door open and the dogs poured in. Russell strolled in after them, scratching his head. 'Blimey, the people are here already.'

Jane looked at her watch and then at Russell. 'What—but it's not even ten o'clock yet.' They could hear the sound of a car door closing and then strange voices drifted into the quiet kitchen. Jane joined Russell at the window. 'All right then. I'll take the dogs upstairs and you go and open the front door to let the people in.' Jane straightened up, untied her apron, and then went upstairs with the dogs.

Russell walked slowly down the narrow hallway to open the front door for the tourists. 'Blimey,' he muttered as he flicked the lights on.

Thomas was carefully opening the double doors of his studio and gallery. He closed his eyes in preparation for the worst; the bright sunlight hit his strangely colourless face. He stood in the doorway with his studio tour sign in one hand and the hammer in the other. Slowly and cautiously he opened his one eye, preparing himself for the instant torture. He groaned and then gradually opened the other eye. He blinked his eyes, waiting for the pain to subside. He looked quite fragile for such a big tall man. He was leaning on his sign trying to collect enough strength to walk to the curb, when he saw the old man and his map-reading wife arguing in the green car on the side of the road, opposite the studio.

'Oh, good god,' was the only thing Thomas could mutter.

The elderly man and his wife were getting out of their car, staring at Thomas. He walked tentatively to the street to greet the couple. Every step made his head hurt; the crunch of the gravel sounded like a sledgehammer in his head.

'Good morning,' Thomas said and winced.

'Good morning. We are a bit early, but can we have a look anyhow,' said the man. It was more a statement than a question. He rubbed his hand across his stomach, leaving his thumbs hooked around his belt.

'Yes, by all means—my gallery is right through those double doors.' Thomas's hand waved in the air. The man walked briskly toward the gallery and Thomas began hammering the studio tour sign into the ground. Every time he hit the hammer, he felt as if his head would fall off. He wondered if it was possible for the brain to hit the walls of the skull. It certainly felt like that. He left the sign standing crookedly, leaning toward the uncut grass and walked into the gallery to find the husband and wife standing there in the darkness. Thomas flicked on the lights and then walked into the studio, where the glory hole was already humming.

The wife remained in the gallery but the husband followed Thomas into the studio. 'Is that hot?' He pointed to the furnace.

'Yes it is quite hot…2000 degrees Fahrenheit.'

'Is it really? Now, how do you do it?'

'I'll start glassblowing demonstrations in half an hour or so.'

'Mind if I wait?'

'No, not at all.'

The husband sat down firmly on an old plastic garden chair that Thomas had in the studio. He folded his arms across his barrel-shaped chest and made himself as comfortable as he could. It looked as if he was there to stay. Thomas was surprised by all of this, but his throbbing head prevented him from thinking too much above the quite complicated task of breathing without hurting his sinuses; he decided to treat the man in the chair as a kind of ugly, unpleasant mascot.

'Now, how hot did you say the oven was, again?' A question came from the depth of the chair.

'About 2000 Fahrenheit.'

It was going to be a very long day with the mascot.

In the Studio Tour Information Centre the doors were opening and closing loudly as people wandered in and out. Linda and Stella were answering as many questions as they possibly could. They were handing out the brochures and giving directions to the different studios, weaving right-hand turns and sharp lefts with their hands.

A group of older women in sensible walking shoes were touching everything in the display area. They were particularly interested in inspecting how Janet Nesmith had knitted her pullovers. They tucked the seams and appraised the evenness of the pattern. The group was also fascinated by the quilt display. They were loudly comparing colours, textures and stitching to the other magnificent quilts they had seen during their long quilt-enthusiast years. The women pointed to certain areas of stitching and then quickly flipped the corner of the quilt to see the underside. They were searching for tips and mistakes; finding mistakes left them far happier than finding special tricks and methods they themselves had never thought of.

'See here how she has done the edge.' One woman pointed to the edge of a quilt and tapped it slightly with her finger.

'Oh, yes…well that is certainly very strange…very unorthodox.' They bent down to have a closer look and a low tut-tut was heard.

Linda was watching all of this. Her eyebrows were almost meeting one another above her nose. She quickly scribbled something on a large piece of paper and then walked to the display area, discreetly putting her sign down. It said in bright red ink: 'Please, do not touch.'

The group of women looked at the sign and then stared at Linda.

Linda returned behind her desk. 'Please, do not touch' had not been her first choice of words, but it was the only politically correct one and therefore the only choice available. Linda glared at the group of older ladies, who slowly backed away from the quilts and went to admire Sheridan's pottery. This time Linda only had to clear her throat loudly and the curious fingers were brought back.

A young couple was looking at the painting of naked Thomas in front of the fridge. The young woman leaned backwards and folded her arms. 'To me, it speaks about the sexuality of food.'

Her companion grunted barely audibly. 'Uh…yes.'

'See the food in the fridge?' The girl pointed.

'Yes. There's'—the young man looked closer—'margarine, milk and,' he paused and then added approvingly, 'beer.'

'To me it screams about sex and hunger…and…lust…and…thirst…and…and…well…hunger.' The girl's voice trailed on as she tried to find the correct word that had somehow slipped her mind as she admired Thomas's perfect backside on the wall.

The young man cleared his throat and thought about how nice it would be to have a beer.

On the edge of the village, Tom and Kevin were standing on the steps of their West End B & B. They were watching a thin older woman walking gingerly down the street.

'Enjoy your tour, Mom,' Kevin called after her.

'Yes dear. I will,' his mother answered.

'Are you sure you don't want me to drive you around, Mom? I could do that. It would be no problem for me.'

'Little walk in the village will do me good.'

'Are you sure, Mom?'

'Yes, I am, Kevin. I am old but not that old.'

'Don't get lost, and lunch will be ready at two,' Kevin hollered to the disappearing back of his mother.

'I will. Don't worry, dear.' And she walked down the street carefully avoiding cracks and loose stones on the pavement.

Kevin was worried, not only because of his mother's health, but also, she might find a brochure they hadn't doctored.

Tom tapped his shoulder quietly. 'It'll be fine Kevin,' he whispered, but Kevin remained anxious.

Jackie was behind her desk in the gallery. There were a few people in the tiny space, squeezed tightly together. Jackie opened a window nearby to get some fresh air.

An older man was turning one of her peppermills in his hands, his knobby fingers touching the smooth surface of the wood. He looked up at Jackie and asked bluntly, 'So you do this all by yourself, then?'

Jackie smiled politely and answered, 'Yes, I do.'

The man stared at her for a moment; 'So, you don't have a bloke doing all the hard work for you behind the scenes?'

Jackie looked at him for a few long hesitating seconds before she answered. 'No, no. I work all by myself.' Then just to make sure the man understood her correctly, she added, 'All the work here is handmade by me.'

The man put the peppermill down on to the shelf and picked up another. 'That's hard to believe.'

Jackie bit her lip, willing herself not to say anything she might regret later.

The man was inspecting the other pepper grinder, turning it again in his broad hands and examining the grinding mechanism. 'So you do not order these from China or anything of that sort?'

'No, no...' Jackie answered quickly. 'I make them all by hand from the beginning to the finish.'

The man grunted. He still didn't believe her. He continued to inspect the pepper grinder. He couldn't figure out how Jackie could have done her wood inlays so precisely.

A young woman and a man were standing beside the overly suspicious, grunting man. They too had their eyes on the grinders. 'This is so cool!' The young girl sighed. 'It would look so cool in the kitchen.'

'Well, why don't you buy it then?' The young man said and scratched his neck. It was hot in the gallery and he had opened his jacket.

The girl turned to look at her boyfriend. 'Really? You think so?'

'Well, yeah—if you like it, you should buy it.' The young man shrugged his shoulders. He needed to take his jacket off.

'All right. I think I will, if you say so. But which one? They are all so cool.'

'How about the red and black one?' The boyfriend suggested.

'No, I can't have that one. I have a blue kitchen.'

'How about the blue and yellow then?'

'No. Lord, no. That's too much blue.'

'Oh,' the boyfriend said and decided not to make any more suggestions.

'Maybe the yellow and orange?' The girl said, pouting.

The boyfriend mumbled something that could be interpreted as yes or no depending on the choice the listener would make. He tried to wriggle free from his jacket.

'Yes. Yellow and purple it is.' The young girl smiled and walked to Jackie with the chosen pepper grinder in her hands. 'I just love your work.' She sighed and put the grinder down on the table carefully.

'Thanks!' Jackie was surprised to make a sale so fast and so easily. She reached under her desk to take out a box, specially designed to hold the grinders and salt shakers. The box had her name stamped on it with black shiny letters: Jacqueline Callaghan Design.

The young woman handed Jackie her credit card. 'Do you make furniture as well?'

'Yes, I do.'

'We are staying at the East End Gays B & B and the man there said that you made their breakfast table.'

Jackie flinched a little when the girl mentioned the mistake in the studio tour brochure. 'Tim and John. Yes, I did make a table for them,' she said.

'It is so brave for the gays to be so open about their sexuality in a small farming community like this. Really, I couldn't believe my eyes when I saw their B & B advertised in the studio tour brochure.

East End Gays B & B! Unbelievable! I called them immediately and
booked a room for the weekend. See, my boyfriend and I have no
problems with gays…or…or lesbians…?' The girl suddenly looked
at Jackie more closely. Jackie had her work clothes on: jeans, T-shirt,
sweater with a hood and steel toed work boots—clothes any sensible
woodworker would wear.

Jackie handed over the receipt for the girl to sign. She didn't
know what to say. Should she correct the hip young girl and tell her
that the brochure had a little mishap with the names or just let it be.
She let it be; the young woman was a very fast talker with a habit of
listening very little.

'And your table is absolutely gorgeous in their breakfast room.
It is so cool!'

'Oh…thank you very much. That's nice to hear.' She closed the
box.

'Did you give me your business card? Great! I'll tell my mom.
She just loves these kinds of things.' The girl signed her name on
the credit card slip. 'Thank you and good luck with the tour.' She
walked away briskly. There were many places for her to visit. This
was just the beginning of the tour. She handed the plastic bag to her
boyfriend and then took out the brochure to see where they were
going next.

'Thanks…bye!' Jackie hollered to the disappearing feet.

The skeptical man approached Jackie. 'Now, when does the wood
turning demonstration start?' He inquired in a low but loud voice.

'In a few minutes.' Jackie answered trying to hide the rising
irritation in her voice.

The man parked himself directly in front of Jackie and stood
there, waiting.

Jackie stared at him for a while expecting him to say something,
but the man remained quiet. He was waiting for the demonstration
to start and he would not budge from his first row place.

A woman customer tried to get by the old man, but he wouldn't
move. He was trying to see into Jackie's studio by stretching his neck
as much as he could. Jackie reached for the woman's hand and took

the pepper grinder from her. She said to the man, 'Excuse me,' but without any effect.

'So you say you don't buy these cheap from China,' he grunted.

'Excuse me sir, but could you move aside a little. You are blocking the desk.' Jackie's voice was straining to be civil.

The woman behind the man cleared her throat but without success. The man stood still, like a gate, dividing the space with his existence.

Jackie put the grinder into the box and came out from behind the desk to hand the package to her customer. She squeezed by the man and the woman customer rolled her eyes. 'Such a brute,' she said under her breath and nodded toward him. All Jackie could do was smile apologetically. It was going to be a long, long day.

Chapter 21

Hot Thomas, Again

In Thomas's studio, the early-bird man was watching as Thomas was blowing glass. The man sat firmly on the very same plastic chair. A group of people were standing around Thomas's roped off work area. They were observing him closely.

'Is that hot?' A man asked and leaned forward to get a better view.

'Yes. It is 2000 Fahrenheit,' Thomas answered.

'Blimey. That is really hot.' The man was amazed. 'You could grill a chicken in there.' He then added and chuckled at himself.

'Yep, I could,' said Thomas and continued working.

'Is it hard to blow? I mean do you need special lungs for that?' A middle-age woman enquired with a high pitched, sharp voice.

'No. No. It is not hard to blow. Normal lungs will do.'

'Well, how much do you have to blow into that pipe?'

'Just enough, depending on how hot the glass is,' Thomas answered.

'How long does it take to learn all this?' Another man hollered from the back row.

'Well, I went to an art school first and I have been blowing glass for about five years now.'

Another woman walked into the studio from the gallery. She looked at Thomas working and then asked. 'Is that hot?'

'Yes…2000 Fahrenheit…' Thomas sat down on his workbench.

'Oh…that's hot.' The woman said and nudged her friend slightly with her elbow. 'You could make a roast in there.'

Sheridan was throwing a small pot on his potter's wheel. He was, simultaneously, lecturing about the importance of the right technique. 'You need to be extremely delicate and firm at the same time. See what I'm going do here? Observe!' Order, discipline and routine, his favourite words sprang into action. Life was a pleasure. Sheridan hummed as he worked his hands over the pliable clay.

There were mostly elderly women around him and they all came closer to have a good look at the work in progress.

Sheridan stopped the wheel and admired his own work. 'Perfect,' he said to himself as he took a long piece of metal string and pulled it through the bottom of the clay pot between the metal plate and the clay. The pot came off easily and he placed it on the table beside him.

The ladies were impressed. 'Would you look at that!' one of them exclaimed.

Sheridan enjoyed this admiration. Nothing better than praise. He used the same metal string to cut the very same piece in half to show the cross section of the cup. The ladies were aghast.

'You shouldn't have done that!'

'It was such a beautiful pot.'

'Now why did you do that?' There were lots of sighs in the studio.

'Watch and learn. See how even this is.' Sheridan instructed and pointed with his dirty finger to the even wall of the cup.

One of older ladies put her glasses on and leaned in to see better.

'That will help in the drying process. The piece will not crack, but of course, as we all know, the drying process has to be slow and monitored ever so carefully. You can never be in a hurry with clay. Patience is a virtue in a potter's studio.' He spoke his last words slowly and glazed with pride. Sheridan was enjoying his captive audience immensely.

Finally he was being appreciated for the whole value of his talent. He smiled at the ladies as they drank in every word he said.

A woman walked into Thomas's studio, flapping her jacket front, trying to cool herself down. She blew air through her lips. 'God, it's hot in here!' She exclaimed and waved her hands in front of her face in an ill attempt to feel cooler air around her burning, flushed face.

Thomas continued working and did not say anything. He waited for the woman's next words and after a few seconds they came as expected.

'How hot is that?'

Janet's old hay barn was rather quiet. People looked at the work under Janet's watchful eyes. There was a low murmur and the sound of scuffing feet on the old stone floor. Kenneth's photographs were on the walls and Janet's pullovers were neatly hanging from hangers near the entrance. The big rustic baskets on the floor were filled with skeins of wool that Janet had dyed herself. She and Kenneth had carried her grandmother's large dresser into the barn. She had opened a few of the drawers and placed some of her pullovers inside. She had also bought bouquets of dried flowers from Nancy and had put them into old tin buckets. They also brought a large tarnished mirror down from the house and placed it beside the dresser. Janet had found an old kitchen table under a tarp in the far corner of the barn, much to her surprise, and they had put Kenneth's Christmas card display on top of it. A few people were asking Janet if the table was for sale.

Janet's sheep were wandering free on the neighbouring field and children were standing by the fence pretending to talk to the sheep by baaing loudly.

Kenneth stood still and tried his best to avoid talking with people. He was looking out the small window. Unfortunately, Janet was not a person to chitchat either.

'Are those your sheep out there?' A woman asked Janet.

'Yes.'

'And you knitted all of these yourself?' The woman pointed to the pullovers and cardigans and smiled, inviting Janet into the conversation. 'Can I try this one on?'

'Yes.' Short and simple answers had always been Janet's favourites. No chance for mistakes and plenty of time for work.

The woman put on the cardigan and looked at herself in the tarnished mirror. 'It is wonderful.' The woman exclaimed.

'Uh-huh.' Was all that Janet said.

'I'll take it.' Her voice carried the sound of happiness that comes from making a quick and sure decision.

'All right then.' Janet folded the cardigan and put it in a paper bag. She had never been one to get openly excited.

Harriet was carrying Winston in her rotund arms and pointing to her vast collection of porcelain paintings. Most of her customers were from the dog show Harriet and Winston had taken part in a few weeks earlier.

'If I were to bring you a photo of Eddie. He's my poodle. Would you paint his portrait?' A woman with very curly hair asked.

'Of course.' Harriet bellowed. 'I love to paint portraits.'

'Marvellous.'

Russell was standing in the middle of his studio. His hair was sticking up every which way and he was talking loudly about his dogs. 'Yes, I have eight dogs...otherwise it would be too quiet in the house. We go to the fields for a walk every day...there...see...by the river.' He pointed to the landscape through the windowpane. 'You see. There is a nice picnic spot right there. The grass is soft...to sit down and...heh heh...you know.'

He had a crowd of dog enthusiasts around him. They all agreed about walking the dogs every day, but they did not quite understand the importance of the soft grass.

Jane was wrapping a painting on a worktable in the middle of the studio. She was talking quietly to a customer and she gave her one of Russell's business cards. 'Yes, he will do commissions...' Jane glanced quickly at Russell, who was in the midst of a deep discussion about dog breeding. Jane turned to her customer and repeated, 'Yes, he will do commissions.'

She was already planning her vacation somewhere warm in the sun. Surely Russell would not object to that. The cold winter bothered her weak back and a change of scenery would be nice.

'Yes, he will be delighted to do commissions,' she said, emphasizing the word delighted.

Nancy was taking a wreath down from her wall. She felt the small drops of sweat run down the middle of her back. She pushed her glasses up on her nose and placed the wreath into a box. She found it hard to breathe normally.

Caroline was talking about art with the young woman and the man who had earlier been admiring Caroline's work at the town hall. They were looking at paintings featuring Thomas in various poses.

The young woman could not compliment the work enough. 'I mean...I just love how you grab the moment in your paintings. I mean...it is so raw and...urgent...hungry and...and...sexual... and...' And she was lost for words again.

Caroline smiled slightly and turned to look at the man who had been quietly observing her paintings. 'Thanks...I will have an exhibition next month at the Williamson's gallery.' Caroline nonchalantly turned and grabbed an invitation from her desk and handed it to the young man. 'If you like, I could give you an invitation for the opening?' She held the young man's nervous gaze and smiled.

The man held the card in his hand and shyly mumbled his thanks. The young woman squealed with excitement. 'Cool, I will bring my mom. She loves openings.'

Caroline looked at the young woman and lit a cigarette. 'There is no sale here,' she thought. 'But the young woman's mother might come to the opening and walk away with a large painting.' She blew smoke into the air. 'Meanwhile I'm stuck with this horny, barely twenty-something, dimwit girl.' She took another drag of her cigarette. 'But the young man is not bad.' She thought as she watched him walk slowly around her gallery. She blew a few smoke rings up in the air. 'Not bad at all.'

Daisy was putting a breadbox into a plastic bag. Her gallery was full of women admiring her delicately painted flowers. One woman was holding a large wooden tray in her hands. She was in the middle of a tantalizing decision. 'It is just so pretty. It would go well with my coffee table.' She sighed and turned to talk to her friend who was looking at the painted mailboxes beside her. 'What do you think?'

Her friend looked up. 'Yes. It would look so good in your living room.' She took a closer look at the tray. 'You know, I think that the colour of those roses is exactly the colour of your sofa.'

'You think so?' The woman tried to picture the exact colour of her sofa. Yes, her sofa was pink, but it might be a bit darker pink than the colour of the roses. She sighed skeptically and studied the tray once more. 'But what if it is a different shade of pink?' She nudged her friend's elbow.

'Well, maybe you could bring a photo of your sofa and she could paint another tray and make the roses match the colour of your sofa?'

The woman held the tray at arm's length. 'Yes, I could do that.' She said thinking deeply. 'Though John said that he is tired of the pink and he would like to have a green sofa.'

'He did?' Her friend turned around, completely shocked at the possibility of a husband wanting to change the colour of the sofa, because the change of the sofa would automatically change everything else—a domestic snowball effect. It just wasn't done like that.

'Yes.' The woman answered cheerlessly. 'So, in that case I need to colour co-ordinate the leaves in this tray to the sofa.' She shook her head sadly. 'Maybe it's better if I don't buy this.' She put the tray down reluctantly. 'You know, if John is going to change the sofa and all.' She sighed. 'It's pretty though.'

'Maybe you could use it in the kitchen?' Her friend suggested.

'Yes, maybe I could.' The woman lit up. 'That's a splendid idea.' She picked up the tray again and looked at it closely once more. 'But, what about the cushions on my chairs?'

'What about them?'

'Well do you think this pink here is too dark for my kitchen?'

'I can't really remember the exact colour of the cushions in your kitchen,' her friend said slowly, trying to imagine the chairs.

The woman put the tray down firmly this time. 'No, I better not buy. I'll come back later.'

'You could bring the fabric of your chairs with you.' Her friend suggested.

'I could, couldn't I?'

'Or the photo of your sofa, unless John gets a green sofa, and in that case you just match the green with the leaves.'

'Yes. That's what I'll do.' She sighed in relief. A decision had been made.

'And in any case, I can always come back tomorrow if I change my mind.'

'That's true.' Her friend said. 'We can always come back just before closing time on Sunday. Maybe you'll even get a discount.'

'Oh, Jenny. You are such a devious woman.'

They both laughed quietly and began examining the mail boxes.

'Oh, look at this. What do think? It matches the shutters of my house, doesn't it?'

Back at Thomas's studio a woman was leaning as close as she could to Thomas's workbench. She wanted to see everything. 'Is that hot?' She asked, breathing in the hot, dusty air.

Thomas lifted his eyes. 'Yes. 2000 Fahrenheit.'

'Oh! That's hot.'

'Yep.'

Jackie was putting one of her peppermills into a box. She was chatting with a customer, when a man pushed past the woman and poked his head into the studio, annoyed that a rope separated the studio from the gallery.

'You do this all yourself then, eh?' He asked abruptly.

'Yes…I make it all from the beginning to the end.' Jackie felt obliged to answer, though she was in the midst of a conversation with her customer.

The man studied her studio for a while longer and then he went to inspect her work in the display area. He turned a peppermill upside down and inspected the bottom, thoroughly poking at the grinder part with his finger.

Jackie gave the box to her customer. 'Thank you. Enjoy your tour.'

'I will. Thank you.' The woman customer gave a disapproving look toward the man with the peppermill in his hands.

'Where do you get the mechanism?' The man enquired from the other side of the room and blew his nose loudly into a large chequered handkerchief, which he then tucked into his pocket.

Jackie stared at the white wall for a while and counted to ten. Then she turned around to face the man and smiled. 'From my supplier.' Luckily she was saved by a lovely couple who wanted to talk about ordering a coffee table.

Rosalind was having a discussion with an important looking man and his wife. She was holding Alistair's biography in her hands and she was proudly pointing out all the art exhibitions Alistair had had. Her finger followed the lines as she recounted out loud the long list.

Alistair was standing beside one his sculptures in the far corner of the studio. He had his hands in his pockets and he was staring at the dancing dust flakes in the bright sunshine when a young man approached him from across the room. Alistair glanced around, but there was nowhere for him to go and hide. If he were to go out the door, he would have to walk in front of Rosalind and the young man was almost there in front of him already. Alistair found himself thinking about cigarettes and that peaceful moment they offered him.

'That is a quite a statement you have made there.' The young man said conversationally, nodding toward a large sculpture in the middle of the room.

Alistair was puzzled. 'Why do you think that?' His eyes glared at the young man from under his eyebrows.

The young man took a deep breath before beginning his lengthy explanation. 'Well, the dimensions are taken to the extreme without diminishing the power of the inner circle, right here.' He pointed to the middle of the sculpture. He let his hand draw a circle in the air. 'To me it speaks of an enormous inner strength and in some strange way of'—he paused for a moment to choose the right words to describe his thoughts—'of primal fear.' He then added slowly, moving his head up and down as if seconding his own opinion. 'Yes…definitely, raw, untouched primal fear.'

'Ahh…' Alistair sighed and nodded his head approvingly. There was almost a smile in the corner of his mouth.

The young man studied the sculpture more closely. He stepped back, tilted his head to the right and then stepped forward again and tilted his head to the left. He closed his one eye and then opened it again. Finally he stood again by Alistair. His arms were folded in front of him; his eyes were narrowed into two slits as he admired the sculpture and gave his final appreciative nod.

'What is the title of this sculpture?' He enquired enthusiastically.

Alistair stared right in front of him and answered slowly: 'Rosalind.'

Jackie was wearing her safety goggles and was about to begin to turn a piece of wood on the lathe. She turned on the power and the gentle humming of the large machine filled the air. Jackie took a long chisel in her hands, stared at the piece of wood fastened well into the machine and began. The wood chips were flying crazily around her and a sharper, louder sound filled the room. Jackie felt the familiar tremulous feeling in her arms as the sharp edge of her chisel cut into the wood grain.

The older man, who had been very interested in the wood turning demonstration, was leaning closer and closer to have a better look at what Jackie was doing.

It was too noisy in the studio to have a conversation or answer any questions, which made Jackie exceedingly happy. The man's mouth was moving rapidly, firing questions but no words were heard through the sharp sound of the lathe. This was a moment when Jackie truly loved turning wood.

Jack Wilkinson drove leisurely to the pub's parking area with his lawnmower. Suddenly he stopped as if he had hit a wall at full speed. He was staring at a bright red car parked in his very own everyday, known to one and all, Jack Wilkinson's parking spot.

He stared at the bright red Volvo in disbelief till his eyes began to hurt. 'How could somebody park in my spot?' He asked—surely, even outsiders visiting the village would know of his birthright. He was getting mad. He needed his parking spot. Otherwise the delicate balance of his life would be disturbed. He left his lawnmower where it was, half on the road and half on the sidewalk, and stormed into the pub. The door slammed loudly shut behind him.

Everybody turned to look in his direction.

Jack Wilkinson stood in front of the closed door and shouted loudly. 'Who the hell has parked their fucking red Volvo on *my* parking spot?'

The pub was quiet.

The locals looked at each other and lifted their shoulders gesturing that they did not know. Why would they park in his parking spot, they seemed to ask. Nobody would do such a crazy thing.

The tourists were staring at this strange, short, raving mad man and they had no idea what he was talking about.

A very well-off looking man stood up, adjusted his jacket front and said, 'I believe I have a red Volvo parked outside.'

'Well, get the damn thing the hell out of my spot, then.' Jack Wilkinson was waving his hands in the air. Despite his strong words, he did not look scary. Instead he looked like a mad bird trying to learn to fly.

Nick came out from behind his bar in an attempt to solve the problem. He hushed Jack Wilkinson so that he could talk civilly with the Volvo owner.

Jack let his hands fall down and stared madly at Nick.

'Is it possible, sir, that you could move your car, just enough to make room for this gentleman's vehicle?' Nick said, and then he stopped briefly to give Jack a warning look that told him to keep on being quiet. 'Because…well you see, at eleven o'clock at night, when this man leaves my pub, he will not be able to find his vehicle unless it is parked right outside the front door.' Nick gave Jack another long threatening look and then continued his explanation. 'It is a tradition that has lasted many years…unfortunately.'

Nick looked at the man apologetically.

The man nodded and tried to understand these complicated, unexplainable island traditions, unknown to any person outside the village. 'Well…hmm…all right then. I'll go and…hmm…move my car.'

'Thank you, sir. I'll pour you another pint…on the house, of course.'

The man walked out of the pub and at the same moment Nick turned toward Jack, who had been triumphantly following the conversation between Nick and the man.

'And you behave…or there will be no more beer for you. You hear me?' Nick talked with a low, surprisingly menacing voice.

Jack looked shocked when he thought about this horrible, incomprehensible possibility.

Jack followed the man outside and Nick returned to his spot behind the bar.

Outside the man had parked his Volvo beside a flowerbed, five metres to the right of his previous parking spot. He was just getting out of his car when Jack Wilkinson pulled in with his rattling, black smoke spewing, patched up lawnmower.

There was dead air. The Volvo owner stared at the sight in front of him and couldn't believe his eyes. His car keys were dangling from his fingers and his mouth was hanging wide open. He stared, trying to organize the thoughts running wild in his head. Finally he locked his car and followed Jack back into the pub and sat heavily down at the bar.

Nick poured him a new pint. 'Here you go sir, and thank you for being so understanding.'

The man accepted his pint and was about to say something, but somehow he couldn't properly frame the question in his mind. He opened and closed his mouth, and finally, with a lengthy sigh, he began drinking his free beer. He shook his head as he put his pint down and looked up at Nick expecting some kind of explanation.

Nick smiled comfortingly back at him. 'This is an island. We don't get out that much.' Nick clarified.

'Ahh…?' It was an answer that made no sense to him whatsoever.

The man stole a glance at Jack Wilkinson, who was sitting at his normal table and talking animatedly to the rest of the boys. Jack lifted his beer up in the air and shouted loudly, 'Thank you, sir.' And then he smiled widely showing his less than perfect teeth.

Thomas was sweating in front of the sweltering glass furnace. He had a large audience in the studio and new people were coming in to have a look at the work in progress. Thomas was happy about the rope that separated him from the audience.

'Is that hot?' A man leaned in and asked, staring suspiciously into the flaming hot furnace.

Thomas looked up agitatedly, bit his lip and then answered. '2000 Fahrenheit.'

'Gee whiz. That is hot!' The man shook his head in disbelief and pulled his pants up by the belt.

'Do you need good lungs to do all that blowing?' A young woman asked and stared at Thomas's chest where the shirtfront had a couple of wet spots.

'No, no. Regular, normal lungs will do.' Thomas still managed to sound cheerful.

Another woman walked into the studio and stopped beside an old couple standing by the safety rope that separated the work area from the viewing area.

'I would like to buy a perfume bottle,' the woman said questioningly, not sure if this was the perfect time to ask such a question, since Thomas looked quite busy.

'I'm almost done here. I'll be with you in couple of seconds.' Thomas flashed his most disarming smile.

The woman was flattered and smiled back at him. 'Oh, I'm not in a hurry...' She dragged out her last words as she looked at him more closely, especially his muscular arms and sweaty chest and then added, clicking her tongue appreciatively, '...at all.'

The church hall was as full as it had ever been. People were admiring the colourful quilt displays and the Bitch and Stitch Club members were selling cakes, cookies and raffle tickets. The first prize was a handmade quilt. Officially the ladies were called the Sycamore Presbyterian Church Quilting Club, though hardly anyone in the village knew their official name.

The visitors, mainly women, were discussing things quietly and pointing to various parts of the quilts. Quilt shows were, by their nature, also an educational event.

The pastor was amazed, when he walked in, by the sheer volume of people filling the church hall. He had never seen it this full, not even during the last year's convention. He held his hands in front of him first, and then he clasped them behind his back. He had no knowledge of quilts, cakes or cookies and he seemed slightly lost amongst the visitors. He clapped his hands together sharply when he saw Muriel and exclaimed with his deep voice: 'And how is everything, Muriel?'

Muriel looked up. She had been straightening 'don't touch' signs in front of the displays of quilts. 'It has been so busy all morning. Why don't you take over from me for a while? I would like to have a cup of tea and put my old feet up for a few minutes.'

She handed the pastor a stack of studio tour brochures before he could say anything and disappeared into the communal kitchen holding her back as she walked. She hated not being able to do things that ten years ago she would have done without even thinking. Old age had its benefits, but it had its numerous downsides as well, and more often Muriel found herself thinking about the downsides. 'What the hell do I do with inner peace when my back is falling apart,' she mumbled. 'I'll just drink a cup of tea and then I'll be fine.' She sighed as she walked to the kitchen leaving the pastor holding the brochures in his hands.

Chapter 22

Hot Sales

The pastor held onto the brochure stack and looked around him. He didn't know where he should stand or where he should keep his hands. It was easy for him in the pulpit. He could always lean against the railing or hold his hands calmly on the ledge by the bible. The bible comforted him. It gave him guidance. It had all of the answers he needed.

In real life he seemed lost, and he felt definitely lost amongst these quilts and amongst these merry ladies.

He slapped the brochures against his one hand and stared at the clock on the wall. He was wondering how long an average tea break was when an older couple asked him a question about the studio tour.

'Well,' the pastor said slowly trying to get the image of the village map into his head. 'Was it now the third street on the left or was it the second?' He really couldn't tell. It was just down the road, but this couple didn't seem to be satisfied with this answer. They wanted details and complained that everybody they had talked to earlier had said the exact same thing: 'It's just down the road.'

The pastor finally walked together with the couple out the door. He gave them the directions with his hands. He was pointing this way and that and he kept referring to the brochure by shaking it vigorously in his hand in midair. There was a strong resemblance to his Sunday sermons, but instead of hell and fire there was the studio tour. The older couple left after thanking the pastor for his help and walked down the road. The pastor drew a deep breath as he leaned against the railing and observed his busy village.

Doors of shops were opening and closing with a steady rhythm, the town hall's door being the busiest. People were standing on its front steps studying the studio tour brochure as they were deciding where to begin their tour. The pub was full, outside Jack's lawnmower was parked in its usual spot and the red Volvo by the flowerbeds. The garden tables of the tearoom were filled with people eating pastries and drinking tea. Honey was running as fast as she could between the kitchen and the outside tables. She had lured her niece, who was much faster on her feet, to help.

It was such a different sight from the normal quiet autumn Saturday that the pastor was beginning to get hopeful that maybe his church would break its attendance record on Sunday morning.

At Jackie's studio, her demonstration had just ended. She turned off her lathe and gradually the studio become quiet again as the motor slowed down and finally stopped altogether. She took off her goggles and walked into the gallery slapping her jeans clean from the woodchips and dust, hoping that the imprint on her face from the goggles wouldn't be too big. She brushed her bare arms with her hands and was ready again for questions.

'How long does it take you to finish one peppermill?' A woman dressed in green and cream asked.

'It's hard to say, because I'm working with quite a few at the same time.'

'But we saw you working only with one during your demonstration?'

'Oh, well...yes...I can only turn one peppermill at one time... but...' Jackie didn't quite know how to explain quickly the different stages of wood turning when her thoughts were interrupted with another question.

'Is it hard to learn?'

'Well, yes I guess...I went to an art and design school and then...'

The woman in green and cream turned to her friend and whispered loudly. 'She did work on only one peppermill, right? So why did she say she works on more than one. I don't get it.'

Her friend's answer disappeared under a thunderous voice of a man. 'How much did you pay for your lathe?' He grunted and cleared his throat.

Jackie turned her head to see who was asking. 'I really can't remember the exact amount...'

'Do you get a discount on your machinery?'

Jackie didn't have time to answer such a personal question when a new question was thrown at her.

'How do you get the different colours and patterns?'

Jackie was getting ready for a lengthy answer when the woman dressed in green and cream spoke over all of the other voices. 'So how many peppermills can you make in one day?'

Jackie felt her cheeks starting to hurt from all the smiling she had done during the day. 'I work with many different pieces at the same time. There are different parts to each and every peppermill. I make them all first and I assemble them later on. It saves money and time.' As soon as she said the words money and time, she regretted it.

'So it's like a production line, then?'

Jackie began to resent the green and cream coloured woman with a passion that can only be acquired after a long day of hard work amidst dozens of people.

'I thought she was selling one of a kind art work here.' The green and cream woman whispered loudly to her friend beside her as they left the gallery. 'Looks like mass production to me.'

Jackie turned to look at the rest of her captive audience and smiled painfully but with an apologetic edge added to it. She wondered if the twitching she felt in her cheeks was visible to the others.

'Excuse me, but how can you...?'

'Maybe I should do another demonstration,' Jackie thought. 'With the lathe running, it was so quiet and peaceful.'

In the full pub Nick was filling up pints and Rose was running in and out of the kitchen. The cook was getting slightly hysterical. She had never served so many people in one day. People were chatting loudly and there were no empty chairs to be found. Jack Wilkinson was in paradise because he had discovered a brand new audience.

'Well…' Jack would let his words hang in the air before diving into the wildly exaggerated story that might or might not have anything to do with reality.

The new celebrity of Sycamore was born.

Rose glanced at him once in a while and snorted loudly when she caught a word of what Jack was talking about. 'UFO…my ass,' she mumbled to Nick and tossed the used paper napkins into the garbage bin.

Nick looked up at her questioningly.

'Have you ever seen a bloody UFO here in the village or, actually, anywhere?' She asked Nick sarcastically, glaring in Jack Wilkinson's direction.

Nick took a quick look at Jack who at the moment was spreading his arms as wide as they could go and making strange screeching sounds.

'Jack Wilkinson is undoubtedly an unidentified object when he drives his lawn tractor home at night.'

Rose snorted. 'What about the flying part?'

'Maybe he's just UO.'

They burst into rowdy laughter. It was the lack of rest and sleep combined with a huge amount of work that made them hysterical.

The people in the pub turned to look at them. Rose nudged Nick when she saw the dozen perplexed faces staring at them. Nick tried to keep his face calm, but Rose's uncontrollable chuckles made him fall about again.

'Sorry,' was all he managed to say.

Rose squeezed her hand tight across her lips. She grunted deeply a few times to try to stop herself from laughing but in vain. There was no stopping. All they had to do was to look at each other or catch a glimpse of Jack Wilkinson and they would convulse with laughter again.

Jack didn't let this interruption disturb his moment of glory and, after a few meaningful looks from under his bushy eyebrows, he continued his story. 'What I was saying…oh, yes…particularly in October they are visible on the eastern sky. My colleagues and I have witnessed these sightings often after midnight.' He pointed his hand to Glenn, Howard and Calvin, who all agreed heartily, giving thumbs up with surprisingly solemn faces.

Thomas was standing behind his desk in the gallery. He was having a well deserved break from glassblowing and he was drinking water. He thought thirstily about drinking a beer, but then he remembered last night's whiskey episode and took another thirsty sip from his water bottle instead.

Most of the men were still in the studio discussing amongst themselves the equipment that was required to blow glass and all the new exciting technological details they had learned during Thomas's many demonstrations.

The women were in the gallery, happy for finally finding something that occupied their husbands and boyfriends while they shopped.

Thomas could hear them admire the colours, designs and forms. He was amused by it all and he was quite pleased with his day so far. He truly did not mind being the centre of attention.

A young woman pointed to a large vase on the shelf and then looked at Thomas shyly and smiled. 'Would you…perhaps…? I'm too scared to pick it up.'

Thomas walked to the woman and lifted the vase down for her to see. The woman stared for a while at Thomas and not at the vase, but then she caught herself doing so and focused her eyes again on the brightly coloured vase.

'It's absolutely stunning. How much is it?'

'Can't really remember.' Thomas laughed. 'Normally I put a price tag on the bottom.' He looked under the vase: '250?'

'I'll take it.' She didn't even hesitate with the price, which in Thomas's mind proved that this Saturday was, after all, charmed.

'Excellent! You have exceptionally good taste.' He smiled and didn't even care that the smiling was beginning to be incredibly painful. His cheeks felt like somebody was pushing sharp pins in them.

'Oh…?' The woman giggled softly.

They walked together to the desk and Thomas carefully wrapped the vase in bubble wrap. She handed him her credit card and Thomas processed it while talking with her, telling her how to take care for her new vase, when another woman approached the desk. She was holding a small delicate bowl from his rainforest series.

Thomas smiled at her. This day was getting better and better. Normally, making a sale felt like trying to get blood out of a stone.

'I'll be with you in a few seconds…'

'That's all right.'

Thomas turned to look the first woman straight in her eyes. 'There, I wrapped it really well for you. Now be very careful. It is quite heavy.' He handed the parcel to her and made sure that she placed one hand on the bottom of the parcel.

'Thank you. I think your work is truly amazing.'

'Thank you. I'm glad to hear that.'

'Bye.' She didn't really want to leave.

'Bye.'

Thomas smiled blissfully. As the young woman left, the other woman moved closer and handed Thomas the small bowl to be wrapped. Thomas was very busy and he liked it. He flashed a big and genuinely happy smile to the other woman. 'You have exceptionally good taste.'

'I know,' said the woman in a matter of fact manner.

Jackie was having a small break, sitting down behind her desk drinking water, when an older woman walked painfully slowly into her gallery. Jackie got quickly up and offered her chair to the woman.

'Oh, that is very kind of you. Are you sure?'

'Yes. Absolutely. Please sit down.'

'I guess my son was right. I have walked a bit too far today.' The older woman sighed and stretched her legs. 'You must know my son?' She asked Jackie with a tired voice. 'Kevin from the bed and breakfast.'

'Oh, yes. Kevin and Tom.' Jackie smiled cheerfully. 'I know them very well.'

'They talked a lot about you last night and said that I should come and visit you. They said you make beautiful things.' She looked around. 'And so you do.'

Jackie offered Kevin's mother a glass of water. Surprisingly, it was a quiet moment. It was almost lunch time and perhaps the people were all going into the pub for a quick bite.

'Thank you, dear,' Kevin's mother said. She had a small sip of water and then picked up the studio tour brochure from the gallery table before Jackie could do anything to stop her.

Kevin's mother glanced at the brochure and let out a small bright laugh. 'Poor Kevin and Tom. Bless their hearts. They forgot to cover up this ad.'

Jackie didn't know what to say. She stood there wringing her hands. She felt sick to her stomach.

'You do know that my son is gay?' Kevin's mother asked Jackie.

'Well…' Jackie was against the wall. 'Yes?' She answered stiffly diverting her eyes.

'Oh, dear. My poor lovely son thinks that I am so old fashioned that I don't know the difference between jolly and gay. Bless his heart.'

Jackie poured more water into her own already empty glass.

'I have known ever since he was small that he was gay. It can be very hard to be openly gay. People don't always treat you with respect. That's why I'm so happy he found Tom.' She sighed and took another small drink of water. 'Tom could not have been a nicer boy. He is the best son-in-law a mother could ever have and I love him like my own son. And come to think about it, they have been together for twenty years. That is a good achievement in any marriage nowadays.'

Kevin's mother put her glass on the table. 'Love is a strange thing. It rarely walks in front of you and announces itself clearly, but if it does, take it, because otherwise you will think about it for the rest of your life and wonder—what if. Life is full of what ifs as it is. No reason to add love-ifs to complicate things. Tom is perfect for Kevin and without him he would not be half as happy.' The old woman shook her head and sighed. 'Like my Marvin. He was a good man and a good father. Oh, how I loved him.'

She sat there for awhile in silence, lost in her thoughts and then asked Jackie if she would be so kind and call Kevin to come and pick her up. 'I think I walked a bit too much today, and I would prefer to lean on my son's arm.' She tapped Jackie's hand gently.

Jackie smiled and picked up the phone.

Harriet had not run out of steam. She carried Winston in her arms while she was proudly showing the vast trophy collection to a new crowd of people gathered in her living room. She filled the room with her booming voice and big bosom. Winston got caught in the excitement, as well, and he barked a few times, which made Harriet scold him tenderly.

'Now this one here is from two years ago.' She pointed to a trophy. 'Winston was magnificent. Absolutely the most beautiful dog. No question about it.'

She walked to the other table. 'And here is the prestigious prize he won last year.' She admired the shining trophy for awhile and inhaled through her nose with pride rumbling in her large chest.

The people followed her through the rest of the house as she pointed out the awards and her porcelain paintings in the highly decorative rooms dedicated mostly to Winston's numerous victories.

Finally they were back in her art room and Harriet brought out her little notebook, tapped her fingers on top of the table and let the ordering begin.

Nancy was frantically packing another wreath, trying to stick a piece of tape on top of a box to close the lid, but her hands were shaking so much that the tape got stuck on top of her hand instead. When she tried to shake the tape off, she somehow managed to get it stuck to her other fingers. She felt her glasses slide down her perspiring nose once again. She took a small moment of rest, just long enough to catch her breath, before beginning another wrapping operation. Her heart was beating rapidly and her face was flushed.

Some of the customers were holding plastic bags that had a painted rolling pin or a flowery tray in it. They had obviously wandered in straight from Daisy's house next door.

Nancy thought about Daisy and wondered how her day had been. She was going to call her after she had closed her front door for the day. Judging by the numerous plastic bags she had seen during the day with Daisy's pieces inside, she could safely guess that she and Daisy might be able to go for a long Christmas shopping spree soon: presents for their grandchildren and maybe something nice for themselves, as well.

Her hands had finally stopped shaking and she took another box out from under the counter and began the whole process again, but this time she would be more careful with the darn tape.

Sheridan was contentedly lecturing a small group of chatty women about the true and amazing facts of pottery. He generously gave information about the history, the different techniques, the glazes and the chemistry of colours. He was standing by a kiln that had its lid slightly open, so that the women were able to have a quick look inside. The air in the small and cramped kiln room was dry and very warm.

Sheridan felt his chest expand with a strange feeling as he looked at his captive audience. He stuck his one hand into his vest pocket and with the other he twirled his moustache. He quickly checked that his Ernest Hemingway beard was still there and then ceremoniously cleared his throat. Instantly he saw that he had the attention of people, and he spoke with a slightly pompous pride echoing in his voice.

'Now then,' he let his words hang in the air, pausing dramatically. 'My kilns are here in this room and I have just opened one of them. I have created these pieces exclusively for the studio tour. They are absolutely one-of-a-kind creations. No, no...no touching!' Sheridan pulled his hand out of his pocket and waved his finger slowly in front of the women.

The women obediently pulled their hands back and looked at him expectantly.

Sheridan continued his well rehearsed monologue. 'The pieces are still hot, so, please no touching.'

The women were sighing in wonder at such magnificent work. They curiously peeked into the kiln.

'I would like to buy one of those special studio tour designs...is that possible?' One of the women shyly asked Sheridan.

'Oh, yes, certainly...but like I said earlier, we'll have to wait for the pieces to cool down to room temperature first. You wouldn't like to burn a hole into your pretty handbag, now would you?'

He chuckled at his own joke and the women began to giggle softly. Sheridan was pleased with his newfound ability to charm women. He continued his lecture with even more enthusiasm and, if possible, in an even louder voice. His Ernest Hemingway look was working very well for him and, judging by the amount of pottery sold, he would be travelling to Africa soon.

Daisy had her reading glasses on while she was painting flowers onto a wooden tray and the chain from her glasses hung down in front of her green apron. Her audience had formed a tight circle around her worktable and she could feel their breath touching her neck. She seemed to have conquered her early morning nervousness surprisingly well and when she added a few bright highlights to the pansy pattern, she even looked as if she was enjoying herself.

Janet and Kenneth had been very busy and they had, to their big surprise, sold quite a few photographs and pullovers. It appeared as though the two of them had remained still, never having stirred from their place by the window, while time itself had moved forward. Their pose was the same, their facial expression was the same, but the surroundings had been somewhat altered. Pullovers had been taken down and new ones had been put up. The photos on the wall were different from earlier. Kenneth and Janet were standing in their chosen place, staring at a spot as far away as possible from any eye contact that might provoke them to have a chat with somebody they did not know. Once in a while Janet nodded slightly toward a customer and Kenneth went and sold a photograph using as few words as possible. If they had engaged in a conversation of any sort, they probably would have used their annual quota of words by the end of the day. So each and every customer got a polite nod, an agreeable grunt and a respectful thank you and they all departed with mutual contentment.

Jackie looked quickly at her watch. It was almost five. 'Thank god! It was almost five!' She felt like singing. The long awaited five o'clock had almost arrived. She was standing behind her desk longing for a nice, soft chair with a foot stool.

Her legs had started to ache an hour earlier. It was a dull and constant ache that can only be achieved by standing on a concrete floor for the entire day without a rest. She wasn't sure if her mouth would ever be able to smile again without pain. She had invisible, agonizing dimples on her cheeks that made her entire face throb.

She looked at her watch again. Twenty minutes to go and then she could sit down, put her feet up and maybe never get up again.

Thomas looked at the clock on the wall as he was sitting down on the workbench. Five! It was almost five. The joy Thomas felt was overwhelming. Only twenty minutes to go and then he could have a cold beer or two.

The man who had arrived in the morning was still sitting comfortably in the plastic garden chair. The man had not uttered a word since his arrival. He had sat there on that very spot for the entire day. He had observed Thomas's every single move and he had watched him make sales. He had seen him flirting with the women and he had kept on staring at him, forcing him to return to the studio and continue the glassblowing demonstration.

'Would you look at that,' Thomas said to the man. 'It's almost closing time.'

The man looked at the clock on the wall and then checked his own watch. He grunted and then leaned back in his chair settling down for an extra twenty minutes of action.

'I'll be closing soon.' Thomas tried again hoping to see some kind of movement, but the man remained seated. There was not even the slightest change in him that would suggest that he was about to leave.

'Well, this is my last piece of the day. After this the show's over.' Thomas tried to make the man understand that the end had finally arrived. The man sat inertly in the discoloured plastic chair.

Thomas finished his work and put the glass piece away. He glanced at the man as he walked past him. 'That's it for the day.' He said, hoping that the man would realize that the show time was definitely over. 'I'm not going to blow any more glass. I'm closing...'

The man sat in the chair. Thomas shrugged his shoulders and went into the gallery.

He was dreaming about a cold beer when the plastic chair man walked by him, said thank you with a loud voice and went out the door.

Thomas stared after him; all he could think of was 'seven hours of show and no sale.' He needed that cold beer badly.

Rosalind was talking to her customers. She loved this more that she could have ever imagined. She had acquired a new kind of voice: proud, busy, organized and, more than anything, important.

'Oh, yes,' she said. How could they even ask that she wondered. 'He was a professor of fine arts at the university.' She listened to their next question and smacked her lips regretfully. 'No, not anymore. He is retired, but'—here she paused for a dramatic effect and then continued, accompanying her sentence with a well-practised long sigh—'geniuses have to keep on working, don't they?' She laughed her light, little, proud laugh. Her small speech had made the effect she was after. She heard the polite laugh from her captive audience and a few words, such as 'Yes, you're quite right.'

Rosalind looked around quickly. She could not see Alistair anywhere. She got slightly agitated by his lack of professionalism and her nose twitched faintly. It was the fifth time he had disappeared today and it was right when she needed him the most.

Alistair was standing behind the studio amongst the tall hollyhocks and sunflowers smoking a cigarette and keeping his ear out for Rosalind's footsteps. He stopped smoking for a second and listened carefully. Fortunately, nobody was coming around the corner. He relaxed again, took a long drag of his cigarette and stared at the bright blue sky. He loved smoking and knew that he would not love it quite so deeply if Rosalind were not so dead against it. It was a well guarded secret with a hint of guilt but not so much that he would feel exceedingly guilty while smoking.

Inside the gallery Rosalind sniffed the air. She had gotten a whiff of Alistair's lingering cigarette smoke. Luckily for Alistair, she was too busy with the customers to be able to leave the studio and investigate the source of the disgusting smell. 'Strange,' she muttered to herself and pointed to the long list of exhibitions on Alistair's biography. 'He had a wonderful sculpture exhibition last year. Yes. Very successful, if I may say so.' She nodded her head. Not a single hair was out of place.

In Harriet's studio, a small cuckoo clock on the wall began chiming five, and it took Harriet completely by surprise. 'Oh, my,' she said. 'Is it really five already?' She opened her little notebook and said, 'I better write down your name and address. You did bring the photo of, what was her name again?' She paused and looked at the man in front of her. 'Juliet, that's right and your other dog's name was…?' She paused again to listen to the quiet man. 'Romeo! I should have guessed that.' She closed her notebook and shook the man's hand strongly. 'I'll call you when the portraits are done.' She walked the man out of her living room while holding tightly onto her precious notebook.

Chapter 23

Closing Time

Linda and Stella escorted the last people out of the town hall and then closed the heavy double doors. 'We'll be open again tomorrow at ten o'clock,' they said. The clock on the wall showed quarter past five and it was high time to close the information centre.

Kenneth closed the barn doors. Inside Janet was putting things in order. She had straightened the pullovers on the hangers and she was sorting out her dyed wool skeins in baskets by colour. She never left anything for the next day if she could do it today.

Kenneth walked to her. 'Well that's that then for today.' He rubbed his hands together and then nervously slapped his thighs. Finally, he put his hands into his pockets when he didn't know what else he could say.

Janet straightened her back and looked at him. 'Yes…that's it.' Janet sighed. Her sigh was not like other peoples sighs when they do not know the answer, or they are worried about something. No, Janet's sigh was to tell her body that the work was done.

'I'm going to fix something easy for supper…would you like to join me?' She asked Kenneth, but kept her eyes on the field where her sheep were grazing.

There was a silence before Kenneth hesitantly answered. 'I would very much so, if it's not too much trouble.' His voice sounded raspy.

'No trouble at all.' She busied herself with the wool again.

They both looked quite happy, though it was hard to tell because they both had weathered stern faces which seldom expressed feelings of any kind.

Russell waved his hand goodbye to the last of the customers, closed the door and sat down on the soft chair beside the front door. He straightened his legs and pulled Jane onto his lap and gave her a big squeeze. 'That was quite a day, I must say.'

'Yes indeed. I'll go and put the teakettle on.' Jane got up and Russell gave her a little pat on her behind as she walked by kicking off her shoes. The cold stone floor felt good against her throbbing feet.

Sheridan walked the last of his customers out. He closed the garden gate behind them. 'Have nice evening ladies.' He said and bowed his head slightly, aiming for a dignified gesture.

'Goodbye…and thank you.' The ladies laughed.

'Goodbye.' He walked slowly back to his house and into the living room. First he put on the marching music and then poured himself a stiff whiskey. He sat down heavily on the sofa under the lion's head and, against all of his own rules, he put his feet up on the coffee table. His hands were folded over his stomach holding the glass of whiskey as he closed his eyes, enjoying the perfect moment of stillness.

Nancy hurried out of her gallery, through the hallway and out the front door to take down the wreath which she had put there just that very morning. She wiped her forehead with the top of her hand, straightened her glasses and scurried back in to put the wreath in a box for a customer who was waiting patiently. Nancy glanced at the clock on the wall at the same time. It was well past five o'clock.

Harriet put Winston down on to the floor and patted his head. 'So there we go, Winston. It is over for today and Mommy will make something for us to eat…but first Mommy needs to have big glass of something strongly alcoholic.'

Winston stared as his owner went into the kitchen and poured herself a drink. The ice cubes rattled in the glass. Harriet sat down, kicked her shoes off and stretched her legs. She took the little order book out from her cardigan's pocket and put it on the table beside her.

'No peeking,' she said to herself as she lovingly patted the cover. 'Only after tomorrow.' She took a long appreciative sip of her drink and rapped her fingers against the table top. 'Don't count your chickens yet.' She told herself. It was hard to resist having just one quick look, but she was, besides being curious, very superstitious and, in this case, being superstitious won. 'Tomorrow, tomorrow.' She sighed and put the book back into her pocket, stroking it absent-mindedly with her strong fingers.

Caroline was watching from her porch as the last car left her driveway. She slowly took a deep breath, turned around and walked into her house. As she closed the door, she kicked off her shoes and walked barefoot into the kitchen. She opened a cupboard and took out a bottle of gin and made herself a drink with tonic water from the fridge. She put the bottle of gin on the kitchen table, sat down, lifted her long shapely legs onto the table and lit a cigarette. She leaned back in her chair and inhaled the first drag, slowly blowing the smoke out. She looked past the doorway, which led into her studio. There were empty places on the walls. She had sold quite a few paintings. Money was always welcome, but she could never admit that out loud to anybody. Today had been very good to her, though, and she had a little more breathing space till her next exhibition. She hated painting when she felt the bank breathing down her neck. Necessity killed the inspiration. Oh, god, how she hated painting those little landscapes, but they sold so well and she needed things to eat and wear. She also needed cigarettes and drinks. It all came down to landscapes at some point.

She blew smoke up in the air and watched it climb toward the ceiling. She was too tired to think.

Rosalind locked the studio door behind her and walked briskly to the house. She stopped on the kitchen steps and pursed her lips tightly together so that the once delicate skin above her lips turned into deep vertical lines. 'Alistair!' She shouted sharply, causing a bird to leave its comfortable perch in a bush just outside the window.

Behind the studio Alistair jumped and threw away his cigarette, straightened his collar and, luckily, found a packet of mints in his pocket. He tossed one into his mouth, washed his hands in the rainwater barrel and walked slowly toward the house. He had much hoped to stay behind the studio a while longer.

Nancy turned round in her foyer as the front door closed behind the last customer of the day and peeked into her gallery shop. To her surprise, it was almost empty. She could only stare speechlessly at her barren walls. 'What an earth could she sell tomorrow?' She asked herself as the panic set in. 'Oh, my word! What will I do now?' She sat down on her chair and for the first time in forty years she thought about smoking a cigarette.

Daisy walked into her kitchen and found her husband standing nervously by the table.

'Are they all gone for the day?' He asked anxiously.

'Thank goodness, yes.' Daisy sighed. She sat down by the table and leaned back in her chair, closed her eyes and massaged her aching temples. Her husband quietly pushed a cup of tea across the table so that it was right in front of her. Daisy opened her eyes slightly. 'Thank you, Dennis.'

Dennis patted the back of her hand gently and Daisy reached for the sugar. Her back ached and she wanted to kick off her shoes and watch telly. Dennis would certainly beat her in the quiz-show tonight. She might even have a nap instead.

The Bitch and Stitch Club members were straightening the things in the church hall after closing up. A woman in a bright red cardigan massaged her back with a painful expression and gladly accepted Muriel's offer of tea. The women compared their different levels of exhaustion in a friendly competition that required no winners.

'I would do just about anything to be able to sit down quietly and rest my old feet.' The woman with a sore lower back sighed.

The teakettle was put on and the tired women sat down around the table in the small church kitchen and kicked off their shoes with immeasurable relief. They wiggled their stockinged toes and laughed.

The pastor strolled into the empty hall and saw a light and heard happy chatter coming from the kitchen. He knocked on the door quietly and then stepped in, surprising the women terribly.

Muriel quickly slipped her shoes back on. 'Ah…Pastor you gave us all a fright!' She held her hand over her pounding heart. 'Would you like to have some tea with us?'

'I would not say no.' He said and pulled out a parcel from behind his back.

'I brought some pastries for us to have with the tea. I think we all deserve something sweet, wouldn't you say?'

The women murmured their approval and Muriel got up to take a plate from the cupboard.

Thomas was turning the glory hole off and the studio once more became quiet. This was the part of the day he enjoyed the most. He walked slowly into the gallery and grabbed himself a beer from the fridge in the office—his other favourite part of the day.

He sat down on the table, stretched his arms above his head and then began leafing through his receipt book. The smile on his face widened as he stared at the numbers written in blue. He closed the receipt book and carefully gave it an affectionate tap.

Jackie was sweeping her studio with an old broom. She dropped the collected woodchips into a dustbin. The studio felt extremely still and quiet after the long and loud day of customers. Somehow it also felt colder. She had gotten a report from Jill about the wedding she had missed. Apparently her mother was still mad and could not understand why Jackie hadn't attended the reception. The groom was drunk and the bride teary eyed. The best man's speech had had a couple of racy bits in it. Not too much to make people choke on their drinks, but just enough to make some of the older women feel uncomfortable. All in all, a good party. Tracy had loved her peppermill and saltshaker set, which Jackie had made especially for her and she had completely understood why Jackie could not attend. It was only Jackie's mother who held a grudge and in a few weeks time, she should be fine as well. Now Jackie would just have to suffer through those weeks. It would be hard and painful and it would involve many irrational phone calls, but it was doable.

Jackie leaned on her broom cupping her hands on top of the broomstick and resting her chin on top of her knuckles. She was tired. She was beyond tired. Her feet were aching and she dreamt about putting them up on her couch. She could almost feel the soft fabric of the cushions touching her tired body and soothing it to sleep. She had done so much smiling and talking that even her face was aching.

Suddenly the gallery door opened and Nick walked carefully in as if not sure if he would be welcomed or not. Jackie was startled. She hadn't been expecting anybody.

'Oh…sorry…did I scare you?' Nick was suddenly apologetic— something else had gone wrong.

'No, no…' Jackie laughed and held her hand over her pounding heart. 'Well, yes actually you did.' She had to admit in the end.

'Sorry about that.' Nick was still standing by the studio door moving his weight from one foot to the other, looking at the pile of dust gathered by Jackie's feet.

Jackie put her broom up against the wall and wiped her hands on the back of her jeans. She was smiling and looking at Nick. Suddenly she noticed a paper bag in Nick's hands. 'What's that?' She asked.

'Well,' Nick hesitated for a very long second and stared at the bag in his hands, trying to form the correct words. 'I thought you might be a bit hungry and I know you probably are too tired to cook something for yourself to eat…so…' He didn't know where to look now; he stared at the heavy ceiling beams. 'So, I brought you some salad, soup and sandwiches from the pub.' He walked to her slowly and handed her the big brown paper bag.

'That was very kind of you. Thank you!' Jackie was surprised by this act of unexpected kindness. She looked at him and he looked at her. They were both holding onto the paper bag. The look went on and Jackie felt her fingers touching Nick's hand. The warmth of his hand moved up along her fingers, reaching every part of her body. They moved slightly closer to each other. The air was escaping from Jackie's lungs and she felt her heart beating heavily. Her feet were no longer tired, but nevertheless, they were about to give out under her. Every part of her body was alert, on the edge of falling. She felt like she was being offered a ticket for a rollercoaster ride in an amusement park, which she was too scared to accept but, at the same time, too curious not to accept. She waited, holding her breath.

Nick leaned closer to her and Jackie felt the warmth of his body encircling her. Through his shirt, she felt his pounding heart. She felt his hand bending carefully behind her back. She felt his breath brush against her cheek. She held her breath and closed her eyes; suddenly the door to the gallery flew open with a violent jolt.

'Jackie! What a day! What a bloody fantastic day!' Harriet's strong booming voice effortlessly filled the tiny space. It hit the walls and bounced back to greet its sender.

Jackie turned swiftly around to fix her horrified eyes on Harriet and at the same time she yanked the paper bag from Nick's hands into her own, thus making Nick lean slightly more forward than he had anticipated.

What came to pass was an unplanned accident that served to refuel the island's thirst for fables and myths within their own jurisdiction. Much cherished fanatic speculation filled the long and dark nights before Christmas brought some light into the world again.

As Nick leaned dangerously forward, Jackie unexpectedly turned her head back to look at him and as she did this, the hard side of her head smashed sharply right into Nick's nose. Nick let out a painful howl and clasped both of his hands around his bleeding nose. He bent down in pain, unable to curse as the sour taste of blood hit his tongue. Jackie stared horrified at Nick.

'Oh my god!' She sobbed. 'Oh, I'm so sorry. I didn't mean to. Oh, oh my god! You're hurt!' Even as she spoke she knew how useless her words were.

She tried to touch his face, but then thought twice about it and let her hands drop; she began looking for handkerchiefs. She might have been more rational if Harriet would not have been standing there in the middle of the gallery waiting for an answer to her loud greeting. Jackie frantically looked for a box of tissues that she had earlier seen somewhere in the studio. Harriet heard the commotion and slowly began to make her way into the studio.

Nick was holding his nose with one hand and the other he was shaking in the air as if to say 'stop fussing.' Jackie held one crumpled handkerchief in her hand. She was afraid to touch him.

'It's okay. I'm okay. Don't worry. Really.' Nick's voice was muffled. He took the offered handkerchief and put it tenderly against his pulsating nose.

'Winston and I went for a walk and…' Harriet was talking as she stepped into the studio. 'And I came to…' Her voice trailed off when she saw Nick doubled over in the dark studio corner, holding a blood soaked handkerchief to his nose. 'What—' Then she realized that there was something odd with the situation and she quickly rephrased her question.

'Nick! What are you doing here? Aren't you supposed to be working at the pub?' She gave him a sharp look. 'What—are you really hurt? Are you bleeding?' Her eyes grew big when she saw the blood drops on the floor. Shocking!

Nick straightened up and winced. The bleeding had slowed down, but his nose was still giving him painful stabs. 'No. I'm fine. I was just leaving. I brought Jackie some dinner.' He leaned backwards and tried to breathe slowly through his nose. The sudden sharp pain made him grimace.

Harriet walked to Nick to have a better look. She was just about to touch Nick's pounding nose when Nick yelled loudly at the sight of Harriet's large hand coming closer to his face. 'No, don't touch my face Harriet! I'm fine.'

'What happened here? Let me have a look, really. I know what I'm doing.' Harriet insisted slightly annoyed by his refusal to let her help him. 'You do know that I'm a qualified nurse.'

'No! Don't touch me!' Nick said with a sharper voice than he had intended, but the pain in his swollen nose was too much. He did not want Harriet or anybody else anywhere near his face. 'I better be going back to the pub anyway.' He walked tentatively to the door, still covering his nose with the blood soaked handkerchief.

Jackie leaned over and spoke with a loud, flat voice that didn't seem to belong to her. 'And thank you for the salad and sandwiches.' Then she added with small and miserable whisper, 'Sorry!'

She looked so sad that Nick stopped by the door and tried to smile despite the pain. 'No problem.' His face contorted with the effort. 'See you tomorrow night at the party. Bye Jackie. Bye Harriet.' He waved his hand and left, walking back to the pub as briskly as his throbbing head allowed him.

'Goodbye, Nick.' Harriet hollered and turned around to look at Jackie and then suddenly a surprising thought came to her. 'Now wait a minute…what was he doing here? Are you two?' She stopped and looked horrified, 'Oh, darn! I interrupted something, didn't I?' She put her hands to her face. 'Gosh, I can be thick sometimes, can't I?'

Jackie put her hand on Harriet's arm. 'No. No. It was nothing. He just brought some salad and sandwiches for me. Really.' Jackie's voice sounded feeble even to her own ears.

Harriet had a sly smile on her face when she spoke. 'Yeah right! And Prince William is madly in love with me.' She stopped and gave Jackie a deep look over her glasses. 'Really now, Jackie. I am not that daft. I do have eyes in my head, though my brain seems to work a bit slower than it used to.' She took a deep breath waiting for Jackie to tell everything in her own words.

Jackie remained quiet. Harriet snorted and a gleeful smile spread over her round and friendly face. 'I see. A new romance has just begun to blossom.' She chuckled merrily. 'I won't tell anyone. You can trust me.' She nodded her head seriously and then added, 'Anyhow, the tour was a hit. It was absolutely bloody fantastic!'

'Great,' Jackie said.

'I was so busy today that I can hardly talk anymore. My calendar is full of orders for canine portraits. So that's what I came to tell you. Winston and I will continue our evening walk now. Won't we, Wilson?' She turned around and left with Winston on her heels, but then put her head right back into the studio.

'Do you want me to call Nick and tell him that the coast is clear and he can come back to finish whatever he was doing here earlier?'

Jackie stared at her and shook her head sideways with an expressionless face.

Harriet smiled wickedly and left, laughing heartily at young romance. The door slammed loudly shut behind her. As she threw herself on a chair, Jackie could hear Harriet in the garden murmuring something to Winston about how sweet young love was.

Jackie could not believe her luck, or more accurately, her non-luck with Nick. She had truly wanted to kiss him. She had wanted to be held more than anything and instead of those things, she had given him a bloody nose. 'Well done,' she muttered to herself with a mocking voice. 'Leave it to me to be the romantic lead. Jesus bloody Christ. God damn shit. Shite. Bugger!' She got up spewing curse words and walked to the front door. She shut off the lights in the gallery more fiercely than she anticipated. 'Bugger,' she said once more, but it didn't make her feel any better.

She stepped outside locking the door behind her. The village was quiet now. The light grey darkness had fallen and the warm day had changed into a cool, damp evening. The garden had lost its sharp daylight outlines and was now wrapped in the blanket of soft misleading contours. The frogs were singing and she missed the early summer fire flies.

She walked into her house carefully carrying Nick's dinner parcel in her hands. She pushed the kitchen door open with a well-practised kick of her knee. Felix was there right by the door, his whole body shaking while his tail thumped loudly against the kitchen cupboards. Jackie scratched him behind his ears and promised to take him for a walk a bit later. She took out a bottle of white wine from the fridge and a glass from a shelf. She put them all on the kitchen table and sat down to open the paper bag to see what Nick had made for her. In the bag was a nice big salad in a plastic container, hot soup in a thermos and sandwiches wrapped in wax paper. A stack of napkins had been slipped in as well. A broad smile spread over Jackie's face. She felt giddy. She was very touched by his caring gesture. She kept on smiling as she took out the salad and the hot soup. She smelled the hot salmon bisque as she poured it out into a bowl. She carefully removed the paper that covered the sandwiches and put them beside her Greek salad. She opened the wine and poured herself a small glass. She again had that funny feeling in the pit of her stomach. She took a sip of wine, looked at the food that she had set on the table and then smiled like a teenager and felt like giggling. She was bursting with happiness. She fought the urge to call Jill and blurt 'Guess what! You'll never guess?' But she wanted to savour this moment, to keep the happiness all to herself, just to make this extraordinary moment last a while longer.

Nick walked slowly back to the pub. Despite his throbbing nose, he smiled as he thought of Jackie.

All of the stores in the village were now closed. It was that strange quiet hour before people go out again and have dinner or an evening walk. The houses were lit and the old village looked charming.

Nick opened the pub's door and the sounds of chatter and laughter poured out onto the silent street and filled the air. Suddenly Nick was no longer alone with his own thoughts. He had been brought back to the centre of things by the loud vivacity of the pub atmosphere.

The small pub was absolutely full. It could hardly contain the people within its old walls. It seemed that everybody who had been on the studio tour wanted to have something to eat and drink and most importantly, somebody to talk to. There was hardly any space for people to walk around.

Rose was busy filling the pints at the bar, and Stella was carrying plates of food. She had been hired to help in the kitchen.

Nick looked at the scene for a second and then apologetically pushed his way through the mass of people and got to work behind the bar. Rose glanced at his nose, which was slightly red and swollen. Her eyes grew big and she let out a small shriek. 'Did you try to kiss that Callaghan girl?'

Nick froze in his tracks and, for a second too long, he stared at Rose. 'What? Well…No! Now why would you say something like that?' Nick was horrified and didn't know what to do with his hands. How come this woman seemed to know everything about his life?

Rose smirked. 'Your nose is a bit red and swollen. That's all— and the island's legend tells us about your grandfather and Jackie's grandmother. And I should not forget to mention your father and Jackie's mother. That's all. And of course Jack Wilkinson has told everybody here how he got his so-called famous crooked nose.'

Nick's mouth fell open. 'For the love of god. Don't you people have anything better to do?' He blurted out.

'No.' Rose grinned knowingly and rushed to the kitchen to tell Stella the latest news, in detail.

Nick was left alone to mutter to himself. 'Bloody Jack Wilkinson and his bloody legends.'

The three men and one woman standing at the bar waiting for their drinks stared at him oddly.

Maximilian's restaurant was very hectic in a lovely, clean and orderly fashion. All the lights were lit. The chandeliers glistened, shedding their light into the garden. As the jazz band was setting up in the west wing of the hotel, notes from the piano drifted slowly into the darkening night—a perfect, glamorous picture from a glossy magazine from some idyllic past. It was a huge contrast to the loud spontaneous disarray of the pub.

Max Woodland himself was very busy at work in his kitchen. He had already used all of his favourite curse words and now he was into his famous combination curse words.

His sous-chef knew by now that during this particular evening Maximilian would easily exceed the triple curse word combination limit. As long as Max did not call him mother fucking useless eejit, he would be fine and he would continue working for him. He found it strangely enticing. All the cursing and direct personal insults in the proximity of the sharpest knifes on the island.

The restaurant was full. The tables were covered with pristine white starched linen. The silver cutlery shined and the scent of fresh cut flowers drifted into the night. Classical music, a low murmur of voices and the occasional clink of toasting glasses filled the room.

Nobody in the restaurant had any idea that the dinner they were going to enjoy was being prepared, according to Maximilian Woodland, by complete and utter mother fucking idiots who couldn't even boil water if their lives depended on it.

There were many other things people enjoying their dinner in the restaurant were not aware of. For example, that Max Woodland had a broken heart and that he was being eaten away by wretched envy. He would have loved to have his arse hanging on the town hall wall. He would not have even minded a full frontal. After all, he was Maximilian Woodland: the Paris educated chef extraordinaire.

So, in his romantic despair, he was coldly abusing his staff while waiting for Caroline to call. Max Woodland was ready to beg and he had never begged for anybody in his entire life, but in Caroline he had found his match. She was even more brutal than Max Woodland could ever be and that fascinated him.

Chapter 24

Tour, Day Two

Sunday arrived peacefully with the cool morning air moving the curtains ever so lightly as it flowed in through the slightly open windows. Then the alarm clock sounded and Jackie tried desperately to shut it off. She opened her sleep encrusted eyes slowly and cried. 'Oh, lord. No!' Her body needed more rest. Her legs were feeling as heavy as if somebody had tied lead weights to them.

She lay in her bed, staring up at the ceiling. Her feet were throbbing, their soles begging her to let them rest a while longer. Her eyes were raw from the lack of sleep and all she wanted to do was to close them.

'Just a few minutes more,' she said to herself and enjoyed the cosy morning warmth of her bed till the clock woke her up a second time and Oscar jumped on her bed, arriving home after his wildcat night out in the neighbourhood. There was no time like present.

Thomas was already in his kitchen making breakfast. He was happy, full of energy and singing Abba's money song as he poured coffee into his large thermos cup. His head was in one piece, his feet were springy and, more importantly, he was ready to make more money. He twirled around and drummed the spoon on top of the counter before licking the sugar remains from it. He felt good.

Sheridan was washing his morning dishes and listening to the top ten marches from his Kenneth Alford album. He hummed along loudly as he rinsed his teacup, plate and a spoon in the sink, setting them down in a straight line on top of a clean and crisp dishtowel.

Caroline was staring out the window. She had a large cup of coffee in her one hand and a cigarette in the other. She felt slightly lonely and since Thomas unfortunately was not talking to her, she thought about giving Maximilian a call. She missed the fresh croissants, the foie gras and good French wine. She should perhaps give him a call just after the tour was finished. By five o'clock she would be hungry for many things.

Rosalind was organizing the papers in Alistair's studio. The tour had given her a new found vigour. She had flushed cheeks as she looked at the receipts from yesterday. She wet her thumb as she flipped through the thin papers. Alistair had disappeared again. Rosalind looked around the studio, but he was nowhere. She was starting to get slightly annoyed with him again. He had left the studio many times yesterday and when he got back, he had had a strange minty smell about him that Rosalind found quite revolting.

'He might as well be wherever he is,' Rosalind thought. 'He hadn't helped much anyway.' She resumed leafing through the receipt book. Alistair's clay reliefs had sold extremely well. 'Thailand or Malaysia.' She deliberated happily and calculated the subtotal on a small piece of paper.

Russell was hugging Jane in the kitchen while she was making their morning tea. She tried to shake him off. 'Oh, Russell. Will you please let me make us some tea? We don't have time for this now.' Whereas, Nancy had already been up and working for a few hours making wreaths in a desperate attempt to fill the empty spaces on her gallery walls. She had curlers in her hair and she was wearing her rose patterned housecoat with bright pink puffy slippers, as she used the hot glue gun to put the little flowers securely in their place. She looked at the clock on the wall and let out a distressed sigh. Time was running faster than she was.

For Janet, the pace of time never changed. She was letting her sheep back onto the field. It was such a glorious morning that she was actually smiling, as she smelled the clean, fresh air. There was no one around. Only birds and her sheep. She liked it that way.

Suddenly she saw Kenneth. He was walking toward her through the fields, hopping over fences and watching the birds. Somehow the company of Kenneth didn't bother Janet. Perhaps it was that he seldom said anything. Kenneth waved his hand to greet her and she answered.

Daisy was biting her bottom lip as she moved things further away from each other around her front mudroom gallery, trying to make the display look fuller. Despite all of this, it remained pathetically sparse. Daisy let her hands fall beside her and shrugged her shoulders. 'What could she do?' She thought and went into the kitchen to make some more tea.

On the street, Muriel was walking through the quiet village. A small group of ladies were waiting for her by the front door of the church hall.

'Good morning, everyone. What a glorious day!' Muriel greeted the ladies cheerfully and fished the key from her cardigan pocket.

'Yes, it certainly is,' said one of the helpers.

'I wonder if we are going to be as busy today as we were yesterday,' said a woman with curly grey hair. She was wearing comfortable house slippers on her feet.

Muriel stared at the woman's feet. 'Irene, what on earth are you wearing?'

'Oh, these,' Irene said and paraded her slippers in front of the group. 'My feet were so tired and they were hurting so much this morning that these were the only shoes I could wear without tears. Fancy or what?' Irene pranced in front of the ladies. 'They do have rubber soles, you know.'

'You'll sit behind the desk today, Irene; not that I don't want anybody to see your flowery footwear, but just so that you can rest your feet,' Muriel said suppressing her laughter. 'Come to think of it, I should have brought my morning slippers as well.'

'At seventy you are too old to think what other people might think about you.' Irene said and laughed. 'I listen to my body. Isn't that what they tell women nowadays?'

Muriel opened the church hall door and let the ladies in. She turned to slip the hook into the ring to keep the door open, when she noticed Stella walking toward her. 'Good morning.' She hollered.

Stella quickened her step and walked to Muriel. 'Good morning, ladies. Are your feet as tired as mine? I feel as if I'm walking on crushed glass.'

'Yes,' Muriel said. 'And Irene is wearing house slippers.'

'Wish I had thought of that,' laughed Stella. 'I even helped Nick at the pub last night. I would have sold my children to be able to sleep in this morning.' Stella turned round and saw Linda walking on the other side of the street.

Stella waved the town hall key that she had taken out of her pocket. 'And, oh yes, here's the money for my raffle ticket.' She suddenly remembered and took out a handful of coins, handing them over to Muriel.

Muriel put the money in her cardigan pocket. 'All right. I'll buy your ticket for you.'

'Thank you, Muriel. Have a good day today. Try to rest your feet.'

'You too.' Muriel wished and then disappeared into the church, walking slightly slower than usual.

'In case we don't have any handsome young men to ogle at today, we can always look at Thomas's picture on the wall.' Stella said to Linda, who was waiting for her in front of the town hall.

'Yes. I think the town should buy it and keep it there. That way we might have more people attending the council meetings.' Linda giggled.

'I would definitely be there every second Thursday, rain or shine.' Stella answered.

They opened the doors to the town hall and, so, their second studio tour day with naked Thomas on the wall began.

Starting the day more slowly, Nick was only now waking up. He felt his body and mind telling him to let them sleep just a bit longer. He opened his eyes, but it felt so comfortable to let them close again. The bed was warm and soft. He almost fell back to sleep, but through his drowsy thoughts, he suddenly remembered the studio tour and that notion woke him up.

He walked slowly into his kitchen and when he looked out the window, he saw Muriel walking by. He stretched his neck to look toward the church hall and he saw all the Bitch and Stitch Club members standing by the door waiting for her. He must have slept too late if Muriel was up and running already. He quickly put the teakettle on and ran into the shower.

At the East End Bed and Breakfast Tim and John were doing the dishes after breakfast. The radio was playing quietly in the corner and the dishwasher was churning energetically.

A young woman guest, with newly blow-dried morning hair, put her head into the kitchen and hollered. 'Thanks. That was a great breakfast again.'

Tim smiled. 'That's nice to hear.'

John put the serving platter into the cupboard and straightened his back. 'Have a nice studio tour day,' he responded.

'I will. Bye!' The young woman was gone out the door.

Tim started scrubbing the frying pan and John poured more coffee for both of them. Their guests were already planning to come back. It had been a good weekend for them, very good.

The main street had begun filling up with cars and people. The shops were opening their doors. The church bell clanged in the bell tower and a lonely rooster notified his flock for the third time. Jack Wilkinson buzzed by on his lawn tractor. Honey was straightening the tables and chairs outside her café and Suzy was opening her Cozy Corner shop. The bookstore's doors were already open and Dan Finch had put a sign out front saying that all summer books were on sale. The fact that the bookstore was open was a miracle itself, since it was not raining.

Jackie opened her gallery doors and hung the open sign on the door. Already a man and a woman were walking through the narrow garden path toward her.

'Good morning.' Jackie was startled and she could not help but to look at her watch. It was only quarter to ten.

'Good morning,' the couple said and Jackie let them go by her into the gallery. She took a deep breath and followed them in, anticipating another day of questions with answers she already knew by heart. It was like going on automatic pilot: 'Yes, made by hand here on the island by me with no offshore manufacturing.' 'Yes, handmade curly maple, cherry and oak.' 'Yes, I do all the work.' 'Yes, the designs are all mine.'

The man looked at her and before he even uttered a word, Jackie answered. 'All the work, here in my gallery, is handmade by me.' She waited for the following question and then pointed to her workshop. 'Every piece is made over there.'

Thomas was whistling as he prepared everything for the day. He cut the strings of colourful glass into equal lengths and then organized his workbench, straightening the tools, putting a new piece of wax on the bench. The gallery doors were wide open allowing the wind to blow gently through the building, disappearing out the back door. He glanced at the beautiful fall day outside just as a remarkably stunning woman walked in. She was dressed elegantly, yet somehow, she managed to look informal. Her shiny shoes tapped sharply against the cement floor and her hair casually fell over her shoulders but none of it was out of place—one hundred percent relaxed elegance finished with a Hermes scarf. She had an odd similarity to Caroline. Maybe it was the same toughness and ruthlessness, accompanied by a beautiful face that seldom smiles unreservedly. Thomas watched her while she observed everything in the gallery.

He wiped his hands on his jeans and then approached her slowly. 'Good morning.'

'Good morning. Are you the artist?' Her voice was sharp like a knife.

'Yes I am, Thomas Stockwell, nice to meet you.' He put out his hand and the woman took it slowly. She seemed to be studying Thomas's handsome features.

'Penelope Lake. I'm the owner of PL-galleries. Would you be interested in selling your work in my galleries?' She was talking slowly emphasizing particular words—the *owner* and *galleries*, not one gallery but galleries. She meant business and Thomas was very interested.

'Yes I would, but it depends on the percentage.' He smiled casually, trying not to let her know that he was very interested.

'Fifty fifty. I'm very fair.' Penelope Lake was staring at Thomas without any expression on her face. 'Payment in thirty days from delivery. No consignment. I'm in business to sell.'

'Then I would be happy to sell my work in your gallery.'

'Good. I know you are busy today. But what if...' Penelope Lake stopped in the middle of her sentence. It wasn't hesitation. Penelope Lake never hesitated. She merely was thinking. She looked at Thomas for a long time and then an idea formed in her mind as she studied his beautiful, angular face and his perfectly sculpted body.

'What if...' She bit her lip ever so lightly. 'I was to come back, let's say next weekend. We could then go through your work, portfolio and biography and so on...and have dinner, perhaps?' She was already planning how to dress Thomas in white shirt and ripped jeans for the photo that was needed for the exhibition invitation to get those middle-aged rich women to flock to her gallery in the hope of having a one on one chat with Thomas. Yes, he would do very well under her guidance. Very well indeed.

She smiled coolly as she waited for Thomas's answer which she already knew would be yes. Nobody had ever said no to Penelope Lake.

'That sounds good to me.' Thomas smiled and nodded.

'Good. Here is my card.' She took her card out from a Louis Vuitton case and handed it over to Thomas. She smiled with her small pearly teeth. It was a smile that never quite reached her eyes. Her smile was more of a reaction to, rather than an expression of, happiness. 'Till next weekend,' she said.

'Bye!' Said Thomas still smiling broadly. He could not believe his good luck.

Penelope turned around and left. Thomas watched her walking back to her car. Penelope knew that his eyes were on her and she sighed contently like a fisherman who knows that his bait has been taken.

Thomas was all smiles. Life could not be more simple and pleasant for him. He had money in his pocket, his work was selling and he had a date for the next weekend with a beautiful gallery owner. Perfect, yes, apart from his arse hanging in the town hall.

The Information centre, with Thomas's infamous arse, was getting busy again. Linda and Stella were giving directions to people while handing out brochures. They looked at each other and rolled their eyes. Sunday was proving to be as busy as Saturday. Already their cheeks were hurting. Smiling was, surprisingly, the hardest part of the tour.

Russell was putting his dogs upstairs when he heard Jane talking downstairs to the first customer of the day.

He stopped at the top of the stairs and looked down. The people were in the hallway walking toward his studio. Russell scratched his head and then looked at his watch. He knew the time already, so he really didn't have to roll up his shirt cuff, but he did so anyway. He was right. It was only a quarter to ten. The same as yesterday. 'Bloody hell.'

'Good morning.' Caroline answered the greeting of a man and woman as they walked into her studio. She straightened a small landscape she was hanging and then took her usual place by the corner of her huge table, nonchalantly stretching her neck. The couple wandered slowly through her gallery looking at the paintings. Caroline idly observed them while swinging her long legs back and forth.

There was one painting of Thomas sleeping in Caroline's bed. This time, though, his body was covered with a white cotton sheet and on the night table was a green apple. Caroline had thought that the space had needed some colour and she had opted for a bright green apple instead of a book. A green book would have repeated the shape of the bed and she had needed a shape and colour contrast.

'He looks so innocent...so peaceful.' The woman stated.

Caroline lit a cigarette. She had a small wry smile on her face in response to the word *innocent*. 'Innocent. Hardly,' she thought just as the woman suggested that there might be a connection to

Paradise and that maybe Caroline was suggesting that in the new world it might be the man who would pick the fruit from the tree of knowledge, instead of the woman.

Caroline was now highly amused. God bless the art critics, she thought. They would find something symbolical in every painting. She smiled as she smoked and nodded encouragingly, suggesting that the woman might be onto something with her new theory.

The woman began explaining her point of view and Caroline heard the words *suppression*, *feminism* and *rebirth*. All Caroline thought about was Thomas's beautiful, strong, naked body pressing hard against her naked body in a bed behind that very same wall where the painting was now hanging.

All the West End B & B customers had left for the day and the house was quiet. Tom had also gone out. He wanted to know how the tour was going and what the town hall looked like, particularly the Thomas painting that had all the guests talking. Kevin was preparing a pot of tea for his mother.

He brought the tea to the breakfast room where his mother was reading a newspaper. He thought about what he and Tom had discussed after the printing accident, and he had admitted that he should have a serious discussion with his mother. He didn't want to hurt her. He had always wanted to protect her, especially after his father had died, but Tom had said that he suspected that his mother was tougher and more up-to-date than they thought. And twenty years of lies was quite enough.

He poured the tea and sat down opposite his mother.

Jackie was putting yet another peppermill into a box. 'Yes, I make everything myself.' She answered as she closed the lid. Her voice revealed none of the tiredness she was feeling.

'Will you turn some wood today?' A man asked her.

'Yes, after I have helped these ladies here. It won't take long.' She smiled at the man. Jackie was feeling happy today. Happy as in giddy happy, smiling-for-no-reason happy. That happy, so that she couldn't even produce a snotty answer to annoying questions that were being asked in her gallery for the second day in a row. In a musical she might have broken into song and begun dancing around her workshop with a peppermill in her hand, swirling elegantly around the machinery, suddenly realizing that she was in love. She was that happy.

Rosalind was also happy in her own command performance. She was talking with a husband and wife who had just walked into the studio.

'So, he could make a sculpture of my wife, you know head and shoulders and such?' The man asked Rosalind.

'Yes, I would think so. He normally does not do commissions, but I'm sure he would be delighted in this case.'

'How long would it take?'

'I will have to consult Alistair to find out. Could you kindly wait a moment? I'll go and fetch my husband.' She hurried off to get Alistair, who was hiding in the far corner of his studio examining his tools. He didn't enjoy being interrupted.

Sheridan wasn't allowing interruptions as he unloaded his kiln. He had a few enthusiastic women around him who were admiring everything he took, slowly and carefully, out of the lukewarm kiln. The women thought very highly of Sheridan's work and they said so incessantly. A showmanship of some kind had slowly taken over Sheridan and his ever expanding ego.

'Do you arrange weekend pottery courses?' One woman asked him.

Sheridan straightened his back and pretended to be hesitant, having read an article about hesitation being the strongest power in negotiations. He rubbed his chin thoughtfully. 'Normally I don't, but'—a theatrical pause—'I guess I could arrange some lessons for a small group.' He let his eyes wander and finally fixed them on the wall opposite, another tip he had picked up from the same article.

The women smiled and one of them exclaimed. 'That would be simply marvellous! I'll leave you my phone number.'

'And you just let us know when we will have our pottery weekend. This will be so exciting.' Another woman chimed in, opening her handbag, looking for a pen.

Sheridan looked around at the group of ladies chatting and smiling and handing him their phone numbers. If only this could have happened in high school, he thought briefly.

The women and men in Harriet's studio were handing her photos of their dogs, as they had done the day before. But today the dogs were different. They all appeared to be so revolting that even their mothers must have had difficulty loving them.

'Could you paint my darling Tony?' The woman in front of Harriet asked.

Harriet kept the photo at arm's length as if studying it meticulously, and then, after composing herself, she answered the question slowly with a strange, tight voice. 'Of course.'

Now, Harriet loved dogs more than anything in the world and she always found them beautiful, but this morning she had been forced to bite her bottom lip in an extreme effort not to laugh out loud. Love was certainly blind, she had concluded. She opened her date book and then followed the weeks with her finger.

'I have a bit of a list here already, but I'm sure I can fit you and Tony in before Christmas.'

'That would be wonderful!' The woman chirped. 'And congratulations for the best in show prize. Winston is a darling.'

'Isn't he?'

Harriet looked at her Winston lovingly. Now Winston was a handsome dog. There was no question about that.

Nancy's early morning wreath-making was not going to carry her through. She dashed out of her house and took down the wreath she had just put up on the front door a moment ago. She was frantic. Her nicely arranged hair was going wild and her stocking had a run in it. She mumbled something as she ran back into the house. The door slammed closed behind her.

Thomas was blowing glass in his studio. He was explaining the technical aspect of glassblowing when a woman cleared her throat and interrupted. 'That must be hot?' She looked at Thomas waiting for his answer.

'Yes.'

'You must need extra big lungs to blow glass?'

'No.'

'Does it take a long time to learn glassblowing?'

'Yes.'

'Is there a special glassblowing school?'

'Yes.'

'Have you been to Murano, Venice, in Italy?'

'Yes.'

'Now, they are the true masters of glassblowing. Isn't that so?'

'Yes.'

'Do you use the same techniques as they do?'

'Yes.'

'We bought so many pieces back from Murano when we were there that my husband said that I am not allowed to buy any more glass.'

Thomas grunted something inaudible.

'We have so much glass at home that I don't know what to do with it.'

'Good for you.' Thomas said through his teeth. 'What the hell am I supposed to say?' He asked himself.

'I do like your work, but you still have a long way to go to be like those Italian masters.'

Thomas got up holding onto his hot glass piece. In his mind he wanted to stick it someplace that was not considered appropriate, but he opted for saying. 'Thank you. It was nice talking with you. Goodbye.' And he turned his back to the woman and walked to the furnace.

He could hear the woman exclaim something about good manners, but he didn't really care at this point. He had been civil long enough. 'Almost a saint,' he thought. 'If you ask me.'

The pastor had finished his morning sermon and he came down to the busy church hall glowing with post-sermon happiness. 'Muriel, any chance of having a cup of coffee?'

'Oh, yes. I think Mabel just made a fresh pot in the kitchen.' The quilters were selling raffle tickets and the bake sale still had a few boxes of cookies left. Muriel turned around to continue answering questions about the raffle. 'The pastor here will draw the winning ticket at four o'clock today.'

The pastor zigzagged through the people in the church hall and headed for the kitchen for a cup of coffee. He was feeling very cheerful and optimistic today. The morning service had been very successful. He had had almost a full church, which was more or less a miracle in Sycamore's church attendance history. He had worked late into the night with his sermon and his feelings had been heightened when he finally had gone to bed at midnight. It had been uplifting to talk to strangers from his pulpit. His sermon had been vigorous, loaded with bible passages filled with fiery hell and holy forgiveness. He had been doing the lord's work today. Yes, indeed he had.

Nick walked into the pub. Rose was already there rolling knives and forks into the napkins and placing them in baskets. She looked up at Nick and hollered happily, 'Hi there! Ready for another day?'

'Yes I am.'

'Stella called from the town hall and told us to expect a large lunch crowd. They are again very busy today.'

'And I heard that all the B & Bs in the village were full and that Maximilian's was fully booked as well. Jackie did a great job.'

'Yes she did.' She looked at him. 'So...'

'So you better get back to work and stop yapping.' Nick smiled a big, wide, happy smile. Rose looked at him in a motherly way and shook her head slightly. It was impossible to get any kind of answer from Nick. She would just have to use her imagination to fill in the gaps. Nick walked to the front door and opened it wide. The bright light flowed into the pub, mercilessly showing the dust particles dancing in the air. He looked out on the street. The tearoom was busy. Honey was bringing fresh pots of tea to the customers sitting outside under the pink umbrellas.

Hilary walked by the pub and shouted happily while trying to keep steady on her high heels on the badly cracked pavement. 'Yoo-hoo...Nick!' She waved her hand and smiled, 'Helloooo!'

'Good morning, Hilary. Lovely day.'

'Yes it is.' Hilary shifted her weight onto her other leg. 'I cut hair like crazy yesterday, but today I'm going on the tour myself.'

'That's good to hear.'

'Tell Jackie thank you for me when you see her. She's a doll.' Hilary clonked toward the town hall. She needed to get her brochure and she needed to see the painting her customers had so ceaselessly talked about all day yesterday.

Nick laughed. It had been a good tour for all of the area businesses, if even Hilary's beauty salon had been busy. Nick stood there by the door and admired the results of Jackie's hard work. He watched his home village's main street that was full of life this Sunday morning. It was a rare moment. Even when the pastor had been on one of his drinking binges and his Sunday sermons had been the main entertainment event of the week, the town had never been this busy on Sundays.

Jackie watched the peppermills disappear from her shelves more quickly than she had thought possible. She wondered if she had enough packaging materials under her counter. She had run out of tape already and the gift wrapping was not available anymore.

'Thank you.' She said to another happy customer and put the money into her pocket tapping it protectively.

She would have to fetch more peppermills from the storage room soon and fill in the empty places on her shelves. She was beginning to feel happily relaxed. It had been a good tour, even if Sunday would prove to be much quieter than Saturday. It had been a success, though Jackie was not ready to let those words escape her lips yet.

Thomas was staring at the wall of his studio.

'Yes, it's pretty hot.' He said and thought about hanging a sign on the wall telling the customers that, yes, the studio is bloody hot because of the glass bloody furnace, which reaches frigging high temperatures of 2000 bloody frigging Fahrenheit. The sweat that formed on his forehead could be a good clue, as well. He didn't do that though. Instead he asked a little boy, who had been watching with his eyes wide open and his little tongue sticking out at the corner of his mouth, if he could get him a water bottle from the gallery. The boy nodded excitedly. He was too scared to say anything.

He ran quickly to the gallery to fetch the bottle and brought it to Thomas. Thomas smiled. 'Thanks pal. You want to help a bit?'

The boy looked at his parents. The father nodded encouragingly and took a camera out of the bag.

Harriet was holding a photograph in her hands. There was no question about it. This was definitely the ugliest dog she had ever seen in her entire life. Tony from before was nothing compared to this dog. She wasn't even sure if it really was a dog.

'I would love to paint your darling Erwin's picture.' Harriet said steadfastly and at the same time she wondered if she was supposed to paint the drool on Erwin's lips as well. 'He's a peach.' She added and she could hardly keep her face straight. She was thinking about how much she and Jackie would laugh at the photo afterwards. 'So you would like to have the painting by Christmas?' She asked her customer, though she knew the answer already.

Chapter 25

Done

There was a routine to things now. People knew what to expect. The wariness of Saturday had changed into knowledge based on experience. The boys had taken their customary seat by the window at the pub. They were giving updated reports on the main street goings-on. Rose tut-tutted at them and called them names, usually including the word *useless*.

By noon Nancy had only small miniature wreaths left in her gallery. Her front door was bare. She didn't even bother to put another wreath on it, because it only meant that she would have to take it down a few minutes later. Her feet could not take any extra steps.

Thomas had started to count how many seconds it would take for a customer to ask the famous question of the tour: 'Is it hot?' He normally only got to five.

Rosalind still enjoyed her all-powerful feeling orchestrating Alistair's studio with an eager and commanding hand. Alistair let her do so freely and enjoyed seeing her happy in her new position. There hadn't been much cheerfulness in Rosalind lately. He used the term *lately* loosely to cover the last twenty years or so and sighed. He felt for the cigarettes in his pocket and began to look for the perfect moment to escape. Alistair had managed to get quite a few cigarette breaks in during Saturday. Now he just needed to get more mint candies to cover up the smell.

Janet and Kenneth had accomplished the impossible. Without much talk and only sparse smiles they had sold quite well. People had sensed that chatting was perhaps not something they did naturally.

Caroline had sold the sleeping Thomas painting and was surprisingly sad when she covered it with thick brown paper.

Daisy was holding two trays in her hands while a woman was trying to decide which one she should buy. The woman's husband stood nearby and wished that he could be in the pub instead. The woman turned to ask him his opinion and it took him a few seconds before he realized that his wife was talking to him.

'Well?' She asked him again and gave him a long look. He quickly agreed with her without knowing what he had agreed to and continued dreaming about drinking a pint. He could almost taste the beer. Daisy was staring right ahead, as if she was merely a display unit.

Jackie was talking about the pair of chairs she had been working on. She flipped one of them over to show the underside.

Sheridan was carefully wrapping a huge ceramic platter for a customer. He proudly explained that his pottery was machine washable and lead free.

Daisy was wrapping the painted tray in her gallery. The husband had disappeared into the pub and the wife was still shopping.

Thomas was blowing glass and his audience had changed, but the questions hadn't.

'Yes, it is really hot.'

Nancy was putting a small wreath into a box.

Rosalind was writing down the information for the ordered sculpture. The couple was standing in the studio chatting with Alistair, who wanted a cigarette now more than anything.

Russell was standing by the window and pointing across the fields to that special picnic spot of his. His audience, luckily, were totally clueless about the significance of this place. Jane was wrapping a painting. She had no comments.

Jackie was turning wood. The lathe was humming loudly and keeping the questions at bay.

Thomas was wiping sweat off his brow and ground his teeth together in an effort to be civil.

'You could say it is hot.' He said and thought about other things he would prefer to say, but could not.

Kenneth and Janet were still standing by the wall in the barn. A woman wanted to buy the tin bucket with dried flowers in it. Nick was filling pints and Rose was running in and out of the kitchen. The cook was so exhausted that she had even forgotten the names of her grandchildren.

Caroline was covering another sleeping Thomas picture with brown paper. The young woman with a flair for sensual descriptions was buying it.

Sheridan was carefully wrapping a butter dish in paper.

Jackie put her goggles away and brushed the sawdust from her jeans.

A woman in the audience sneezed loudly.

Daisy wanted to have a cup of tea.

Thomas stopped his glassblowing demonstration for a split second to answer a question. 'It is really, *really* hot.'

Nancy had glue stuck to her hair and she was a nursing a paper cut.

Jackie ran out of packaging material.

Kenneth sold the last of the Christmas cards.

Thomas wiped the sweat off his brow. 'Really, I mean really hot.'

Alistair sat on a block of wood behind the studio and lit a cigarette.

'Machine washable,' boasted Sheridan.

Russell moved is hips.

The pastor put his hand into the raffle jar and shook it around before pulling the winning ticket out of the jar. 'Number 244.' He said slowly and clearly. The church hall was quiet as people checked the numbers on their tickets.

All of a sudden an older woman shrieked. 'It's me! It's me!'

She pushed through the crowd and handed her winning ticket to the pastor and he handed the folded quilt to the woman. People applauded. The two of them posed for a second for the local newspaper photographer. The woman was beaming with happiness. She had red dots on her cheeks as she held her quilt tightly in her arms.

Nancy sat down.

Thomas was leaning against the gallery table and drinking water from the bottle. He was staring at the clock on the wall willing the time to go forward.

Janet was folding a pullover and Kenneth was inspecting the fields through the window.

Jackie's eyes were burning holes into the clock on her studio wall.

Sheridan was twirling his moustache.

Jane called Russell to come and help her.

Harriet put her glasses on and examined a photograph in front of her.

'Alistair is a very well-known artist,' Rosalind stated with a smile.

'2000 Fahrenheit,' Thomas explained.

'What a lovely dog,' Harriet said with a well-practised smile.

'Yes, I am the designer and the maker,' Jackie answered.

'Goodbye.' Caroline waved her hand.

'Pretty hot.' Thomas wiped his sweaty forehead.

'Dishwasher safe,' Sheridan mumbled.

'Bye,' said Janet.

'Handmade,' Jackie muttered.

'It is very very hot,' Thomas grunted.

'Oh, dear!' Sighed Daisy.

Stella closed the door of the town hall. She felt a surge of relief as she turned the key in the lock. Linda was already sitting on a chair by the information table. She looked fatigued and she was trying to hold her feet up so that her soles would not touch the floor. The throbbing pain was pulsing through her feet.

'That's it. The town is empty.' Stella walked slowly to the information table, pulled out a chair and sat down heavily.

'So that's it for the studio tour, then,' Linda said and stretched her neck from side to side with closed eyes.

'Seems like it,' Stella said and kicked off her shoes. The relief was unimaginable. Stella smiled and exhaled deeply.

'Look! I still have toes.' Linda laughed and pointed to her feet.' I thought I had definitely worn them out.'

'It sure feels like it.' Stella wiggled her toes and yawned trying to cover it by placing a hand over her mouth. 'Lord I'm tired.' She sighed sounding exhausted beyond words.

Linda stretched her arms over her head and then let them fall. 'One thing I'm not too tired of though,' she said.

'I know...I love that painting, too.' Stella replied as they both rested their tired eyes on Thomas's perfect body on the wall.

Jackie held the door open for a couple who were leaving. She turned around to see her gallery and the clock on the wall. It was five past five.

She turned to peak out the door. The small stony path through her garden was empty. There was nobody walking toward her gallery. She saw the couple disappear behind the tall hedge. The husband was carrying the heavy bags. They had bought Christmas gifts for all their four children. It was a good finale for the tour, she had thought, while apologizing for the lack of gift boxes.

Jackie went back into the studio and sat down on her office chair. She was exhausted. She leaned back, put her hands behind her head and stared at the ceiling. Her body felt so heavy that she could barely lift her legs onto the table. She wanted to sit quietly and not move at all for a good long while.

Sheridan was straightening the display in his gallery. There was nobody in his gallery anymore. No more admiring ladies swarming around Sheridan's stout body. He felt the loss more than he could have ever imagined.

Daisy was sitting down in her gallery. Her head was still buzzing. She pondered if it would be too foolish to call her husband on her cell phone and ask him to bring her some tea because she had no energy to walk around the house trying to find him. It was a big house after all.

Nancy was closing her gallery's door. There was nothing left, only a floor full of shoe prints and pieces of crushed dried flowers.

Rosalind was writing something down in the black gold edged book and Alistair was smoking a cigarette secretly behind the studio. He had found new mints after searching through all of his jackets hanging in the hallway closet.

Kenneth and Janet were standing in front of the barn door looking out onto the long and empty driveway. A lovely stillness had settled in.

'Well, I guess that's it, then.' Janet stated with her both arms folded against her chest.

'So it seems.' Kenneth was staring at the sky where a hawk was peacefully circling, calling for its partner.

Caroline was in her kitchen making herself a drink. She looked at her watch and then leaned backwards in her chair to see her driveway through the open door—nobody. She poured an exceedingly generous amount of gin into her glass of tonic water and reached for a phone. It was time to call Maximilian. She was getting hungry.

Harriet picked up Winston and walked toward her kitchen. 'I think, Winston, that it is time for Mommy to have a wee drink.' Now it was time to count the money the orders would bring in just before Christmas.

Jackie closed her studio door and flipped the sign on her door to say 'Closed'. She felt like grinning even though her cheeks were hurting.

Russell closed the front door and walked into the kitchen where Jane was making tea. He walked up to her and put his arms around her and buried his head in the crook of Jane's neck. Jane shook him off and told him to let the dogs out from the guest bedroom. She was already planning their holiday, but first she needed to count the money. Today love and affection came only after money.

Muriel was sitting in the church hall kitchen with all of the other quilters. They were drinking tea and laughing hysterically. Some of the ladies had lifted their tired feet onto the chairs and they were contemplating the idea of calling a taxi to take them home. Walking was not at the moment an option.

Harriet stared at the little notebook in front of her. The glass beside her was still untouched. Winston was looking at his owner cocking his head to the left and then to the right, expecting a loving pat on his head. Harriet took a deep breath and tapped her round fingers against the table. She stared at the little numbers that she had scribbled on a piece of paper in front of her.

'Good lord Jesus and Mary!' Harriet finally blurted out. 'My god!' She took a sip from her glass and patted Winston while closing her little book. A gigantic smile was beginning to form in the corners of her mouth.

Thomas was flamboyantly leading two women into his studio. He had his hands around their waists and he was happily giving them a private tour of his studio. The young women were giggling. Thomas was back in his very own element again. Caroline seemed like a bad dream from the past. Thomas was a very lucky man in that respect—he had a very short and forgiving memory and a mind that treasured the present moment more than bad past experiences. He appeared to be completely incapable of carrying ill will with him.

Jackie was sitting in her kitchen drinking a glass of white wine. She had her old metal moneybox, her receipt book and a calculator on the table by her. She looked at them, took a sip of wine and then leaned forward. Slowly she opened the box and began counting her studio tour earnings.

Nick was hanging a sign on the front door of the pub that said 'Tonight Private Party' and then he went back in. He was going to be busy for a moment longer.

Jackie stared at the note pad in front of her. She could not believe her eyes. She calculated the receipts and the loose money in the box again, arranging the bills and coins into piles. She added the last numbers and then let the pencil roll from her hand. A shock! A beautiful magical shock!

'Holy shit and a half!' She grabbed the money, jumped up and started dancing with a bunch of crumpled bills in both of her hands. She danced badly following some kind of Motown music in her head. She shook her hips, took salsa steps back and forth and then rattled the bills victoriously in the air while jumping up and down.

'I love money!' She yelled and then held the money tightly against her body. 'Love it. Love it! Love it!' She said again and again, grinning blissfully. Never mind that her cheeks were hurting. She had money now. She had money even before the Christmas rush was going to begin. Money! It was a historical moment. Magnificent moment. It was almost a religious experience. 'Money,' she repeated the word slowly savouring every single syllable.

She began planning what she would do with this extra income. New sink for the kitchen, perhaps. The porcelain one she had seen in a magazine. Perhaps, or maybe new tools for the studio, a trip or maybe she should fix her car first. It seemed a shame, though, to use this money to fix a car. A new kitchen sink, perhaps. She could always fix the car later with the rest of the money—maybe or maybe not.

Oh, how welcome the extra income was in October.

Chapter 26

Rose Calls It

The feeling in the pub was rowdy. It was a mix of celebratory exhaustion and hard earned pride. The pride was shared evenly among everybody who had taken part in the tour. It wasn't a feeling that could be felt alone. Exhaustion was the complementary, unavoidable byproduct.

Jackie looked around her and smiled broadly. She couldn't stop smiling. She was so happy. Her eyes had vanished into two small slits as her lips turned upwards into a permanent grin. Everybody had come to the pub to celebrate. All the people who had been a valuable part of the volunteer force for the tour were there. The Bitch and Stitch Club members sat in the corner with the pastor. Stella and Linda were talking with Jane, who was definitely travelling to Spain after Christmas, and of course the boys were there, sitting in their usual place by the window. Whether the boys had actually helped or not had not yet been agreed upon.

Despite the massive, never ending arguments and accidental disasters, these people together had achieved something very special. Jackie gulped and felt oddly sentimental and at the same time giddy.

The weekend had been very long, filled with hours and hours of hard work, and now the physical exhaustion was turning into relaxed hysterical laughter. A big buffet table had been set up in the middle of the pub, and people stood around it chatting with each other, telling tales from the tour and comparing experiences.

Rose was bringing glasses and wine bottles to the centre table. Nick was behind the bar pouring champagne. Russell was helping him by delivering the filled glasses to everybody. He walked around the room with the tray in his big hairy hands and chatted boisterously with everyone. The room was filled with loud laughter and chatter.

Jackie got a glass of champagne and a wink from Russell. She was in such high spirits. Life was good. Champagne was good. The studio tour was over and she had money stashed away in a shoebox under her bed and, last but not the least, Nick had made her lunch yesterday. Yes, life was as good as it could get right now. 'Thanks, Russell.' Jackie tried to shout over the noise.

'You're welcome. You would make a perfect Colgate commercial my girl...with a big grin like that on that pretty face of yours.'

Russell nudged Jackie's arm and smiled. He looked around the room packed with people trying to see if there was still somebody without champagne. He grabbed the last remaining glass for himself and then put the tray on the table beside the wall. 'All right then. Are we ready?' Russell glanced at Jackie questioningly, nodding toward his tall drink.

Jackie looked around and decided that this was the time to thank everybody for their efforts. She cleared her throat. 'If I could just say a few words.' She started hesitantly.

People slowly stopped talking and turned to look at Jackie.

'Does everybody have a glass of champagne?' Jackie asked.

Thomas beamed at her from the bar with two champagne flutes in his hands. He pretended to make a toast. Jackie shook her head and then continued. 'I promise to be quick. Don't worry. I'm not going to make any long speeches. You all know me by now. Long winded speeches are not me.'

People laughed encouragingly. Jackie felt nostalgic and took a deep breath. It had been many months of preparation, but now when it all had come to an end, it was sad to say goodbye to those hectic, life filled moments.

'I would like to thank everybody here for all the hard work you have done. We had a fantastic tour—sometimes quite strange and chaotic, I admit, but nevertheless, it was fun, especially now when it is officially behind us.'

People chuckled. Russell's loud voice was heard above the crowd. 'Strange is an odd choice of words, Jackie dear. I would call it a bloody mad house.' The room filled with roaring laughter.

'So to all of us. We did it!' Jackie lifted her glass. 'Cheers! And thanks to Maximilian for supplying us with the champagne,' she added.

'Cheers to Maximilian!' A cacophonic ovation filled the small pub.

After one long sip of champagne, Russell cleared his throat. 'We would like to thank you, Jackie, for organizing everything. You're one grand lady. Let me tell you that.' He lifted his glass and then bellowed to his heart's content. 'To Jackie!'

'To Jackie!' Everybody shouted simultaneously.

Jackie beamed and felt an aching warm feeling where her heart was. She took a sip from her tall glass and bowed her head slightly. The champagne was delicious. She felt as if she was sitting on the edge of a silver cloud. 'Thank you, thank you, thank you.' Jackie turned to look at Nick and then lifted her glass high up in the air. 'And thank you, Nick, for the lovely buffet you made for us, and thank you for your absolutely generous help and your bighearted support.' Now she couldn't stop smiling. 'We could not have done it without you!' She gazed into Nick's eyes across the room.

'Thank you, Nick!' The people in the pub shouted. Jackie could almost see the ceiling of the room lifting.

'It takes a superhuman strength to deal with this bunch on a weekly basis.' Russell yelled over the noise.

'Thank you all. You have all brought me pain and…well…some happiness.' Nick added with a wide grin on his face. He took a sip of his champagne. Tonight he was not the bartender. Tonight he was part of the crowd. 'And now let's eat, everybody! There's wine on the table and Rose has promised to bring out some beer, as well. So help yourselves.' He pointed to the table filled with food.

'In heaven there's no beer, that's why we drink it here.' Russell grabbed a pint from Rose's tray as she walked by. Rose smiled at him and shook her head slightly in a friendly but pitiful manner.

People began filling their plates with food. There hadn't been much of a chance or time to cook during the tour. They were all bored with simple sandwiches and looked forward to the already prepared excellent dinner. Everybody was in high spirits. Even Rosalind seemed more relaxed than normal, although that might have been only a figment emanating from Russell's exhausted mind which swiftly disappeared again into thin air.

Nick walked slowly to Jackie. He walked tentatively as if buying time. Jackie smiled cheerfully at him. There was again that unmistakable feeling. The sweet ache that wrapped itself around her throat.

'Everything looks great, Nick. Thank you so much for all of this.' Her words came out slower than normal. She could almost feel them leave her lips, one syllable after the other.

Nick studied her flushed smiling face for a moment. It was pure joy that was reflected in Jackie's eyes.

'No problem and because of you I had the busiest weekend ever in the history of this pub.' He finally said, still gazing into her eyes. Jackie felt suddenly oddly nervous and the words stuck in her throat.

She looked quietly at the people gathered around the table eating, drinking and laughing, being merry and happy, all the time feeling Nick standing so close to her. She thought of things to say and when no words came to her mind, she drank more champagne, feeling her heart beat loudly in her ears.

'Come with me!' Nick whispered suddenly and took Jackie's hand tightly into his and led her outside. Nobody except Jack Wilkinson noticed that they were walking out the door.

Nick pulled the heavy door open, guided Jackie out and then closed the door quietly behind them. They stood on the front steps of the pub. Nick turned Jackie around to face him, holding her by her shoulders.

The stars were out in the clear sky and Nick wondered if his pounding heart was audible to Jackie. He took a deep breath and looked into Jackie's flushed face.

'If I were to kiss you right now, you wouldn't punch me like all of your female relatives have done to the men in my family'—Nick hesitated slightly—'now would you?' He was staring deep into Jackie's eyes.

'No I wouldn't. Absolutely not.' The words fell out from Jackie's frozen lips.

A joyous smile spread over Nick's face. 'Good and I locked the bloody door as well, so nobody can come out and interrupt us this time.'

They both glanced at the second door leading into the pub. It had been locked with an old rusty hook while the outside door remained open. They both laughed and then nervously turned to look at each other again.

Nick put his arms around Jackie. She could feel his pounding heart through his shirt. He felt so warm. It was good. Nick leaned forward and Jackie looked at him seriously. Nick moved closer and their noses touched slightly. There was still the slight uncertainty between them. Jackie smiled nervously and then she closed her eyes. She felt Nick's warm lips on hers. At first it was a slow, hesitant kiss, but then it turned into a long, passionate kiss banishing any doubt left lurking in their minds. Nick tightened his arms around Jackie and pulled her closer. He felt her hair on his face and her body against his. Jackie put her arms right around him and pressed her ear against his chest inhaling the familiar smell of him. It was good. It was all right. It was as it should be. There was love to be found and she had found hers.

Nick whispered in her hair, 'I love you, Jacqueline Victoria Callaghan.'

Jack Wilkinson's face appeared in the window. He was trying to see past the glare of the glass by pressing his face as close as possible to the cold window.

Nick kissed Jackie again to Jack Wilkinson's utmost delight. Jack Wilkinson swirled around like lightning and yelled with a booming voice that could be heard even outside. 'Callaghan and O'Neill are kissing!'

Suddenly there was a lot of commotion in the pub. Howard, Calvin and Glenn verified the kiss with solemn faces pressed against the window pane. It was ten past seven.

Rose looked first at the calendar on the wall and then she looked at the clock. She let out an excited scream. 'And that makes me the winner!' She smacked her lips knowingly. 'I knew. I just knew it. Damn! I knew it!'

'Well, let's see what the book says before we go on announcing the winners.' Thomas yelled and pointed toward Howard.

Howard took a small weathered book out of his pocket and opened it slowly. He put on his reading glasses, which nobody even knew he owned, and leafed through by wetting his thumb as he turned the dog-eared pages of his notebook.

Everybody waited for his verdict.

'Yes, she is the winner, all right.' He finally said with a deep juridical voice.

'Start handing over the money, people.' Rose rubbed her big palms together and then laid her hands open in front of her. She was flexing her fingers as if inviting the money to flow in.

Russell was heard cursing about how he just missed it by one day and three bloody measly hours. The pastor was shaking his head in a disapproving manner, until he too took his wallet out from his pocket and began counting the bills. Muriel sighed and flicked her handbag's lock open to take out her wallet. Nancy and Daisy murmured 'oh well' and then giggled taking out their money as well. Harriet cursed freely about young people who cannot control their hormones and jump at each other a full two hours before they are suppose to.

'Now, 9 p.m. That's the time to start kissing,' she exclaimed with her booming voice, but she paid her share nevertheless. Kenneth's cheeks were flushed from the champagne and he mumbled something close to jolly good and handed Rose his money. Janet congratulated Rose and said that she had only been beaten by fifteen minutes. Stella called Rose her best sister but Rose replied quickly that she was not inclined to nepotism. Stella put a fiver into Rose's waiting hands.

Thomas laughed until he had tears streaming from his eyes. 'They were much faster than I expected.' He finally managed to say to Rose who grabbed his money and held it against her large chest. 'Female intuition, my dear,' she said smugly and continued collecting her winnings.

Even Alistair gave money to Rose. Rosalind stared at him with unflinching eyes. She was utterly surprised and shocked. 'You surely did not participate in this uncivilized, ridiculous bet?' Her nasal voice demanded to know. Alistair had a few drinks under his belt and he felt indestructible.

'I did indeed, darling!' He grabbed a bottle from the table. 'Have some more champagne, dear.' He filled Rosalind's champagne glass, while she speechlessly stared at her husband. Russell grabbed Rosalind by her waist and twirled her around.

Rosalind didn't anymore know what was more disturbing: her husband's gambling problem or another man's hands around her waist. Russell pulled a chair out for her and helped her sit down. Alistair put a glass of champagne in her hand and then the two men left, headed to the bar, their arms around each other's shoulders. Rosalind held the glass tightly in her hands and stared at the scene in front of her. For the first time in her life Rosalind McKay felt that drinking could be a good replacement for reality.

Caroline came to sit by her but Rosalind barely noticed. Caroline thought about calling Maximilian again as she fingered her glass. Thomas hardly would come home with her now. It was a shame, really. He had been her best model and she had sold almost all of the paintings she had painted of him. Pity, because the sex had been good as well. She poured some more champagne into her glass. Maximilian had good taste in champagne anyway, she thought as she pulled out her cell phone. Hopefully, he would answer this time. Caroline didn't want to call in vain.

Rose approached the boys by the window. She encouraged them to pay immediately, reminding them all that she did work in this very pub and she did control the beer taps at the bar. Reluctantly the boys dipped their hands into their pockets and started counting the coins between them.

Nick and Jackie could hear Rose's voice as she demanded what rightfully was hers. They both looked in through the brightly lit pub windows and saw Rose's hands receiving a mound of coins and crumpled bills. A couple of bent nails and broken screws found their way into the money pile as well.

Jackie burst out laughing. 'Well, we should have guessed it. They bet on almost anything.' She pressed her face against Nick's sweater and then looked up at him. She was smiling. Nick brushed one unruly curl from her face and then held her tightly against him, not wanting to let go of her, now that he finally had her in his arms.

Jackie smiled, put her arms tightly around him and looked up at Nick and the starry sky. Life was good.